SHOES FOR
ANTHONY

SHOES FOR ANTHONY

EMMA KENNEDY

Thomas Dunne Books
St. Martin's Press
New York

THOMAS DUNNE BOOKS.
An imprint of St. Martin's Press.

SHOES FOR ANTHONY. Copyright © 2015 by Emma Kennedy. All rights reserved. Printed in the United States of America. For information, address St. Martin's Press, 175 Fifth Avenue, New York, N.Y. 10010.

www.thomasdunnebooks.com
www.stmartins.com

Library of Congress Cataloging-in-Publication Data

Names: Kennedy, Emma, 1967– author.
Title: Shoes for Anthony : a novel / Emma Kennedy.
Description: First U.S. edition. | New York : Thomas Dunne Books, 2017.
Identifiers: LCCN 2016037250| ISBN 9781250090966 (hardcover) | ISBN 9781250090973 (e-book)
Subjects: LCSH: World War, 1939–1945—Wales—Fiction. | Interpersonal relations—Fiction. | Prisoners of war—Fiction. | BISAC: FICTION / Historical. | FICTION / War & Military. | GSAFD: Historical fiction. | War stories.
Classification: LCC PR6111.E543 S56 2017 | DDC 823/.92—dc23
LC record available at https://lccn.loc.gov/2016037250

First published in Great Britain by Ebury Press, an imprint of Ebury Publishing, a Penguin Random House company

First U.S. Edition: January 2017

10 9 8 7 6 5 4 3 2 1

For Georgie, Geoffrey and Sarah

GLOSSARY OF WELSH PHRASES

Uffarn den – hell fire
Uffach wyllt – wild wind
Cera yffarn – go to hell
Diawl – devil
Duw – God

CHAPTER ONE

Pen Pych, our mountain: here she came, rising out from the fog, ground up, like a woman quietly raising her petticoats. I loved this time in the morning, when the mountain made her presence felt. The wind blew away the haze of night and there she was, the Queen of the Valley. We were standing, the five of us, stolen tea trays tucked into our armpits, staring up towards the spoil tip that sat at her base. It was such a blot on the landscape, and yet, in a way, it fitted right in: muck and beauty, side by side.

'Race up, then race down, right, boys?' said Ade, spitting into his hand. Ade was my best bud. He had a face so ingrained with dirt he looked like the inside of a teapot. He was wearing a pair of muddied shorts and a jumper so oversized it floated round him as if he were suspended in a well. Nobody had had new clothes in years, certainly not since the start of the war. All the kids on Scott Street were reliant on hand-me-downs and the clothes of the dead.

'Onesies, right?' said Thomas Evans, scrap of a thing, tough as hell. He was like gristle – a chewy lad, we called him – forever breaking his limbs. 'Starting b'there.' He pointed up

1

to a flat section to the left of the heaped-up spoil tip. 'But feet up, like. No brakes.'

We all nodded.

'Who's doing starters, then?' asked Bozo, shoving his glasses up his nose. One of the lenses was covered in sticking plaster, on account of him having a lazy eye. Plaster was supposed to make his lazy eye less lazy. None of us understood how that worked, mind, but there it was.

'I will,' said Fez, glancing sideways. Fez was a stick of a lad, all knees and elbows, with an explosion of curly blond hair. He looked like a firework. He lived three doors down and was an only child, something that was virtually unheard of in Treherbert. There'd been something wrong with his mam and she couldn't have any more; that's what Bopa Jackson said. Bopa lived next door to us. She knew everything about everyone. 'Better than the *Pathé News*,' Mam said. Still, it meant Fez always had stuff. He was good to hang around.

When it came to clambering up spoil tips, the general rule was low and fast. There was a knack to it: light on the toes, no digging the heels in, don't stand still for any length of time. Easier said than done in rubber wellingtons, but I'd been climbing spoil tips for as long as I could remember. Up and at it. There was no other way.

The five of us took up position, slightly bent at the shoulders, one leg forward. We cast each other a sideways glance. 'On your mark …' I began, getting ready to crouch.

'Go!' yelled Fez, and off he dashed, his plimsolls digging in.

'*Uffarn den*!' yelled Bozo, clambering after him. 'That's not starters! That's cheating, you bastard!'

I got off to a bad start. My first footfall slid away from me and I tumbled at the off. Falling down into a crouch position, I used my free hand to stabilise and began to make inroads upwards. Fez was already a quarter of the way up. He was darting left and right, taking a leaping zigzag approach towards the summit. I'd seen him do that before. I knew it tired him out. He'd have to stop, and when he did, he'd slide down.

Bozo was struggling: for every two steps forward, he was slipping a step back. He had good balance on his left side, but his right was letting him down. That would be his lazy eye, I thought.

Ade and Thomas were neck and neck, just below Fez but higher up than me. I glanced up. There were miniature gullies in the spoil tip. You didn't want to run up those. The clinkers tended to be finer, less stable. You wanted to run up the harder stuff. It had less of a tendency to fall away.

I looked over towards Fez. He was slowing down. I clawed myself forwards with my free hand and tried to push myself up on to my toe tips. A light touch and high knees, that's what was needed. It wouldn't look pretty, but it would get the job done.

I got myself into a rhythm: high knees, touch and up. I was passing Thomas. He looked red in the face, exhausted already. Ade was within reaching distance. I checked his position. He was about ten feet from the top but almost at a standstill. Touch and up. My left foot hit a gully and slid away. I managed to stay upright but the heels of my wellingtons wanted to dig backwards. I had to push forwards.

Bozo was nowhere. He was out of it. Ade and Thomas were flagging. It was just me and Fez. I could hear him breathing, heavy, laboured. He was finished. He'd have to crawl the last bit. My legs felt strong. I had him. Push, jump and past Fez I went. The summit was mine.

I let out a cheer and straightened up, arms aloft. 'Bad luck, Fez,' I said, watching him crawl over the top edge. He flopped down on his back, his chest heaving.

'Well done, man,' he panted. 'I got stuck at the top bit, couldn't get a grip.'

'You got sticks of dyno up your arse, Ant?' said Ade, heaving himself onto the flat. 'You went by like a rocket.'

'Bloody plimsoll came off, dinnit?' yelled Thomas, holding the offending item aloft. He slumped down onto the ground and pulled it back on. 'Where's Bozo?' he said, lifting his head.

'Coming,' I answered. 'He's on his belly, mind. About to come over.'

A cry went up. 'Giz a hand!'

I went to the edge, crouched down onto my haunches and, grabbing Bozo's hand, pulled him onto the top. '*Uffach wyllt*,' he said, breathing heavily. 'That's harder than it looks.'

The five of us sat catching our breath. It wasn't much of a vantage point but just enough to look down over the village, the uniform rows of pitmen's houses, smoke gently rising from the chimneys. I imagined it had always looked this way, from the day it was first built, a village for miners: functional, no fuss, at one with the mountain.

'Well,' said Thomas, standing. 'Let's get at it.'

I placed my tea tray on the lip of the spoil tip and straddled it; the heels of my wellies dug down into the clinkers. Bozo went to place his down next to me but, in his exhaustion, he fumbled it and his tray skittered away. 'No!' he cried, grasping for a corner, but it was too late. We watched as it slid and bounced its way inevitably back to the bottom.

'Oh, for fuck's sake,' said Bozo, hands on hips. 'That's a bad business, like.'

'You massive tit, Bozo,' said Thomas, laughing. 'Chuckin' your tray down, is it? It's not a throwing contest.'

'*Cera yffarn*, Evans,' snapped Bozo, his one eye darkening. 'Bloody accident, innit?'

'Climb on behind me,' I said, sitting down and shifting my weight forward to the front of the tray. 'Mine's a bit bigger. You'll fit on. We'll go quicker, 'n' all.'

'Hang on!' yelled Thomas. 'Onesies, innit? We never said twosies.'

'Yeah, but his tray's down b'there, innit?' I replied.

'And he's proper knacked,' added Ade. 'He needs a lift, like.'

'S'pose,' said Thomas. 'But you have to do feet down, like. Make it fair.'

'All right,' I replied, with a nod.

I felt Bozo's arms come about me, his fingers interlocking just below my ribcage. 'Everyone ready?' I cast a glance to my left and right. Ade, Thomas and Fez were astride their chariots, each holding up the top end of their tea tray to stop it slipping away.

'Ready,' they all yelled.

'Kick off, then!' I cried, and with that, I lifted my heels onto the top rim of the tea tray and we were off, sliding down the spoil tip, clinkers scattering, bumping and jolting.

To our left, Thomas let out a whoop, followed by Ade, their excited yelps filling the air. To our right, Fez, screaming, hit a ridge and literally flew through the air, like a man on a magic carpet, his hair whipping backwards and his cheeks flushed pink. Everything else around us was a blur, the distant mountains a smudge of green zipping past as we skeltered downwards. Bozo was yelling something in my ear, but I couldn't hear him, the noise of the slag beneath us scraping and grumbling. I tried to look sideways, to see if we were in the lead, but the bottom was coming up fast, faster than I would have liked. 'Hold on!' I yelled, grabbing the sides of the tea tray. Wind whipping at our faces, we span off the spoil and skidded onto patchy scrub, and as we hit, the tea tray tipped sideways and sent us spilling.

'Cut my leg,' said Fez, holding his shin. He licked his forefinger and rubbed at the long scrape of red dribbling down towards his sock.

I pushed myself up and checked myself for obvious wounds. None to report. Bozo was still lying on his back, his face black from the spoil. We were all pretty filthy. It was the single advantage of being brought up round a mine: nobody minded the dirt. We'd had some chalk, once, spent ages marking out roads for Fez's Dinkies on the flagstones. The mams had gone mental, furious with us for making a clean, white mess on their paving. We couldn't understand it: mad with us for a bit of white when we spent all our days covered in black.

Ade was pushing himself up and dusting coal off his knees. Beyond him, a small, pained moan went up. Ade turned and looked over his shoulder towards Thomas. 'What's up, man?'

'Ankle, twisted, dunno, hurts like hell.' He sat up and pulled off his plimsoll.

'Bet you've bloody broken it again,' said Ade, pointing towards his leg. 'Your mam'll have your guts. You only just got out of the last cast.'

We gathered round him and stared down. There was no denying it. He'd knacked his leg right up.

''Ere, boys,' said Thomas, staring down at his swelling ankle. 'Don't tell me mam it was the tip, mind. I didn't tell her I was taking the tea tray.'

We all nodded and helped him up. We may have liked a scrape, but we weren't stupid.

'Born of a scorpion!' said Bopa, folding her arms. 'Can you even imagine it, Em? Stealing ration books! Three gone in Scott Street alone!'

My mother shook her head. 'Who'd steal a ration book? It's wicked, Bopa. Wicked.'

'They may as well knock on doors and tell people to starve! Beryl Morris has been in tears. She's only got half an ounce of kidneys. How do you make that last a fortnight?'

'Is that how long it's going to take to get replacements?'

'Well,' said Bopa, reaching for the kettle that was starting to whistle, 'that's how long Arthur Pryce said it would take. But that's Arthur Pryce. I wouldn't be surprised if Beryl Morris doesn't see another lump of meat for a month.'

'We'll have to help her out. I can ask Alwyn to catch her some rabbits.'

'I've given her two eggs. They're appetite suppressants. Pass me the pot. I'll get it warmed.'

Bopa, our immediate neighbour, was an irascible widow. She kept a clean flagstone and a keen eye on everyone else. She had brown hair, flecked with grey, cut short and hidden under a blue checked headscarf. Her face had a rough quality to it, like a pumice stone, her features sharp and pointed. Some boys reckoned she was directly descended from that dinosaur that can fly – a pterodactyl, it's called. Mam wouldn't hear chat like that in her earshot, mind. Disrespectful, she said.

'I hope you're listening, Anthony!' Bopa barked. 'Keep your whistle clean. Do something wrong and bad things happen! Mark my words. There was a boy from Blaencwm, doing the rounds for the milkie, turned out he was pocketing half the pennies. Guess what happened to him, Anthony?'

I shrugged. 'Don't know,' I mumbled.

'He got polio and died, that's what.'

'Bopa!' protested Mam. 'Stealing doesn't cause polio!'

'Bad things happen!' she cried, raising a finger into the air. 'Bad. Things. Happen! Young boys round here would do well to remember it.' She palmed the side of the teapot. 'That's warm enough. Let's get the tea in.'

Bopa came round at 11.00 a.m. on the dot every single day. She'd bang on the adjoining wall to signal her imminent arrival and in she would come, morning chores completed, ready to update my mother on every scandal and bowel movement troubling anyone in Scott Street.

'I think it's his liver,' she said, blowing into her cup. 'He's got that bilious look to him. Mind you, he's not eaten a vegetable since 1937. "Margaret," I said, "Margaret, you've got to put a carrot in a pie. Trick him into it." He picks leeks out of cawl, Em. The very thought! I think it's traitorous wasting food when there's a war on. Hitler wants us to starve. He's doing his job for him.'

My mother nodded silently and cupped her tea between her hands.

'You're a bit filthy, aren't you?' said Bopa, her beams turning towards me. 'I mean, I know you're a mucky lot, but if I didn't know you were a boy, I'd be chucking you on the compost.'

'Yes,' said Mam, turning towards me. 'You're in a proper muck. Have you been sliding down that spoil tip again? You better not have had my tray.'

Her eyes darted towards the place on the counter where she kept her tea trays. I said nothing. I'd snuck it back in and wiped it clean using the inside of my jumper.

'Dr Mitchell's round at Anne Evans'. Don't know why yet. Thought I'd pop over after seeing you. Don't like to intrude. He'll be snaffling up any cake that's going. He's a card, ain't he? I swear he can smell a cake from half a mile away. He's like those pigs that can sniff out treats.'

'A truffle pig,' I said, picking dirt out from under my fingernails.

'That's it. A truffle pig. But for sponge. Clever lad, your Anthony, ain't he?'

Mam nodded and shot me a small smile. 'He's always got his nose in that encyclopaedia of his. He loves reading that.'

'Dr Mitchell's seeing Thomas. He's bust his leg up again,' I said.

Bopa raised an eyebrow. 'Look out, Em. Your boy's on the button. Bust his leg, has he? How he do that, then?'

'Don't know,' I said, staring intently at my nails. I slightly wished I hadn't said anything.

'Didn't he only just finish breaking his leg?' I could feel her eyes boring into me.

'Hmmm,' I mumbled.

'He did,' Bopa rolled on. 'Well. Good job Anne hasn't sent that wheelchair off to salvage, innit? He'll be needing that again. How did he do it? Didn't catch it.' She took a long slurp of her tea.

I blew out my cheeks a little and pulled my bottom lip tight. It was an unspoken rule if you were a Scott Street boy: You didn't tell. 'Running or something,' I murmured.

'Running or something,' said Bopa, with a sharp nod. 'It's this war, Em. They're running wild. Feral. He'll have been up to no good. If I had a shilling for every time a Scott Street boy said he was doing something when he was doing something entirely different, I'd be living in Cardiff in a house made of Lardy cake. What did I say? Bad things happen!'

I looked up towards the old clock that sat on the back kitchen mantelpiece. It only had one arm, the long hour one, so as clocks go it wasn't much cop. All the same, I liked to guess what the time was just by looking at its tip. Twenty past eleven, I reckoned.

'Right, then,' said Bopa, thumping her cup down onto the table. 'I've got some cloths to wash. I'll pop into Anne Evans'. Let you know what's what. Ta-ra, then. Ta-ra, Anthony.'

'Ta-ra,' I said, pushing myself up from the table.

'Ta-ra, Bopa,' said Mam, standing to place the tea things in the sink. 'See you later.'

But she was already gone.

'Wash up those cups for me, Ant,' said Mam. 'Now, then,' she added, wiping her hands on the bottom of her housecoat. 'Let's think about your father's lunch.'

The tommy box was a battered old thing, the only family relic I think we ever had. It had been handed down from father to eldest son, pitmen all, for three generations, and I knew to be entrusted with it was a responsibility of some significance.

It was sitting, opened and empty, in front of me on the kitchen table. Chin resting on my crossed forearms, I watched as Mam opened the larder door beyond. 'Your father's forgotten his lunch again. Right, then,' she said, standing with one hand on her hip. 'What shall he have today?'

She stared at the near-empty shelves. There wasn't a lot to choose from. We never had much, but then, as Mam said, if we'd never had it, we'd never miss it.

'Lord knows it's hard enough feeding three men at the best of times, let alone with a war on. He can have that trotter,' Mam mumbled, picking up a gelatinous nub from a slippery plate. 'A slice of bread and … get me some jibbons from the veg box, Ant.' I slid backwards from the table and pulled out two long spring onions from a tangle of muddied home-grown vegetables. I passed them up to Mam, who quickly took her knife to the end of them. Peering into the tommy box, I snuck my forefinger into the trotter jelly.

'I can see you,' said Mam, slapping my hand away. She tucked the jibbons into the side of the open tin. 'Did you get that quarter of twist?'

I licked the stolen, meaty smear from the end of my finger and pulled out a small wrap of chewing tobacco from my shorts pocket. 'Mr Hughes told me to ask you to go in so you can square the bill.'

'He'll have to wait. I haven't got it. No more going in the shop until I get some wages from the boys. That means no penny chews on tick, Ant. Are you listening?' I nodded. Mam took the roll of tobacco, pressed it into the top, rounded section of the tommy box, then laid a slice of buttered bread over the trotter and onions, the soft seal to my father's lunch.

'There you go,' she said, pressing down the tin lid. 'Get that to the pit. And no nicking bits. Quick sharp.'

At the top end of the street, before the houses ended and our mountain began, a gaggle of Scott Street kids were huddled in a tight knot on the pavement. Something was going on. I had time, I reckoned, so I squeezed in. Two matchboxes were being poked with sticks. 'Give 'em a rattle, man,' said Fez, not looking up. 'Then we let 'em go.'

I tapped Ade on the shoulder. 'What's in 'em?'

'Red Indians. Fez's dad brought some back from the pit to give his mam a scare. Fez got hold of them. Reckon they'll fight.'

I pushed further into the circle and crouched down on my haunches. 'Let 'em go, Fez. Come on!'

Fez pushed his finger into the middle of one matchbox and eased the drawer open. Two red antennae popped upwards. The girls in the group gave out small, theatrical screams. 'Don't let it loose, Fez!' wailed one, staring wide-eyed at the tiny, probing feelers.

12

'Come on, Fez,' urged Ade, 'get at it, man!'

'They'll never stay out,' I said. 'They only like the dark down the pit.'

'We'll see,' said Fez, poking both matchboxes fully open.

For a moment, the cockroaches seemed stunned, as if daylight had shocked them rigid, but then, in the blink of an eye, they were scuttling, feelers swathing from left to right. The circle of children burst backwards like a flower exploding into bloom. 'Stop 'em!' shouted Ade. 'Make the buggers fight!'

'Look out!' screamed one of the girls, covering her face with her hands. 'They eat your eyes!'

The largest Red Indian had scuttled left, but as a defensive plimsoll shot down in its direction, it turned sharply back on itself and headed towards me and Ade. 'Watch out!' cried Ade, standing up suddenly. 'They're bloody at it!'

I was momentarily caught off balance and fell sideways onto my elbow. Around me there were more hysterical screams. A sharp tingling sensation coursed down my shin.

'It's in your boot, Ant!' shouted Ade. 'Get it off, man!'

Fez grabbed the heel of my wellington and tossed it across the street. Nobody moved.

I looked down at my bare foot. No Red Indian. 'Where is it?' I said, panting.

'It'll still be in there,' said Ade, gesturing towards the discarded wellington as if it were an unexploded bomb. 'Go get it.'

'Where's the other one?' I said, scrabbling upwards.

'Over there by the drain,' said Fez. 'Do you want my stick to pick up your wellie?' He held out a whittled branch.

I shook my head.

My wellington was resting at an angle against the kerb. I hopped over towards it and peered into the opening.

'Flick it, Ant,' encouraged Ade. 'Pick it up. Flick it out.'

'I don't know how to do it.' I said, my cheeks reddening.

'Oh, *duw*, he can't do it,' murmured Fez. 'You do it, Ade. You don't mind a Red Indian.'

'Move aside,' said Ade, crossing the street towards me. 'And give me that.'

He took my father's tommy box in his left hand. Bending down, he took the heel of my wellington, banged it sharp on the kerb and upturned it. The cockroach fell out. Slam went the tommy box. A crunch. A grind. A peek. He looked over to the others. 'I killed it,' he announced.

A cheer went up and everyone ran over to stare down at the pulpy mess smeared across the bottom of my father's tommy box. 'There you go,' said Ade, handing it back to me. 'That's how you finish a Red Indian.'

I took my wellington and pulled it back on. Ade was having his back slapped, the hero of the hour. I stared down at the splattered innards smeared across the tin box's bottom. Father wouldn't want that for his lunch.

'Wanna try and catch the other one, Ant?' said Ade, beaming.

'Can't. Got to take this for Father.'

He nudged his head upwards. 'Ta-ra, then.'

'Ta-ra.'

Nobody watched me go and I turned away, slightly embarrassed. I looked down at the mess of splintered legs and yellow gore. I couldn't wipe it clean with my jumper sleeve so I'd wait until I'd crossed the black tinder track that served as the marker between street and mountain. I'd clean it in the brook.

Beyond the tinder track was a stream that tumbled down between the hillside crevasses and veered left, away from the top of the village. Dropping down over a thick tussock, I splashed into the cold waters. The depth was deceptive, and water cascaded over the rim of my wellingtons. I leapt backwards but it was too late. My feet were soaked. No matter. I was used to it.

This part of the stream was always clean. The river changed as it passed the colliery, picking up coal dust and clinkers, a black bubbling mass that drifted onwards, but here it was still as the mountain intended: clear, crisp.

I bent down and scooped some water onto the bottom of the tommy box, but the innards proved sticky and stubborn. I reached into the water for one of the flat pieces of flint that covered the riverbed and, wiping it first on the leg of my shorts, scraped off the remains of the cockroach. Such a squashed mess. A small surge of annoyance flushed through me and I tossed the mucky flint downstream.

The Tydraw Colliery was situated in a narrow part of the valley between our mountain, Pen Pych, and her sister, Graig-Y-Ddelw. If the wind was blowing towards you, you could taste it coming: a thick, deep tang of black stuff that stuck to the back of your throat. I hopped over a rail track where a few empty drams were sitting idle, and made my way, between grey stone buildings and corrugated iron structures, towards two large pithead wheels. There was a constant beat of shunting coal trucks and grinding cable, and a cloud of steam, the trusted marker for the prevailing wind, billowed low, whipping across the rooftops of the outbuildings. I watched its thick bloom lick across the valley. The wind was coming from the west.

A group of pitmen, about four or five miners, was sitting on some upturned drams to the left of the pithead. The tallyman, a short, stocky fellow with a cap pulled low over his forehead, was standing above them, gesturing back towards the lamp house.

'*Cera yffarn*! I'm going back down after I've had my buttie, man!' said a blackened man, legs splayed either side of the end of the dram. 'You'll only have to give it me back.'

'Stop being daft, hand it over. You know full well – if you're up, you hand it in.'

'Christ, man,' said the fellow, reaching into his waistcoat pocket and pulling out a small metal coin. 'There. Now leave me be, daft bugger.'

He took a bite from his sandwich and grimaced. 'Bloody jam again,' he said, his cheeks bulging outwards.

'Every day you get jam,' said another man, sitting on the floor with his back against the dram. 'Every day you moan. Ask your sweetheart to put something else in your sandwiches, for Christ's sake.'

'I would,' the first man replied, 'but I make them myself.'

Groans rang out. I found myself grinning. 'Bloody hell, Alf,' said the man sitting on the floor. 'Your jokes don't get any better. No wonder you haven't got a sweetheart.'

'Don't need a sweetheart these days, innit?' said Alf. 'You can get a tup easy enough. Pretend you're a soldier on furlough, the girls throw themselves at you.'

'Every girl in Treherbert knows you're a pitman!'

'Doesn't matter. Go doe-eyed, tell 'em you've signed up. Being sent to France or Africa, like. Might not be back for Christmas, you say. Might not be back at all. If only I'd had a tup with a girl, like! Oh, to die a virgin!' He clutched at his chest, dramatically.

'And they give you tups? For telling 'em that?' said the man on the floor.

'Works like a dream,' said Alf, leaning back.

'And what happens when they see you the next day in your pit kit?'

Alf shrugged. 'Jobs done b'then, innit?'

'*Uffarn den*! You're a menace, Alf Davies,' said the man sitting on the floor, shaking his head. 'I wouldn't let a woman anywhere near you.'

'Aye, aye,' said Alf spying me. 'What's this? You're Davey's boy, aren't you? Scott Street? Bethan's brother?'

I nodded and came to a standstill.

'Brought his tommy box? Forgotten it again, has he?' Alf continued. '*Duw*, he'll forget his trousers one of these days. He's underground. You taking it down?'

I shook my head. He shoved the last of his sandwich into his mouth and tilted his head as he stared at me. A thick, bready grin stretched across his face.

'You ever been underground, boy?'

I shook my head again.

'Fancy going down? Would you like to?'

I nodded.

'Ignore him,' the man sitting on the floor said in my direction. 'Lampy'll never allow it.'

'Course he will. We all had to go down a first time,' said Alf, sliding off the dram and coming towards me. 'I'll keep an eye on him. You going to be a miner, then?'

I nodded one more time.

'Course you are. Good Welsh lad. Black stuff is in your blood. Come on, then. Let's get a token from the lamp house. I'm Alf. What's your name? Tallyman will want it.'

'Anthony Jones,' I said, holding tight to the tommy box. 'I don't know if I can go down, though. Father might not like it.'

'There comes a time when all sons must go against their father's wishes, young Anthony. It's how we become men. And besides, you want to see underground, don't you? See what it's like?'

I did want to see it. From the six o'clock siren that rang over the rooftops, to the clattering of hobnailed boots coming back at night, underground was the driving heart of our village. It was spoken of every evening, ingrained into every crease of my father's face. It was our way of life. It was my future and I had never even seen it. 'Yes,' I said. 'I do.'

'Come on, then,' said Alf, wiping his fingers on the bottom of his dust-covered shirt. He pressed his hand into the middle of my back. 'Let's go down.'

'He'll have your guts for garters!' shouted the man sitting on the floor.

'Ignore him,' said Alf, pushing me forwards. 'It's an adventure, innit?'

I followed him to the lamp house, a small outbuilding to the left of the pithead. It had no door, and I stood in the open frame, hanging back. Alf went forward.

'Give us two tokens,' he said, leaning across a scarred wooden counter. 'I'm taking Davey's boy down. He's brought his father's tommy box.' He nudged his head back in my direction.

'Are you mad? I'm not letting a boy down. How old is he? Ten? Eleven? Get away, man. Finish your butties. And you …' He strained round to look at me. 'If you want to leave your father's box with me, you can.'

'Don't trust him. There's a reason he's that fat,' said Alf, leaning back against the counter and grinning. 'Come on, Lampy. Let him go. He wants to see it. I'll not let him out of my sight. Take him down for five minutes. No more.'

'No, Alf,' said the lamp man, shaking his head. 'It's not happening.'

'I'll trade you a coupon,' said Alf, shooting me a wink.

'For what?' answered the lamp man, his tone softening.

'Dunno. Something you need, something you'd look good in … stockings?'

I suppressed a giggle. The lamp man rolled his eyes. 'Alf Davies, you're a right card. Give me a coupon for cheese and you've got a deal.'

'Cheese? Hate the stuff.' He spat on his hand and held it out.

'All right,' said the lamp man, taking Alf's hand and shaking it. 'Five minutes, mind. No more. Straight down. Straight up. And I want that coupon first thing, Alf. Got it?'

'Got it,' said Alf. He turned and gave me a lopsided grin.

Alf took the helmets from the lamp man and gestured for me to go outside. 'Now, then,' he began, fixing me with intensely blue eyes, 'here's your helmet and that there's your lamp.' He held up a heavy metal pack that was attached to the helmet by a cord. 'And this is the battery for the lamp. Tuck that onto the back of your belt.'

'Haven't got a belt,' I said, struggling to keep the front end of the helmet from falling down over my eyes.

'Then shove it down the back of your shorts,' said Alf. 'Or hold on to it. Here's your token. Stick that in your pocket. Before you go underground, you hand that to the pit cage tallyman. That's how he knows how many men are down.'

I tried slipping the battery pack down the back of my shorts, but it was so heavy it fell out the hole of my right leg and dangled behind my knee. I looked towards Alf, who was clipping his own to the back of his belt. I didn't want him to think I was stupid, so I pulled the cord upwards and decided to carry it instead.

'Right, then,' said Alf, patting me on the back, 'let's get to the pit cage.'

The cages hung from the base of the pithead wheels, and as we walked towards them I felt strangely elated. I was going underground. We'd find Father and he'd see me and p'raps, even though I wasn't allowed, like, he'd be pleased? It showed gumption, spirit. He admired those things in a man. P'raps he'd admire them in me?

'Your sister, Bethan,' said Alf, casually, as we walked towards the cages, 'she stepping out with anyone?'

I shook my head. 'Don't think so. She hasn't brought anyone home.'

Alf sniffed. 'She up at RAF St Athan, isn't she? In the WAAF. Not fallen for any of those fancy airmen, then?'

I shrugged.

'What's all this, then, Alf?' said a man sitting by the cages reading a paper.

'Taking Davey's boy down. It's all right. Lampy's said so. He's got a token. Five minutes down, and then we're up.'

The man frowned. 'Your father know about this, does he?' he said, looking straight at me.

I looked down at my wellingtons and my helmet slid towards the bottom of my nose. I shoved it upwards. 'No,' I said. 'But I've got his tommy box. And he likes gumption.'

'Gumption, is it?' said the tallyman, his forehead frowning. 'More like bloody madness. Lampy said yes? Has he lost his mind?'

'Quit blathering!' said Alf. 'He's only going down for five minutes. I'm not taking him down to do a shift. Besides, he'll be down here for good, soon enough. May as well see his home from home, innit?'

'I don't like it,' said the man, folding his paper and standing up. 'Five minutes and no more, mind. They're blasting this afternoon. I want him back up before they start.'

'On my word,' said Alf, reaching for the metal bar that spanned the large empty cage in front of us. 'Anthony, give the man your token.'

I reached into my pocket and pulled out the small, scratched circle of metal.

'In you get, then,' said the tallyman, taking it. 'Don't put your hands outside the cage. Drams coming up. They make a racket.'

I stepped inside the cage and stood next to Alf. To our left was a cavernous hole, the shaft that held the larger cage for shuttling coal drams. Our cage was big enough for about ten men and, instinctively, I shuffled myself into one corner. Alf slotted down the horizontal metal bar in front of us, then reached up and fixed a vertical bar across it.

With no solid walls to the cage, I felt exposed, as if the mountain could eat me up at any moment. My stomach bubbled and I found myself rushing forward to cleave into Alf's side. He glanced down and let his arm drift around my shoulders. 'Ready?' he said. I nodded. 'Away, then!'

A sudden jolt and we plunged downwards into the pit, blasts of warm air shooting through my fringe. It was blacker than I'd imagined and I narrowed my eyes, hoping they'd acclimatise to the gloom. I raised my hand in front of my face. I couldn't even make out a shape. I felt disorientated, anxious, and my nails dug into Alf's shirt, desperate to hold on to anything for a scrap of comfort. The noise! Metal on metal, grinding, ugly sounds filling the air. I wanted to block it all out, but I was paralysed with fear, as if I'd been punched, very suddenly, and couldn't move. My ears popped and an odd sense of weightlessness overwhelmed me, as if my feet were bobbing in water. We were now going so fast I couldn't tell if we were going down or coming back up again. I wanted to call out for it to stop. I didn't like it.

A light sparked above me. Alf had turned on his helmet lamp. 'Twist that,' he yelled over the rattling. He pointed towards a large dial on the top of my battery box. I turned it and a small round light appeared in front of me, catching the contours of the rock as we descended.

I grimaced. 'Not long now,' shouted Alf, seeing my expression.

A deep rumbling tumbled upwards, like a train, a wave of dark noise. The cage shook and I stumbled away from Alf, falling into the side rail. My head jerked forward, sending the beam from my helmet shining down into the shaft. The light caught something metallic, the noise roared louder, I felt the breath catch in my throat, and my eyes widened. Something was coming up and it was coming fast. I heard a voice shouting, felt a hand gripping me in the middle of my shirt. Alf yanked me backwards, there was a sudden dazzle of lamps, and the coal dram cage with its men on board shot past us. It knocked the breath from my lungs. I gasped for air, shut my eyes tight and buried my face deep into Alf's smoky shirt.

A bump. A pat on my shoulder.

'That's it,' said Alf. 'We're down.'

He undid the two metal bars at the front of the cage and we walked out into a tunnel. It was about fifteen feet wide. Small electrical lamps ran along the walls either side of us, and below my feet were tracks that disappeared off into pitch black. The smell was dense, claggy, warm earth and coal, the air filled with dust. I lifted a hand to my forehead. I was sweating. It was hot. I hadn't expected that.

'There's a fallen section that way,' said Alf, pointing off down a side tunnel. 'They're working it up with timbers. Your da's b'there. It's not far.'

'Will my brothers be there n'all?' I asked.

Alf shook his head. 'Nah, they're loading drams down by the seam.'

A series of loud thuds rumbled above us and the tunnel shook, sending small grumbling waves up through my legs. I looked towards Alf. 'Was that thunder?' I said.

23

'Bumpers,' he told me. 'It's the mountain settling after the seams are worked. Happens all the time. Come on. Follow me.' He strode off.

I kept as close as I could, occasionally breaking into a trot when I had to. Ahead of us, the dark, black circle tightened and I began to feel the dank creep of something claustrophobic. Skewed timbers held up roof falls, moisture dripped from the ceiling, creatures scuttled as we passed, and the hair on the back of my neck began to bristle. A sharp chill was icing up my spine. I didn't want to be afraid. But I was.

'Conveyor belt's running,' said Alf, as another intense rumble sounded from inside the walls. 'It runs down the seam. Brings the coal up, men down.'

We walked on, indecipherable voices drifting up through the dark. Ahead of us, the tiny black pinhole began to open out, larger with every step nearer, until we found ourselves stepping into a chamber filled with light. A group of men was fixing interlocking timbers. It was bright. I blinked.

I heard a voice call out. 'Pass me that cleat!' I recognised it. It was Father.

A tight ball of panic surged through me. I wanted him to be impressed, to be proud of how brave I'd been, to pat me on the back, call me 'his boy', but now, standing here, waiting for him to turn round, I knew exactly how he was going to react. I looked back the way I'd come. If I ran now, I'd get back to the cage without him seeing me. I turned. A hand fell on my shoulder.

'Someone to see you, Davey!' called out Alf, a laugh in his voice. 'You'll never guess who.'

A bundle of hunched, blackened men all turned round, the whites of their eyes dancing in the lamplight.

'*Uffach wyllt*,' said one of them, nearest me. 'He's brought your boy down.'

My father stepped forward, sledgehammer in hand. His face, black with coal dust, was as dark as I had ever seen it. I stared up at him. Father was a tall man, broad across the shoulders, a rugby player in his youth. Could have played for Wales, they said, but he broke an ankle and that was the end of that.

'I've brought your tommy box, Father,' I said, holding it up.

He raised the back of his hand and struck me, sending a sharp sting throbbing across my cheek. I raised my arm to protect myself. 'I just thought I'd—'

'Not another word, Anthony.'

My father stared down at me, livid, and then his eyes darted towards Alf. 'Was this your doing, Davies?'

'He wanted to come down,' said Alf, lightly. 'I was merely obliging.'

'You bloody idiot. They're blasting shortly. Take him back and get him up.' Taking me roughly by the shoulder, he drew me to one side. 'Anthony. You must never come down here again. Do you understand?'

I stared into his eyes. 'I'm sorry, Father. I wanted to see—'

'Get out of here!' he yelled. 'Now! I don't want to see you underground again.' He bundled me forcibly back towards the tunnel and pushed me so that I nearly fell. Turning towards Alf, his jaw tightened. 'I'll speak with you later, Davies. Now get him out of here.'

'Looks like we're not wanted,' said Alf, pulling his hands from his pockets. 'No need to get a cob on, Davey. Boy was only bringing you stuff to feed that belly. 'Ere,' he added, taking the tommy box from me, 'best not forget why we came, eh?' He tossed it towards my father. 'Ta-ra, then. Enjoy your lunch.'

Father surged forwards but was held back by a man behind him. 'Leave it, Davey,' he said. 'You can square it with him later.'

Alf tipped his cap. 'Come on, then, young Ant. Adventure over.'

'I'll catch it later,' I said, following him back down the tunnel. 'I'll get the belt for this. And I've got you in trouble, 'n' all.'

'Don't mither yourself,' he said, shooting me a glance. 'I've had worse. He'll give you some snaps, tell me off. I'll shrug and take it. We'll shake hands and that'll be that. Tell you what, how's about you say hello from me to your sister Bethan? That's a fair trade, I say.'

'All right,' I agreed with a nod.

'Shake on it, then,' he said, holding out a filthy hand.

I took his hand and we shook. 'No telling the other lads, mind. Or they'll all want to come down. Anyway,' Alf added, 'more important … how do you like underground?'

I looked around me. It was filthy, hot and cramped, and yet something about it called to me. 'I like it very much.'

CHAPTER TWO

Ade clattered in through our front door and slid towards the kitchen, boots squeaking across the linoleum. Catching himself with one hand on the doorframe, he stopped and looked towards me. He was panting. 'Mrs Reece has got a banana!' he yelled. 'She's going to show it to all the kids in Scott Street. Come on, Ant. We're going up b'there now.'

I cast a glance towards Mam. She had a loaf of bread tucked under one arm and was buttering the cut end with the back of a wooden spoon.

'Can I go, Mam?' I asked, leaning across the kitchen table. 'Mrs Reece has got a banana.'

'Do you know what a banana is?' she asked, not looking up.

I shook my head.

'Well, go and find out, then. But don't be long. Father and the boys will be back soon, and I want that tin bath out.'

'Come on, Ant!' yelled Ade, running back out towards the street. 'Or we'll miss it.'

Pushing back my stool, I jumped up and ran across the kitchen towards my wellies. I'd put them by Mam's stove, hoping they might dry out. But they never did. 'You've got the feet of an eighty-year-old man,' Mam would tell me, when my toes were white and wrinkled from the wet.

I grabbed a boot and let my foot be sucked downwards. A faint aroma of something deep and damp wafted up, and a familiar cold, clammy sensation flooded across my sole. The boots smelled hot and wet, the way bogs up the mountain do in summer. The stink breathed up my leg, like thick smoke clinging to a pipe. They were black and two sizes too big. They used to belong to Mrs Morris's father, but he died and Mam gave Mrs Morris a pie for them, so now they were mine. My eldest brother Alwyn said the old fella died wearing them, which meant they were haunted. Bopa told me to pay no attention. 'Wellington boots are not receptacles for spirits,' she said, although she did hear of a woman who swore blind her dead cat was spending eternity in her coal scuttle. I didn't know if my wellies were haunted, but I did know they'd left dark smudged rings around my shins that I couldn't get rid of. 'It's the rubber,' Bopa always said.

'Here,' said Mam, handing me a just-cut slice of buttered bread. 'Take that. And don't be long, mind.'

'I won't, Mam,' I replied, squashing the soft white bread between my fingers. It was still warm, the butter melting on the top, and as I raced to the door, I shovelled the crusty end into the side of my mouth.

Kids were pelting past me, hobnailed boots sparking off the flagstones, plimsolls scuffing up the clinkers, all helter-skeltering towards the bottom end of Scott Street, where a small crowd of boys and the odd girl were mustering themselves around the doorway of Mrs Reece. I could see Ade, his jumper flapping behind him like a cape. Swallowing the bread, I made after him, my feet squelching along the paving stones.

'Mrs Reece has got a banana!' Kids were shouting, lumps of chalk discarded, marbles gathered. The air bristled with excitement. Children tumbling up the road like leaves in the wind. Nobody had ever seen a banana. I wasn't entirely sure what one was. I had a vague notion that it might be something massive that had to be held like a baby.

I ran harder to reach the jostling group, head down, arms working like pistons. My feet rattled inside my wellies, flopping about like just-landed fish. I hadn't had proper shoes in over a year. 'Wear those till you grow out of them,' Mam had said when she first handed them to me.

'He'll be wearing them until he's old and buried. No chance of him ever growing,' said Alwyn. Everyone laughed. I had always been small for my age. Mam put it down to an infection when I was a baby and a lack of meat since the war started. 'You're my rations baby,' she said, ruffling my fringe.

'Runt of the litter, more like,' said Alwyn.

Ade was pushing through the bigger kids at the back. 'Come on, Ant!' he yelled, gesturing for me to follow him. I slipped through a small pool of elbows and shoulders, kids standing on their tiptoes, straining for the best view of Mrs Reece's front door. Ade reached back and grabbed the sleeve of my jumper to pull me through. 'Littl'uns up front,' he said, his eyes wide with excitement.

'She's coming!' cried out Bronwyn Pryce, her face blushing pink.

'Ssshhh, everyone! The banana's coming!' shouted Ade.

You could hear a pin drop. All eyes were fixed on the door, unblinking.

Mrs Reece appeared, arms folded in a knot, lips pursed tight. She was a stout woman, built like a pit pony, dress sleeves shoved up hard past her elbows, with a faded blue housecoat clinging to every curve. Her hair was dark brown, piled high into a functional topknot, her face soft and full with a hint of colour in the cheeks. Her eyes darted over the group. 'Now, what's all this?' she said, standing a little taller.

One of the bigger boys behind me shoved me forward. 'You're the littlest. You ask her,' he said.

'Mrs Reece,' I said, staring up at her, 'can we see your banana?'

'It's the banana, is it?' she replied, one eyebrow raising. 'Well, now. How many of you want to see it?'

'I do!' shouted Ade, his hand shooting into the air.

'And me!' yelled Bronwyn, nodding her head furiously. A small cacophony of excited yelps filled the air.

'Right,' she continued. 'Then I suppose I can show it to you.'

I felt Ade's hand on my shoulder as he went up on his toes to get a better view. All eyes were on Mrs Reece as she unfolded her arms and reached into the large front pocket of her housecoat. Pulling the centre of the pocket forward, she lifted out a long, slightly bent yellow thing and held it aloft.

'There it is. That's my banana!' she said, triumphantly.

A collective gasp rippled through us.

'What do you do with it?' said Ade, his eyes as wide as plates.

'You eat it.'

'How do you eat it?' asked Bronwyn, stepping closer to get a better look.

'I don't know,' said Mrs Reece, a little sheepishly. 'I've written to my sister in Cardiff to find out. Until I hear, I'm going to put it on a plate and keep it.'

'Can I touch your banana, Mrs Reece,' I asked, stepping closer.

She looked down at me and thought about that. 'All right,' she replied. 'But a quick touch, mind. And only a feel. You're not allowed to hold it.'

The kids behind me gathered in, jostling from all sides. She lowered the banana and held it out in her palm. I looked at it. It was so peculiar. 'What's it made of?' asked Ade, his face pushing low into my armpit.

'It's made of banana,' answered Mrs Reece.

I reached out with my forefinger and let it hover. I didn't know what to expect. I'd touched a grass snake once up our mountain. I thought it would be scaly, raspy, but it was as smooth as silk. 'Go on,' said Ade, nudging me in the ribs. 'Touch it!'

I let my finger drop onto the banana's surface. It felt tough, like old leather, but fibrous, the way celery feels in your mouth. I ran my finger along its length, watching the way it curved 'It's bendy,' said Ade. 'Is it broken? Can I touch it too?'

'No, you can't,' said Mrs Reece, withdrawing the banana and popping it back into her housecoat pocket. 'They're supposed to be bendy. Right. Fun's over. Off you all go.'

'Where are you going to keep it?' asked Bronwyn, rubbing the back of her hand across her nose.

'On a plate in the parlour,' said Mrs Reece, retreating back into her hallway. 'I'll place it near the window. So you can see it.'

Ade cast me a glance and yanked me towards Mrs Reece's parlour window. Pressing his nose hard against it, he peered in. Joining him, I rested my elbows on the stone sill and watched as Mrs Reece took one of her best flowery plates from her dresser, placed the banana in its centre and presented it on a small round table in front of the window.

'Let us have a look!' shouted Gwyn Williams, shoving me to one side. Gwyn was a year older than me, taller and broader. He had a squashed-in face, as if someone had pressed him into a flat tin. He elbowed Ade out of his way and raised his hands to cup his eyes against the pane. 'I'm going to try and eat that banana,' he said. 'See if I don't.'

'Don't be daft,' responded Ade, trying to push his way back to the window. 'Mrs Reece doesn't even know how to eat it. Maybe you can't eat it? Maybe bananas are German tricks?'

'Did a German give Mrs Reece that banana?' said Gwyn, turning to stare at Ade.

Ade screwed up his nose. He was on unsure ground, but Gwyn was turning nasty and he had to show no weakness.

'Don't be daft, man. There's no Germans in Treherbert.'

A tight fist popped across Ade's nose, sending him sprawling. 'Call me daft, is it? I'll show you how daft I am. Get up!'

I bent down to help Ade to his feet. A small drop of blood fell from the tip of his nose, and he rolled his hand into the sleeve of his jumper to wipe it away. His eyes were watering and I could tell he was trying hard not to cry.

'You didn't have to hit him,' I said, 'he's half your size.'

Gwyn's knuckles crunched across my cheek and I fell down

on one knee. Without looking up, I dived towards Gwyn's knees and tackled him backwards.

'Fight!' I heard Bronwyn yell.

Fists pummelled into my side, sending a sharp pain ricocheting up my spine. I cried out but held on, kicking down on his ankle in an effort to push myself upwards. My wellingtons scrabbled backwards on the cobbles, but they were wet and I couldn't get a grip. As I slid away, a fat knee came sharp and upwards into my belly. I doubled up, the wind knocked out of me, and as I rolled into the kerb, I felt another fist land on my left side. I looked up into a tight circle of faces.

'Get up, Ant!' I heard Ade yelling.

Gwyn loomed downwards, I felt my shirt collars being grabbed, and I was hauled upwards. I saw his arm go back but as it did, I swung my right arm and jabbed it forward, catching him on the nose. He reeled away, clutching his face.

'Leg it!' shouted Ade. 'He'll kill you!'

But the circle was too tight. There was no escape route. Spitting blood out from his mouth, Gwyn came for me again, his face scowling with fury. My back tumbled against gathered bodies, and Gwyn came in, both fists pummelling, and then, with one fulsome punch, he had me down.

My head hit the cobbles and the world spun away, the taste of clinkers filling my mouth. Everything went quiet and, for a moment, I was utterly at peace, deep and lost, and then a voice, familiar and anxious, floated somewhere above me. 'You've killed him. You've killed Ant.'

I felt hands pulling me up, there was a smell I knew but couldn't place, and then I opened my eyes and saw my sister Bethan. She was pushing hair from my eyes. 'Are you all right, Ant?' she said, peering down at me.

'Dunno,' I said, tasting a tang of blood.

'Bugger off, Gwyn Williams,' she turned and yelled. 'If you want a fight, you can have one with me!' I raised my head and narrowed one eye. I could see the back of Gwyn Williams sparking off up Scott Street.

'He was sticking up for me,' said Ade, leaning in to take a look. 'Gwyn Williams punched me first. Look …' He stuck an index finger up his nostril, pulled it out and showed Bethan. There was blood on the end of it.

'You shouldn't hang round him,' Bethan answered. 'You know what he's like.'

'Is Ant going to die?'

'No,' said Bethan, putting an arm round me to support me. 'Few bruises. Sit on the kerb, Ant. Let me have a look at you.'

She picked up the gas mask box she'd dropped on the flagstone and clicked the hinge in its centre. Pulling out a small pink handkerchief, she spat on it and rubbed at my eyebrow. 'Got coal dust in that cut,' she said, frowning. 'I can't take my eye off you for a minute, can I?' She smiled and I felt a familiar warmth course through me. I wanted to fold into her, but I didn't want to make a soft show in front of the other Scott Street boys. I sat on my hands and raised my knees upwards. My left wellington had come off in the scuffle and my bare foot was covered in grey muck.

'Here y'aar,' said Bronwyn, handing me my lost boot. 'Does your face hurt?' She stared down at me.

I shook my head. I was lying and everyone knew it, but Treherbert boys didn't moan and I wasn't about to start.

'There,' said Bethan, giving me a short tap on my knee. 'That's the best I can do out here. Let's get you home and I can tidy you up proper.'

She reached down, took my hand in hers and pulled me up from the kerb.

'Thanks, Ant,' said Ade, with a small nod and a manly pat to my back. 'I owe you one. He fought Gwyn Williams off me!' he shouted to the kids still clustering round. 'Did you see him? Did you see?'

I pulled my wellington back on and let Bethan steer me homewards. My head was hung low, despite the cries of my heroics scattering behind me. I had fought Gwyn Williams and lost. Again.

'Look at you,' Bethan said, stuffing the bloodied hanky back into her gas mask box. 'Fighting again. Father won't be pleased. If that eye comes up with a shiner, there'll be no hiding it from him.'

'I'm already in trouble with Father,' I said, rubbing blood from my nose with the back of my hand. 'I went underground. I'll get a leathering for it when he gets back.'

'Sorry?' said Bethan, stopping in her tracks and staring at me. 'You went underground? How did you manage that?'

'Alf Davies took me. And then he asked me to say hello to you.'

'Bloody cheek!' Bethan rolled her eyes and gave a long sigh. 'Alf Davies. You stay away from Alf Davies. He's a bad influence. Took you underground? Of all the irresponsible ...'

I looked up at her, my eyes brimming with tears. I'd managed not to cry in front of the others, but now, as our front door loomed, I felt the weight of the trouble I was in.

'Shall I tell you something to cheer you up? It's secret, mind, so no blabbing,' said Bethan, fixing me with her green eyes.

'What secret?' I said, rubbing at my eye with my sleeve.

She leant down and held her mouth close to my ear. 'The Americans are coming.' She straightened and shot me a wink.

'Where?' I said, looking up at her. 'To here? To Treherbert?'

'Maybe,' she said, hooking her gas mask box back into the crook of her left elbow. 'They're coming to Porthcawl and then they'll be stationed all over. We were told today. They're being billeted. But it's top secret, mind. So no loose lips.'

'Why are they coming? Are the Germans invading Wales?'

'Hope not!' snorted Bethan, pushing open our front door. 'Can you imagine Emrys if he was ever face-to-face with an actual German? He'd eat him. Eat him all up!' She dropped her gas mask box over the banister and grabbed me suddenly about my waist and shook me. 'Eat him up! Eat him up!'

'Get off!' I laughed, trying to push her off.

Bethan stood back up and put her hands on her hips. 'You're a good boy, Ant. Looking after Ade.' She stared down at me, smiling, and ran her fingers through my fringe. 'Don't worry about Father. I'll tell Mam.'

'That you, Ant?' came a call from the kitchen. 'I want that tub out!'

'It's me too, Mam!' Bethan shouted out. 'I'll get out of my uniform and come help! Come on,' she added, looking back down at me. 'I'll lend a hand. And leave telling what happened to me. You'll get flustered and it'll come out wrong. Go get the tub. I'll start the water.'

She kicked off her shoes, pulled on her slippers and headed up the stairs.

The tin tub hung on the outside wall in the back garden. It was bigger than I was, and I always had to carry it with the top end hooked over my head. Being the youngest, it was my job to get it in front of the fire and filled with water so that Father, Alwyn and my other brother Emrys could get washed when they came back from the pit. If they had to wait around, I'd catch it.

I flipped the tub over onto the rug in front of the hearth. Mam tipped more coal onto the fire from the scuttle, a grand clatter followed by a blast of heat, and then placed the coal soap, the bar that was only for Father and the boys, into the bottom of the tin bath. 'Get a lick on,' she said, wiping her hands on the bottom of her housecoat. 'They'll be here any minute.'

I ran through to the kitchen, almost bumping into Bethan. She was carrying the first of the large pots of water that had been boiling on the stove. 'Look out, Ant!' she yelled, lifting the pot above my head. I took a tea cloth from the front of the stove, doubled it over and lifted the second pan of hot water, taking care not to spill any. It took four pans to get the water to a reasonable level, with one pan of cold so that Father wouldn't have to wait for it to cool down before he could get in.

Mam stood, hand on hip by the parlour window, gazing out. 'Have you got something you want to tell me, Anthony?' she said, not looking at me.

I shot a glance towards Bethan. 'It's all right,' she mouthed.

'I went underground, Mam,' I said, my voice soft and quiet. 'Father wasn't pleased.'

'No. I expect not. I'm not pleased, either,' she said. 'That Alf Davies is reckless. An idiot. The best favour you can ever do yourself is to pick out the idiots and steer well clear of them. Do you understand, Ant?'

'Yes, Mam,' I said, leaning against the arm of Father's chair. 'Will I get a leathering?'

She turned and looked at me, her eyes resigned to the inevitable. She gave a small sigh. 'Probably. I'll do my best.'

My heart sank. Mam could never bear to see us beaten, but Father said it was the only way we'd learn. You got his belt over your upturned palm five times. There was no escaping it. It hurt like hell.

'Here they come!' Mam said, as miners began pouring past the parlour window. 'Paper down!'

Bethan grabbed yesterday's paper and began laying out the double sheets, creating a temporary bridge from tub to door. Two sheets were laid next to the paper trail, small islands for Alwyn and Emrys, who would have to stand, waiting for their turn in the tub. All eyes on the parlour door and then in they came, three great, blackened men, the smell of coal dust filling the air. Helmets were tossed in my direction, Davy lamps lined up, clothes peeled off to be surgically removed to the back room washtub by Mam, every day the same, the household moving as one slick machine until Father was in the tub and my two elder brothers were standing in their long johns.

But today's routine was to be different.

'Hand out, Anthony,' said Father, pulling his belt out from his trousers.

'It wasn't his fault, Davey,' said Mam, stepping towards me. 'It's Alf Davies'. He took him down.'

'Hand out.'

I let my arm drift upwards and span my palm to face the ceiling. Mam turned away, her hand resting on the mantelpiece behind me, and Bethan cast her eyes towards the floor. I looked up into Father's face, stern, furrowed. There was no animosity. We'd just get this done. I braced. His arm went up, and down it came, the bent-over leather thwacking onto my skin. I winced. Four more times, the only noise in the room the leather slicing through the air, biting into my flesh, and short, tiny grunts from Father. I didn't look down at my hand. Instead, I focused on Father's face. No pleasure lay there, and for all the times I'd had this done, I was always left with the overwhelming sense that I had hurt him, not the other way round. It was the disappointment I couldn't bear. That was the real wound.

As the last blow sounded, Mam's shoulders relaxed. 'Get him something cold, Bethan,' she said, quietly.

My hand burned, prickly and painful red welts swelling across my palm, and as Father turned away, I cradled it and blew into it.

'No more going underground,' he said, quietly, as he pulled his clothes off. 'No matter who offers to take you down. Now come and shake my hand.'

I held out my good hand and he took it, a shake, a small firm nod, and he was back to taking his pit clothes off.

'What's the matter with your eye?' said Alwyn, casting me a glance as Father lowered himself into the tub. 'You been in a fight with another girl?'

Emrys snorted. 'Fighting and sneaking underground? Christ, man, you know how to get yourself in trouble, innit?'

'Leave him be, you two,' said Bethan, handing me a small, wet rag. 'He was sticking up for Ade. Got punched by Gwyn Williams. That boy's a thug.'

'Then bloody punch the bugger back!' said Alwyn, reaching on top of the mantelpiece for a pair of cigarettes. 'That's how a boy becomes a man.'

'He's only eleven,' said Bethan. 'He's got plenty of time to be a boy yet.'

'He'd have done well to remember that this morning. Come b'here, Ant,' said Father, gesturing towards the front end of the tub.

I went and stood in front of him, my hand wrapped in the cold cloth. Father had one foot in his hands and was working the coal dust out from between his toes. 'Did he hurt you?' he asked.

'He did, Father,' I replied.

'And did you hurt him?'

'I did, Father.'

'Well, then. You're all even. Boys will take tumbles and knock heads and tangle fists. It's what boys do. But always shake the hand of the man you've tangled with, especially if you were the better man.'

'I wasn't the better man, Father. He beat me. He was too big for me.'

'Did you stand back up and accept it?'

I nodded. 'But I didn't shake his hand, though. He ran off.'

'That wasn't right of him. Always do what is right rather than what is popular, Anthony, and you will never fail. Something you forgot to do this morning.'

'Load of bloody rubbish,' grumbled Alwyn behind me, striking a match against the mantel stone. 'If I was you, I'd jump him up the back alley. Right when he wasn't expecting it.'

'Don't give him ideas,' said Emrys, taking one lit cigarette from his brother's mouth. 'He's already obsessed with those gangster films. What's that film you keep talking about?'

'*Double Indemnity*,' I said. 'It's dead good.'

'Hang on,' said Mam, laying out three piles of clean clothes. 'How have you seen that? That's not a film for children.'

'They all creep in the side door on a Wednesday, Mam. It's when Gwennie Morgan is ushering. Wednesdays are when the magazines come into the post office. She just sits reading them.' Emrys took a long drag of his cigarette. 'What's it about again, Ant?'

'It's about a woman who's up to no good with a man called Neff, who isn't her husband,' I said, passing a towel to Father.

'Oh, *duw*,' mumbled Mam. 'I don't want to hear this already.'

'Keep going,' said Alwyn, nodding. 'This sounds like my sort of film.'

'She comes up with a scam to kill her husband so she can get double money, and Neff says he'll help her do it after she kisses him.'

'So she has to kiss him to get his help?' said Alwyn, with a wry smile. 'I'd get on with this Neff. Smart fella.'

'Ade said this is how all boys get in trouble and we should all make a pact that we would never kiss a girl. So we did.'

'Smart lad is Ade.' Emrys grinned.

'You're never going to kiss a girl, Ant?' said Bethan, from the kitchen. 'You might regret that!'

'Anyway, it all went wrong. And Neff killed the husband, then pretended to be the husband. Then the lady kissed another man, and Neff's boss, who was called Keyes and was, like, the detective boss at the insurance firm, smelled a rat, and that's how the whole thing came undone. So at the end, the lady shot Neff and then Neff shot the lady and she died and then he died and that was it. Bozo and Ade were a bit bored, and Fez said it didn't have enough shooting in it. I thought it was all right.'

'That woman sounds a right kettle of fish,' said Mam, passing Father his clean shirt. 'Kissing all sorts and going round shooting people. What a do. And pretending to be someone you're not! The devil of it.'

'I'd never die for a woman,' said Alwyn, climbing into the tin bath for his turn. 'Especially not Gwennie Morgan.'

'Not since she knocked you back, anyhow,' said Emrys, blowing a plume of smoke from the side of his mouth.

'That was only because her father doesn't like me since I punched that lad from Tonypandy. Don't know why, mind. Bastard had it coming.'

'You broke that boy's jaw, Alwyn,' said Father, in his sterner tone. 'And that was after you already had him beat. If you learned to control that temper of yours, you'd present a better prospect.'

Alwyn scowled into the darkening tub water and silence fell in the room. Emrys picked a speck of tobacco from his tongue while Mam set to work on the black spot on her son's back. The burn in my hand was deepening, but it wasn't too bad. I'd had worse. I unwrapped the cloth and had a look at it. Skin not broken. It would smart for a day and that would be that. I shifted the cloth so that a fresh, cold bit was lying against the welts.

'Bethan says there'll be Americans at Porthcawl!' I said, looking towards Father.

'Ant!' she yelled, from the kitchen. 'I told you that in secret!'

'Americans?' said Mam, her eyes widening. 'Is that true?'

'So we've been told. They're arriving in two days. Something must be up, we reckon. But we don't know what.'

'Getting ready to push into France. I'd put money on it,' said Father. 'But if Bethan has been told to keep it quiet, I want the rest of you to do the same. Once they're here, that's another matter. But not a word until they've come. Careless talk costs lives, remember.'

'Christ, I wish I could go to France,' moaned Emrys. 'Stuck down the bloody pit when we could be out fighting. We'll see none of the war. It's not fair.'

'I'd rather be underground than in it,' said Alwyn.

'We get to see the Mosquitoes from RAF St Athan,' I said. 'That's seeing the war.'

'I don't want to sit on the bloody mountain watching it,' said Emrys, 'I want to be doing it!'

'Be careful what you wish for, Emrys. War's a nasty business. Anyway, we've got one member of the family in uniform,' said Father, smiling towards Bethan. 'And you boys are helping the war effort. You're doing your duty.'

'Some duty when you have to salute your own sister,' said Alwyn, rubbing the coal soap between his hands.

'Talking of duty, can I borrow a sheet, Mam?' said Emrys, flicking the end of his cigarette into the open fire. 'We've been told to take one to training.'

'What do they want sheets for?' said Mam, frowning.

'Perhaps they're going to dress up as ghosts. Scare the Germans to death?' grumbled Alwyn. 'That's all the Look, Duck and Vanish brigade can hope for. Fucking useless.'

'Shut up, Alwyn,' said Emrys. 'At least I'm in the Home Guard. More than you can say.'

'Why would I want to be in the Home Guard? You're all just mucking about. No guns. No clue. I do my hours down the pit and they want me to be up all night pretending Germans are coming? No thanks.'

'All right,' said Mam, quietly. 'That's enough. Take the blue one from the top shelf of the airing cupboard. Not any of my white ones, mind. And I don't want it coming back covered in grease.'

'Thanks, Mam,' said Emrys, tapping out another cigarette.

'Do you think they'll bring chocolate? And silk stockings?' said Bethan, her face breaking into a smile from the kitchen doorway. 'They do look so handsome. And American! Imagine that? Americans in Porthcawl!'

'What's that smell?' said Father, sniffing the air.

'Ant's wellingtons,' said Mam, handing him his tie. 'They're always bad after he's been running.'

'Can't we get him a pair of shoes?' said Bethan. 'He smells like a mouldy log.'

'He's worked his way through all the hand-me-downs. The only spare pair of shoes left in this house is an old pair of mine,' said Mam. 'If he wants them, he's welcome to them. If not, he's stuck with the boots.'

Bethan shrugged in my direction. 'Ah, well,' she said. 'You'll just have to hope the war ends. Or an American brings a pair of shoes for an eleven-year-old boy.'

'Or someone else dies,' said Alwyn, darkly. 'Here you go,' he added, throwing the coal soap towards Emrys. 'Your turn.'

CHAPTER THREE

The Treherbert 2nd Platoon of the Welsh Home Guard gathered every Tuesday evening at the local Men's Club for training. Being a unit that was off the beaten track, they had never been furnished with a grand arsenal. Between them, there was one rifle that was taken home each week on a rota basis and an assortment of broom handles and sticks that passed for guns. Instead of grenades, they had brown paper bags filled with flour; or at least they did have, until all the mams started complaining about the stuff going to waste. 'What would you rather have?' Mam asked Emrys. 'Bread or bombs?' And that put an end to that. One week, a man from Cardiff came with a Bren gun for them to have a go on, but he'd brought the wrong ammunition so they all just stood around staring at it. Not that anyone was that bothered; the likelihood of the Germans invading Treherbert was as slim a chance as any.

Ade and I climbed onto the broken brick wall at the back of the Men's Club to watch the platoon. The early evening sun was casting a golden swathe of light across our mountain. I stared up and watched the ridges shifting. The contours of the mountain were as familiar to me as the lines on the palms of my hands, but I would always marvel at how differing lights could change its personality entirely. I cupped my hand over my eyes to stare into the low evening sun. The black silhouette of a bird of prey floated in and out, soaring on the wind as it eddied above the rocks. There were two of them up our mountain, a breeding pair, I reckoned. I nudged Ade, pointing upwards. 'There's that red kite again,' I said. 'Father says there's not many left. You only get them in South Wales, he says.'

'We should find the eggs,' said Ade, kicking at a loose brick in the wall with the end of his shoe. 'You can get good money for rare bird eggs.'

'Who'd you sell 'em to?' I said, frowning. 'No one round b'here's got money to buy 'em with.'

'Dunno,' said Ade, with a shrug. 'P'raps someone up Cardiff way. Or old Pughsy. He owns a factory. Got to be worth a bob.' Ade nudged his head down towards the backyard of the club.

Old Pughsy was Captain Pugh, leader of the Treherbert 2nd Platoon Home Guard, or, if you'd known him before the war, Mr Pugh, manager and owner of Polikoff Sewing Factory. He lived in a detached house, an unimaginable luxury, and was rumoured to have an indoor toilet. 'He shits INSIDE,' Bopa once told Mam, shaking her head in wonder.

Below us, the platoon was scattered about the backyard. Emrys was standing, leaning against an empty beer barrel and staring up at us. 'You two got nothing better to do?' he said, pulling out a pack of rolling tobacco.

'Better than the radio, watching you lot,' answered Ade. 'Better than the pictures, even. What you doing tonight? Knitting?'

Emrys picked up a broken bit of slate and chucked it at us. We ducked. Missed. 'Bugger off,' he said. 'Home Guard's important business. You'll be glad of us if the Germans come. We're your only hope.'

'Yeah,' said Ade, 'they'll surrender the minute they see your broom handle.'

I laughed. Emrys scowled. 'We've got a rifle. It's my turn with it, 'n' all. You watch on, Adrian Jenkins. Or I might confuse you for a German.' He mimed holding up a rifle. 'Bang. Bang.'

'Right. You two. Be quiet and you can stay. If you're going to be chucking insults, you can be off.' Captain Pugh strode out towards the back of the yard. He turned his back to us and faced the platoon. 'Attention!' Ten men hurriedly arranged themselves into two lines and tried their best to look efficient.

'Your Emrys really got the rifle?' whispered Ade, leaning in.

I nodded. 'Only for a bit, mind, while it's his turn. Mam made him keep it in the outtie. She doesn't want it in the house.'

'You had a go on it?'

'No, man. Don't be daft. Besides, I don't know where he keeps the bullets. And even if I did find 'em, he's only got five. He'd miss any if they were gone.'

Ade sniffed and carried on working the loose brick with his toe. 'P'raps we should go have a look at it, like?'

Ade was always for having his fingers into everything, but I was naturally more cautious. I stared up again towards the mountain to catch the last glimpses of the sun skimming off its peak. The red kite was circling again. Hunting. She liked mice. Saw her catch one, once, those russet wings hovering then the sudden dive, the flash of light eyes, grab and away, the slow beat of mighty wings thumping through the air. Beautiful, graceful, deadly.

'Come on,' I said, hopping down from the wall. 'They're going to do something with sheets up the street. Let's get up there.'

Captain Pugh did not really know what he was doing. Everybody knew this, even Captain Pugh, but he was the epitome of enthusiasm over talent, so everyone forgave him. He was an odd-looking fellow: hunched shoulders, a pinched, bird-like face and then a mass of black curly hair greased down so it undulated like the coal-filled waters of the village river. He had married once but rumour had it that within weeks of walking his bride up the aisle, she'd skipped off with a man who sold cockles. Bopa said she'd lost her mind. 'She's given up a life of luxury!' she wailed. 'He's got electricity upstairs. And now what has she got to look forward to? Stinking of fish till the end of days.'

'Right, boys,' Captain Pugh said, staring into his Home Guard handbook. 'Hang your sheets at random intervals all the way up the street.'

'On what?' asked Emrys, shaking out Mam's blue sheet. 'There's no washing lines.'

'Did you bring that ball of string, Malcolm?' Pugh asked a thin lad in thick glasses.

'No, Mr Pugh,' said Malcolm, looking sheepish. 'I couldn't find it. I brought my mam's wool. She wants it back, mind.' He reached into his pocket and pulled out a bright red ball.

'Right,' said Pugh, nodding. 'Then that will have to do. String it up. And don't cut it. And when we're in our uniform, what am I, Malcolm?'

Malcolm stood very still, thinking. 'Very handsome?'

Everyone stifled a laugh. Pugh blinked. 'No, Malcolm, I am *Captain* Pugh. Not Mr. Although thank you for the compliment.'

'Can I get the rifle, Captain?' asked Emrys, pushing his blond fringe out of his eyes. 'For training, like?'

'Yes, let's have it out,' said Captain Pugh, turning a few pages of his treasured handbook. 'No bullets, mind. Not with the sheets.'

Ade nudged me. 'We'll get to see the gun,' he said, grinning as Emrys ran past us and in through our front door.

I heard a short burst of shrill admonishment from my mother, and then Emrys reappeared, holding the rifle like a flag.

'Bear that arm properly,' said Captain Pugh, frowning. 'I don't want you waving it about as if you're frightening crows. Now, then. Your objective, Emrys, is to advance up the street with your four men, and take the five men up at the top. Think you'll manage that?'

'Course he will, he's got the only gun,' shouted Ade. 'Just don't tell 'em he's got no bullets!'

There was an outburst of laughter. Ade and I had joined the usual concentrated bunch of Scott Street kids who hung about waiting for anything to happen. The weekly Home Guard training session was the highlight of the week.

'Ignore them,' said Captain Pugh, reaching into his pocket. 'On my whistle. Begin!' He blew down and off Emrys went, crouching behind a billowing sheet.

Fez had some cigarette cards out, looking for swapsies. 'Got that one?' he said, holding up a card with two people on it dressed head to toe in what looked like yellow mackintoshes. 'Rubber Clothing,' said Fez, tapping it with another card.

'Nah, I've got Anti-Gas Suit,' said Bozo. 'Wanna swap it for that?'

Fez shook his head. 'I've got three Anti-Gas. If you've got Respirators I'll have that. You got any ciggie cards, Ant?' He turned towards me.

I shook my head. 'Father don't get packet cigs,' I said, peeking over his shoulder into his battered Strepsil tin full of cards. 'Can I have a look?'

He handed me the card he wanted to swap. It was a man and a woman, running away from a house. They looked posh. They were running up a pathway leading away from some fancy windows. A tall, creeping plant was edging up the side of the house wall, and either side of the pathway were beds filled with decorative flowers. The pair both wore yellow rubber coats, the woman's coming with a fashionable belt, and they were in matching yellow sou'wester hats. Each wore a gas mask. Above them, in the daylight sky, there was a German plane and a small, smoky explosion just behind it.

I flipped the card over and looked at the words on the back.

During an air raid, the safety of the citizen may depend to a considerable extent on his knowledge of how to behave. Splashing from the liquid liberated from certain gas bombs, or subsequent contact with it, produces a serious blistering of the skin. The Government provides each individual with a respirator, which is complete protection for the eyes, throat and lungs. Prudent persons, if forced to go out of doors during air raids, should provide themselves with rubber or oilskin coats and hats and rubber boots.

I looked down at my own rubber wellingtons. 'What does "prudent" mean?' I asked Ade, showing him the card.

He shrugged. 'Isn't that when girls won't kiss a lad? Maybe that's why she's wearing the gas mask?'

I stared back at the picture. It was impossible not to feel a twinge of regret. We'd never get to run away from German gas bombs dressed up in rubber outfits. Perhaps they got to do that in Cardiff?

'Emrys!' shouted Captain Pugh. 'It's no good just crouching there! You need to advance! You've got to make your way up the street using the sheets as cover! Pull your finger out and crack on, man!'

'Does he think sheets are going to stop Germans?' asked Ade, scratching his neck. 'The man's mad. Come on, let's jump 'em.'

Ade dropped down to a stoop and gestured back towards Fez and Bozo. Tucking their Strepsil tins of ciggie cards into their pockets, the two of them joined Ade, crawling along the house fronts. Stopping at the mid point, Ade picked up a clinker from the gutter and rubbed it under his nose, making a small black smear. Grinning, he passed it back to Fez and Bozo, urging them to do the same.

Emrys was almost at the halfway point. He was in a crouched position, cradling the rifle. Behind him were four others, two lads from the pit of about the same age, then two much older men. One of the older men kept standing up and shouting 'Bang, bang, bang!' while pointing a garden fork in the direction of the opposing team.

'Covering fire, Private Jenkins!' shouted Captain Pugh. 'Keep it up!'

'Look at them, playing soldiers,' said a voice just behind me. I turned round. It was Alf. He stared down at me and gave a small smile. 'All right, young Anthony? Did you catch it?'

I held my hand out. 'Got the belt,' I said, showing him the welts. 'But it wasn't too bad. They're all proper mad with you, mind.'

'Hmmm,' he said, looking off down the street. 'I don't mind. It was a lark right and proper. Sometimes it's worth taking the punishment, innit?'

I nodded, but tried to remember my Mam thought he was an idiot.

'My Mam thinks you're an idiot,' I said, out loud. 'And Bethan thinks you're irresponsible. They say I shouldn't hang round you.'

Alf gave a wry smile. 'Irresponsible, is it? Well, well. If I was a betting man, I'd say your sister was starting to go soft on me.'

I blinked. I didn't think that was very likely, but I decided not to tell him that bit.

'Anyway,' he said, sticking his thumbs into his waistcoat pocket, 'I'm all right. You're all right. All's well that ends well, innit?'

'That's a Shakespeare play.'

'Is it, now? Shakespeare, eh? You're a gentleman and a scholar.'

I looked him up and down. Suit on, white shirt, waistcoat, polished shoes, cap. 'Why you togged up?' I asked. 'It ain't Sunday.'

'Thought I'd pay a visit to your father,' he said, 'bring him some twist. Make amends, like. See, I'm not all bad.'

'You don't have to get dressed up to give my father baccy,' I said, frowning.

'Well ...' said Alf, with a small smirk. 'There might be other people in the house.'

Ahead of us there was a commotion. Raised voices. A sound of tearing. I jumped down from the pavement and stood out in the middle of the street so I could see up through the line of sheets. Ade, Fez and Bozo had leapt out on Emrys and his team. They were all strutting about pretending to be Hitler. Emrys was on the floor, trying to extricate himself from a sheet. Captain Pugh was blowing his whistle.

'You lot better scarper,' said Alf, adjusting his cap, 'Before old Pughsy blows a gasket. I'll be off in, then. Ta-ra.'

'Ta-ra,' I said, watching him walk on to our front door. He stood for a moment, knocked twice on the doorframe, and then disappeared inside.

I looked back up the street towards Ade and the others. They were being chased in circles by Emrys, but the boys were pulling down sheets as they went. It was chaos.

'Come on, Ant!' yelled Ade, sprinting towards me. 'They'll have us!'

Fez and Bozo were hard behind him, and then I saw Emrys, emerging from a wave of floating sheets, red-faced and furious. I didn't need asking twice. I turned on my heels and ran.

The den was beneath the Big Stone that faced south over the valley. On a clear day, Fez reckoned you could see all the way to Cardiff, but I wasn't so sure. We'd seen lights from bombing raids, but that was different from actually seeing the city. All the same, it was a grand viewing platform. Behind us towered the peak of our mountain and, beyond that, a mighty panorama of rolling green. The Big Stone was a large, flat-faced boulder, a relic from a long-ago rockfall that had embedded itself in an upright position. Beneath it was a shallow hollow that someone, probably a shepherd, had once built up with smaller stones. It had a weather-beaten wooden roof, but to mend the holes, Ade and I had covered it with planks we'd found by the coal tips. It was our place, now.

Inside, we had two wooden planks resting on three upturned tin buckets we'd nicked from the back of the Men's Club. They all had T.M.C. painted on the side, but nobody had ever asked after them, so we reckoned they'd been chucked out for salvage and forgotten about. We had a few wooden crates, too. One for sticks set aside for whittling, and another for mountain treasure: a sheep's skull, a few jaw bones, a clay pipe we'd dug up by the stream, an old bottle – green with a marble inside the neck – an atlas we'd found, and a lump of fool's gold we used to start fires.

Tucked at the back of the den, we had an old biscuit tin that was used to keep sandwiches in. If we were lucky, Fez might bring up a bag of toffees sent by an aunt who lived somewhere near Reading. She'd married a doctor, right posh, like, and was given to sending unexpected parcels. Fez had seen their house, once. It had a garden front and back and a bath you didn't have to carry. I hardly ever got to have sweets, but if Mam was feeling generous, she'd spoon some sugar into a cone and let me have it. She'd squeeze lemon juice into it, and I'd sit, legs dangling off the Big Stone, licking the sharp sweet sugar off my finger. Sweets were a rarity, these days, what with rationing being so tight.

'You still got a Hitler moustache, man,' said Fez, pointing towards Ade. 'If the Mozzies see you, you're done for.'

Ade put a hand to his top lip and rubbed. 'They can't see it from up b'there, man!' He threw his other arm up towards the clouds.

'They can,' said Fez, pulling an army knife from his pocket. 'They've got magnifiers. For when they're doing the bombing runs. Pilot looks down, sees Hitler's moustache. He's not going to take chances.' He reached into the whittling box and took his pick.

Ade checked the back of his hand. A long, black smudge was smeared across it. 'Has it gone, Ant?' he said, looking towards me.

'Sort of. It's more Errol Flynn now.'

'Pilots don't want to kill *him*, though, do they?' said Ade. 'We got anything in the tin?'

I went to the back of the den and pulled the lid off the old biscuit tin. There was a half-eaten jam sandwich with a few ants on it. I picked it out and flicked the ants off. 'There you go,' I said, handing it to him.

'Ta,' he said and bit into it.

'Here they come!' said Bozo, standing a few feet from the den. He was pointing up into the evening dusk. 'At least three squadrons.'

Ade and I scrambled outside. The sky was dappled with a deep pink blush. The birds had stopped calling and over the bottomless quiet of our mountain we heard the first rumble of the aircraft. Mosquito bombers, all in formation. Their snub noses sitting squat between shoulder-mounted wings, twin engines humming, bearing the heart-lifting insignia of the RAF.

'Where to, d'you reckon?' said Bozo, face turned upwards.

'Germany. Must be,' said Fez, still stripping the bark from his whittling stick. 'They've been on night raids for ages. Ever since Little Blitz.'

'Yeah, but where in Germany? Get out the atlas, Ant,' said Bozo, his one good eye locked on the aircraft. 'Did you know Mozzies are made all from wood. D'you think we could make one? How long do you reckon it would take us to make a plane out of wood?'

Fez looked at his stripped twig. 'Dunno.'

'I made a shove ha'penny board once,' said Ade, crouching and poking at an ant nest. 'That took two weeks.'

Bozo scrunched his face into a ball. 'Probably take us ages, then. For a plane.'

Everyone nodded.

I'd pulled the atlas out from the crate of mountain treasure. The cover was faded blue, with *Colliers World Atlas and Gazetteer* printed across it in broken gold lettering. Many of the pages were missing, either torn out to start fires or ruined by damp. I flicked through to the European section. We'd taken care not to rip out any page of mainland Europe, so that if there was a place mentioned on the *Pathé News*, we could come up to the den and find it.

'Germany. There you go.' I placed the atlas down on a patch of moss, and crouched, knees by my ears, to investigate. Bozo sat cross-legged beside me.

'Flick back to Britain,' he said. 'Then we can work out the route.'

I turned back a few pages and Bozo, seeing Wales, laid his finger on the planes' starting point. 'What direction d'you reckon, Fez?' he said, squinting upwards.

'More that way this time,' said Fez, holding his arm out and pointing left.

Bozo trailed his finger across the page until he reached its edge. I flicked it over for him. 'Going over the Netherlands, I reckon,' he said. 'Might be Belgium. Must be doing a drop over the top end. Hamburg? Berlin?'

'I bet it's Berlin,' said Ade. 'About time we got 'em back for Cardiff, like.'

'And London,' I said, hooking my hands over my knees.

'Yeah, but mostly Cardiff.'

We all stood up and watched in silence as the formation faded into the dusk. Fez, as he always did, saluted them for luck. We followed suit and as the planes disappeared beyond the horizon, the deep quiet of our mountain settled back into itself.

I turned to pick up the atlas and put it back in the treasure box. I felt the wind first, a rush of air through my fringe, and then the noise. I looked up. A Mosquito, no more than fifty feet above our heads, ripped over us with a deafening roar. I clamped my hands to my ears and stared up at the grey underbelly tearing over me. Ade and the others were jumping and cheering. I instinctively flinched as if I would get caught up in the wheels like a mouse picked off by the kite, adrenalin coursing through me, and in a heartbeat, it was gone, flying away over the valley to join the formation and find its prey in other lands: beautiful, graceful, deadly.

'*Wish me luck as you wave me goodbye!*' sang Bozo, jumping up and down.

'*Cheerio, here I go on my way!*' we all sang out, exhilarated.

The lone Mosquito cut across the sky, leaving plumes of billowing clouds in its trail. Ripples, murmurs, then gone, swallowed into the black.

'That,' said Ade, his eyes wide and staring, 'is the toppest thing that's ever happened in the whole of my life.'

And as we stared after it, the smell of aviation fuel in our nostrils, I knew, more than ever, that I never wanted the war to end.

'What time do you call this?' said Bopa, as I slumped onto the floor in front of the fire. 'What did I tell you, Em? Feral.'

'I heard about you boys mucking up the Home Guard tonight,' said Mam. 'Emrys is fuming.'

'Where is he?' I said, half getting up to avoid a clouting.

'Up the waterworks, on bivouac,' said Alwyn, who was sitting polishing a pair of shoes. 'If you're lucky, he might have forgotten when he comes back tomorrow. I doubt it, though. Best stick a book down the back of your pants.'

Bethan appeared in the doorway into the kitchen. She was carrying a tray with a teapot and a few mugs. 'Gonna listen to *Appointment with Fear*, Ant?' she said, placing the tray down. 'It's starting in a minute.'

'Oh, I hate that show,' said Bopa, 'gives me the willies. I don't think it's right or natural to be so obsessed with dark matters. It's positively ghoulish.'

Father, who was sitting in his armchair reading a paper, took out his pocket watch and looked at the time. 'Turn the wireless on, boy.'

I got up. The wireless was set high on a set of drawers. It was an old one, saved after a clear-out from another neighbour who'd died. Her daughter already had a wireless, so she'd given it to Mam. 'A Mosquito went right over our heads up by the Big Stone, Father,' I said, switching it on. 'Not high up. Right low, like. Almost so you could touch it.'

'Oh, *newl*,' said Alwyn, curling his lip. 'You're making that up.'

'Am not. Right over the top of us. Came from nowhere.' I stood, waiting for Father to respond, but he didn't lift his eyes from the paper.

'Came from nowhere? Like someone else, eh, Bethan?' Bopa shot my sister a knowing look.

'The front of him,' said Mam, unpicking wool from an old jumper. 'Coming round here after what he did.'

'He's got some brass,' said Bopa, folding her arms. 'I'll give him that. You need to mind yourself, Bethan. You're not stepping out. The wolves will gather until you pick a beau. Mark my words.'

I looked over towards Bethan. Her cheeks were flushing. Behind me, lone bells began to sound. '*Appointment with Fear,*' said a low, sonorous voice. '*This is your storyteller. The Man in Black. Here again to bring you another … placid evening.*'

'Ugh,' said Bopa. 'Let's sit in the back kitchen. I can't bear to listen to it. Gives me chills. I went round to Anne Evans. Found out everything. Come on, we can have another brew.'

Mam stood up and followed her.

'Turn the lights down, Ant,' said Alwyn. 'All spooky, like.'

I reached over Mam's chair and turned down the gas lamp that was on the table next to it, so that the only light in the room came from the flickering embers in the hearth.

'*Loss of memory,*' the voice rang out. '*The eerie darkness which closes on the brain is a subject that often amuses me. Tonight, I bring a guest, Mr Gideon Barton, to tell you all about it. He's here with me now, eyeglasses on a black ribbon, his face pinched and drawn, and when he tells you about the horrors that unfold, we shall satisfy our promise to bring you …*'

A sudden, dramatic chord belted out from the wireless.

'Oh!' cried out Bopa from the kitchen. 'Makes me jump every time!'

'*An Appointment with Fear!*'

A surge of dramatic strings punctuated the gloom, followed by a single, tolling bell.

'*It was a grim business …*'

'I'll just go sit with Mam,' I mumbled.

Bopa and Mam were sitting on wooden chairs by the back kitchen fire. It wasn't as comfy as the parlour, but was as good a gossiping spot as any. Father would only speak when he had something important to say, but Bopa had an endless capacity for chit-chat, and Mam loved to listen.

'*Where am I?*' the voice of a young woman, agitated, cried out from the wireless behind me. '*My head feels queer and I want to cry.*'

'You were right, Anthony,' said Bopa, balancing her teacup on her forearm. 'Thomas Evans fractured his ankle. That's twice in two months. He's had another cast put on. Doctor reckons it was the same place as before. Hadn't healed proper, like. It's the lack of red meat. That, and being a right little bastard.'

'Bopa!' said Mam, stifling a laugh.

'Well,' said Bopa. 'Thomas Evans. He's an absolute terror. If it turns out it was him stealing the ration books, I wouldn't bat an eyelid. I watched him once, up the veg patches taking bites out of tomatoes. Didn't pick them off and eat the whole thing like a normal person. Took bites out of them. Like a maggot. He's not normal. I don't know why you like him, Anthony.'

I gave a shrug and leant against the kitchen table.

'*This isn't an ordinary cell,*' an older woman's voice rang out. '*This is the condemned cell. They're going to hang you in the morning.*'

A terrible scream filled the room.

'I wish they'd turn that down a bit,' said Bopa, with a shiver. 'I'm going back to an empty house, later!'

'Might not be empty for long. Bethan reckons there'll be Americans billeted round the valley,' said Mam, wrapping a strand of wool around her finger. 'P'raps you'll end up with one? Be nice company.'

'Or more. I've got room for at least two. Maybe three if I have one bunk up with me!' She gave a wink. 'Can you imagine! Ha!' She threw her head back and gave a deep, throaty laugh.

'Pipe down in there, you two!' shouted Alwyn. 'We're trying to listen!'

Bopa raised her eyebrows and leant in to whisper, 'You know what they say about Americans, though, Em. Gangsters. The lot of 'em. With their rough talk and swaggering ways. We'll have to have our wits about us. Make sure they don't take us for Indians. Try and kill us.'

'That's cowboys,' I said.

Bopa nudged Mam. 'Cowboys,' she said. 'That's it. We'll have to get Ant to whittle us a bow and arrow. Protect ourselves, like.' She laughed again.

I drifted back towards the parlour. Bethan was sitting on the floor, clutching a cushion to her chest. Alwyn was on the sofa, leaning forwards, his head resting in an upturned hand. Father melted into the back of his chair, his fingers locked together, his eyes fixed on the fire.

'*Got herself mixed up with a thorough-going swine called Philip Gayle. Threw her over for a woman with money. They argued, he chased her out. She took a revolver, told him to beg for mercy. He raised his arms, she shot him. Cold and callous, in a way only a woman can be. After that, she couldn't remember a thing.*'

Behind me, Bopa was still laughing.

'I wish they'd stop their bloody yapping,' said Alwyn, irritably. 'I can only hear every other word. Father, tell 'em.'

'Be quiet, Alwyn,' he said, his voice low and steady. 'You're making as much noise as they are.'

'*I'm not lying. I'm not.*'

''Ere, Ant,' called Bopa. I turned and looked towards the two women, heads huddled together. They were whispering. 'Ant!' She gestured to me to come back into the kitchen.

'*The prisoner has been told there is no hope. It's cruel to raise her hopes where there is none!*'

'I think she did it,' I heard Alwyn mutter. 'She was found with the revolver in her hand. And the brother saw her do the shooting. This fella's had his head turned because she's pretty, or something.'

'Ssshhhh,' said Bethan.

'You watch the flicks, don't you?' said Bopa, poking me on the upper arm as I came to stand next to her. I nodded. 'What are they called? Those fellas that run around Chicago chasing people who shoot policemen?'

'G Men,' I replied.

'That's it. G Men.' She shoved Mam in the knee. 'That's what we need round here. Some proper G Men. They'd sort out the likes of Thomas Evans. Bites out of tomatoes, indeed.'

'Bit harsh to get shot through with bullets just for snaffling a tomato,' Mam said, frowning.

Bopa nodded. 'Fair do's,' she replied. 'It would be excessive. Deserved. But excessive.'

'*Come with us now! To the condemned cell!*'

The sound of soaring strings resounded from the parlour. A clock struck six times.

'What's the time?' said Bopa, squinting towards the one-handed kitchen clock.

'About quarter past nine,' I said, glancing at the familiar face.

'Getting late,' said Bopa, looking into her teacup. 'Well, well,' she added, turning the cup in her hand, 'interesting leaves …'

Mam shot me a glance and a small, wry smile. Bopa often liked to convince us that she could read tea leaves. She had the 'gift', she said. 'Gift of the bloody gab, more like,' said Alwyn, who didn't believe in any of her nonsense. All the same, Bopa once said the leaves had told her Mam was going to come into money, and then, on the same day, Mam found a shilling in the back garden. 'The leaves have spoken!' declared Bopa, and we'd all laughed.

'See those leaves,' said Bopa, gesturing for me to look. 'What can you see, Anthony?'

I stared down into the wilted mass of shredded tea. Just looked like tea to me. Nothing special. 'Dunno. It's tea leaves, innit?'

'Quieten your mind, boy!' she whispered, slowly rotating the cup in her hand. 'Let the leaves speak to you. Empty your head of all thoughts! Now, then, what do you see?'

I squinted down into the cup. 'Dunno. That bit there looks like a crocodile.'

'Crocodile, Em!' declared Bopa. 'A vision of false friendships and deception! And look there … an exclamation mark. Beware of impulsive actions, Anthony. The cup is speaking.'

'I don't really know what it means,' I said, with a shrug.

'Trouble!' said Bopa, jabbing her finger upwards. 'That's what! And the tea never lies.'

She grabbed my chin between her hands and squeezed my cheeks with her long fingers. 'Look at you! He's such a good boy, Em, inne? Bright as a button. Make sure you keep it that way. Americans coming. Wind shifting. All change. Trouble in the tea! Bad things happen, Anthony!' She smiled and patted me on the cheek. 'Right, then, I best be off.'

She stood and rinsed her cup out at the sink. 'That's that, then. Ta-ra! See you tomorrow.'

'Ta-ra!' said Mam.

'What's in your cup?' I said to Mam, as she stood and walked towards the sink.

'Just leaves, Ant,' she said, giving her cup a swirl. 'It's all silly nonsense. Just fun, remember.'

The front door slammed shut. Bopa always had a heavy hand.

'Could that woman make any more noise?' complained Alwyn. 'Seriously? It's like having a bloody magpie in the house. Jabbering on, and then, Boom! goes the door.'

'*And so ...*' returned the voice of the Man in Black, '*we come to the end of the* Appointment with Fear. *If you can say that only the graveyard has yawned, then we are deeply grateful. I shall return to tell you more stories of corpses and the midnight hour, but until that happy day when we meet by some evil crossroads of the future, this is your storyteller, the Man in Black, saying goodnight and goodbye.*'

Father stood up and switched off the wireless. 'Right,' he said. 'That's enough silly entertainment. Off to bed with you, Ant. School in the morning.'

'I prefer it when it's ghosts and stuff. Dead people walking about, like,' said Alwyn, spitting on the toecap of his shoe.

'Hang on,' said Bethan, 'I'm confused. So she didn't kill her fella? It was the brother?'

'Aye,' said Alwyn, bringing up the shine with a chamois leather. 'Second son, wan'he? Nobody took any notice of him. Don't you be getting any ideas, Ant. You're the third son. You're even further down the pecking order. Small boys are to be ignored at all costs, but that doesn't mean they can go about shooting their elder brothers.'

'Mean,' said Bethan. 'Don't mind him, Ant. I notice you.'

Father sat back down in his chair and folded his paper so he could read it more easily. He had turned the gas lamp back on and he sat, illuminated, looking more like a bookish librarian than a hardened pitman. 'Get to bed, Anthony,' he muttered, without looking up. 'I'll not tell you again.'

'Can I take a candle up, Mam?' I asked, as she walked into the room.

Mam reached for one of the candleholders lined up on the mantelpiece. Sticking the wick into the embers, she passed it to me. 'Don't burn it for long, mind,' she said. 'Those are my last candles until we can get some more.'

I shared a bedroom with Alwyn and Emrys. Being bigger than me, they always shoved me to the end of the bed to sleep by their feet like a dog. So instead, I slept under the bed on some old jumpers Father didn't wear any more. I could have chosen to sleep on the floor next to the bed, but I preferred it underneath: it felt more like a den, my space. I had a pillow and a blanket and a shoebox where I kept my own treasures: a tooth I'd knocked out playing football, a flint, a seashell I'd brought back from a day trip to Porthcawl, and a comic,

The Dandy, I'd been given on a birthday by an uncle from Tonypandy. I also had an encyclopaedia, a brown, battered old thing that Mam had picked up at a jumble sale. It was the only book I owned, and I loved it.

On the wall between the bottom of the mattress and the skirting board, there was an advert for a pair of men's shoes, cut out from one of Bethan's American magazines and stuck up with a splash of wallpaper glue. 'Regal Shoes!' the advert exclaimed. 'A rugged Scotch grain brogue! As ultra correct in the swankiest clubs as on the busiest sidewalks from Boston to Hollywood!' The shoes were the grandest things I'd ever seen: a rich, nut brown with fancy stitching on the toes. They had wooden shoe trees inside to keep their shape, and were sitting between a fine tweed jacket and some smart leather driving gloves. I would lie staring at that picture, wondering what it might be like to walk into a 'swankiest club' or along a 'busy sidewalk'. If I had shoes such as these, I'd feel ten feet tall. But then, I didn't have any shoes. I had my stinking wellingtons.

The bedroom door opened. I turned over and watched Alwyn's trousers flying onto the wooden chair in the corner by the window. It was never warm in our room. The window was north facing so, even in the hottest summers, no warmth permeated it. There was always a damp, reluctant chill that hung heavy in the air. Not having anything fancy, like pyjamas, I'd sleep in my clothes and old jumpers.

The mattress springs gave a creak and sank towards me.

'Blow that candle out, boy,' said Alwyn. 'Down in your condemned cell.'

I took one last look at the Regal Shoes, then leant over and blew out the candle. Pitch black, cold, sleep.

CHAPTER FOUR

I wiped the blood from my nose.

'*Uffarn den*! Whaddya do that for, man?' yelled Ade, frowning angrily at Gwyn Williams.

'Finishing business, innit?' he yelled back, gesturing towards me. 'Come on, then.' He raised his fists. 'Let's have it.'

I had fallen backwards, trapped up against the wall of the schoolhouse. I'd scraped a knuckle against the brickwork as I fell, and it was hard to know whether the blood on the back of my hand was from my nose or my fist. He'd caught me unawares, jumping out from the culvert by the main building and landing me with a punch that had found its mark.

I squinted upwards. Gwyn was standing in front of the sun, his silhouette dark and flat. There was a metallic taste in my mouth. 'I don't want to fight,' I mumbled. 'Leave off.'

'What?' said Ade, staring at me. 'Come on, man! He lamped you!'

'I don't want to,' I said, pushing myself upwards. I shielded my eyes against the sun and saw other bodies crowding in behind Gwyn's black frame.

'Won't fight?' said Gwyn, jabbing me in the shoulder. I recoiled away.

'No,' I said, my eyes casting downwards. 'I won't.'

Someone at the back of the pack made an exaggerated clucking noise. 'Chicken!' Gwyn yelled. 'Chicken!'

I stood, my head hung low, back against the wall. A drop of blood fell onto the toe of my wellington. I felt another poke, into my shoulder, but I didn't look up.

'Lamp him, Gwyn!' I heard, and then another crunch, deep into my belly. The breath exploded out of me and I went down again, doubled over, my face contorted into a look of pained surprise as I gasped for air. Shoes clattered on the cobbled courtyard around my head. Yells. The smell of earth and wet stone. I gasped again. A hand on my shoulder. Tugged upwards. A smell of lavender. The sun in my eyes. A kite circling.

'Everyone to your classrooms!' shouted Miss Evans, her arm shoved under my armpit. 'Who hit him?'

'Gwyn Williams, Miss,' said Bronwyn, her brown hair scraped back into a ponytail. She was pointing towards him. He'd backed off and was skulking by the entrance to the culvert.

'I'll speak to you later, Gwyn Williams,' said Miss Evans. 'Picking on boys smaller than you! This isn't how we're trying to win a war, is it? Get inside. Go on!' She shooed her hand towards the other loitering children. 'Inside, the lot of you. Stand up, Anthony. Hold the top of your nose. Pinch it.'

From the corner of my eye I could see Ade peering round the back of our teacher. 'He wouldn't fight him, Miss,' he said. 'Is his nose broken, like? Gwyn tried to break it yesterday, 'n' all.'

'No,' said Miss Evans, squinting at me through her glasses. 'Got your breath back? Right, then. Inside. The pair of you.'

She took out a small handkerchief and wiped her fingers. She was always meticulously presented, a rarity for the women in our village, whom we were only used to seeing dressed up on a Sunday for chapel. There was an accepted dress code for weekdays – stout shoes, thick stockings, shapeless skirt, jumper with sleeves shoved just past the elbows, and a checked blue housecoat pulled tight at the waist – but none of this would do for Miss Evans. She was thoroughly modern, wore trousers and was rumoured to smoke a pipe. She'd been to a university in England, drank wine and had once been to a party in London where she had briefly stood five feet away from Alec Guinness.

It was often commented on, with surprise, that she had returned to Treherbert at all after such worldly experiences, but she always gave the same response. 'I'd miss our mountain,' she'd say, and then look up at it the same way I did.

'You gone soft?' said Ade, nudging me as we followed her into the schoolhouse. I shook my head. I couldn't explain why I hadn't fought back.

'Is it cos he's bigger, like? He did play dirty. Jumping out. All same, you'll have to do something. Show 'em you're not chicken, like.' Ade stared at me and reached into his pocket. 'Bung this up the left one,' he said, holding a bit of mangled cloth towards my nostrils. 'You're still dripping.'

The schoolhouse had once been the village chapel, but following a fire and a religious relocation, the building was reborn. It was a drafty building with an odour of wood polish, chalk and ink. Our classroom was towards the back end, where the windows looked out towards our mountain. I sat halfway from the front, sharing a double desk with Ade. We'd tossed a coin for the window seat and I'd won, so I carved my name into the windowsill to show I'd always be there.

'Right,' said Miss Evans, back turned to us and writing on the blackboard. 'Sphagnum moss. Who knows what it looks like?'

I cast an eye around the room. No hands up.

'What colour do you think it might be?' said Miss Evans, turning towards us. 'Fester, cigarette cards away, please, and tell me what colour sphagnum moss is.'

Fez squirrelled his tin into the front of his desk and sat stock still in concentration, staring at the ceiling. 'Is it blue, Miss?'

'No, Fester, sphagnum moss is not blue. What colour is normal moss?'

'Green, Miss.'

'Correct. And so is sphagnum moss. Now, does anyone know what's special about sphagnum moss?'

Everyone shook their head.

'Do you all remember how we went up the mountain and gathered wool from hedges for the war effort? We've been asked to do the same with sphagnum moss.'

'What do they want moss for, Miss?' asked Ade.

'It's got medicinal properties. It helps dress wounds and also makes them heal quicker. Sphagnum moss is going to be sent to look after wounded soldiers. So this morning, instead of writing, we're going up the mountain and we're going to find as much sphagnum moss as we can.'

A great cheer rang out.

'Now, so that we know what we're looking for,' said Miss Evans, reaching into a hessian bag, 'I gathered some this morning. So I want you all to come up and have a look at it.'

There was a surge towards her. 'Desk at a time!' shouted Miss Evans. 'And no pushing.'

I shoved my chair back and joined the queue. Bozo was in front of me. He turned round. 'Why didn't you fight Gwyn, man?' he asked, frowning. 'Everyone's calling you chicken, like. You're going to have to do a forfeit, or something.'

'Forfeit will sort it,' said Ade, behind me. 'Do a forfeit.'

My nose was still sore from the punch, and I dabbed at it with Ade's cloth.

'Ant,' said Ade, again, 'for serious, man. You have to do one.'

'All right,' I said, staring down at another drop of blood. 'I'll do a forfeit.'

Bozo tapped Fez on the shoulder. 'Ant's up for a forfeit. To prove he's not chicken, like.'

Fez nodded and passed it on. One by one, everyone ahead of me turned and looked at me.

'It's an acidic moss,' I heard Miss Evans explaining. 'So it stops bacteria growing.'

'Who's deciding the forfeit?' I asked Ade, with a sniff.

'It'll have to be Gwyn, wannit? He's the one that's called you chicken. You'll have to do what he says.'

My heart sank. Forfeits were to be avoided at all costs, let alone ones set by Gwyn Williams. My father's words rang in my ears: 'It's better to do what is right rather than what is popular.' No chance of that now. The class would be baying for blood.

Gwyn pushed his way up the line towards me. 'You gonna forfeit, like?' he said, fixing me with his small, black eyes. I nodded. 'Right, then. You gotta steal Mrs Reece's banana.'

Bozo gave a short gasp.

Gwyn spat onto his hand and held it out. I stared down at the thick sputum in his palm and felt Ade nudge me in the back. I had no choice. I placed my hand in his. The forfeit was on.

My pockets were filled with moss. Behind me stood fifteen children. Ahead of me, Scott Street. Someone, somewhere, had found something to bake. Smelled like Welsh cakes. Perhaps some sugar had come in, down the shop? My mind raced. Mrs Reece's house was ten doors up from mine. What if Mam came out looking for me and saw? What then? What if Mrs Reece caught me doing it? I looked over my shoulder. Gwyn Williams was standing with his arms crossed. Ade stood squinting, the noonday sun beating into his eyes. I looked up towards our mountain. Somewhere, in its depths, my father and brothers would be working. Stealing wasn't right.

'Hell of a forfeit,' said Thomas Evans, sitting in his wheelchair. His left leg was in plaster up to his knee. He was all right if he was on the flagstones – cobbles, not so much. Mind you, he'd already broken his ankle once this year. He was a dab hand.

'Window's open,' said Gwyn, nudging his head upwards.

I stared into the cool shadows of Mrs Reece's front parlour. There was the display table. The lace cloth. The fancy plate she'd brought from her dresser. And there, on top, resplendent, glorious: the mighty banana. All I had to do was reach in and take it. Nothing difficult. Just put my arm in through her open window and quietly remove the banana from its pedestal. That was it. I felt as if I were putting my arm into a den of vipers.

The curtains either side of the window fluttered gently outwards, licking up the side of the outside wall. I thought about the cigarette card, the couple running away from the poison, and I thrust my arm in, grabbed the banana and ran.

'Away!' yelled Ade, clattering down the street after me.

I didn't look back. I glanced down into my hand. I stuffed the banana into the top of my shorts, skidded round the corner and ducked into the back alley behind the houses. I leant up against a wall, my chest bursting. Like a swarm of bees, the others appeared and surrounded me.

'He's bloody done it,' said Ade, banging me on the shoulder. 'He took the banana. He's done the forfeit.'

A sea of hands came pattering down, but one hand, flattened and facing up, stuck stubbornly in front of me. 'Let's have it, then,' said Gwyn. 'Give me the banana.'

'It's his, man!' said Ade, frowning. 'Fuck off!'

The others muttered. Gwyn fixed me with a stare. I stared back at him. An ugly boy. Squashed and lopsided, like a face pressed up against a window. His was a face you could imagine floating up out of a peat bog: primitive, base, barely formed. He curled his lip. He had no more cards to play. He'd demanded the forfeit and it was done.

'Bloody bastards,' said Thomas Evans, the wheels of his chair squeaking up behind us. 'What's wrong with yers?

Nobody giving me a bloody shove. I've had to crank meself all the bloody way.'

'Sorry,' we all said, a little sheepishly.

'You gonna eat it, then?' Thomas said, nudging his head in the direction of the banana, his chest still heaving with effort.

'Dunno,' I said, fingering the top of it where it poked up from my shorts.

'Well, take it out your knackers, at least,' said Thomas. 'Or no one'll want a bit.'

'Anthony!' My mother's voice rang across the fences. I looked sideways to see her head poking over the back gates. She was standing on a stool, hanging out the washing. 'What are you all up to?'

'Nothing, Mam!' I yelled back.

'Nothing, Mrs Jones!' the rest behind me chimed in.

My mother's eyes narrowed. 'When boys of a certain age tell me they're doing nothing, they're clearly doing something. Get in for your lunch! All of you!'

Nobody needed telling twice, and the boys dispersed like dandelion seeds on the wind. I was left, standing, Thomas Evans behind me.

'Christ alive,' he yelled, looking over his shoulder. 'They've all naffed off again. *Diawl*, man. I'm bloody knacked.'

'I'll push you home,' I said, and, taking the handles, I twisted him round.

I ran straight up the stairs. Taking the banana from the top of my shorts, I reached under the bed for my shoebox. I could hide it under *The Dandy*. That way, even if someone looked, they wouldn't see it. The skin was a darker yellow than I had remembered, and it had an odour, a bit like a pear, but deeper, odder. I crouched by the bed and wondered if I should eat it there and then, have done with it. Raising it to my nose, I sniffed it again: such an unfamiliar smell. I let the tip of my tongue touch it: bitter, weird. I threw the banana into the shoebox and covered it with my comic. I'd work out what to do with it later.

'Anthony!' I heard my mother calling.

'Coming!' I shouted back.

'Bread and jam,' said Mam, gesturing towards the kitchen table. I looked out of the window towards the washing line. The wind was picking up. Father's shirts looked like they were trying to escape. I picked up my bread and bit into it. I liked to save the crusts till last, so I ate into the middle and then bent out the slice so I could finish off the centre.

Mam bent down to the veg box. 'Don't think much of my crop this year, do you?' she said, holding up a few wizened carrots. 'Need some more compost. Mind you, there's hardly anything to make a compost with. I put it down, it gets eaten.'

'Has Emrys been home yet, Mam?' I asked, licking some jam from my finger.

'Came in, got changed, went off to pit. I don't think he's slept. They spent most of the night catching rabbits. Look b'there. He's brought me three.'

Three dead rabbits were lying by the sink.

'Did he say he was still after me, like? About Ade and the boys and the sheets?'

'He asked where you were,' said Mam, running some muddied potatoes under the tap. 'And then he said something about melting you down for glue ...'

I swallowed a mouthful of bread.

'But I've got something else to tell you. Your teacher, Miss Evans, wants to see me. She's sent me a note.'

I stopped chewing and stared up. 'Why?'

'I dunno. You done something rotten?' She turned and raised an eyebrow at me. 'You better not have. Remember what Bopa told you ...? If you do something wrong, bad things happen.'

I said nothing, my face frozen.

'If you have, you best tell me now, Ant,' Mam said, putting the washed potatoes into a bowl and wiping her hands on the bottom of her housecoat. She fixed me with her pale-blue eyes.

I stared down towards my plate, my fingers clutching the elongated crust. My mind raced. It can't be about the banana. Miss Evans couldn't know about that. It would be about the fight with Gwyn. 'I had another scrap with Gwyn, Mam,' I said. 'But I didn't start it. Honest.'

Mam nodded. 'I believe you,' she said, unbuttoning her housecoat and slipping it off. 'All the same, I'm to come up to school with you. No doubt Gwyn Williams' mother will be there, too. So we shall have to deal with that. Bopa had a run-in with her last week. The woman shoved in the queue at the butchers, took the last of the sausages. Bopa said there was almost a fight. A bag of parsnips got knocked over. Finish that bread up. I'll spruce myself into something presentable.'

She hung her housecoat on the hook by the back door and stood in front of the kitchen fireplace. There was an old mirror that hung above the mantelpiece, a rare find in a back alley. Thrown-away treasure – just like the one-handed clock – that's what she called it. It was a mottled old thing, covered in dark black spots, as if the glass was slowly dying. Mam stared into it and began to tidy her hair into a topknot. She had long, dark-brown hair with a natural curl, but it wasn't often we ever saw it down. I watched as she deftly pinned it up into a swirling bun, pouting her lips without thinking, as she always did when she was staring into a mirror. It was the only time she ever concentrated on herself. Her face was lived in, every line a testament to the endless effort of her life: her hands were red raw from scrubbing, she was as thin as a whippet, her demeanour scuffed about the edges. She might have been attractive if life had led her down a different path. I could imagine her on the arm of a swanky fellow wearing those Regal Brogues. What would she look like in a fancy frock, a fur wrapped about her shoulders, a cigarette at the end of a holder?

'Right, then,' she said, reaching for her overcoat. 'You done? Fetch my handbag and let's get this over with.'

It was a portent of something deep and terrible to be seen walking with your mother towards the school. The only time mothers were seen anywhere near the gates was when there'd been an accident at the pit, or you were in dire trouble. 'We'll go the long way round,' said Mam, shifting her hat to sit more comfortably. 'I don't want to go past the shop and be seen.'

I felt anxious. Kids were starting to make their way back, having had lunch, and their glances were boring into me. We had to cross the playing area in front of the schoolhouse, girls sectioned off to the right, boys to the left, and my mother swept through the centre, a maternal Moses cutting a swathe through a sea of small jumpers. I was lagging behind, trying not to look as if I was hanging on to my mother's apron strings, but Mam stopped and pressed her palm into the middle of my back to hurry me up. She had better things to be doing, and I knew it.

I stopped. Mam reached for the door into the schoolhouse signposted for girls. I couldn't be seen going through that, so I hung back again, not quite sure what to do. 'Mam,' I said, with some urgency. 'I'm not allowed in b'there.' I pointed towards the sign carved into the stone above the doorway. She glanced upwards.

'Well, I am,' she said. 'You go in whichever door you please.' And in she went. I dithered, torn between following my mother and being seen by any of the boys in my class. I looked back across the yard. They were all staring. Get on with it. I plunged through the girls' door, a vein of panic pumping through me. I heard jeers echoing around the yard. I'd suffer for that.

Mam had stopped at the end of the corridor. 'Schools. They always smell exactly the same,' she said, lifting her nose.

'Ah! Mrs Jones. Thanks for coming in.' Miss Evans strode into view, her hand extended.

My mother stood staring at Miss Evans' flared slacks, blinked, then carefully placed her hand into the one offered.

'How do you do,' she said, in an unfamiliar posh voice. I frowned at her. She ignored me.

'Let's go to my classroom. Come on, Anthony. Don't dawdle.'

A brief discussion about the weather covered the gap between corridor and classroom. I said nothing, still none the wiser as to what this might be about. There was no sign of Gwyn or his mother; in fact, I think I'd seen him in the yard kicking a ball against the far wall. I followed Miss Evans and my mother into my classroom and, from habit, began to make my way to my own desk.

'Come and sit up front, Anthony,' said Miss Evans, placing two chairs opposite her own. My mother sat, her handbag clutched tightly on her lap. I slid onto the chair next to her and sat on my hands.

'I expect you're wondering why I asked to see you?' said Miss Evans, smiling at my mother.

'Ant told me about the fight,' said Mam, her lips taut. 'But he tells me he didn't start it.'

'No,' said Miss Evans, casting me a glance. 'He didn't. But that's not why I wanted to speak with you.'

My eyes widened. She does know about the banana. My mother's back stiffened.

'The thing is, Mrs Jones,' said Miss Evans, crossing her legs and leaning forward, 'I think Anthony should be put up for scholarship. He's a clever boy and it would be quite wrong for me to encourage him on a path to the pit. With your agreement, I'd like to put him up for the 11-plus and see if we can get him to the Grammar.'

I turned and looked at my mother. She turned and looked back at me. We hadn't expected this.

'Up for the Grammar?' said Mam, as if the wind had been taken out of her. 'Nobody from our family has ever done that. I don't know how ... I mean, I don't know if we could afford it.'

'Anthony would be a scholarship boy,' Miss Evans cut in. 'So that would mean his education would be paid for. You'd simply have to find the funds for his uniform and shoes.'

'Simply?' said Mam, with a small laugh. 'We haven't got funds to buy him shoes now.' She nodded down towards my wellingtons.

'Well,' said Miss Evans, 'there's a war on. Times are tough. But let's see if we can get him in first, shall we? If he does extra well, we can apply for a Special Place. Then you won't need to shell out a single shilling. There's no harm in trying. How do you feel about it, Anthony?'

'I don't know anyone at the Grammar,' I said, looking up towards Mam.

'Not yet, you don't,' said Miss Evans, placing her hand on my forearm. 'But you're an affable lad. You'll make new friends.'

'I don't know,' said Mam, her face troubled. 'I wouldn't want to give him hopes and have him disappointed. And besides, his brothers are down the pit, his father too, and his father before him. It's what we know. He went underground the other day didn't you, Ant?'

I nodded.

'Wasn't supposed to, mind, but there it is. When it's in your blood, it's in your blood.'

'Mrs Jones,' said Miss Evans, her face softening, 'there is nothing harder than changing a pattern. But it doesn't mean we should shut ourselves off from the possibility of change. Anthony has the chance of a different life. A better life. Wouldn't you want that for him?' She stopped and held my mother's gaze.

Mam's fingers tightened on her handbag. 'Better life? My boys have a good life,' she said, quietly. 'It may be hard but at least it's honest.'

'But you've said it yourself, it's a hard life, a terribly hard life, and if Anthony makes it to the Grammar, he can be anything he wants to be. What would you like to be, Anthony?' She turned her gaze towards me.

I looked up at my mother, her eyes perplexed. I wasn't sure what I should do so I thought about what I'd say if Father was with me. I should do what was right. 'Miner,' I said, looking back towards Miss Evans.

Miss Evans sat back and unfolded her legs. 'You don't have to say yes now. We've got a while before I have to send off for the papers. But have a think about it over the Whitsun half-term break. It's just an exam. If you don't get in, you don't get in. But I think you can do it, Anthony. I wouldn't ask you otherwise.'

My mother rose. 'Well, you've given me plenty to think about,' she said, with a terse nod. 'Anthony' – she nudged her head towards the door – 'you go back out to the yard. I'd like to chat to your teacher alone, please.'

I headed towards the door, twisting my head round to look over my shoulder as my hand turned the knob. Both Mam and Miss Evans were standing watching me, silent, coiled. Things would be said that I wouldn't hear. I slipped out through the door and stood for a moment trying to listen. Muffled. Low. Gentle. Like hearing a bee somewhere out of sight. I leant back against the wall and turned my head to look down the corridor. The lime-green tiles behind me were cold to the touch, chipped, faded. Everything about the school was run down, worn out. I wondered what the Grammar was like. I thought about the uniform, a pair of shoes …

A pair of shoes.

I stared down at my wellingtons. The blood from earlier was dried now. It looked like a strange, flattened flower. If I leant back on my heels, I could see the ring of rubber on my shins.

'*Uffach wyllt*,' I mumbled to myself. 'A pair of shoes.'

The mumble was coming closer. Mam was moving towards the door. Couldn't be caught loitering. So I scarpered.

'Take that, you little shit!' yelled Emrys, giving me a clout. I fell sideways onto the kitchen table. 'Showing me up in the street. Who do you think you are? You're nobody. A bloody runt. That's who.'

'Enough of that!' said Mam, sharply, picking up their coal-dirty clothes from the floor. 'It was the other boys who made a show of you, not your brother.'

'He's part of 'em, though, inne?' said Emrys, his face contorted. 'Mucking about with official war business! You lot need to learn.'

'Why are you so moithered?' said Bethan, arms crossed and standing in the doorway of the kitchen. 'It's only boys. Not like you didn't scrap about when you were a young'un.'

'He's just fouled up after the pit, in't he?' said Alwyn, pulling up the braces on his trousers. 'Almost fell out of the lift today. Bloody Home Guard. Up all night, he's been. Falling asleep on the job. And for what? So you can make yourself feel better you're not killing Germans? The only person you've got a chance of killing is yourself. You'll be looking after no one when you're dead and in a box. Do as I do, Emrys. I look after one person – myself.'

'You what?' said Mam, stopping what she was doing. 'Almost fell out of a lift? That true, Emrys?'

Emrys shrugged and reached for a cigarette from the kitchen mantelpiece. 'We were going down. Dram lift coming up. One of the drams went loose, lift smashed into ours. I wasn't concentrating. Two lads went over the rail. Broken legs, both of 'em.'

'One was Penwyth Collins,' said Father from the back step, where he was standing staring up at the mountain. 'He'll not work again.'

Mam clutched the dirty work clothes to her. 'Oh, no, Davey. His wife's expecting.'

'Perhaps you can put together something,' said Father, turning to Mam. 'Anything extra you might have. We should give them what we can.'

Mam stared at him. 'I don't know if we have got …'

'Whatever we can, Em,' said Father.

A heavy silence filled the kitchen.

'It's only a matter of time before something worse happens,' said Alwyn, who was now stretching out a discarded rabbit skin onto a wooden board. 'Mark my words. More coal needed. Not enough men. We're going too deep into seams. Blasting without manholes. Cutting corners. When men are told to speed things up, safety is the first thing out the window. Pit owners don't care. All they care about is shifting seams and reaching quotas. Well, bugger that. It's not worth it.'

'Without us, the war effort grinds to a halt,' said Father, his expression dark and his brow furrowed. 'No engine runs without coal. No machinery builds armaments. Everything needs power, energy. This is how we serve. Never lose sight of that, Alwyn. There are men, neighbours, people we know, fighting in fields abroad. They risk their lives gladly. We can do the same. Don't tell me it's not worth it.'

'Tell me it's worth it when one of us is in a wooden box,' Alwyn grumbled, taking a nail and piercing the stretched rabbit skin.

Mam cast a glance towards me. 'Pass me the hot water, Ant,' she said, softly.

She let the clothes in her arms fall into the washtub. She'd let them soak overnight, scrub them in the morning, hang them on the line if it was dry, hang them by the fire if it was wet. I had never known any different. Neither had she. There were comforts to be had in the familiar, the everyday rituals of our lives, and yet ... I passed her the pan of water. Our eyes met and I felt consumed with a small, burning terror that something bad was going to happen.

I snuck upstairs, tucked the banana under my jumper, took it out into the garden and threw it down the outtie.

CHAPTER FIVE

'Fancy coming to the pictures?' said Bethan, hand on hip, head tilted to one side.

I stared up at her from under the bed.

'Thought you could do with a treat, what with all the scraps you've been in.'

'What's on?'

'Dunno,' she said with a shrug. 'Let's go and see, shall we? Besides, I need a beau to take me. May as well be you?'

I slid sideways and pushed myself up. 'Thought Alf might be your beau,' I said, following her from the room.

Bethan stopped and turned to face me. 'Are you mad? What gave you that idea? I've not stepped out with him. Nor am I going to.'

'Dunno,' I said. 'He's asked after you, been round, like. Reckon he's sweet on you. Alwyn says so.'

'Yeah, well,' said Bethan, with a snort, 'he can be as sweet on me as he likes. Doesn't mean I'm going to like him back. Come on. If we get a lick on, we can make the six-thirty. You've got a proper shiner coming up.' She stood back and regarded my face. 'Does it hurt?'

'Bit,' I said. I was in a strange mood. I felt out of sorts. So many thoughts swirling through me, full of feelings I didn't know what to do with. Bad things happen. I felt haunted by the idea.

As we came down the stairs, I could hear my brothers laughing. 'So he bites into his sandwich,' said Alwyn, 'and there's no filling. Instead, there's a handwritten note. And he spits it out, opens his sandwich, pulls it out, reads it. It says, "I hope you choke on it, you bastard!"' He let out a loud laugh.

'No!' said Mam, sitting in her usual spot in the parlour, unravelling the never-ending jumper.

'Honest, like!' said Alwyn, his face animated. 'Wife had stuck it in his sarnie. Turns out he's been having it away with one of the women up at Polikoff's.'

'Who?' said Mam, frowning.

'Dunno. But her fella's away fighting, ain't he?'

'No way to behave.' Mam tutted and shook her head.

'All the same, funny, ain't it? "I hope you choke on it, you bastard!" Ha! That'll teach him!'

Father was sitting in his chair, legs turned towards the fire, glasses on, reading *David Copperfield*. He stopped and looked up. 'There is no fun to be had from other people's bad choices, Alwyn. Mistakes are things we learn from. Make a mistake once, and learn from it. Make the same mistake twice, and that's a choice. It's by our choices we are judged. You'd do well to remember that.'

Alwyn's smile stiffened. Mam gave him a small shake of her head. 'Put another lump on for me, there's a good lad.'

'You off out?' asked Emrys, seeing Bethan reaching for her coat.

'Ant's taking me to the pictures, aren't you?' She looked down at me. I nodded.

Emrys stood up. 'I'll come with you. Nothing worth listening to on the wireless, anyhow. You coming, Alwyn?'

Alwyn was standing by the hearth, lump of coal in hand. He shook his head. 'Nah. I'm gonna stretch out the rest of them skins.' He nodded back towards the kitchen.

Emrys walked towards the door and, ducking suddenly, raised the back of his hand towards my face. I flinched but he didn't hit me. 'I'm messing with you, boy,' he said, pushing past me to lift his coat and cap off the rack of hooks in the hallway. 'Look at the state of you. You need to toughen up if you're going undergound. You won't last five minutes.'

I cast a glance towards Mam, but if she'd heard, she didn't show it. She was staring into the fire, the fresh coal sending new flames crackling upwards. She looked tired, her head gently falling onto one shoulder. The half-unravelled jumper sat limply in her lap.

'I'll have a cup of tea, Em,' said Father, turning another page in his book.

Mam blinked and, for a moment, looked around the room as if she didn't quite know where she was. She didn't reply, simply got up and disappeared into the kitchen.

'Right, then,' said Emrys, opening the front door, 'let's get going. What's the film, anyway?'

'Dunno,' I said, turning to follow him.

'Better not be none of your soppy nonsense, Bethan. If it is, I shall snore loudly and show you right up.'

Bethan gave him a sharp stare. 'Good, I like you better when you're asleep.'

The Gaiety was our local fleapit: fourpence wooden seats at the front, sixpence cushy seats towards the back. Before the war, the picture house frontage had been lit up with grand announcements, but I was too young to remember all that. Instead, there was a board with a poster on that came with that week's reel. The one for *Double Indemnity* had Barbara Stanwyck sitting in a chair with her leg in the air. It caused a bit of a to-do, as lots of mams thought it was racey. I liked it.

The poster on display was for that night's film – *A Canterbury Tale*. It didn't give much away, just three faces, two men and a woman set against a rolling green field. A dark figure lurked at the bottom. Couldn't make out what he was.

'Look at that lot,' said Emrys, nodding towards a group of boys round Thomas Evans' wheelchair. 'Like they've struck gold, or something.'

I glanced in his direction. Thomas, having had to complain endlessly that nobody was pushing him anywhere, was now smothered with offers of help. Funny, that; but anyone with a lad in a wheelchair got in for free. The trick was to stand with your hand on the back of his chair. It meant you were with him and had a pass into the flicks. I had a quick count. There were seven hands.

'I don't know why Gwennie Morgan puts up with it,' said Bethan, laughing. 'Look at them! They're like flies!'

'Here,' said Emrys, nudging me, 'get over b'there. Then we won't have to pay fourpence for you.'

'Actually,' said Bethan, opening her purse and peering in, 'that's not a bad idea. I'm a bit short. Go on, Ant, hop to it.'

I did as I was told and slipped between two of the larger boys at the back of the cluster. Reaching forward, I managed to slip a finger over the back of Thomas's chair. Gwennie Morgan was staring down from her glass-fronted booth. She was sucking on a boiled sweet, her blood-red lips squeezed into a pout. Gwennie was a great favourite with Treherbert lads. She had platinum blonde hair, cut short and waved, always worn with a ribbon bow. Her face was plump and cherubic, large blue eyes framed with turquoise half-moon glasses. Her lofty status as the giver of the tickets gave her an authoritative air, but Mam said the way lads behaved round her was more to do with the size of her bosom. 'They're mesmerised,' she would say. 'She's a viper.'

I was too short to see the full glory of Gwennie Morgan's bosom. I just wanted to get into the flicks for nothing. So I stood, finger hanging off the canvas back of the wheelchair, waiting.

'How many is it, then?' said Gwennie, with a sniff. 'Stand still. I can't see all of you. Right. So, you in the chair. Then one, two, three ...' Her red-taloned finger counted us off. '... seven ... Wait. Is there one down b'there? Right. Start again. One, two ...'

Behind me, Emrys was laughing. Another gaggle of boys had joined the group.

'Hang on. Were you there before?' said Gwennie, counting to eleven. 'It was seven a minute ago.'

'I've been here all the time,' said a ginger-haired lad.

'And me,' rang a chorus of voices.

'Oh, just get in, the lot of you,' said Gwennie, waving her hand towards the cinema doors. 'I can't be bothered with it.'

Everyone ran towards the doors to get the front seats. I was left, standing behind the wheelchair.

'Someone give us a shove, then!' said Thomas, who had been abandoned, again.

'Two fourpence tickets, please, Gwennie,' said Emrys, leaning into the booth. He glanced down towards the wheelchair. 'Where've all your pals gone?'

'They've all buggered off!' said Thomas, staring up. 'I get 'em in. They all bugger off!'

Emrys laughed. 'Our Ant'll shove you in. *Diawl*! What a scam! Don't know why you stand for it, Gwennie.'

'Well, I don't usually,' said Gwennie, handing Emrys two cardboard tickets. 'I just happen to be in a good mood today, that's all. The Americans are coming. Have you heard? Soldiers in proper uniform. None of you dirty lot!'

'Better not let Alwyn hear you say that, Gwennie Morgan. And besides, I'm in the Home Guard. I wear a uniform.'

'I said proper uniform,' said Gwennie, 'not something that's come out of a dressing-up box. Next!'

Emrys screwed his mouth sideways and gave me a poke in the shoulder. 'Go on, then, get him inside. And hurry up. Or we'll miss the newsreel.'

The inside of the Gaiety was a dark mess of a room, the projector light crawling to the screen through a blanket of swirling cigarette smoke. The screen was in constant motion, with anonymous objects – bits of orange peel, chewed-up wads of paper, discarded butt ends – all flicked up into the beam using elastic bands. The general rule was that mucking about was tolerated during the newsreel, unless the King appeared, in which case you all had to stop and show respect; and if you didn't chuck something up every time a German appeared, you were a traitor.

'Do you want to sit with us?' Bethan said to Thomas, as we pushed him down the central aisle.

'No, ta,' he replied, reaching into his pocket. 'Down the front, please.'

I pushed him to the edge of the first wooden bench, where all the boys were flicking stuff up into the projector beam. Someone had brought a bag of woodlice. 'Flick 'em up b'there,' said the ginger-haired lad, gesturing to where some girls were sitting. They all did. Screams.

'Guess what I've got,' said Bethan, as I slid onto the bench beside her. 'Bag of humbugs.' She pulled out a small white paper bag and I could instantly smell a sweet, heady vapour.

'Get away, man!' said Emrys, his face lighting up. 'Where d'ya get 'em from?'

'Work. I did a favour for one of the WAAF. She wanted someone to do her shift so she could see her fella on furlough. I volunteered. She gave me these as a thank you. Want one?'

'Do I ever!' said Emrys, sticking his fingers into the bag in her hand.

'Come on, Ant, help yourself.'

I peered into the top of the bag and saw the glorious striped chaos of beloved humbugs. Oh! It was proper lovely: the sweetness on the tongue, my spit turning thick and minty. It was like a long-forgotten memory running to meet me.

'Remember,' said Bethan, popping one into her own mouth, 'suck it so it lasts.'

The *Pathé News* newsreel was in full swing. Something about French civilians being allowed to evacuate during a truce between the British and Germans. I wasn't really paying attention, but there must have been a German on screen as a sudden flurry of catcalls and missiles filled the air. I shifted on the bench and cast a look back towards the rear of the cinema. A hand waved in my direction. I peered through the smoky gloom. It was Alf. I waved back.

'What you looking at?' said Bethan. 'Watch the news.'

I twisted back round and let the humbug rattle behind my teeth. Emrys, having lit a cigarette, was picking strands of tobacco from his tongue. Down at the front, Thomas had a catapult out. Up on the screen, Princess Elizabeth appeared. Someone wolf whistled, only to be scolded immediately by everyone around him. I felt a hand land on my shoulder. I looked up.

'Shove over,' said Alf, with a grin. 'All right, Emrys? Evening, Bethan.' He sat down. Bethan gave me a sharp stare.

Nobody said anything.

'Bethan's got humbugs,' I said, pulling mine out and showing him. 'Do you want one?'

'Not that one, I don't,' said Alf, eyes fixed on my half-sucked sweet. I popped it back in my mouth and licked my fingers. 'Gonna offer me one or what, Bethan? All in it together, and all that.'

Bethan offered up her bag without looking at him. She said nothing.

'Thank you very much,' said Alf, popping one into his mouth and shooting me a wink.

'Heard you almost took a tumble down the shaft today, Emrys,' said Alf. 'No harm done, I hope?'

'I'm fine,' said Emrys, blowing a puff of smoke upwards. 'I was just tired, what with being up all night. Home Guard, see. Surprised you're not mucking in with that. You should join.'

'Well,' said Alf, settling into the back of the bench. 'I was thinking more about joining up for proper, like.' He shot a quick, sideways glance towards Bethan.

My mind cast back to the first time I'd seen him, and his chat of charming girls into giving him tups. I frowned. 'He's not really, Bethan,' I said, tugging her sleeve.

'I know,' she replied, curtly.

Alf smirked. 'Anyways, Americans coming, eh? Talk of the village. They'll be turning all the girls' heads, I expect.'

'Why are you looking furious?' said Emrys, noticing my sister's expression.

'Shut up,' she said, staring determinedly forward. Emrys raised an eyebrow and sat back with a grin.

Ahead of us, in the dark, there was another small commotion. Thomas Evans was catapulting spitballs at the girls – small, chewed-up lumps of tissue that were cold and wet as they landed. 'Not surprised no one wants to push him anywhere,' said Emrys. 'He's a right proper shit.'

'Emrys!' yelled Bethan.

The *Pathé News* ended and the cinema was plunged into a deeper black as the reel was changed to the main feature. It was traditional to hurl as many insults at the projectionist as possible while he did the switchover. You could call him anything you liked, as nobody could see you.

'Get on with it, ya bastard!' yelled someone just behind us.

'Bet you can't wait to see 'em, can you?' said Alf, giving me a nudge. 'D'you know what to say if you see an American?'

I shook my head.

'Can I have some gum, chum?' said Alf. 'They haven't had rationing. They're like walking treasure chests.'

'Film's starting,' said Bethan, clearing her throat.

A wave of shushes rippled through the cinema, all faces upturned. Title card, a peel of church bells, a swell of strings, a narrator reading out some poem, a load of people in medieval costumes on horses. Someone falls off.

A gust of laughter bellowed up from the benches.

Suddenly, a Spitfire. Cheers as it roared out from the screen.

'Thank God for that,' whispered Alf. 'Thought it was going to be all old-fashioned, like.'

I sat, staring up, sucking my humbug as slowly as I could. An American soldier had got off at the wrong train station and found himself walking in the dark with an English soldier and a young lady, but someone attacked the lady and threw glue in her hair.

'Who throws glue in a girl's hair?' whispered Alf.

'I did that to Bethan, once,' said Emrys, leaning across. 'Got the belt for it, 'n' all.'

The American was trying to get to Canterbury. People were suspicious of him but I reckoned he was all right. We didn't get many strangers in Treherbert, but Father always said: If you meet a man you don't know, treat him how you'd like to be treated. 'There's nothing warmer than a welcome.' Mam says that, too. But the people in the film weren't giving that warm a welcome to the American. I felt sorry for him and resolved that if I ever met a stranger, I'd be as kind to him as I possibly could.

It turned out some posh fella had been chucking glue in girls' hair during blackouts so soldiers wouldn't be distracted from doing their jobs. The American got to Canterbury with his pal, another American soldier, who asked for tea loudly. And the girl who'd been attacked at the start found out her Tommy beau was alive after all. Bethan cried during that bit, but I tried not to notice. It was all right.

'Didn't think much of the pal,' said Emrys, standing ready for the National Anthem. 'Bit brash. Full of himself.'

We all stood for the National Anthem. Alf's voice rang out. I glanced up at him. He was smiling as he sang, chest puffed out, cap in hand. A lusty sense of national pride swelled through the room. 'There is nothing a Welshman loves more than to sing his devotion,' said Alf, grinning down at me. He slipped his cap onto the back of his head. 'Mind if I walk you up the street, Bethan?' he asked, turning to my sister.

'You can walk us all up the street,' she said, buttoning her coat. 'We're all going in the same direction.'

'Oh, don't mind us,' said Emrys, putting his arm on my shoulder as we walked towards the exit door. 'Ant and me can manage in the dark, can't we?'

'I'm the only one with a torch,' said Bethan, shooting Emrys a glare. 'And you know how clumsy Ant is. He best stay with me. He's been hurt enough for one day.'

'Don't tell me I didn't try,' said Emrys, shrugging his shoulders towards Alf.

'The more, the merrier!' said Alf, unfazed. 'Besides, I haven't got a torch. I shall have to take your arm, Bethan. You can save us all.'

My sister gave a small, exasperated snort.

The wind had picked up, bringing with it a sharp nighttime chill. I'd come out without my coat so I pulled the sleeves of my jumper down over my hands, made fists and stuck them into my armpits. There was nothing to be done about my knees. I didn't own a pair of long trousers. I would have to endure the air biting up my shorts.

There was no moon that night, no stars to walk home by, and Bethan reached into her handbag for the small low-beamed torch she always carried with her. 'Come on, then,' she said, rather briskly. 'Let's get off.'

Voices and footsteps sounded around us as people from the cinema peeled off down side streets. As we made our way further up the village, the only sounds were our own footfalls: Emrys and Alf's hobnailed boots, Bethan's sensible heels and my wellingtons providing a base-like squelch to underpin the hometime symphony.

'So when are the Yanks coming?' said Emrys, breaking the silence. 'Are they actually coming here, like? Or just to the base?'

'I really don't know,' said Bethan, her voice clipped. 'I doubt if they'll come here. Why would they?'

'To take our women!' yelled Emrys. 'By God, Alf, can you imagine the punch-ups? They won't stand a chance. Not against pitmen.'

'Don't be so sure, Emrys,' said Bethan. 'They're trained soldiers, remember? And they've not been on rations for years on end.'

'What you talking about?' said Alf. 'Jam sandwiches are the food of the gods. I shall fight them to the death.'

I let out a laugh. I looked up towards Bethan and saw a small smile mustering in the torchlight.

'What's that noise?' said Emrys, coming up sharp.

We all stopped. An odd thick whine was coming up behind us, but in the pitch black it was impossible to see what it was. I peered down the street. 'Can't see anything,' I said.

'Sounds like a van coming,' said Bethan, tugging at my jumper. 'Get off the road, Ant.'

'Why would a van be coming up at this time ...?' began Emrys, narrowing his eyes in an effort to penetrate the gloom.

And then I realised. It wasn't something coming up the street. It was something going over it. It was the same noise I'd heard up the mountain.

'It's a plane!' I shouted. 'Told you about the Mozzie. Must be the same one!'

I stared up into the sky, bursting with excitement. It was quite something to see a Mozzie so low once ... but twice? A deep, penetrating rumble rolled closer. It was coming right over the rooftops. Bethan shone her torch upwards in the hope we might catch sight of something, but I could only make out the chimney tops, the constant wafts of smoke making strange shifting shapes across the night sky.

'Beam's too weak,' said Bethan, tapping at the end of it.

I peered into the black; was that a shadow moving towards us?

'There!' I shouted. 'Up there!'

The rumble turned into an ear-splitting roar. I clamped my hands to my ears as the plane, louder than I remembered, passed over us. I couldn't make out any details; it was just a large, dark mass. A sudden, sharp wind blew across us and Bethan had to grab her hat to stop it rolling up the street.

'Christ, it's low,' said Alf.

There was a strange whining noise, splutters and cracks, as if the engines were faltering.

'They need to pull up,' said Emrys. 'They're going to hit the mountain! Pull up, man!' he yelled. 'Pull up!'

Odd-sounding, fractured glitches echoed off the rooftops followed by a crunching, disturbing mechanical death rattle. I strained to hear more, but there was nothing, nothing at all. A terrible, deadly silence filled the gloom. It felt like an eternity but in reality it must only have lasted seconds.

'Oh, God, no,' whispered Bethan.

A thumping boom and a ball of flame shot upwards into the night sky.

We felt the energy of it, an invisible wave that sent me reeling, a massive explosion that illuminated the mountain, sending great orbs of fire raging outwards. The air was thick with the bitter smell of burning fuel, and a wall of sour, choking smoke billowed towards us.

'Cover your face!' yelled Bethan, groping for her gas mask.

I grabbed the bottom of my jumper and pulled it over my nose.

'Get down!' shouted Emrys, and all of us threw ourselves onto the cobbles.

My mind was racing. Bad things happen.

Bad things happen.

CHAPTER SIX

The first thick wave of smoke had rolled over us. I was coughing and it was difficult to see.

'Knock up as many men as you can!' yelled Alf, pushing himself up. 'Come on, Emrys! We've got to get up there!'

I felt Bethan's hand tighten around mine. 'Don't be afraid,' she said, getting to her feet. 'Quickly, we need to get help.'

I picked myself up and ran alongside her, my hand tight in hers. The street was filled with smoke, making my eyes burn. I rubbed at them and looked beyond the rooftops, my gaze fixed on the mountain. I was consumed by a strange, hollow sense of dread. A dark cloud billowed upwards. There was another explosion. I flinched.

People were coming out from their front doors, wrapping themselves in heavy dressing gowns. It was as if time was suspended: people frozen, staring up, soundless. Bethan punctuated the silence, yelling as we ran, 'A plane's gone down! Everyone do what you can!'

'Is it a Mozzie?' someone called out as we flew past. A cry went up. I glanced sideways: a face, hands clutched over a mouth; it was all smudged shadows.

'Ant,' said Bethan, looking down at me and letting go of my hand. 'Run to Mr Pugh's. Tell him to call out the Home Guard. I'll get to the cop shop and use their telephone to ring the base.'

I nodded and watched as she ran off down a side street towards the police station. There was just one telephone in the village. I'd only heard of it being used once before, when a tunnel had collapsed underground, a charge having gone off by accident. Ten men had been killed, one of them Bopa's husband.

My heart was thumping, my mouth dry. My legs felt heavy, rooted to the spot. I knew I had to run but it was like being in a wet bog, every step an effort. Pugh's house was towards the top end of the village, past Scott Street. I saw Father and Alwyn running towards the tinder track, but they were ahead of me and didn't hear me call. I dodged right and could make out Mr Pugh's solitary rooftop, black against a sky that was burning orange. A flash of light from a door opening, and then a silhouette moved towards me.

'Mr Pugh,' I panted, realising it was him. 'A plane's crashed up the mountain.'

'I know that, boy,' said Mr Pugh, pulling on his Home Guard tunic and picking up a bucket that sat by his front door. 'We'll need buckets. And lots of them. Follow me.'

I ran behind him back to the tinder track. 'Stand there,' Mr Pugh told me, pointing to the spot that led up the mountain. 'Tell anyone coming to fetch a bucket, fill it in the stream and bring it up.' I looked down into the stream. Father was standing in it, up to his knees. He was filling pans as fast as he could.

Mr Pugh disappeared away through some bracken and I turned, still trying to catch my breath. Footsteps were clattering towards me. 'Buckets!' I called out. 'Mr Pugh says bring buckets!'

I ran towards Father. 'We saw it go down!' I said, my eyes filling with tears. 'Right over us, it came. Like the other day but ...'

'Go home and fetch my Davy lamp. Alwyn's, too,' said Father. He didn't look down at me. He was staring up at the scramble of bodies making their way towards us.

'Let's get organised!' he called out, holding his arms up. 'We need to get water up the mountain. Start making a line! We'll pass it up!'

I pushed my way down the street, a salmon swimming against the tide. The press of bodies was relentless, the air filled with urgent calls, wild, worried eyes. I needed to get out from the scrum, and elbowed my way sideways. A familiar face loomed out at me. Ade. 'Christ, man,' he said, his mouth gaping open. 'Think it was that plane flew over us? Let's get up there.'

'Got to get Father's lamp. Come with me.' I grabbed his jumper by the sleeve and heaved him after me.

Mam was standing on the front step, hands high, trying to tie her hair up. Her gaze was unflinching. I cast a glance over my shoulder. The black cloud was spreading wider. 'God help them,' mumbled Mam as I pushed past her. She blinked and noticed me. 'Hang on, where are you going?'

'Getting the Davys!' I called out. They were in the back kitchen, on the ledge below the window. I grabbed them and turned to run back.

'Should we get the rifle?' said Ade, nodding towards the back door.

'What for?' I said. 'Take a pan off the stove. It'll do for a bucket.'

'Wait!' shouted my mother, coming in as Ade pulled a saucepan off the top of the oven. 'That one's got a loose handle. You'll need something bigger. Take this.' She handed Ade a large double-handled pan. Then, taking another pot herself, she headed after us.

Father was standing, up to his knees, in the stream, filling buckets as they were passed to him. Looking up and seeing me, he gestured to another man, who took his place. Taking a box of matches from his waistcoat pocket, he lit both the lamps and handed one to Alwyn. 'Come on,' said Father, his face grave. 'Let's get up there.'

I cast a glance back towards Mam. She was joining the long line of people waiting to fill their pots, pans and buckets. Ade nudged me. 'Let's follow. We're too small to carry water all the way up.' I nodded. Ade passed Mam's saucepan to a woman at the stream's edge, and we struck upwards, following the misty lights from the Davy lamps.

There was a wretched stench in the air, bitter and acrid, that burned into my nostrils. Behind us, voices called out, but as we climbed higher they faded on the wind. There was a sharp, mean edge to the wind that whipped up the path, making me tremble. I climbed faster. Ade was just ahead of me. I could hear him breathing.

The plane had crashed into the ridge below the mountain peak, and as Father and Alwyn reached the plateau, I looked up to see them lit by the fire burning against the hillside. Alwyn raised his arm to shield his face from the heat. 'It's in two pieces!' I heard Father shout. 'Front end is gone. Back end's not alight. There's a chance we may have survivors!'

Survivors. It was the first time I'd contemplated that someone might be alive. I was expecting nothing but death. I'd seen a dead body. Mam was taking a fruit cake round to a neighbour and I'd gone with her. We'd let ourselves in – nobody locked their front doors in Treherbert – and we'd found her in an armchair, sitting, head slumped gently backwards onto the headrest, her mouth falling open, her eyes half-closed. She looked grey and asleep, as if she'd dozed off listening to the wireless. I hadn't been frightened then, but now I was. If there was a dead body on our mountain, it wasn't going to be sitting and it wasn't going to be grey. It was going to be bloody and violent and real.

I felt dizzy and as we reached the top of the ridge, I rested my hand on an old stone wall and stopped for a moment. I looked down towards my feet and tried to catch my breath. My chest was thumping. I needed courage. As soon as I looked up, I would see it, and it would be burned into my memory for ever. I would never be able to unsee what I was about to see.

'Bloody hell,' I heard Ade mumble. He stumbled back towards me and pointed upwards, his hand trembling.

I looked up. Above me was the tail fin, broken off and caught on a rock. A chill coursed through me. I wasn't looking up at an RAF insignia. I was looking up at a swastika. The plane was German. Ade was still staring upwards. A swastika. A bloody swastika. Father had said there might be survivors. 'Christ,' I heard Ade whisper. 'It's Germans. On our mountain.'

Voices were coming up towards us: the line of buckets and pans making their way up the path. Ahead, I could hear people calling out, then a terrible pained cry. Ade turned and stared at me, his eyes wide. We climbed the final incline on the ridge and, steeling ourselves, turned to look on to the plateau. The heat was tremendous. The plane broken in two, the front half ablaze, the rear section further down the hillside and rolled onto its side. Ash filled the air, small black pieces fluttering down like burnt blossom. I could make out the silhouettes of a few men: one was standing, arm against his forehead towards the blazing cockpit, the others around the broken fuselage. I could just make out Father and Alwyn. They were carrying something. I couldn't make out what.

'Come on,' said Ade, edging forward.

A figure ran towards us. It was Emrys. 'Hurry with those buckets!' he yelled down the ridge path.

Had he even realised? I reached out and pulled the sleeve of his jacket. He glanced down at me, his face frowning and anxious. 'It's a German plane, Emrys,' I said, wind blowing through my fringe.

'What?' he said, looking again down the hill path. 'What you talking about?'

'The plane,' I said, dragging him to the tail fin. 'Look.'

Flames licking the skyline illuminated his face. There was another small explosion, a popping bang that sent me ducking. Emrys stood stock still, gazing upwards towards the swastika. 'But how ...?' he began, his words trailing away to a mumble.

People were running past us, water sloshing over the rims of buckets and pans.

'Form a line!' I heard Mr Pugh shouting behind us.

Emrys turned, his breath shallow. Pushing past, as if he could no longer see me, he stumbled upwards. Mr Pugh was standing, waving on the line of people stretching down the mountain. Emrys grabbed him and pointed back towards the fin. Pugh's face contorted. He glanced towards the burning cockpit, then over to Father and Alwyn. They were bent over something, but in the dark it was hard to tell what it was.

Something in me made me do it. As if a metal thread was pulling me towards them. Everything else faded away. My eyes fixed on one spot, the bundle at Father's feet. What was it? Father bent down, his face intense. Alwyn stood over him, his hands resting on his knees. Pugh and Emrys ran over. Father looked up. I was closer. What was it?

'Stay back, Anthony!' I heard Father shout, but the words evaporated into the surrounding din.

What was it?

Father straightened up and came towards me, and at that moment I saw a red pulp, a hole, hair, white stuff, a length of curling rope. Emrys was retching onto the grass. I looked again and I saw the jacket, blown open at the bottom, an impossible mess of intestines, legs gone, something that might have been a face, a mass of clots, a chunk of skull missing and deep red bubbles frothing from a nose and mouth.

I felt my father's arm come about me and turn me away. 'Don't look at him,' he shouted over the din. 'Don't look at him.'

Alwyn strode over to the first man in the line and knocked his bucket to the floor. 'Let them burn,' he said.

I hadn't slept well. Images of the dead airman had returned to me through the night until I'd woken, sweating and frightened. Five bodies had been found in all. Two were in the cockpit. Three had come from the fuselage. They were still up the mountain. The decision had been made to let the cockpit burn itself out. It was too dark to do anything, so a few members of the Home Guard had been left to mind the site, and everyone else had gone home.

It was a sombre breakfast. Emrys, in particular, seemed shaken, almost embarrassed. 'First sign of a German,' said Alwyn, reaching for the butter, 'and you throw your guts up. Good job you're not in the proper army, eh?'

'Shut up, Alwyn,' said Emrys, scowling.

'What'll happen with it all?' said Mam. 'The plane? The bodies? Sends me cold thinking of Germans lying up there. Even if they are dead.'

'They'll send someone up from the base this morning, I expect,' said Bethan, pouring herself a cup of tea, 'check over the wreckage. They might have been carrying documents. Might be useful?'

'Yes,' said Father, shooting me a look. 'I don't want to hear of you boys being up there scrumping stuff, Anthony. What's mountain treasure to you might be vital information for the war effort.'

I said nothing. Mam put a boiled egg in front of me. 'There you go. Treat. Bopa's hens laid a bumper crop this morning. She gave me one.'

'How come he gets it?' said Alwyn. 'It's bigger than he is!'

'It's his turn,' said Mam, handing me a teaspoon. 'Make it last. You might not have another one in a while.'

She ran her fingers through my hair before turning to the sink to get the tap running.

Everyone was staring at me in silence, their eyes darting between my mouth and the egg.

'Give me the top bit?' said Alwyn, as I shoved the edge of my teaspoon into the tip.

'No. It's mine.'

I flipped the end off and sucked out the white. Emrys leant over. 'Look at the colour on that yolk. Liquid gold. C'mon, Ant, give us dipsies.'

'Get away,' I said. 'Mam, tell 'em.'

'Let him eat his egg in peace,' said Mam, washing a pan. 'He didn't bother you when it was your turn.'

'He bloody did,' said Alwyn, protesting. 'Moaned with every mouthful. Hey, remember when it was Emrys' turn and he went to the outtie? I ate it, turned the shell over. He comes back in, smashes it all cocky, like. Empty. *Diawl*, I thought he was going to cry.'

'That was proper rotten,' said Bethan, standing and taking her quickly drained cup to Mam. 'Right. I best be off. I'll let you know if I hear anything about that plane. Ta-ra.'

A thick globule of yolk dripped off the end of my bread onto my knee. 'Look at him wasting it!' said Alwyn. 'Eggs are for men, Mam. Not boys!'

I scraped the bread across my knee to catch every scrap. 'Waste not, want not,' I said, stuffing it into my mouth.

'Right, then,' said Mam, drying her hands on a tea towel before planting a goodbye kiss on Father's cheek. 'Your tommy box is in the larder, Davey. Don't forget it. Boys, I've wrapped your lunches in wax paper. I've run out of paper bags. Ant, you come with me. You can say thank you to Bopa for the egg.'

I took the eggshell and peered into it, making sure I'd had every last scrap, then turned it over in the egg cup and pushed it towards Alwyn. 'You can have it now,' I said. 'All yours, like.'

'Can you hear a noise, Emrys?' said Alwyn, fixing me with a glare. 'Some sort of annoying buzzing sound. Must be a fly. Roll up the paper, let's kill it.'

Emrys reached for Father's discarded newspaper and scrunched it into a baton. He made a swipe for me, but I was too quick for him, and with the sound of my brothers swearing, I scarpered after Mam.

'Say thank you for the egg, Anthony,' said Mam, shoving me in the back as we stood at Bopa's open door.

'Thank you for the egg, Bopa,' I said.

'Big one, wasn't it? Almost as big as a duck's! Must have been the shock. Frightened the hens. All that noise, what with the plane. Terrible business last night, Em. Terrible.'

'I can't stop thinking about Germans being up our mountain,' said Mam, folding her arms.

'Germans up our mountain,' said Bopa, shaking her head. 'Imagine if they'd survived. Mind you,' she added, giving Mam a tap on her forearm, 'my sister, who's in Cardiff, told me a German plane landed down b'there. The German crew walked out, went to the nearest house, knocked and asked for tea.'

'Never,' said Mam, with a tut.

'My sister said the woman invited them in.'

'No.'

'She did. And she gave them tea.'

'I don't believe it.'

'Not in her best china, mind. That would have been wrong.' Mam nodded.

'What did she do with them then?' I asked, all ears.

'Her husband came down, put his Home Guard uniform on over his pyjamas, got his garden fork and marched them to the cop shop.'

Mam mumbled her approval.

'I expect the copper had a fit. Can you imagine what Arthur Pryce would do if Germans were marched into our cop shop?'

They both laughed.

Arthur Pryce was the police officer in charge of Treherbert. He was well regarded but considered lazy, given there was never any trouble for him to deal with. Fights between lads were sorted out on the spot, and bar one occasion when a cricket ball had smashed a window, I couldn't recall a single instance when he'd been required to do anything.

'I saw him the other day,' said Mam. 'He was buying a paper. I asked him if he was busy. He told me he was up to his eyes because they've made him Regional Officer in charge of Exotic Animals.'

'Exotic animals?' said Bopa, frowning.

'That's what *I* said. I said, "Exotic animals, Arthur? Are there any exotic animals in Treherbert?" And he said, "No, no there aren't." Still. If it keeps him busy.'

'He'll be busy with that lot, up the mountain,' said Bopa, folding her arms. 'Oh. And there's been a theft.'

'A theft? What of?'

'Mrs Reece's banana. Someone stole it, in broad daylight. Bold as brass.'

A hot surge of discomfort rose through me.

'Never. Where from?'

'Right out of her parlour. Window was open. Someone must have reached in and taken it, she reckons. She was proper upset. She was saving it for a fritter.'

Mam shook her head. 'It's this war, Bopa. It's bringing out the worst in people. Well. Let's hope Arthur catches whoever did it. That'll teach them wrong from right.'

Their chatter was as constant as birdsong and, seeing Ade, Fez and Bozo running towards the tinder track, I edged away to join them, leaving Mam and Bopa still gossiping. Ade was slinging a blue hessian satchel across his chest. 'Ant!' he said, seeing me approach. 'We're heading up the plane. Fez saw the Home Guard coming down for their breakfast. There's nobody up there till the RAF get here. If we get up b'there now, we can get treasure.'

'Father says we shouldn't. In case there's stuff they need for the war.'

'Get away, man! It's finders, keepers! Come on!'

Tendrils of smoke were still creeping upwards from the cockpit, whispers of the night before. In daylight, the crash was ever more real: a burnt black metal skeleton strutting out from the hillside, as out of place as a thing could be. Below it, the splintered remains of the fuselage lying on its side, one wing still on. From where we were standing, it looked as if the wreckage was surrounded by butterflies, but as we got nearer, the butterflies turned out to be scraps of paper fluttering up from the broken innards.

Ade touched my arm and pointed towards a large tarpaulin spread on the grass. Underneath it, five lumpen shapes ending in splayed boots. 'Germans,' mumbled Bozo, picking up a stone and throwing it. 'Bloody Germans.'

'Hey!' called Fez, bending down. 'Look at this!' He picked up something shiny. 'Compass. Still works, too.'

'What do you reckon it is, Bozo?' said Ade, bending down near the dead bodies and nodding up towards the burnt-out plane.

'It's not a bomber,' he said. 'Can't see any gun ports. Must be reconnaissance. Or transport? Maybe a Heinkel? Hard to tell with the front end all gone.'

'Reconnaissance?' said Fez, holding the compass up and swivelling around. 'Why would a reconnaissance plane be over Wales, like?'

'Dunno. Maybe they are planning on invading,' said Ade, pulling at something. 'Or looking for things to bomb. There you go, Ant,' he added, chucking two dirty brown boots in my direction. 'Pair of shoes for you at last.'

I picked one up. It was weathered, with a split heel and no laces. 'Too big for me,' I said, dropping it back to the floor.

'Wanna look at the Germans, like?' said Ade, standing. 'Proper, like? Come on.'

He took one end of the top edge of the tarpaulin and flipped it over. Instinctively, I looked away. 'That's disgusting!'

said Ade, sounding thrilled. 'That one's got no eyeballs. Must have burnt out.'

I turned round and looked down. Five faces, contorted. Two burnt beyond recognition. One was the man I had already seen, his face a bruised red mass. The others, mouths hanging open. They looked as if they were screaming. Details, my eyes were drawn to details: two had long boots, better boots, the others visibly more down at heel, a tear on a tunic, a blackened hand, half of a face clean as a whistle, hands held up, like when a baby sleeps, photos on the floor, leather braces holding up trousers that had no legs in them, and a hat, peaked, its rim decorated with braid, an eagle, a swastika.

I picked up the cap and tried it on, its smell – perfumed, almost sticky – the memory of a man's daily habits. A lone bird cried out above me. I raised an arm to shield my eyes from the sun. It was the red kite again. Circling.

'Look at all this stuff, man!' said Fez, filling his pockets. 'Let's get inside that bit. See if we can find a gun.'

'They're wearing different uniforms,' said Bozo, still staring down at the dead bodies. 'Look. Those two in grey. This lot in blue.'

'Never mind that,' said Ade, running after Fez. 'Let's find some weapons!'

We grabbed everything we could get our hands on inside the plane. Anything that wasn't bolted down was ours: lengths of rope, a pair of leather flying goggles, a tin of what looked like peaches, a few books, a magazine with women in very few clothes, a poster of Betty Grable, maps, rulers, dials we chipped off with rocks, half a loaf of bread, a round of cheese, and then Ade let out a yell.

'Pistol!' he said, holding it aloft. 'We've got a bloody pistol!'

'Got bullets?' said Fez, as we circled round. Bozo crawled into the mass of debris behind us.

Ade held the pistol in the palm of his hand and examined it. 'Dunno,' he said, 'stand back.'

He held the pistol out and squeezed the trigger. A loud shot exploded and a rogue bullet zinged about the plane's interior. We all ducked.

'Christ, man,' said Fez, standing back up again. 'Be careful. Shoot it outside.'

Ade jumped down from the fuselage and aimed towards a boulder. He squeezed again. Nothing. 'Think that's it,' he said, turning back to us. 'Quick. Find some more bullets.'

'Hey!' came a shout behind us. We turned to see an older member of the Home Guard puffing up the hill. 'What d'you think you're doing? Get out of it, bloody scamps!'

'Scarper,' said Ade, tucking the pistol into his hessian bag. 'Let's get to the den.'

We tumbled down the hillside, confident that we wouldn't be caught. A few sharp admonishments floated away behind us, but we weren't bothered. Old men would never catch young boys, and besides, we were scrumping mountain treasure. The stuff was ours.

We bounded down a tussock-covered incline, avoiding a ewe and two lambs, then ran along a narrow path that meandered its way around the mountain. There were no trees here – although plenty of heather and the odd windswept gorse bush – so our line of vision across the valley was unimpeded.

The cold wind of the previous night had been replaced by a warm south-westerly breeze, and the air was slightly heady with the smell of flowers coming into bloom. The mountain seemed so beautiful, so welcoming, it was hard to imagine the scene we'd left behind.

I was bringing up the rear, as usual, weighed down by my wellingtons, dodging rabbit holes and small, treacherous rocks. I could see the Big Stone, rearing up in the sunshine, and below it, the speckled roof of our den. Ade was in the lead, pointing the pistol at imaginary foes every now and again, and popping them with invisible bullets. He'd almost reached the drop down to the den's entrance when he slowed and came to a halt. He was staring at something.

Bozo was panting. 'What's matter?'

Ade bent down and picked up what looked like a harness. 'Wass'is?' he said, holding it up and showing us.

'Dunno,' said Fez, taking it from him. 'Must have blown down the mountain from the plane.'

'All this way, man?' said Ade, his face crunching. 'Must be half a mile.'

He let his toes tip over the small ridge, and jumped down with a thud. Bozo, Fez and I followed. 'Funny, innit?' said Ade, still trying to work out what it was. 'That must buckle into that, I reckon. But what is …'

He stopped dead in his tracks. We all did.

There was someone in our den.

CHAPTER SEVEN

There he was, inside our den, lying face down, legs splayed apart, his head hidden in the crook of an elbow.

Ade held out the pistol and edged closer. 'Kick his foot,' he whispered in my direction.

I inched towards the den entrance, swiped at the end of one shoe with my wellington, and ran back to Ade. Nothing.

'P'rhaps he's dead, like?' said Bozo. 'Crawled here and died?'

'Chuck a stone at him,' said Ade, still holding out the pistol.

Bozo bent down and picked up a small flint. It bounced off the man's back. Still nothing. We all crept closer.

'Oi!' called out Ade. 'You're in our den. And you're under arrest, innit?' We all turned and stared at him. Ade shrugged. 'Grab some sticks, in case he comes alive.'

I took a metre-long switch from our den stick box and held it, end tucked into my armpit, whittled end pointing towards the man on the floor. He still hadn't moved.

'Kick him again, harder, like,' said Fez, going down onto one knee and holding his stick out. 'And speak in German. He might not understand otherwise.'

'*Achtung* Hitler!' Ade shouted. 'You're our prisoner. We've captured you!' He kicked the man's boot again, this time landing a harder blow. There was a groan.

'He's alive,' said Fez, crouching. 'Stay sharp, boys.'

'Christ,' said Bozo, shoving his glasses up his nose. 'We've caught a bloody German.'

'Don't take your eyes off him,' said Ade, taking the pistol with both hands. 'There's no knowing how slippery he is.'

The man let out a long pained breath, coughed and turned his head towards us. He was squinting, the morning sun shining in his eyes.

'Steady, Adolf,' said Ade, squeezing the pistol tightly. 'I've got a gun. So no funny business.'

The man rolled onto his back and sat up. He coughed again and spat onto the floor. He looked at us all in turn. 'I surrender,' he said, putting his arms up into the air.

'He speaks English,' said Bozo. 'We've got a gun!' he shouted, pointing towards the pistol.

'Yes,' said the man, 'I see that.'

There was a short, awkward silence. Nobody blinked.

'Right, then,' said Ade, waving the pistol towards him. 'Shall we march him up the mountain to the Home Guard? Or down the mountain to the cop shop?'

'Or take him to the RAF?' said Fez. 'They're probably the best when it comes to Germans.'

'I'm not German,' said the man, still squinting. 'Do you have water?'

We all stared at him. 'Slipperiness,' said Ade, shooting us a sideways glance. 'He is a German. We all saw the swastika.'

'No. Polish. I'm Polish prisoner of war. I was just in a German plane. Please. Do you have water? Very thirsty.'

'I don't trust him,' said Bozo, clutching his crotch.

'There's a stream runs down between two rocks over there,' I said, pointing over my shoulder. 'I can get you some water from that.'

'Don't be mad, man!' yelled Ade. 'He's a German. It'll be a trick.'

'It's okay to give Germans drinks. Bopa told me,' I said, reaching into the den box for an old tin. 'I'll get it now.'

The man smiled at me. 'Thank you,' he said. 'Really, not German. Not even German uniform. Check my tags.' He reached into his shirt and pulled out two metal tags on a leather necklace. Pulling them over his head, he threw them towards us. 'There. Read them.'

Ade, still keeping the pistol trained on the man, bent down and picked them up. He tossed them to Fez. 'What do they say?'

'Dunno. Can't make it out. Skar ... bow ... itz. Piotr. What does that mean?'

'My name. Piotr Skarbowitz. Polish.'

Ade was shaking his head. 'I don't like it. We need to get someone up from the village. Ant, run down and fetch someone.'

'He's the slowest in his wellies,' said Fez. 'You go, Ade. You're the fastest.'

'You're right,' said Ade. 'Ant, you take the gun. Keep it pointed at him. I'll tell your mam. All the men are underground. She'll know what to do. I'll be back!' And with that, he pelted off across the hillside, like a fox with a scent.

I stared down at the gun in my hand. I wasn't entirely sure I wanted this responsibility. I looked at the man sitting on the floor. He didn't have a bad face, an evil face. He had the face of a working man – straightforward, strong jaw. His eyes were pale green in the sunlight, his hands dirty, stubble coming through on the edges of his chin, his lips dry and cracked. He looked tired. I still had the empty can in one hand. I saw him glance at it. 'I'm really very thirsty,' he said. 'And I think ankle is twisted. I can't run away.'

'Fill that up with water, Fez,' I said, passing him the can. 'It's all right. I'll watch him.'

Fez nodded and clambered back up the hillside towards the thin stream. Bozo sat down on his haunches, elbows on knees, and stared at our prisoner. 'If you are Polish,' he began, 'how come you were on a German plane, like?'

'We were being transported. Me and also other Polish soldiers. We were picked up in France and were to fly to camps. But we overpowered the guard, took gun from him. This gun.' Piotr nodded his head towards my hand. 'One of Polish soldiers said he could fly plane. Fly to Scotland. Polish army in exile there. But flying by night, we got lost. We didn't know where we were. In fact, where am I?'

'Don't tell him, Ant,' said Bozo, seeing me open my mouth. 'We don't know he's telling the truth yet.'

Piotr smiled. 'Quite right! Don't tell me. We ran out of fuel. Plane started coming down. I grabbed parachute and managed to jump out. I'm guessing the others weren't so lucky?'

I shook my head.

'Ah,' said Piotr. He fell silent, his eyes drifting off skywards.

Bozo stood up. 'Parachute? That's proper treasure, that is! Where'bouts is it, then?'

'I'm not sure. I landed badly, hurt ankle. I crawled quite a distance then found this shelter.'

'It's our den. Not a shelter,' said Bozo.

'It was dark. Up the hillside. That way, I think ...' He gestured with his thumb. 'Go find it.'

'If there is a parachute, that means he did jump out the plane,' I said, letting the pistol fall to my side. Piotr eyed it. I raised it again.

'Doesn't mean he's Polish, though,' said Bozo, pulling himself up onto the ridge to see if he could see silk billowing anywhere. 'Hey, Fez!' he called out. 'Can you see a parachute up b'there?'

'No!' I heard him call back. I looked again at Piotr. Father says you can always tell a man by his face: whether he's a man of the land, or a man underground, or a man who's never had to sweat and toil, smart types, like. Perhaps there was a smart man inside that uniform, an honest man? He was so dirty and scuffed and crumpled it was hard to tell.

Bozo jumped back down. 'Can't see nothing. Sounds like cock and bull to me.'

Piotr shrugged. 'I can't make you believe. I'm not sure where I landed. Wind carried it. It could be a mile away.'

Fez had returned with the water. 'There you go,' he said, handing the tin down.

Piotr took it and drank voraciously. Water dripped down his chin and onto his shirt. He ran a hand over his mouth.

'Thank you,' he said, handing the tin back. 'Do you mind if I try and stand? I'm a little stiff.'

I shot a glance towards Fez and Bozo. I wasn't sure what to say. Piotr placed one hand on the makeshift bench beside him and pushed himself upwards with a grunt. We all instinctively took a step backwards. 'I'm not going to hurt you,' he said. 'You're the one with gun. Could you pass me bigger stick?' he added, gesturing towards the whittling box. 'Perhaps I could use this as crutch?'

'Your English is dead good,' said Bozo, tilting his head to one side. 'Whys'at, then?'

'English grandmother,' Piotr explained, hopping uncomfortably. 'She brought me up, really. So my accent isn't that terrible. Perhaps it is.'

I could feel myself softening. Even if he was our enemy, he wasn't so bad. He hadn't been unkind or aggressive. He hadn't told us off or shouted at us to go away. Perhaps he was who he said he was? I let the pistol drift downwards again.

'Keep the gun on him,' said Fez, handing him a lengthy stick.

'Nah,' I said. 'He's all right. Besides, my arm is aching.' I slipped the pistol into the waistband of my shorts, the butt tucked out, just like I'd seen in the flicks.

'Have you knife?' said Piotr, examining the stick.

'There's one in the—' I said, pointing towards a tin near the back of the den.

'Shuddup, man!' yelled Fez. 'That's a weapon, like!'

'I like to cut this bit down,' said Piotr, holding out the stick and pointing to a few twig-like branches gathered round a gnarled knot. 'Then I can put it under armpit. For support.'

'It's in the tin at the back,' I said, ignoring Fez. 'I'll get it for you.'

I went past him to the old biscuit tin that was tucked under the bench, and pulled out the penknife we used for whittling. 'There you go,' I said, handing it to him. I stood back.

Piotr lowered himself onto the bench, stretching out his bad leg. He placed the stick between his thighs and, opening the penknife, ran his thumb over the blade. 'Not bad,' he said. 'This should do it.'

Bozo had crouched down again, as if he wanted to be ready to spring into action. Fez was hanging back, biting his nails. He looked anxious and kept glancing down the mountain. I stood, quietly staring. I wondered what Father would make of this man, this situation. Piotr took the penknife and began trimming the bark from the top end of the stick. His face was relaxed. He was not worried or afraid. These were the things Father would notice, I thought. I believed him.

The sun felt so warm. I stared up, a few thin trailing clouds lacing across the sky, and looked for the red kite. No sign. A songbird was trilling somewhere, busy and purposeful; below, another ewe was leading her lamb downwards, over the purple heather sparkling with dew-covered webs. Our mountain was still our mountain. And yet …

I lay down, hands behind my head, and closed my eyes. Behind me I could hear Piotr whittling; to my left, Fez shuffling, Bozo sniffing. I bent my knees upwards, my wellingtons making that dull rubbery squeak they always did. I could feel the metallic cold of the pistol against my belly. I was tired. I'd have liked to drift off, sun on my face, birdsong in my ears. It was odd I felt so relaxed, so unagitated, but no one is your enemy until they prove themselves to be, and nothing about this man made me afraid.

I don't know how long we all sat, waiting, but I stayed lying on my back, watching the sun shift in the sky. Fez saw them first and called out, and I sat up and turned to see Ade running back towards us with Mam and two old men in tow. I raised a hand to my brow to shield my eyes from the sun. It was the Baptist minister, Jones the Bible, and the grocer, Mr Hughes. Jones the Bible was carrying a large candle, Hughes had a spade, and Mam, I could see, had brought her rolling pin. They were creeping down the path to the den, weapons aloft.

'He's in here,' said Ade, panting.

'Right, then, right, then,' said the minister, brandishing his candle. 'What have we here? Boys, get behind me. Now, then. Steady on. Steady on.'

His shoulders were hunched, his arms splayed, candle in one hand, the other open-palmed as if preparing to wrestle. Dressed in a black three-piece suit, he was a stout man, his drum of a belly protruding from the edges of his jacket. He had greased-down hair, a thin moustache that tended to disappear when he sang, and little round spectacles that were far too small for his face.

Behind him, Mr Hughes was similarly bent over, spade in both hands and held aloft. He was in his shop scrubs, apron on, and had a brown felt cap teetering on the side of his head. He also had a moustache, but his was more fulsome, melting down over either side of his mouth like cheese dripping off a crust.

I glanced at Mam. She had a wild look in her eye as if she had no idea how this was going to play out. To be honest, neither did I.

Piotr, who was still whittling, saw them and stood up, penknife in hand.

'He's got a knife!' yelled Ade, pointing.

Jones the Bible let out a short, shrill scream, at which Mr Hughes leapt forward and made a swipe at Piotr with the spade. Piotr recoiled back, avoiding a blow, and Mr Hughes, losing his footing, stumbled sideways, whereupon the spade slipped out of his hands and hit the minister on the shin.

'Good grief, man!' yelled Jones the Bible, clutching his leg. 'What you do that for? Bloody hole in my trousers, now. And I'm bleeding. Look at that!'

'Sorry 'bout that,' said Mr Hughes, picking his spade back up. 'I panicked.'

'He's just trimming the stick, Mam!' I called out. 'He's not even German.'

'So he says,' said Ade, eycing Piotr suspiciously.

Piotr placed the penknife on the bench and held his arms out, palms of his hands facing up. 'There,' he said. 'Nothing that can hurt you.'

The minister lowered his candle and straightened his back. 'Now, then,' he said, clearing his throat. 'I am the Baptist Minister of Treherbert. I trust that you will respect my standing as a man of the cloth. We shall have no bloodshed here.'

'Apart from your leg, Mr Jones,' said Fez, hands in pockets.

Jones the Bible shot Mr Hughes, who was looking sheepish, a sharp look. 'Yes, well,' he said. 'Mr Hughes was a little over enthusiastic, but there it is. Now, young Adrian here tells me you are claiming not to be a German, is that correct?'

'Yes. Polish POW. The boys have my tags. No official papers. Germans took them in France.'

'Let me see, lad,' said Mr Jones, holding out his hand in Ade's direction.

'I've got them, Mr Jones,' said Fez, pulling them out of his pocket.

'I see ...' said Jones, holding the tags in the palm of his hand. 'Actually, I can't see. These aren't my reading glasses. Hughes, can you ...?' He passed them across, gave another cough and put his thumb into his waistcoat pocket.

'Can't make head nor tail of these,' said Mr Hughes, frowning.

'There, look,' said Mam, leaning over to have a closer look. 'That's the name, see? There.'

'Can't make it out,' said Hughes, turning the tags upside down.

'Piotr Skarbowitz,' said Piotr, taking the stick and placing it under his armpit. 'My name.'

'Obviously,' said Jones the Bible, with a purposeful nod, 'we'll need to verify with the relevant authorities that you are who you say you are.'

'We should definitely treat him like a proper German until we're sure, like,' said Hughes, lifting up his spade again. 'Take him down the cop shop.'

'Put that down, Mr Hughes,' said Jones, rolling his eyes.

'Not sure the cop shop's the best place for him, what with that leg,' said Mam, gesturing towards the homemade crutch. 'What you done? Broken ankle, is it?'

'I think just bad sprain.' Piotr smiled at my mother. She blushed and looked away.

'He'll have to stay somewhere,' said Jones the Bible. 'We can't have him wandering round the village like a wraith.'

'What about at the chapel?' said Mr Hughes, taking his cap off and scratching his forehead. 'Or the back room at the pub?'

'Neither are much comfier than here,' said Jones, gesturing into the den.

'I'll have him,' said Mam. 'We can make room for him. Davey won't mind. And if he is a Polish soldier, then he's a war hero. We should be looking after him. Not marching him from pillar to post. In fact, we should be ashamed of ourselves, coming up here armed to the teeth. Look at the poor man. He needs our help.'

Jones and Mr Hughes exchanged a short, nervous glance. 'Yes,' said Jones the Bible, nodding furiously. 'Yes. You're quite right, Mrs Jones. We must help him immediately. Come, now, Mr Skarbowitz, place your hand on my shoulder. I'll help you down the mountain.'

'Sorry about trying to hit you with my spade,' said Mr Hughes, taking Piotr by the elbow. 'You put your weight on me. It's not far. We'll have you down in no time.'

'I'll go ahead and get the kettle on. I expect you'd like a cup of tea?'

'I would, thank you,' said Piotr. 'Thank you. Thank you.'

'Right,' said Mam, with a nod. 'Come with me, Ant. I'll need you to help get your sister's room ready for our guest.'

I pushed myself up from the grass and dusted down my backside.

'Bloody hell, man,' said Ade, nudging me. 'You've got a bloody German staying at your house.'

I didn't reply. Instead, I handed him back the pistol and ran off after Mam. Sometimes, I thought, Ade could be quite annoying. Besides, he was wrong. Piotr was Polish.

CHAPTER EIGHT

'What do you mean there's a man upstairs in my bed?' said Bethan, frowning as she took her cap off.

'He survived the crash. He's Polish,' I said, holding a cup of tea in a saucer to take up to him. 'They were trying to escape. But the plane went down. Everyone's up there with him.'

Bethan put her hands on her hips and paused. She tilted her head to one side. 'Really?' she said, as if she wasn't quite sure whether to believe me.

'Honest, B,' I said, carefully ascending the stairs. 'Mam's making him cawl. And he's going to get to eat it upstairs. And nobody's eaten upstairs since Alwyn had rheumatic fever and almost died. So that's how serious it is.'

'And he's in my bed?' said Bethan, following me up the stairs. 'Where am I going to sleep?'

'In our room. Alwyn and Emrys are going to sleep on some camp beds from the Home Guard.' A peal of laughter came from the bedroom above us. Bethan pressed at my back. 'Don't rush me,' I said, 'or I'll spill his tea.'

Piotr was sitting on Bethan's bed, propped up by some pillows. He was wearing a pair of Father's best pyjamas, blue stripes, and his foot was raised onto a cushion. He'd had a wash and a shave and looked entirely different, a smart type, even; some might say handsome. Bozo and Fez were sitting facing him at the bottom of the bed, and Ade was behind the backboard, leaning over it. Jones the Bible was sitting on a wooden chair in the corner of the room, arms folded. He looked very pleased with himself. I placed the cup and saucer down on the small cabinet next to the bed. Piotr turned and smiled to me. 'Thank you!' he said. 'Such service! I can't get over it. I should crash in Wales more often.'

Jones the Bible let out a small chortle.

Piotr picked up the saucer and took a sip from the cup. 'Mam's best china, goodness,' said Bethan, coming in behind me. 'Hello,' she added, holding out her hand. 'I'm Bethan. This one's big sister.'

Piotr took her hand in his and shook it. 'He's been looking after me well,' said Piotr, smiling in my direction. 'You're army?' he added, seeing Bethan's uniform.

'WAAF, based up at RAF St Athan. I'm a paper shuffler, really. Don't get to do anything that exciting.'

'You're helping out with the Americans coming,' I said, joining Fez at the edge of the bed.

'Americans?' said Piotr, taking another sip. 'Really? In Wales?'

'Father reckons it's for something big in Europe,' I said, nodding.

Piotr raised an eyebrow. Bethan shuffled on her feet. 'Well, I wouldn't say helping out. I just type up stuff. Anyway. How's your leg?' She nodded down towards the raised foot.

'Sore. Bruise coming.'

'Show us again,' said Fez, grinning. 'It's a right whopper.'

'There's a lady,' said Piotr, taking another sip of his tea. 'I'm sure she doesn't want to see.'

'Oh, don't mind me,' said Bethan, leaning against the wardrobe and folding her arms. 'With three brothers, I've seen most things.'

'Well ...' said Piotr, casting a look at us.

'Go on, Piotr,' I said, sitting on the edge of the bed. 'Show us your bruise again.'

'All right, then,' he said. 'Don't say I didn't warn you,' he added, throwing a look to Bethan. 'Not nice.'

Putting his cup down he leaned forward and pulled off the large knitted sock Mam had given him to keep his toes warm. As it slipped off his foot, Fez, Bozo and Ade gave out a large 'Errrrrrrrr' to signify how impressed they were. The bruise was a medley of tones ranging from a halo-like yellow fringe through to a compote of blues, reds and purples. It stretched from the bottom of his toes, across his foot and slid sideways around his ankle and up to the midpoint of his calf. It was the greatest bruise I had ever seen.

'Goodness,' said Bethan, behind me. 'That looks terrible.'

'And disgusting,' said Ade, grinning.

'Does it hurt?' I said.

'Yes, it does,' said Piotr. 'But not too bad. I think I'll live.'

'Take note, boys,' said Jones the Bible, resting his hands on his belly. 'That's bravery right there. Did Jesus complain on the cross?'

'He did a bit,' said Ade, thinking about that.

Jones the Bible blinked. 'No, Adrian, he did not. Expressions of regret for mankind are not the same as complaining.'

Ade shrugged.

'You haven't complained once,' said Fez, leaning closer to get a better look. 'That means you're braver than Jesus.'

'Well, hang on,' said Jones the Bible, who looked as if he wished he hadn't started this.

'Can you help me get sock back on?' said Piotr, changing the subject. 'I can't quite reach.'

'Here,' said Bethan, stepping forward, 'I'll do it.'

She took the sock and gently pulled it back over Piotr's foot. 'Thank you,' he said, smiling. He laughed. 'All I've done since I got here is say thank you. But truly, thank you!'

'Right then,' said Mam, coming in holding a tray. 'Cawl! It's Welsh penicillin. Eat that up and you'll be right as rain in no time.' She placed the tray on Piotr's lap and handed him a spoon.

'Thank you,' said Piotr, then looked at everyone in the room and burst out laughing.

I sat, on the edge of the bed, laughing along with him. Everyone was laughing. Ade, Fez, Bozo, Bethan, Mam too. It felt wonderful. I looked back at Piotr. He was the single most exciting thing ever to happen to our house. 'There's nothing warmer than a welcome,' I remembered, and there and then, I resolved to look after him. No matter what.

Arthur Pryce arrived at half past three. He was sweating and looked anxious. Mam had asked him if he wanted to take his helmet off, as he was a tall man and we had low ceilings, but he'd declined, politely. He was here on official business and was to see the gentleman from the plane immediately. The boys were still hanging about. There was a real buzz of excitement, and with the men not back yet from underground, it was like we were holding the fort, in charge, like. A small crowd was gathered by our front door. I felt important, famous.

'He's upstairs, Arthur,' said Mam, wiping her hands on the end of her housecoat. 'I hope there's nothing wrong?'

Arthur, who wasn't used to being sent on official business anywhere, swallowed deeply and gave a non-committal shake of his head. 'If you could show me to the gentleman, I'd be greatly obliged,' said Arthur.

'Right, then,' said Mam, with a firm nod. 'Follow me.'

A small army of children flooded in and up the stairs after Arthur. There was no point telling them to leave. This was the single most thrilling thing that had ever happened in Scott Street.

'Mind your …' Mam began, pointing back towards the doorframe. Arthur's helmet banged off the wood and tipped backwards. 'Well. Here we are. This is Arthur. He's from the cop shop. He wants to speak to you. Official, like.' Mam went and stood by Piotr's side and crossed her arms. 'Go on, then, Arthur. Get on with it.'

Arthur's helmet fell onto the floor and rolled towards the wardrobe. He bent down to catch it, picked it up and tried putting it back on, but the tip scraped the ceiling and it fell off again.

'Let me take that for you,' said Mam, taking it and putting it on the bed.

Arthur looked desperate and uncomfortable. 'Right, then,' he said, reaching into his breast pocket. Pulling out a small notepad, he opened it and cleared his throat. 'At ten this morning, I was informed that a man, you' – Arthur stopped and gestured towards Piotr – 'had been found up Pen Pych mountain, and that this man, you, made claims that he was a Polish Prisoner of War captured by Germans and flown here during an attempt to escape.' He stopped, licked his finger and turned the page. 'In my capacity as the police officer in charge of this area' – his eyes darted about the room, and Mam nodded encouragingly – 'I made a telephone call to headquarters in Cardiff. They then rang someone in London.'

'Who's that, then?' said Ade, who was standing behind me at the front of the small gaggle of onlookers.

Arthur stopped and thought. 'I don't know. Anyway, someone in London then made enquiries of the Polish Army based in Scotland. And then the person in London rang back the headquarters in Cardiff.'

'Person in London's quite busy, isn't he?' said Mam, with a sniff.

Arthur swallowed. 'And then headquarters in Cardiff rang me and I can confirm that one Piotr Skarbowitz, that's you, was reported as being captured by Germans four years ago.' He closed the notepad and put it back in his pocket. 'That's it.'

'Is that it?' said Ade, in disbelief.

'What does that mean, then?' said a small girl towards the back.

'It means Arthur's come to tell Piotr who he is,' said Mam, 'and Piotr is who he says he is, which, everyone take note, is a

proper war hero who we are very lucky to be able to look after.'
A cheer rang round the room. She gave Piotr a comforting pat
on the forearm. 'And what's more, I couldn't be more proud
that he's in my house. So everyone here, go tell your mams.
Arthur's made it official. Now off, the lot of you. This man
needs rest.'

She shooed everyone down the stairs, then turned back
into the room. 'Never doubted it for a minute,' she said,
quietly, patting down the quilt.

'Nor me,' I said, leaning on the bedpost. Piotr smiled.

'Em!' came a call from downstairs. 'Yoohoo! Only me!'

'Come up, Bopa!' shouted Mam. 'Bopa Jackson, lives next
door. She'll be wanting to meet you.'

Bopa came in, all wide-eyed and smiling. 'Arthur,' she said,
giving the policeman a nod. 'Now, then. Is this him?'

She came and stood at the edge of the bed and stared at
Piotr as if he were a brand-new sofa. 'Handsome, inne? Bet
you've noticed that already, Bethan!' she said, casting a glance
back towards my sister. Bethan blushed. 'You know she's not
courting at the moment, don't you?' she said, turning back
to Piotr. 'Wait till you're up on your feet, you can ask her to
a dance.'

'I think I'll just pop downstairs,' said Bethan, with some
urgency. 'Put the kettle on. Do you want a brew, Arthur?'

'Oh, no, thank you,' said Arthur, shuffling uncomfortably.
'I'm on official business, see.'

'The official business is over now, Arthur,' said Mam,
sticking her hands in the pockets of her housecoat. 'Have a
cup of tea. Sit down, man.'

Arthur gave a small, awkward smile. 'All right, then. One sugar, please. Two if you can spare it.'

Mam rolled her eyes. 'You'll have half, Arthur, and make do and mend. Off you go, Bethan. Bring a tray up. We'll all have one.'

'I wish I had some more sugar,' said Bopa, nudging Piotr in the leg. 'If I did, I'd make you quite the cake. I've got the eggs. I've got the flour. I've even got the butter. Em makes her own, you know. But sugar?' She closed her eyes and shook her head. 'Harder to find than a hen's tooth. We should have a whip round, Em. Ask everyone for a little bit of their sugar rations, then I can bake him a cake!'

Piotr frowned as if trying to grasp hold of a distant memory. 'Actually,' he said, pointing his finger upwards, 'I know recipe for cake that doesn't need sugar at all. Prunes and a little orange juice instead. Warm prunes with juice, blend it to paste. Add melted chocolate and butter. Stir in egg yolks and beaten egg whites. Cook for twenty minutes.'

Mam and Bopa stared at him, mouths open.

'How come you know cake recipes, then?' asked Arthur, still trying to find somewhere to sit down.

'My grandmother had me sit with her when she baked. Always sit with your mother when she bakes, Anthony,' he said, shooting me a look. 'That way you always get to be person who licks spoon.'

'Well, I never,' said Bopa, shaking her head. 'A man giving me a recipe. Did you ever think you'd see the day, Em?'

My mother shook her head then gave Piotr a look I don't think I'd ever seen before. She was thrilled, bursting like a spring flower. She looked ten years younger, her face lit up with joy, lifted with smiling. She'd even put lipstick on. 'You're a tonic, Piotr,' she said, agreeing with Bopa. 'I can't remember the last time we had quite so much to talk about.'

'How long will you be stopping? You off up to Scotland, are you? Be with the rest of your Polish lot?' said Bopa, leaning closer.

'I hope so,' said Piotr. 'I'm not sure of when and how. Do you know?' Piotr shifted in the bed so he had a clear view of Arthur.

Arthur was trying to move some towels from a chair, but he wasn't sure where to place them.

'Arthur!' barked Bopa. 'Did you hear that? He wants to know if you know when he can go to Scotland.'

Arthur stopped, towels hovering in mid-air. He glanced round. 'No. No I don't.'

Bopa turned back to Piotr and mouthed, 'Useless,' while gesturing back towards Arthur with her thumb. Arthur frowned.

'Put them over there,' I said, pointing towards the dressing table. 'The towels, I mean.'

Arthur gave me a small appreciative nod, gently laid the towels down, and then sat on the small chair in the corner.

'Tea up!' said Bethan, carrying in a large tray. 'And you've got another visitor.' She gestured behind her with her head.

'It's like having royalty to stay, isn't it, Em?' said Bopa, tapping Mam on the forearm. 'Actual royalty.'

We all peered past Bethan to see Captain Pugh, poking his head round the bedroom door. 'Knock, knock,' he said, rapping the doorframe with his knuckles. 'Come to see the patient!'

He strode into the bedroom, which was becoming quite the squeeze, and stood, full Home Guard uniform on, with his chest puffed out. He stood at the bottom of the bed and saluted Piotr who, looking rather bemused, saluted back.

'He owns the local sewing factory,' said Bopa, taking a cup of tea from Bethan. 'His name is Pugh. He's got an inside toilet.'

Captain Pugh shot Bopa a stern look, and cleared his throat. 'Good afternoon. I am Captain Pugh, head of the local Home Guard, and, as such, I thought it best to present myself as an official delegation of His Majesty's Government.' He then saluted again.

'You can't be a delegation when there's only one of you,' said Bopa, taking another slurp of tea.

'Well, Emrys will be home soon, so that'll make two of us,' said Captain Pugh. 'May I enquire of your rank?'

'I'm captain,' said Piotr.

'Captain,' said Mam, beaming. 'That's higher than you, isn't it, Mr Pugh, because he's a proper captain and you're not?'

'I am too a proper captain!' protested Pugh, his face reddening.

'He's not,' mouthed Bopa.

I tried to stifle a laugh.

'Tell them, Arthur!' said Pugh, voice slightly raised.

Arthur, who had just received his tea from Bethan, looked startled and confused. 'I'm a constable,' he said, not really understanding what had been asked of him.

'Oh, never mind,' said Pugh. 'Now, then. Our first consideration is what is to be done with you. Does he come under your protection, Arthur? Or is he the responsibility of my platoon? It is a military matter so I'm of a mind that he might be ours.'

Arthur's eyes narrowed as he tried to think about that. It was like watching a large, confused dog.

'There'll be someone to see him from St Athan, I expect,' said Bethan, putting the tea tray down on the end of the bed. 'They might take you up the base, keep you there till you can transport to Scotland.'

'No, no, no,' said Mam, interjecting. 'He's not going anywhere. He needs rest and looking after.'

'He does,' said Bopa, nodding.

'He can't go anywhere until he's feeling better. And nobody is going to look after him better than the people in this village. Dealing with the authorities can wait. Father will agree with me. School's on Whitsun holidays so Ant can be his minder. If Piotr needs anything, Ant can come and fetch me. You'll do that, won't you, Ant?'

I nodded.

'Well, there it is, then.' Mam nodded decisively, then continued, 'Could you look after him down the cop shop, Arthur?'

'No, I could not,' said Arthur, shaking his head.

'He couldn't,' said Bopa, shaking her head in agreement.

'Could you look after him up the factory? Or in your house, Mr Pugh?'

'Well, I ...' began Pugh, shuffling a little.

'No, you could not,' said Mam, standing firm. 'He'll stay here until he's stronger, and then we'll think about where he goes. Right, then. That's settled. Now, finish up your tea and be off. There's men due home.'

CHAPTER NINE

There were many things that Father had the final word on, but going upstairs in your coal clothes wasn't one of them. I had set up the bath as I always did, and waited till Father was dried and dressed. He stood in front of the kitchen mirror, combing his wet hair, and asked for a tie. I passed him his only tie, a black one that came out on Sundays and whenever someone died, and he took it, flipping the thick end over the thin and tying the knot into a solid triangle just below his collar. He had shaved in the tub and, despite the ingrained coal dust that could never be cleaned from under his nails, he was as spick and span as I'd ever seen him. 'Right, then,' he said. 'Take me to our guest.'

I inched open the door into Bethan's bedroom. I'd given Piotr my *Dandy* to read. He was the only person I'd ever lent it to, and as we came in, he was frowning slightly at the open comic. 'This man,' he said, seeing me come in. 'Desperate Dan. Explain him to me.'

'He's a cowboy and he likes pie,' I said. 'Father is here. He wants to meet you.'

Piotr closed the comic and sat up.

'Excuse my wet hair,' said Father, holding out his hand. 'Welcome, Mr Skarbowitz. It's a pleasure to have you in our home.'

Piotr took his hand and smiled. 'You have all been so kind. Your wife, especially. She's given me some clothes of yours to wear. I hope you're not inconvenienced. And young Ant hasn't taken eyes off me. He's my guardian angel.'

Father cast a glance down towards me and stuck his thumbs into his waistcoat pockets. 'You're welcome to any shirt or pair of trousers. We don't have much, but what we have is yours. I'm told you're a Polish prisoner of war. See much action before you were captured?'

Piotr nodded. 'Signed up first day. I seem to have dodged every bullet. My mother says I have nine lives, like a cat. Do you know that expression?' he said to me.

I shook my head.

'It means he's very lucky,' explained Father.

'He jumped out of a plane that crashed, and survived,' I said, jumping up onto the edge of the bed. 'I can't think of anything more lucky.'

'Well, let's hope his luck rubs off. Pipe down now, Ant. We're talking. Anyway, you were saying?'

'I was posted to France. Holding up Maginot Line. Then it fell. We fought corridor to Dunkirk, where I was captured by the Germans.'

'That long ago?' said Father, leaning into the back of his shoes. 'Goodness.'

'We were in POW camp in Northern France, but they began moving us month ago. Worried about Allies coming and liberating us. They were marching us somewhere. Four of us managed slip away. But we were picked up by another platoon. I don't think they realised we were already POWs. If they had, they would have shot us. Another of my nine lives. So we found ourselves in plane.'

'Quite the adventure,' said Father, his voice softening. 'You're a brave man. I was too old to enlist in 1939. My middle boy would have liked to. But he's a Bevan Boy – made to work down the pit for the war effort. He sees the newsreels, hears about boys his age out in the world, fighting for their country, and he resents it, but the way I see it, he's already fighting for his country. The only difference is our army works underground.'

'Middle boy? You have another?'

'Alwyn's my eldest. He's got no stomach for putting on a uniform. Good job, really, he's not one for discipline.'

'Dangerous work, mining,' said Piotr, shifting in his bed. He winced. Father cast a look down at his swollen ankle.

'Bethan's sent for Dr Mitchell. A fine sort, he'll take a look at that leg for you. Is there anything else we can help you with? You mentioned your mother. Is there some way we can get her word that you're alive, if not quite well?'

Piotr's eyes lit up. 'Actually, yes,' he said, pushing himself up a little. 'Do you have paper and pen? I could write her letter. I would like that very much.'

'Of course,' said Father. 'Ant. Fetch up some paper from the top drawer in the kitchen cupboard. And there's a pen in the inside pocket of my jacket in the hallway. Ask your mother for a tray. Mr Skarbowitz can use that to lean on.'

I jumped from the bed and clattered downstairs. Alwyn was standing in the parlour, towel wrapped round his waist; Emrys was in the tub, foot in air, rubbing it with the coal soap. 'What's he like, Ant?' said Emrys, seeing me in the hallway. 'Bethan's gone a bit moony. Can't get any sense out of her.'

'Keep quiet, you,' said Bethan, handing Alwyn a clean shirt. 'I only said he was nice.'

'And handsome. Handsome this, handsome that, if I remember correctly,' said Alwyn, pulling his shirt on.

'Shut up, Alwyn,' said Bethan, ignoring him. 'If Emrys was hurt and in Poland, some family would do the same for him.'

'You must be joking,' said Alwyn. 'Look how ugly he is. Nobody'd touch him with a bargepole. They'd run away, more like. Anyway, I'm glad you're moony on him. Keeps him away from Gwennie Morgan, dunnit?'

'What about Alf?' I said, reaching inside Father's jacket for his pen. 'He's a bit moony on you, B.'

'How many times do I have to tell you, I don't like Alf Davies?' said Bethan, turning away to unfold a pair of trousers. 'There's more fellas in Treherbert, you know?'

'There is now,' said Emrys, winking at Alwyn.

'Here,' said Alwyn, seeing me forage, 'what you doing in other people's pockets?'

'Father wants me to get his pen and a piece of paper so Piotr can write his Mam and tell her he's all right.'

'I hope you're taking note, you lot,' shouted Mam from the kitchen. 'Writing to his mother. Who is probably worried sick, I expect. Do I ever get letters from my children? No. I do not.'

Alwyn and Emrys exchanged a puzzled glance. 'We live with you in the same house, Mam,' said Alwyn, calling back. 'I'd write you a letter, but I can't think of a single thing you don't know already.'

'She doesn't know how sweet you are on Gwennie Morgan,' said Emrys.

'Yes, I do,' shouted Mam.

'Here,' said Emrys to me, 'chuck us that towel.'

I picked up one of the towels from a small pile that sat on Father's armchair. They would have been white once, but the coal had taken its toll. Mam could scrub for all eternity and she'd never shift the stain of underground.

'Mam,' I yelled. 'Father says there's paper in the kitchen cupboard. Can I have some?'

Paper was a luxury and letter writing, a great pastime of Father's, was now restricted to emergencies only until further notice. 'Births, deaths and marriages, that's it,' Father had said almost a year ago, as he'd tucked away his precious Basildon Bond.

I walked through to the kitchen and leaned against the doorframe. Mam was pulling out a pale-blue pad. 'There you go,' she said, carefully tearing out a couple of pages. 'Two sheets. I expect he's got lots to say.'

'Father asked if Piotr can have a tray to lean on, 'n' all?' I asked, rubbing my fingers on my shorts before taking the paper. I didn't want to get mucky prints on it.

'Take that small green one,' said Mam, pointing over towards the corner of the counter. 'And give it a wipe. Piotr's Mam won't want Welsh grease spots all over her lovely letter, I half expect.'

By the time I'd cleaned the tray and taken it upstairs, both Emrys and Alwyn were in the bedroom with Piotr. Alwyn was perched on the edge of Bethan's dressing table; Emrys was leaning against the far bedpost. Both had their arms tightly folded, as if important business was being done.

'How many Germans you killed, then?' Emrys was saying as I squeezed in, next to Father.

Piotr's eyes drifted towards the ceiling and he cleared his throat. 'I suppose I have killed many people. But as to how many, I don't know. I'm not sure I want to know.'

'I'd give anything to kill a German,' mumbled Emrys, with a sniff.

'My middle son is something of the hothead, Mr Skarbowitz,' said Father. 'I put it down to an excess of energy. We're not city people, Mr Skarbowitz. Village life isn't suited to everyone. I think, perhaps, after the war, Emrys would be better placed somewhere with a racier pace of life. Be the man you want to be, not the man you think you are.'

Emrys shifted on his feet and turned to look at the open window. There was a warm evening breeze, and the lace curtain was fluttering. I placed the tray with the paper and pen down on the bed by Piotr's hand. 'Mam gave you two pieces. In case you had lots to say,' I said.

Piotr smiled down at me. 'I haven't seen or spoken with my mother in over four years. I could fill book.'

'Well, then,' said Father, 'we must leave you to it. When you're done, Ant can run it to the postie for you. Downstairs, boys. If you need anything else, shout for Ant.'

*

148

'It's magnificent, Bopa,' said Mam, standing back and admiring the large Victoria sponge that was now sitting on our back kitchen table.

'Everyone mucked in,' she said. 'Quarter of a cup of sugar from most people in the street. Proper butter cream, 'n' all. Worth it, innit? With a hero in the house?'

'Christ,' said Alwyn, coming in behind me. 'Is that a cake? Can I have a bit?'

'Not yet,' said Bopa, lifting it and taking it to the larder. 'Got to cool. Besides, we're going to give it to Piotr later, innit? Make a surprise out of it. And here,' she added, pressing some coupons into Mam's hand, 'we had a whip round. It's not much, but everyone's given a little something to help you feed him.'

Mam looked down into her hand, her eyes smiling. 'Thank you, Bopa,' she said, quietly. 'Tell everyone thank you.'

Behind us, we heard footsteps coming up the hallway. 'Hello, there!' a voice rang out. 'Hello!'

We all exchanged small, anxious glances. It was Dr Mitchell.

Dr Mitchell had a penchant for anything sweet. Before the war, when visiting a patient, he would settle himself into a chair, wait until asked if he wanted tea, feign pleasant surprise when offered and then, after being handed cup and saucer, would stir the tea meticulously before asking, 'I don't suppose you've got a slice of cake going spare?' in a soft, conspiratorial whisper. If there was one golden rule, it was this: Don't call out the doctor when there's a buttered sponge in the house.

He had come in and was sitting, case on knees, in Mam's chair in the parlour. The clock on the mantelpiece – this one with two hands – was ticking. Father was in his chair, legs crossed, fingers laced together in his lap. Alwyn and Emrys were sitting looking awkward on the sofa. Bethan was standing next to the wireless, Bopa next to her, hands held behind her back. Everybody, bar Dr Mitchell, knew there was a Victoria sponge minding its own business in the larder. Nobody spoke.

'There you go, Dr Mitchell,' said Mam, coming in from the kitchen with a tray. 'Imagine if the Germans stopped us getting our tea! Britain would surrender in a day!'

Dr Mitchell let out a small, appreciative snort. Taking a cup and saucer, he began the ritual of slowly stirring. Everybody watched him like a hawk. 'I wonder,' he began, in a low hush, 'if there might be something to soak up the wet?'

Mam stared at him, momentarily frozen, and then, to our collective horror, said, 'There's a bit of sponge in the larder,' she began. 'Bopa made it, for Piotr.'

Dr Mitchell's face lit up. 'Sponge?' he said, eyes widening. 'That would be delightful.'

Mam turned back towards the kitchen.

'It's all gone, Mam,' said Alwyn, cutting in. 'That cake. All gone, Dr Mitchell.'

'What you talking about? Bopa only just …' said Mam, frowning.

'No. It's definitely all gone, Mam,' Alwyn said again, more forcefully.

Bethan stifled a smile, and Emrys stared resolutely at his shirt cuffs. Father raised an eyebrow and I sat on my hands on the floor. Bopa was staring at Mam and not blinking. We were all willing her to understand. She stood, motionless, like a trout in the mountain stream. Penny dropping, she turned slowly back towards Dr Mitchell. 'Oh, yes,' she said, 'last of it went half an hour back. How forgetful of me. But that's cakes, for you. I can cut you a slice of bread instead?'

'Oh. Well. No, thank you,' said Dr Mitchell, his smile fading. 'I should have come earlier! A sponge, you say? Well.'

'It's him upstairs,' said Alwyn, hands on knees. 'Like a bloody gannet. Never seen a man consume so much cake.'

'Surprised if he'll eat for a week,' said Bopa, nodding slowly. Bethan coughed.

Dr Mitchell nodded. 'That'll be the shock. The body craves sweet things, you see.'

Everyone murmured in agreement.

'Right, then,' said Dr Mitchell, draining his cup. 'Let's see the patient.'

The examination was short and precise. Having ascertained there were no broken bones, Dr Mitchell was satisfied that a few days' rest with the leg elevated would be more than sufficient to see him back on his feet.

'It's a nasty sprain, but the bruise is already good and out. That's a sign everything is on the mend,' said Dr Mitchell. 'Here,' he added, taking a small ceramic pot from his medical bag. 'Rub this into the ankle twice a day. It's a balm. Puts heat into the muscle. Helps it mend faster.'

'I can do that for you,' said Bethan, taking the pot. 'Save you having to try and reach.' She gave Piotr a small smile and tucked the balm into an embroidered bag on her dressing table.

'Well, Mr Skarbowitz!' said Dr Mitchell, tidying away his equipment. 'You've given us plenty to talk about. It's not every day we get crashed planes, Germans and escaped prisoners of war! It's like something you'd see up the Gaiety! Except, instead of Clark Gable, you're the featured star!'

'It's like having someone famous in our house, like,' I said, nodding in agreement.

'And I'm glad to hear your appetite is so healthy,' added Dr Mitchell, snapping the clasp of his bag shut.

Piotr frowned. Bethan shot me a glance.

'Did you enjoy the sponge?' Dr Mitchell stood upright and fixed Piotr with a solid stare.

Piotr shook his head a little. 'Sponge? I had flannel.'

Dr Mitchell tilted his head to one side. 'Flannel? Do you mean flan? You had a flan as well?'

Bethan took Dr Mitchell by the elbow. 'Well, thank you for coming,' she said, bustling him towards the door. 'I'll make sure he uses the balm. I'll send Ant to fetch you if there are any problems. I'll see you out. Down the stairs, after you.'

Piotr turned and looked at me, his eyebrows knitted together. 'What was that about?' he said, seeing me convulsed with laughter on the bedspread.

'It's about cake,' I laughed. 'He's always desperate for cake.'

'Like your man, Dan,' said Piotr, tapping at *The Dandy* with his finger. 'Pie, cake, what else are people desperate for round here?'

Bethan reappeared in the doorway and folded her arms. 'That would be telling,' she said. 'You'll have to find out, won't you?'

They exchanged a small, silent stare, and for the first time since Piotr had arrived, I felt left out.

*

'An actual jeep!' yelled Ade, jumping up into the passenger seat and bouncing up and down. 'Cor, you're lucky you've got a sister in the WAAF, Ant. An actual jeep!'

Bethan had been lent a service vehicle in order to dispatch important documents from St Athan to a field office in Tonypandy. I was to go along to keep her company, but mainly so I could see the first wave of Americans who had arrived the night before. The arrival of the jeep outside our house had caused a flurry of activity, and the car was smothered in a swarm of children, like ants on a blob of jam on a summer day.

'Right,' said Bethan, gesturing with her thumb. 'You lot, off.'

'Can't we come 'n' all?' said Ade, who was now sitting in the driver's seat, trying to turn the steering wheel.

'No,' said Bethan, slinging her bag into a shallow well behind the front seat. 'You can't. There are only two seats. Hop it. I've got official business to attend to.'

'Get some gum, Ant,' said Fez, as I climbed up onto the passenger seat. 'Off the Americans, like. Got any gum, chum? That's what you say, remember.'

'Tell 'em we captured a German,' said Ade, swinging off the front side mirror.

'We didn't,' I said. 'He's Polish.'

'I know. But they don't know that, do they, man?' said Ade, scrunching his nose up. 'They might give you more gum if they think you've captured Germans, like. Besides. We sort of did capture Germans. Or, at least, our mountain did. And that's sort of the same, innit?'

Bethan was hunting in her handbag. 'Where did I put the key?' she mumbled. 'Could have sworn it was in this side pocket.'

'It's there,' said Alf Davies, appearing from behind a gaggle of kids, 'in the ignition. *Diawl*, Bethan. Sure you don't want me to drive?' He leant on the window frame of the door and gave a toothy grin.

'Why aren't you down the pit?' said Bethan, tossing her handbag into my lap.

'On shifts, innit?' said Alf. He glanced over to me. 'All right, little man?'

I nodded. 'We've got a war hero in Bethan's bed.'

Alf raised an eyebrow. 'In Bethan's bed, you say? Well, well. And what does Bethan think about that?'

'I've got to sleep in my brothers' dirty bedsheets. That's what I think about that, Alf Davies.'

'Bethan's gone a bit moony,' I said.

Bethan turned and gave me a sharp stare. Something in Alf's eyes dulled a little, and his smile fell. 'And who can blame her?' he said quietly. 'What with him being a war hero, 'n' all. Well. My shift won't be over until I start it. I'll bid you a good day. Drive careful, Bethan. And keep an eye on the keys, Ant.'

He tipped his cap towards Bethan and slung his bag back over his shoulder. I turned to watch him go, one hand in a trouser pocket, picking his way through jumping children, his normal swagger a little jaded.

'You shouldn't have said that, Ant,' said Bethan, turning the key in the jeep's ignition. 'You know he's sweet on me.'

'But I thought you said you didn't like him,' I said, twisting back towards her.

'Never mind what I said,' said Bethan, casting a quick look over her shoulder before moving off. 'Lads have hearts too.' She shoved the gearstick forward, and off we roared, the cheers of all of Scott Street ringing in our ears.

CHAPTER TEN

They were different, all right. It was the confidence, the energy, the size of them, the teeth. Slick, smart, caps at a jaunty angle, the way they leant against walls; Americans weren't us, of that there was no doubt.

We'd driven up onto the long high road that looked down into the next valley and, looking down, I was stunned by the activity. I could barely remember seeing a car before, other than the old Morris Minor owned by Hughes the Grocer, but now the valley road was crammed with large green wagons carrying troops, weapons and ambulances, all bearing the badge of the white five-pointed star. America had come to the Rhondda.

Tonypandy was full to bursting. The town was swarming with personnel: soldiers in shiny round helmets smoking cigarettes, guns slung over one shoulder, and smaller vehicles, jeeps like the one we were in, dotted up and down the streets. Large trucks were being waved on towards the town hall, where boxes of oranges and other provisions were being unloaded. It was a scene of endless bustle. Everywhere there were Americans, local children clustered round, women waving to trucks as they passed. It was electric. The hope was electric.

'Exciting, isn't it?' said Bethan, sticking her arm out to indicate left. 'Looks like Hitler's going to get a fight.'

'How come they're all here, though, B?' I said. 'France is miles away.'

'Training up the mountain, I think. They won't be here long. Couple of weeks, tops, I reckon. They're going to spread all over. That's what I'm taking in – all the billeting orders. We've got a few coming to Treherbert. Not with us, mind. We haven't got the room. There's going to be Nissen huts going up over by the big field behind the sheep dip, canteen for the Americans. They're having all their food sent from America, cos of rations. That way, none of us will have to feed 'em.'

It was so enormous, I couldn't quite take it all in: an invading army, here in the valley. A week ago it would have been unthinkable. Bethan pulled the jeep over to the kerb outside a large, white building. 'Right,' she said, yanking the handbrake upwards. 'Thistle Hotel. We're here. You stop b'there. I'll take the billet orders in, and then we'll be off.'

She jumped out from the jeep and reached behind the driver's seat for a thin red file. An American, standing at the entrance, saluted her as she approached. He looked proper smart: shining metal helmet, white leather gaiters and a gun, a real one, not like the useless one Emrys had stashed in the outtie. Bethan saluted back. I grinned. It was a sharp thrill. The war was happening and it was here.

I was too tumbling with excitement to stay sitting in the jeep. Bethan would be a while, I reckoned, so I opened the door and hopped down, the rumble of trucks vibrating up through my wellingtons. I looked over my shoulder. Another convoy was rolling in: covered wagons filled with soldiers. Local children ran along behind the open backs, hands outstretched ready to catch whatever the Americans tossed down. The air was filled with young voices yelling, 'Give us some gum, chum!', faces of American soldiers grinning down towards them, sweets scattering out from the backs of the trucks. I ran after them, joining in the concentrated gaggle of children, my hands reached out. Something flew past my face and bounced off behind me on to the pavement. I twisted round, ready to dive down, but I was beaten to it. We were like ducks being fed.

A whistle sounded from up ahead and the bottleneck of lorries began to pick up pace. The trucks pulled away, making running with them near impossible, and I eased up to a walk, chest heaving. I stopped for a moment to catch my breath, hands on hips and panting. Kids were on the other side of the street, heads bowed, hands cupped, all assessing their bounty. I had come away with nothing. I scanned the road and the kerbside to see if anything was still to be claimed, but the cobbles had been picked clean.

Ahead of me, a wagon pulled over, a large gun barrel protruding from the green canvas roof. I wandered towards it and walked directly under the barrel, staring up. It looked powerful, deadly. Pushing myself onto the tips of my toes, I reached up to try and touch it, but I was too small and my fingers flailed just beneath. Ahead of me, there was a loud clank and I dropped down and dodged sideways to see a leg swinging out from the driver's side door. I ran forwards. 'Give us some gum, chum?' I said, holding my hand out.

'Hang on, kid,' I heard a voice say. The soldier was turned away from me. He was reaching for something in the cabin. His arm came back and then he turned, his teeth flashing white. 'There you go, kid,' he said. 'You like chocolate?'

I stared up at him, my eyes wide. He was a black man, the first I'd ever seen in the flesh. I felt the chocolate bar being pressed into my upturned palm, but I couldn't take my eyes off his face.

'Cat caught your tongue, little fella?' he said. 'Or would you like some gum instead?'

I blinked. 'No, thank you. Good luck with the Germans.'

'Thanks, pal,' said the soldier. He jumped down, patted me on the shoulder and walked off towards a man with a clipboard.

I stood, staring after him, as if my eyes couldn't get enough. He was standing, hands in pockets, waiting to speak to a sergeant who was directing drivers to various locations around the town. Other black servicemen were waiting with him. They shared a joke, heads thrown back and laughing.

'Ant!' I heard a voice behind me shouting. I cast a glance back over my shoulder. It was Bethan, standing on the footplate of the jeep and gesturing for me to come back.

'What's that?' said Bethan, as I ran over and hopped into the passenger seat. 'Chocolate, is it?'

I nodded. 'I saw a black man, B,' I said, fingering the bar in my lap.

'What was that like, then?' said Bethan, smiling.

'Smashin'.'

*

Piotr wasn't just sitting up; he was sitting downstairs in Mam's chair, leaning into a heap of plumped cushions. I'd come running in, all full of news, and Mam had had to tell me to slow down so she could understand a single word I was saying.

'And then he gave me this,' I said, holding out the chocolate bar. 'Look at that. Hershey's Tropical Chocolate. And what's even more amazin' is the American who gave it to me had a black face. A black face, Mam!'

'You see black faces every day,' said Bopa, who was sitting next to the wireless, knitting.

'Not from coal, though,' I said. 'A proper black man. Like in the films.'

'How exotic!' said Mam, shaking her head in wonder.

'Exotic, you say?' said Bopa, putting down her needles. 'Arthur Pryce will be pleased! Exotic animals!'

Mam gave out a short hoot. I handed Piotr the chocolate bar. 'You can have that, Piotr,' I said. 'I got it for you.'

'For me?' said Piotr, taking the Hershey bar. 'Surely I've done nothing to deserve such a treat. My goodness. Look at it. What a wrapper. Pretty fancy.'

He turned it over in his hand and lifted it to his nose to smell it.

'There were thousands of Americans, Mam. All in wagons. And massive guns, too. And they're going to have huts for food. Bethan says they're coming here, Mam. And they're going to train up the mountain.'

'I haven't seen you this excited since that time you ate a bag of sugar in one go,' said Mam, shaking her head. 'You were sick on my shoes. P'raps try sitting down for a bit. Calm down, like.' She patted the seat next to her.

'I don't want to sit down, Mam,' I said, fidgeting. 'I feel all full of beans.'

'Hop it out,' said Bopa. 'Go on!' She gestured towards the hallway.

I stood up and began hopping on one leg. 'I'm desperate for hopping,' I explained to Piotr, who was looking at me, puzzled.

'It calms him down,' said Mam. 'Pay no attention. He'll be worn out in a minute. Who'd have thought it, proper Americans, here in the valleys? I can't get my head round it. When was the last time we ever had posh visitors, Bopa?'

'We had that man from the Swansea Rotary Club. Said he could speak to the spirit world, wore a turban. He was quite posh.'

'But nothing like Americans,' said Mam.

'No,' agreed Bopa. 'Nothing like. Bethan said they'd be training up the mountain, did she?'

I nodded, still hopping.

'They'll be getting ready for push into France,' said Piotr, taking another deep sniff of the chocolate. 'Good time to do it, too. Hitler's pinned down in East. Might be beginning of end.'

'*Diawl*, I hope so,' said Bopa. 'I'm fed up with bloody rations. Oh, Em. Can you imagine what a feast we'll have when we don't have to scrimp and stretch every last bloody bit of meat?'

'And tea!' said Mam.

'And sugar!'

'And clothes!'

'And proper cheese!' wailed Bopa. 'Oh, what would I give for a chunky lump of Cheddar?'

'That man's days are numbered now,' said Mam, giving a small nod. 'There's no way the Germans will hold off Americans. No way.'

'No way,' I said, panting as I stopped hopping. 'They've got crates of oranges.'

Bopa let out a throaty laugh. 'Oranges, is it? Well! Hitler will be quaking in his boots.'

'Here, Ant,' said Piotr, handing me back the chocolate. 'You do honours. Break everyone off bit.'

The smell was wonderful: deep, heady, dark, a hint of sweet. It had been so long since any of us had tasted chocolate, and I let the small square I'd broken off sit on the top of my tongue.

'Chewing that would be ungodly,' said Bopa, popping a square into her mouth. 'I shall make this last as long as possible.'

I handed another square to Piotr and the four of us sat, silently sucking, eyes sporadically closing. I was expecting the chocolate to melt, like liquid velvet, but instead, it remained stubbornly solid. I frowned.

'Is your chocolate melting?' I said, shoving the lump into the side of my mouth.

Mam shook her head. 'I've given up not chewing. Not that that's doing much good, either.'

'It's chewier than a pig's foot,' complained Bopa. 'Tastes nothing like chocolate. Are you sure it's proper, like?'

I looked again at the wrapper. 'It says it's chocolate,' I said, trying to bite into my square.

'Have a tooth out with that,' said Mam, picking the mangled lump out from her mouth. She stood up and threw it into the fire. I watched as it landed on a burning coal.

'*Uffach wyllt*,' said Bopa, staring in astonishment. 'It's indestructible. Look at it. It's not even melting!'

Piotr frowned. 'Rations chocolate,' he said, picking at a back tooth with his finger. 'Made to withstand heat. I'm afraid you got bad trade, Anthony. Next time, get some gum!'

'Who'd have thought,' laughed Mam. 'Chocolate tougher than a shoe sole. I'd have had a better time sucking that lump of coal!'

There was a knock at the front door and we all turned to see who would appear in the sitting-room doorway. I was picking at the chocolate glued to the back of my teeth, but when no one appeared, Mam straightened and threw me a puzzled look.

'Must be a proper visitor,' said Bopa. 'Everyone we know just walks in.'

Mam quickly patted the underside of her tied-up hair and, licking her finger, wiped down her eyebrows. 'It's probably for Piotr. Help him sit up straight, Ant. And tuck my knitting away.'

I quickly bundled Mam's unfinished jumper into a small wicker basket below the wireless. Piotr was pushing himself up in the armchair, and as I helped him sit more upright, Bopa rearranged the cushions behind his back.

Voices were coming up the hallway. 'He's through here,' I heard Mam say. 'Can I get you some tea? I've got a little Teisen Lap, local cake, if you don't know it. My neighbour brought it round. It's very good.' She was talking in that odd, posh voice she'd used before at the school. I looked at Bopa. We frowned.

Mam reappeared in the doorway and flashed us both with wide, impressed eyes. Behind her was a man in an RAF uniform. He was taking his cap off and tucking it into his armpit. 'Here's a gentleman from RAF St Athan,' said Mam, gesturing towards him. 'Come to see you, Piotr.'

The man stepped forward: clean-shaven, bright-eyed, brown hair, recently clipped and oiled. There was a faint, rosy hue to his cheeks, a hint of something cherubic. He held a hand out. 'How do you do,' he said.

'English,' mouthed Bopa, then pulled a face.

'Captain Willis,' said the man, extending his hand. 'Liaison Officer up at RAF St Athan. I hear you've had quite the adventure.'

Piotr took Willis's hand and shook it, gratefully. 'You could say that,' he said, smiling. 'But I've had such welcome, I've quite forgotten all bad bits.'

'Hope you haven't forgotten *all* the bad bits,' said Willis, looking keen. 'Hoping you can give us some useful intel.' He looked around the room. 'I wonder, Mrs Jones, if I might be able to sit down? I've got a lot of questions to ask.'

'Ant, clean away that paper from your father's chair. I'll get the tea and cake.'

Willis shot me a smile as I cleared Father's chair for him. 'Thanks awfully. Very kind.'

'Know Bethan, do you?' asked Bopa, giving him a good look up and down.

'Bethan Jones?' said Willis, meeting her gaze. 'Vaguely. She works over in the secretarial pool. Pretty girl, I recall.'

'You married, are you?' asked Bopa, folding her arms.

'Ummm,' said Willis, a slightly puzzled look passing across his face. 'No, I haven't yet had that pleasure …'

'Bopa!' called Mam. 'Would you be so kind as to lend me a hand?'

'Oh!' replied Bopa, throwing her arms up and putting on an equally fake accent. 'I should be delighted, to be sure.'

Captain Willis had a brown leather attaché case, and as he sat, he pulled it onto his lap. He undid the clasp and pulled out a file of papers and a notepad. 'We checked all your details with Polish HQ. Turns out you're quite the hero. Wouldn't be surprised if a medal was coming your way.'

'What did he do?' I asked, folding Father's paper and placing it on top of the mantelpiece.

'Took out a German position single-handed, and pulled out five injured men. If you were British, you'd be getting the Victoria Cross!' I turned and beamed at Piotr. I knew it. He really was a hero. 'I've made some arrangements for you to receive some back pay,' said Captain Willis, smiling. 'Should be quite a sum. But until that comes, I've been authorised to give you some cash, to tide you over, so to speak.' He reached into the attaché case and pulled out a small yellow envelope. 'There you go. Don't spend it all at once!'

'Thank you,' said Piotr, taking the envelope.

Willis took an ink pen from the inside pocket of his jacket. It had a jade top and looked heavy, expensive. He opened his pad and wrote the date at the top of a blank page, followed by what looked like Piotr's name. He held the pad towards him. 'I think I have the spelling right, but I'd be grateful if you'd check.'

Piotr peered at it. 'Quite right,' he said, with a small nod.

'Super,' said Willis, taking the pad back and leaning it against his attaché case. 'So if you don't mind, we'll go over the basics. And then I'd like to discuss your time after capture. Whether you heard anything, saw anything, that sort of thing.'

'Is there going to be a push into France, then?' I said. 'I saw all the Americans, like.'

'Well,' said Willis, casting me a glance. 'It's supposed to be classified, of course, but it's impossible to keep a secret with three thousand Americans running round the Rhondda.'

'Hit them hard through Normandy,' said Piotr. 'You'll need to. Their strength is in Panzer divisions. And Luftwaffe.' He stopped and tapped his finger methodically along the arm of the chair.

Willis stared at him, then made a quick, urgent scribble. 'Yes,' he said, nodding, then stopped and looked up. 'Sorry ... why would you say Normandy?'

'Well, you're not going to land troops in St Tropez,' said Piotr, letting his palm float upwards.

Willis gave out a short snort. 'No! Ha! Quite!'

'They'll expect you at Calais. That's most heavily fortified. Go either side, and you'll have better odds.'

Mam returned with a tray of tea things. 'Here you go, gentlemen,' she said, placing it down on the occasional table.

'Would you like me to pour?' added Bopa, following her in with the pot.

'Actually,' said Willis, placing his attaché case on the floor, 'I'm afraid I'm going to have to ask you to leave. Bit awkward, I know. But what I'll be asking is classified. Loose talk costs lives, and all that. Is there somewhere you could go for an hour?'

Bopa stared at him. 'Leave? And miss everything?'

Willis blinked. 'That's sort of the point ...'

'Oh,' said Mam, looking a little crestfallen. 'Well, if it's classified, I suppose ...'

'Come on,' said Bopa, putting down the teapot. 'We can go round mine. I've got tumblers ...' She mimed holding them up against the wall, and winked.

'You too, I'm afraid,' said Willis, towards me.

'You can run some errands for me,' said Mam. 'I need all those old newspapers taken to salvage. And then you can pick me up a cob loaf from the baker's.'

She reached for her handbag and pulled out her purse. 'There,' she said, handing me a coupon and a shilling. 'That's for the bread. And bring me back the change.'

'Thank you,' said Willis, standing as my mother went to leave. 'I'm very much obliged.'

Mam nodded in return. 'Come on, then, let's leave the gentlemen to it.'

I glanced towards Piotr, who gave me a quick, reassuring wink. Willis seemed an all right sort. He'd be fine.

Old Morris' salvage shop was in Blaencwm, the next village over, past the colliery. Normally, I'd have taken a shortcut over the mountain, but with a large pile of newspapers to carry, it made more sense to stick to the road.

As I walked, I passed girls standing on the pavements, plaiting each other's hair. They paid little attention to me, but that was nothing out of the ordinary. We never played with them and they never played with us. I could see Ade and the boys beyond them, gathering near the bottom end of the street and sorting themselves into teams.

'Ant!' yelled Fez, waving at me. 'Catty and Doggy. Come on. We need another player.'

Ade was swiping a metre-long wooden stick through the air, trying to hit a much smaller stick with tapered ends. 'Getting my eye in,' he said, as everyone laughed when he missed. 'I got two more goes, mind! Hey, Ant. Stick your paper over b'there. You're in next.'

Catty and Doggy was a Scott Street favourite, 'Poor man's cricket,' Father used to call it. I dumped the bundle on the flagstones and stood next to Bozo.

'What's happening with the prisoner, then?' he asked, taking his specs off and folding them into his pocket.

'He's not a prisoner,' I said, reaching into my wellingtons and pulling my socks up. 'He's a war hero. Fella from St Athan said so. He's killed masses of Germans and saved loads of people, like.'

'Smashin',' said Bozo, giving a manly nod.

'Fella from the RAF is round our house now. They're talking all secret stuff, like. So Mam's sent us up the salvage. Not allowed back for an hour.'

'Christ, man,' said Ade, blowing his fringe away from his eyes. 'You should have stayed and listened in. You'd have top secrets and everything. He'are. Have the doggy.' He handed me the stick. 'I missed every time. Your turn.'

Taking the doggy, the smaller, tapered catty was thrown down in front of me. The object was to strike its end as hard as you could, sending the catty into the air. Then, when it was airborne, you had to hit it as far as possible. I had three attempts and, if I managed to hit it, the distance would be measured with the longer stick. One length of the doggy counted as one run.

'Come on, Ant,' yelled Ade. 'Hit the catty!'

I thumped the doggy down onto the tapered end of the catty, but it didn't connect properly and the smaller stick skewed sideways across the street. A groan went up behind me. 'Second go!' yelled Ade. I ran over and struck downwards again. This time I struck true, and the catty spun up into the air. Pulling my arm back, I swung again at the smaller stick. A sweet, pleasing thwack filled the air and I stood watching as the catty spun away from me.

'Cracking hit, Ant!' yelled Ade. 'Get it measured.'

Taking the doggy, I measured out the distance to the landed catty. 'Four!' I shouted.

'We're in the lead,' said Ade, hands on hips. 'You're up, Fez.'

Fez was a decent player, probably the best we had, and with his first go he whacked it down the street. We all ran after it, waiting for him to measure it out. 'Five!' he yelled.

We played until a mam appeared in a doorway, shouting at us for putting her windows at risk. It was a common complaint and one we always answered by simply running away.

'If my windows end up broken,' shouted Mrs Evans, shaking her fist at us, 'I'll have you all in a pie.'

'Wanna come up the mountain?' said Ade, as we scarpered.

'Can't,' I said, bending to retrieve my pile of newspapers, 'gotta get up the salvage.'

Old Morris never seemed to know quite what to do with all the rubbish we dumped on him. I'd been taking him paper and old tins, even an old iron gate, once, for as long as I could remember, and as far as I could tell, it was all still sitting there. In the window, there was a large, faded poster of a soldier, tin hat on, hand cupped about his mouth and shouting, and emblazoned above him, the clarion call, 'I need your waste paper!' But for what, I don't think any of us would ever know. Father said it was something to do with making matches. Mam tried to work out how they made matches from old newspapers, but gave in saying she 'couldn't get her head round it'.

Old Morris was the perfect front man for a heap of waste. He had a faded appearance: eyes grey like rainwater and a general dusty demeanour, as if he'd been put in a cupboard and forgotten. Like an old family hand-me-down, everything about him had seen better days. He was sitting, as he always was, towards the back of the shop in a rocking chair, slippers on, pipe in mouth, staring at a chessboard, where he was locked in an eternal struggle with his most fiendish opponent, namely, himself.

'Who's winning, Mr Morris?' I said, as the bell above me gave a tinkle. It was a standard joke, like a secret password for locals coming into the shop.

'The good news,' began Old Morris, casting a brief glance in my direction, 'is that I am winning. The bad news is, I'm up against a better man.' He took his pipe out from his mouth and tapped the end into a blackened saucer. 'Paper, is it?' he said, pushing himself up from his chair. 'Stick it in that corner, if you can. You might have to use the ladder.'

He gestured over towards a small mountain of newspapers piled almost up to the ceiling. Bundles of flattened cardboard boxes were dotted about the shop, along with baskets of crushed and rusting tins. There was a smell of neglect, old and musty, a bit like an ancient bookshop, but damper. Leaning up against the wall was the cast-iron gate I'd dragged here a year ago. I pointed towards it. 'When they coming to take that, then?' I said.

Old Morris shrugged. 'No idea. Nobody's been to collect anything in months. Not that I've heard they're stopping salvage, mind. To be honest, I think they've forgotten about us. We're not like Cardiff, are we?'

'Better than Cardiff,' I said, clearing some space to get out the wooden ladder. 'Got no proper mountain in Cardiff. What's the good of that? Father says he doesn't understand people who want to live on the flat. They've got nothing to look up to. That's what he says.'

Old Morris gave a considered nod. 'Wise man, your father. Here, hang on. I'll hold the bottom for you.'

I leant the ladder against the column of stacked papers and heaved my bundle under my armpit. Old Morris held on to one side and watched as I climbed upwards. 'I hear you've got a visitor staying at your house. Village is buzzing with it. Injured, is he? That why we not seen him out and about?'

I heaved the bundle up over my head and shoved it into a space above me. 'He's got a sprained ankle,' I said, pushing the newspapers towards the wall as best I could. 'Mam reckons he'll be up tomorrow. He's managed to get downstairs.'

'Sprained ankle, is it?' said Old Morris, looking over his shoulder. 'I've got something he can have for that. You all done? Down you come and I'll get it.'

I jumped back onto the floor and watched as Old Morris began rooting through a maelstrom of junk. 'It's back here somewhere,' he mumbled, bending over.

Teapots with bent spouts, pans with holes in their sides and chewed-up rolls of string came tumbling out onto the shop floor, a flood of wartime flotsam.

'It's in here, I think,' he said, leaning over and reaching into a battered tea chest. 'There we go,' he said, pulling out a walking stick. 'That might help. Good one, too. Can't recall who threw that out. All the same, your visitor's welcome to it.'

He handed me the stick. It was a dark brown wood, a round tapering length with a handle carved in the shape of a bird. 'That's right posh, that,' I said, marvelling at it. 'Shall I get Father to give you some money for it?'

Old Morris shook his head. 'Don't be daft, boy,' he said. 'Right and proper we all lend a hand. Besides, I'm glad to get rid of it. It was cluttering the place up.'

I frowned. It was always hard to tell when Old Morris was having a laugh, but as I stared up at him, I saw a glint of something in his eye, and he smiled. 'Want to help me make my next move?' he said, gesturing back towards his chessboard. 'I'm up against a devil.'

I peered over. 'Queen to bishop four,' I said.

Old Morris frowned. 'Well, I'll be damned,' he said, making the move. 'Checkmate. Clever lad!'

'Mam wants me to get her a cob loaf,' I said, making for the door. 'The baker won't be open long.'

Old Morris nodded and popped his pipe back into the corner of his mouth. 'Send your mother and father my regards. And I'll see our new friend at chapel this Sunday. Quite the stir, he's caused. Quite the stir.'

The walking stick was too tall for me to walk with a swagger, so I tossed it over my shoulder and ran down the hill from Blaencwm back to the baker's in Tynewydd. The stick was about the same length as a doggy, I reckoned, and I found myself hoping that the game I'd left was still underway. I'd smash that catty for six if I was able to use the walking stick. But the boys were all long gone; tangled up somewhere in our mountain, I expected.

The baker's ovens were so hot you could feel them before you got to the shop. On a cold winter's day, it wasn't unusual for our gang to play right outside, mostly for the warmth but occasionally, at closing-up time, the baker would chuck us stuff that had gone unsold. In summer, you'd avoid it like the plague: it was hellish hot and whenever I was sent by my mother, I'd stand in the doorway, listening to the crickets singing in the rear and breaking into a sweat just waiting for a loaf.

'What's your mother wanting?' shouted the baker, seeing me standing in the doorway. His face was cherry red, his shirt wet with sweat.

'Cob loaf, please,' I said, coming forward and handing him my coupon.

He reached for a pile of dusted bread and pulled one from the top. 'You Emily Jones' boy, ain't you?' he said, eyeing me as he wrapped the bread in some waxy paper.

I nodded.

'Got that crashed airman staying, still?'

I nodded. 'He's a Polish war hero,' I said.

'Here,' he added, wrapping up a few sweet buns. 'You give your mother those from me. No charge, mind. In fact, she can have the bread 'n' all.'

He handed me the large rectangular packet. The bread inside was still warm, the sugary aroma from the buns heady. Nobody had ever treated us special, but now, because of Piotr, they were. I had the sense of something I'd never felt before: importance. That's what it was. I felt important.

I felt like I mattered.

CHAPTER ELEVEN

'Careful now,' said Mam, holding on to Piotr's elbow. 'Ant, pass him that.'

I handed him the wooden walking stick and Piotr, taking it, gently lowered his left foot onto the floor. Gingerly, he took a step: a wince, then another step, better.

'How's that feelin'?' said Mam.

'Not too bad. Little sore, but actually, feels good to move it. I might even try walk.'

'Are you sure?' said Mam, frowning. 'I don't want you overdoing it or you'll be right back at square one.'

'It'll be good for me. Get out. Get fresh air. Perhaps young Anthony can come with me? Make sure I don't do myself damage?'

I grinned. 'I can go with him, Mam,' I said. 'Unless you've got errands you want doing, like?'

Mam shook her head. 'No,' she said, 'you go off. I suspect he'll be proud to show you off, Piotr. Just mind you don't be getting him into trouble, Ant.'

'I won't, Mam. Promise.'

There'd been deep rumbles sounding from beyond the valley road all morning, and, as we came out of the house, a large green wagon slowly made its way up the street towards us. People were coming out from their houses to stare, women were waving and the Scott Street kids, ever atune to the slightest scrap of excitement, were running alongside and cheering.

'Here they come,' said Mam, folding her arms and leaning against the front doorframe. 'Bopa!' she yelled. 'They're here!'

Arthur Pryce was sitting in the front seat looking anxious, and as the wagon came to a stop, he jumped down and stared at a clipboard.

Bopa appeared in her doorway and raised her eyebrows towards Mam. 'Do you think I'll get a film star, Em?' she shouted. 'Clark Gable, please, Arthur!'

Arthur Pryce didn't reply; he was blinking rapidly and trailing a forefinger down the list in front of him. His cheeks were burning scarlet and he seemed flustered.

'Christ, Arthur,' chided Bopa, 'let's be having you. Who am I getting?'

Arthur raised his head and yelled towards the back of the wagon. 'Robert Paine! Andrew Janko!'

Bopa's eyes widened. 'Robert Paine and Andrew Janko. Did you hear that, Em? Two!'

Two American soldiers appeared from within the wagon, both holding kit bags over a shoulder. They looked very young, a little nervous. 'Wet behind the ears,' Father would call them.

Arthur reached into a satchel slung across his chest and handed them a small booklet each. 'Wassat, 'en?' asked Bopa, taking one and having a gander. '"Instructions for American Servicemen in Britain!"' she read out loud. 'We'll have a

178

read of that later! Well, come on, you two! Robert Paine and Andrew Janko. Which one's which?'

'I'm Andrew,' said the taller one.

'And I'm Robert.'

'Got any gum, chum?' said Ade, leading a small knot of children who'd gathered behind them.

'You can ask for gum later,' said Bopa, shooing them away. 'Let's get 'em in, get 'em settled. Thank you, Arthur. I'll take over from here.'

Arthur gave an awkward nod, went to shake the hands of the Americans but thought better of it, turned and climbed back into the front of the wagon. He consulted his clipboard. 'Number sixty-seven,' he shouted, and the wagon rolled onwards, the children running after it, like gulls following a trawler.

'Look at us, Em,' said Bopa, jerking her thumbs towards her two new charges. 'Soldiers coming out our ears. Tea's on. Fancy a cup?'

'Not half,' said Mam, patting her hair upwards. 'Don't worry,' she whispered towards Piotr. 'You're still my favourite.'

I looked up at Piotr and rolled my eyes. He let out a loud laugh. 'This is how it will be. Nobody can compete with Americans. They're too glamorous.'

'They're not heroes, though,' I said, 'not proper ones, like you.'

'Not yet,' said Piotr, looking down at me. 'Now, then. I have request. I would like you help me return to your den. Take me up your mountain.'

I frowned. 'But your ankle,' I said, 'it's not better enough ...'

'With the stick and your help, I'll be fine,' said Piotr, placing his free hand on my shoulder. 'Besides, I have reason for wanting to go. I lost something very precious to me, my father's watch. And I am certain it fell out of my pocket. Would you like to help me find it?'

'I would,' I said, nodding. 'If it's not there, it might be still up by the plane? We took loads of stuff out of it. Don't remember seeing a watch, mind. But perhaps one of the other lads took it. It'll be in the mountain treasure box if they did.'

Piotr smiled. 'Thank you,' he said, his hand still firmly on my shoulder. 'Boys are like magpies. Always drawn to something shiny.'

'You can lean on me 'n' all,' I said, smiling. 'If you feel tired, like.'

I led Piotr up across the tinder path and on to the trail that wound around our mountain. The weather was particularly fine, a buttermilk sky high above us, with a warm south-westerly blowing through the heather. I made Piotr sit as often as I could, taking trouble to point out the mountain flowers. 'This is sphagnum,' I said, picking some moss from the base of a rock and shoving it into my pocket. 'It heals wounds. Stops bleeding. We had to pick a load for the war, like.' I picked some more and held it out for him to see.

Piotr took it in his hand and rubbed it between his fingers. 'How clever and unexpected,' he said. 'I like odd remedies. Be sure to always have some in your pocket, Anthony. You never know when it'll come in handy. When we were fighting and had smelly feet, we rubbed vodka into them. Cured the stink.

Although, to be honest, when you're fighting, it's probably better to drink it.'

I shielded my eyes from the sun and cast a long glance upwards. The red kite was circling, about a mile to our left. 'See that bird,' I said, pointing. 'It's proper rare. Red kite. You only get them in the valley.'

Piotr stared up, following my finger. 'Beautiful. Out hunting, like us. Birds of prey are so efficient. A vulture can smell something dying from mile away. Brilliant opportunists. Scavengers always find way to survive.'

'She likes hovering over the bracken on the lower slope,' I said, eyes still fixed upwards. 'It's where the little mammals hide.'

The red kite dived down. We waited to see her rise again but she didn't reappear. 'Looks like she's found something. Eating it, I expect.'

Piotr stood. 'Come,' he said, placing his hand on my shoulder. 'Let's carry on.'

The boys had been in the den, that was clear. Another heap of plundered stuff was stacked towards the back. There was a screwdriver lying on the floor and next to it, a panel of dials Somehow, they'd managed to pull out the plane's steering gear. 'Little magpies,' said Piotr, as he rifled through it. 'I can't believe how much they've managed to take.'

'Can you see your watch?' I asked, picking up what looked like a small suitcase. I went to open it, but it was locked. I placed it on the bench and, taking the screwdriver, tried to pick at the hinge.

'No, not yet,' said Piotr, his back to me. 'Your boys have been thorough. I'll give them that. They've got enough here to build their own plane.'

He stood, and turned to face me. 'What have you got there?' he asked, taking a step towards me.

'Dunno,' I said, trying to wedge the screwdriver into a small gap so I could lever the hinge open. 'Suitcase. It's heavy. Must be stuff in it.'

'Here,' said Piotr, holding his hand out for the screwdriver. 'Let me try.'

I passed him the screwdriver and sat on my haunches, watching as he placed the tip into the centre of the lock. With one sharp punch downwards, it gave a small crack and the suitcase popped open. I leant forwards and peered in. It was equipment of some sort, knobs, dials, a meter with a needle in it, bright orange tubes wrapped in copper coils and a pair of headphones. 'Crikey,' I said, giving a knob a twiddle. 'What's that, d'you reckon?'

'Radio,' said Piotr, flicking a few switches. 'Doesn't look as if it's working. I expect it broke in crash.'

'Can you fix it?' I said, tapping a larger black knob that was attached to a metal arm.

'Not sure,' said Piotr, taking one of the coils and examining it. 'It'll need a working receiver and a power supply unit. Looks like it's carrying spares. Perhaps I could? We can try.' He smiled down at me. I smiled back.

I'd never spent this much time with a man, a grown-up one, certainly not one who paid any attention to what I said. Youngest sons don't get minded. That's what Alwyn always said. I looked up to Father, and always did what he told me as best I could, but we weren't friends. At least, I didn't think of him that way. But with Piotr, it was different. He was like Ade or Fez or Bozo.

'Do you think you can stay here, like?' I said, watching as he fiddled with a screw at the back of the panel. 'Live here, I mean. In the village.'

'Live here?' answered Piotr, his face tense with concentration. 'I don't think so. Captain Willis said I'll be transferred to Polish headquarters in Scotland. I don't know when. With all preparations for France, I expect I'm quite low down list.'

'Does that mean you'll live with us for longer, then?' I asked. 'Till the end of the war, like?'

'I don't know about till end of war,' said Piotr, pulling out a tangled wire. 'If they're pushing into France, then who knows? I might be sent there. War isn't over for me yet, Ant.'

I picked up a small stick and swirled it into the dry earth between my feet. My chin fell into the crook of my left elbow, my thoughts tumbling away. 'It'll be dangerous in France, won't it, Piotr?' I said, my voice soft and low.

Piotr shot me a glance. 'That it will. The Germans will be waiting. They are strong, well fortified, organised.'

'But they're not as brave as you,' I said.

'I'm not brave,' said Piotr. 'I try to survive. Like the vulture. There,' he added, holding up a small crystal, 'I think that was problem. The crystal was dislodged. If I put it back in, we might have working radio.'

I leant forward to watch as Piotr slotted the crystal back into place. He twisted a few wires back together, and replaced a few screws. Shooting me a small wink, he sat back, crossed his fingers and flicked a switch on the bottom right of the unit. There was a small crackle.

'Look!' I said, pointing at the dial. 'Did you see the needle move?'

'I did!' laughed Piotr. 'Looks like we've fixed it.'

'You fixed it,' I corrected.

'And you found it. Your den now has working radio. Not bad for gang of small boys, eh? Here, try headphones.'

I slipped the headphones over my head. The earpieces were hard and uncomfortable, but I could just make out a distant fuzz of noise. 'It's like a buzzing,' I said, 'but far away.'

'You can increase volume there,' said Piotr, tapping another dial. He gave it a small twist to the right.

My eyes widened. 'I can hear it!' I said. 'I mean the buzzing, that is. How do you listen to people talking?'

'Big dial on left is for tuning into frequencies. You'll need to be gentle and precise. It's careful operation.'

I held the headphone tighter to the side of my head and turned the frequency dial. Noises faded in and out, things I couldn't quite put my finger on, and then suddenly, ' … rain, moving in from the east …'

'It's the weather!' I declared. 'I can hear the weather forecast!'

'Good boy,' said Piotr, standing up. 'You can play with it as much as you like. Now, then, back to my lost watch …'

'There's a small box,' I said, slipping the headphones off, 'an old cigar box Fez brought from home. We use it for special stuff. If the boys found a watch, that's where they would put it.' I pointed under the bench towards it. 'Can you reach it? It's just b'there.'

Piotr bent down and picked it up, flicking off some dry earth across its top with the back of his hand. He flipped open the lid and stared in.

'Is it in there?' I said, stepping towards him.

He shook his head and reached into the box. 'No, but I'm not sure you should keep this up here,' he said, pulling out a revolver. 'Bullets, too. Anthony, listen to me. War isn't game. If you or any of the others hurt yourself with this, I would never forgive myself. Please, allow me to keep safe for you? It's still yours. But let me look after it.'

I shifted where I stood. 'It's Ade's, really,' I said. He must have hidden it here after I gave it back to him. 'I can't give away what's not mine. Please, Piotr. If we leave it here for now, then I can ask him. See if he minds, like.'

Piotr fixed me with a steady gaze then blinked. 'All right,' he said. 'But I'll take bullets. At least then I know you can't hurt yourself. Deal?'

He held out his hand to shake.

'Deal,' I replied, placing my hand in his.

'I don't think my watch is in here,' said Piotr, pocketing the bullets and replacing the cigar box. 'I think it might be lost for ever …'

'We could have a walk about. It might be under the bracken.'

'We need the red kite,' said Piotr, making his way to the entrance. 'Picking out small treasures from great heights.'

He stood and stared out across the valley, leaning onto his stick and raising a hand to his forehead to shield his eyes from the sun. I came and stood next to him. Before the Americans came, it was all rolling green, but now it was a different sort of green: wagons, huts, troops. The valley was a mass of activity.

'Three thousand Americans, Captain Willis said,' I muttered. I picked a long blade of grass at its stem and swished it through the air.

Piotr looked down at me. 'Did you ever think you'd see American troops up your mountain?'

I shook my head. 'Didn't think we'd have a Polish hero, neither. Or a load of crashed Germans. Nothing ever happens round here, and now it's all happened at once.'

Piotr cast a look over his shoulder towards the ledge that dropped down onto the den. He paused for a moment, frowned and then walked towards its lip. 'I fell down this, that night,' he said, scanning the rim.

'I already looked there,' I said, stripping the long grass of its outer blades.

'Hang on,' said Piotr, bending down and reaching into a patch of bracken. 'Well, I never,' he added, straightening. 'Look. I've found it.'

He let a fob watch fall by its chain from his hand.

'You're like the red kite!' I said, excitedly.

'You must be lucky charm, Anthony,' said Piotr, grinning as he palmed the watch. 'Come on, then, let's make our way back.'

'Please can I go, Father?' said Bethan, hands practically clamped in supplication. 'Mam, ask him for me. Everyone's going. There's going to be an American band playing. And I'll be with Alwyn and Emrys. They'll make sure nothing bad happens to me.'

Saturday night was Dance Night, and with the Americans billeted all through the valley, there was a sense of something tantalising in the air. Normally, everyone would head off to a dance at the local Labour Club, but tonight was different: there was a special Forces Dance down in Porthcawl.

'I'm not worried about anything bad happening to you, Bethan,' said Alwyn, lighting a cigarette. 'I'd be more worried about the trouble you'll be causing.'

'Shut up, Alwyn,' retorted Bethan, her eyes flashing. 'You're the one most likely to be causing trouble. Especially when you see Gwennie Morgan dancing with a Yank.'

Alwyn scowled and took a long draw on his cigarette.

'Let her go, Davey,' interjected Mam, poking at the fire to get some life into it. 'Besides, it would be nice for Piotr to go. Have a bit of fun. They can all go.'

'What about his ankle, Mam?' I said. 'I know he can stand on it, but never dancin'.'

'He's right,' said Piotr, nodding towards me. 'I don't think I'm up to foxtrot yet. I can go if I've got someone to keep eye on me. Is Anthony allowed to go to dances? Or is he too young?'

My eyes lit up. I'd never been to a fancy do. Not properly. We used to hang round the Labour Club when a dance was on, but we never ventured in. We'd stand on the outside wall and peer in through the window. It wasn't that we weren't allowed; it was because we weren't wanted. Dances were for courting, not being laughed at.

'Please, Father,' said Bethan again. 'If Ant's going, I'll spend most my time keeping an eye on him.'

Father raised an eyebrow. He was strict when it came to Bethan, her being his only daughter, but the odds were stacked against him. Every girl in the valley would be going.

'All right,' he said, with a heavy sigh. 'You can all go. But I don't want anyone getting carried away. Excitement is one thing, but you don't need to lose your dignity. And if Anthony's going, someone smarten him up a bit. He looks like he's been spat out of a bog.'

I glanced down at myself. My wellingtons were covered in dried mud and slime, my shorts were ingrained with dirt and my jumper was fleabitten and threadbare. I didn't have anything smart to wear. 'I can wash my wellies in the sink,' I offered.

'No, you bloody can't,' Mam replied, turning to look at me. 'You can wash them under the garden tap. Emrys, find him one of your old shirts. If we put a tank top on him and tuck everything in, he might not look so bad. I'll get the iron out. There's nothing that's not instantly improved by the presence of a sharp crease. Anthony, get those shorts off.'

I was used to helping my sister get ready when she went to dances, but the attention being on me was a first-time experience. Normally, I would spend half an hour on my knees helping Bethan apply gravy browning to her legs before painting a fake seam up the back of her calves with an eyebrow pencil. Turns out I had a good eye. 'He's good at drawing, inne?' Bopa would say, standing behind me, watching.

Emrys had taken me to the back kitchen and sat me down with a hand towel wrapped around my shoulders. 'I think we'll have to give you a pompy,' he said, dipping his comb into a tin of Brylcreem. 'Christ, man, you've got so much hair we could ask Bethan to stick some curlers in.'

Piotr laughed. 'Get side parting as straight as possible. Then pile it over. Don't you worry, Anthony. We'll have you looking like dapper swag in no time.'

'A little dab'll do it,' said Emrys, dragging the comb as best he could through my fringe. 'And keep still. Or you'll end up looking like Rita Hayworth.'

Piotr was unwrapping a blade from a blue Gillette packet. 'Have you ever had shave, Anthony?' he asked, holding the blade between two fingers. 'Not close one, of course. Real one.'

I shook my head.

'Keep bloody still,' moaned Emrys, dragging the comb sideways.

'So,' began Piotr, 'we place blade in head, like this.' He held out the head of the razor and slotted in the blade. 'Then we attach it.' He screwed the head into a patterned silver handle. 'And so you have razor. Now, what to do with it? Do you know?'

'No,' I said, mesmerised.

'You need to make foam. For this, you take scuttle.' He took a dark ceramic pot that looked like a small bowl with a spout. 'Pour hot water into reservoir and let it stand. Get it warm.' He filled the spout with hot water from the kettle then took a small shaving soap pot and nestled it in his palm. 'Now you make your lather. So we circle soapy brush in scuttle bowl. And see, in no time, you have thick lather.' He held up the shaving brush that was now coated in a rich, silky cream. 'Spread that all over your chin and upper lip, take your razor, draw skin tight and let razor slide downwards. Don't drag it. You'll cut yourself. Watch as I finish.'

I'd lived in a house with two older brothers and my father for eleven years and I had never, not once, actually seen them shaving other than in the tub in front of the fire. It was an afterthought, a chore as ordinary as cleaning between your toes, but watching Piotr, shaving felt like the most magical treat. I didn't even know we had a shaving kit in the house, let alone seen anyone use it.

'There,' said Piotr, patting his face dry with a towel. 'What do you think?'

'Very handsome,' said Bethan, wandering into the kitchen. 'Ant. I need you to do my seams. Well, well!' she added, on seeing my emerging hairdo. 'I hardly recognised you. I didn't know I had a little sister …'

I screwed my mouth sideways. 'I'm going to have a shave first,' I said. 'I'll do your legs after, like.'

'A shave? When did my little brother become a little man?' said Bethan, registering mock surprise. 'Look at the effect you've had on him,' she added, looking towards Piotr. 'My goodness. You can stay for ever.'

'This book they've given 'em's amazin',' said Bopa, who had brought her GI guests round so we could take them to the dance. She waved a small grey booklet in the air. 'Listen to this, now … *"The British have phrases and colloquialisms of their own that may sound funny to you. You can make just as many boners in their eyes. It isn't a good idea, for instance, to say 'bloody' in mixed company in Britain — it is one of their worst swear words."* Ha! Can you believe it? We say it all the bloody time! Christ! Good job they don't know about the Welsh swear words, innit? *Uffarn den!*'

Father gave a small tut and reached for his book.

'And this, listen to this bit … *"Don't be misled by the British tendency to be soft-spoken and polite. If they need to be, they can be plenty tough. The English language didn't spread across the oceans and over the mountains and jungles and swamps of the world because the people were panty-waists."'*

'What's a panty-waist?' asked Mam, casting a glance towards the two Americans. They were both standing by the fireplace, clutching their caps in front of them, looking awkward.

'It means you're sort of lily-livered,' said the taller one, his voice soft and quiet. 'You know, panty-waists …'

We all stared at him, none the wiser.

I didn't look good: I was covered in razor cuts, my hair, full of pomade, leant sideways and drew to a point which, from a certain angle, made me look as if I was wearing a large, hairy dunce cap; I was swimming inside Emrys' shirt and tank top, despite the addition of a belt, and my shorts, now with a knife-sharp crease, were still as ingrained with dirt as they ever were. My wellingtons, however, were sparkling.

'Shame about the boots,' said Bopa, putting the book down and giving me the once-over. 'But for your first time out, I don't think you look half bad.'

'If I'd looked that terrible first time I went out,' said Alwyn, who hadn't stopped laughing since seeing me, 'I'd have never left the house again.'

Bethan gave him a sharp nudge. 'You look lovely, Ant,' she said, putting her arm round my shoulders. 'Don't you mind him. He's just jealous.'

'Alf's here!' said Emrys, who was standing at the parlour window looking out. 'You can relax, Bethan. He's hasn't got the grocer's van.'

'Thank God for that,' said Bethan, with a sigh. 'Now we'll not arrive stinking of onions.'

'You look after my boys, now,' said Bopa, shoving her two American GIs towards the door. They hadn't really spoken yet, but that was no surprise. Bopa had barely stopped to breathe. 'And don't be bringin' 'em back in any sort of dopey state! We'll want all the stories when you get back, won't we, Em?'

'Everything!' said Mam, pushing herself up from her chair.

Alf had managed to cadge the use of a delivery van from Polikoff's sewing factory. A fella he knew owed him a favour, and Alf had seen fit to cash it in.

'I've put some cushies on the sidebenches,' he said, helping us all in. 'So it's comfy, like. Nice to make your acquaintance,' he added, to the two Americans. 'I'm Alf. *Diawl*, Emrys,' he added, squaring them up and down. 'We can't compete with them togs, is it? We shall have to up the charm offensive if we're going to get any dances tonight.'

The mood was affable, animated. Alwyn had taken the passenger seat up front with Alf, while our American visitors, Emrys, Piotr and Bethan were in the back with me. We had stopped off on the corner of Blaencwm Terrace to pick up the last passenger.

'I can't get up there!' protested Gwennie Morgan, staring into the back of the van.

'I'll give you a leg up,' said Alf, cupping his hands. 'Come on, 'en.'

'Leg up? Who do you think I am? The scrum half for Treorchy? Haven't you got some steps, or something?' She peered into the van. She wasn't wearing her glasses and without them, her eyesight wasn't what it might be.

'Can I help you up, ma'am?' said the taller American, standing to help her.

Gwennie's expression changed in an instant. 'Oh!' she declared, her face breaking into a beatific grin. 'That's an accent I don't recognise ...' She gave a small giggle. Alf rolled his eyes.

'Do you want this bunk up or what, then?' he asked. 'There's no other way in. It's that or I'm leaving you here.'

Gwennie flashed him an irritated look. 'You will not bloody leave me here,' she snapped, then, turning to the American, 'Thank you kindly. If I could take your hands I'd be much obliged.'

The GI – I think he was Andrew – took both of Gwennie's outstretched hands and pulled her up, with Alf giving her an unceremonious shove up the backside to get her in. She gave out a small, startled yelp and then, once inside, set about presenting herself to the best advantage.

'All right, Gwennie?' said Bethan, opening her handbag. 'Sit beside me, if you want. There's a cushion.'

We were sitting on wooden sidebenches facing each other, the Welsh contingent on one side, foreigners on the other. Alf banged the side of the van. 'Everybody in! We're off!'

'It's not too far,' said Bethan, pulling out her compact. 'Shame we've got no windows, mind. You won't see the view.'

'They'll have to enjoy the view they've got, then, won't they?' said Gwennie, pursing her lips.

'Did I hear you say earlier you're from Texas?' said Emrys, tapping Andrew on the knee. 'Isn't that where cowboys come from, like?'

'Yes, sir,' replied Andrew with a nod. 'We're both from a small town called Webberville. You won't know it. Only got three hundred and fifty-four residents. It's just outside Austin. That's a proper city. Me and Robert went to school together, joined up together, trained in Wisconsin. Then they moved us to Orangeburg. That's in the state of New York. We got Port Call orders early October last year. Sailed to Belfast, Ireland. And now we're here.'

'I didn't care for the sea voyage,' said Robert, shaking his head. 'Sick as a dog. We all were.'

'Nice you've known each other for so long, like,' said Emrys, with an appreciative nod. 'I'd have joined up with my brother if we'd been allowed. But we're miners, see. Essential work, innit?'

'You talk so funny,' I said, staring at them.

'To me, you talk funny!' said Andrew, smiling.

'And to me,' said Piotr, 'you *all* talk funny!' We laughed.

The girls were acting giddy, cooing over everything the Americans said, but the men weren't what you'd call flash. The taller one, Andrew, had teeth that wouldn't look out of place on a sheep, while Robert had one eye that seemed to have a mind of its own. I wondered if it might be a bit lazy. He needed a go on Bozo's glasses.

They'd seemed out of their depth when we saw them the previous day, but now, sitting in close proximity, they had an air of men well travelled. The furthest I'd ever been was a day trip to Tenby. We'd gone on the bus and Mam had bought me an ice cream in a cone. I fell in a rock pool and we had to come home an hour after arriving. As day trips go, it wasn't much cop. Travelling an ocean seemed unimaginable to me.

Gwennie Morgan had not stopped crossing and uncrossing her legs since getting in. She was wearing a bright-red swing dress, white polka dots, a thick red belt pulling her waist in tighter than looked comfortable, and her hair was swirled up like a dollop of cream. If I'd been older, I'd have been terrified.

'You got sweethearts, then?' she asked, batting her eyelids. 'Back home, like?' She lay her hands on her knees and stretched her legs out, I guessed to show off her calves.

'Yes, ma'am,' said Robert. 'In fact, we're both engaged to be married. Just as soon as we get home.'

'That's the second time you've called me "mam",' said Gwennie Morgan, sitting upright abruptly. 'I don't look that old, do I?'

'It's what they call ladies,' said Emrys, laughing. 'Short for madam. Ma'am. Not mam. Ain't that right, boys?'

'Yes, ma'am,' said Andrew.

'Sounds the same to me,' said Gwennie, looking umbraged.

'So how long you here for?' said Piotr, both hands resting on the top of his walking stick.

'They don't tell us nothing,' said Andrew, leaning forward so his elbows were on his knees. 'All I know is, today we had to do digging. That's it. I know where the mess is. I guess I know where we're headed, and that's about it. Infantry men are the last people to hear anything.'

Piotr laughed. 'It was same for me. We'd get in truck, be driven somewhere, told to get out, commander would point at something on map, tell us to hold it or take it, and that was that. You get on with it then check you've got all your limbs at end.'

'What's it like?' asked Robert, his voice dropping. 'Action, I mean. Proper fightin'.'

'You're so terrified you haven't got time to be terrified,' said Piotr. 'If that makes sense?'

The Americans both nodded.

'Piotr saved people,' I said. 'A man from the RAF said he's probably going to get a medal.'

'Pay no attention,' said Piotr, waving a hand through the air. 'I didn't do anything out of ordinary. When you're in thick of it, last thing you're thinking about is medals. All you're thinking about is how you get out as quickly as possible. That's not bravery. That's necessity.'

'All the same,' I persisted, 'he definitely said medal.'

'Too easily impressed, Anthony,' said Piotr. 'You should be impressed by your brothers! Going underground day in day out. They're the engine that drives us all. They are just as brave. More brave!'

'Shame you can't dance, Piotr,' said Bethan, who was touching up her lipstick. 'I'd have asked for the first one.' She snapped her compact shut and pressed her lips together.

'Don't you worry, Bethan,' yelled Alf, from the front. 'I'll stand in for him.'

Bethan shot Alf a quick glance and then turned to look at Piotr. Their eyes met, Bethan blushed, and as quickly as she had stared at him, she turned away. If I didn't know better, I'd have thought my sister was going soft.

*

The town hall was jumping. As we arrived, a mass of people stretched up to the large double doors, crowding to get in. Blaring from inside was a noise so vital and urgent that couples, not able to contain themselves, had started dancing on the pavements. I didn't recognise the moves. In Treherbert, the standard dance was mostly ballroom, but Mrs Collins, who was paid a shilling to man the piano every Saturday, had heard about a new dance, swing, and had sent off for the sheet music. It had taken everyone ages to learn the new steps. We were many things in our valley, but up to the minute wasn't one of them.

Alf stood at the back of the van, doors open, and held up his hand towards Bethan. 'Take my hand,' he said. 'It's quite a gap.'

'I'm fine,' said Bethan, steadying herself on the doorframe, but then, shooting a glance towards her heels, added, 'Actually, I might need your help after all.' She held her hand out and let him take it.

Alf grinned. 'There you go,' he said, helping her down. 'Let's hope that's not the last time you need it.'

Bethan dusted down her jacket and ignored him. 'Gwennie'll need a hand as well,' she said, not looking up. 'She's got higher heels than I have.'

'I'm not sure if I should try and jump it at all,' said Gwennie, twisting her mouth into an anxious knot. 'If I break a heel, I'll have an emotional collapse. Perhaps,' she added, batting her eyelids towards the Americans, 'you gentlemen could lift me down ...'

Robert and Andrew leapt up, ready to oblige, but Alwyn appeared and held his arms out. 'I can manage,' he said. 'Come on Gwennie, down you come.'

Gwennie's face fell. 'But ...' she said, her disappointment palpable, as Alwyn stood waiting below her. 'I asked ...'

Alwyn reached up and grabbed her. 'Come on,' he said, squaring a sharp look in the Americans' direction. 'There's people waiting to get out.' Gwennie let out a small, high-pitched squeak and as Alywn placed her on the floor, she was a picture of indignation.

'Really, Alwyn,' she said, smoothing her dress down. 'If I want your help, I'll ask for it. Come on, Bethan,' she said, hooking her arm through my sister's, 'let's go see who we can dance with.'

She shot a sharp, mean glance at Alwyn and flounced off. I looked towards my eldest brother, a dark shadow passing across his eyes. That wouldn't go down well, I thought, and a tiny knot of apprehension quietly tied itself in the pit of my stomach.

I noticed the noise first; it was incredible, and even louder close up. There was a piano, some drums, two lines of brass – trumpets and trombones – and a singer, hugging a microphone, leaning back and belting out a high note. The musicians were blasting out a relentless, uninhibited sound, while on the floor, in front of them, GIs, jackets off, hair slicked back, were dancing. It was like nothing I'd ever seen. They were jumping in the air, throwing girls over their backs, going crazy.

Welsh and American flags hung overhead, with red, white and blue bunting adorning every wall. Everywhere I looked, people were wide-eyed and animated. The atmosphere was joyous, alive with people crammed into every available nook and cranny, drinking, dancing, laughing or smoking. It was a large room, and there was a balcony above us – reached by a staircase – that looked down onto the dance floor. To the right of the room, there was a refreshment stand serving drinks, and ahead of us, at the far end, the stage.

'What are they doing?' I said, staring at the dance floor.

'Jitterbug,' said Emrys, reaching into his jacket pocket for his cigarettes. 'They look like they've lost their minds.'

'Look at them,' said Gwennie, eyes sparkling. 'Look at their hips, Bethan. Look at them. Hopping. Bouncing. It's almost obscene.'

Gwennie and Bethan had taken up a vantage spot on the staircase above us, staring down into the bubbling mass below. Gwennie, I noticed, was wearing an expression of sheer determination. 'Right, then, Bethan,' she said, primping the underside of her hair. 'Let's mingle.'

'Would you like to dance?' said a sweating GI, gliding over.

Gwennie's eyes lit up. 'Delighted, I'm sure,' she said, letting her hand fall into his. 'Hold that,' she added, thrusting her handbag backwards into my arms, and off she twirled.

Alwyn made a deep, guttural grunt and surged forward, but was held back by Emrys. 'Steady, man,' he said, quietly, 'it's only a dance.'

'I need a drink,' said Alwyn, his face dark and brooding. 'Where are they selling it?'

'Bar's over there,' said Piotr, pointing off to the right. 'I'll come help you. Bethan, can I get you something?'

'Bitter lemon, please,' said Bethan. 'And something fizzy for him,' she added, pointing in my direction.

'Can you do that dance?' I said, nodding towards the gyrating couples below us.

Bethan shook her head. 'Wouldn't know where to start,' she said, taking off her jacket. 'Wait here,' she added. 'I'm just going to the coat check.'

I stood and looked around me. Andrew and Robert had wandered over to a cluster of GIs they clearly knew. Andrew was being slapped on the shoulder by a laughing corporal. Next to him, another infantryman, cigarette hanging from the centre of his mouth, was clapping along to the music. Robert shook the hand of another, who then turned towards the stage, pressed his fingers into the sides of his mouth, and let rip with a loud whistle. Goodness, they were confident.

Welsh girls stood nervously around the edges of the dance floor, waiting to be swept up: some were swaying enthusiastically, others more apprehensive, not quite sure what they should be doing. They reminded me of the border flowers on the cigarette card, pretty girls all in a row.

The Welsh lads, on the other hand, looked mildly furious. They were being out-classed left, right and centre. They didn't have a hope. Some were trying to ask girls to dance, but were getting nowhere: the girls wanted to save themselves so they could be asked by an American. Instead, the Welsh lads stood in tight, angry clusters, beers in hand and staring. If there wasn't a fight, I thought, it would be a miracle.

I wandered away from the entrance, pushing myself gently through swaying hips and girls staring up towards the stage. A black trombonist had moved front and centre, clicking his fingers, smile dazzling, his head shaking from side to side. The drummer, just behind him, had his tongue out, and was pulsing out an almost manic beat, while the pianist, standing at the baby grand, was thumping the keys and tapping his foot on the wooden boards. Below them, there was a whirling sea of movement: girls being tossed into the air, skirts flapping, hands shaking, heads pecking. It was wild.

I stared down at my wellingtons. I wished I could dance.

The trombonist on the stage stepped forward and grabbed the microphone. 'Ready for the group jive?' he yelled. A cheer went up. 'I said, READY FOR THE GROUP JIIIIIVE?' A roar.

As he clicked his fingers three times, the brass section stood and began to blare out a furious riff. Below him, couples organised themselves into lines, bobbing and swaying on the spot. Then, under the brass, came the drums and the piano, and the tempo quickened.

'Send out!' yelled the trombonist. The boys took the girls by the hands and flung them forwards.

'Through!' he yelled, and back they all curled.

'Shoulder twist! Release!' he yowled. Everyone spun round.

'Switch! Change places. Quick stop!' Everyone froze.

'Now let's hit that jive!' The dance floor exploded, girls were spinning, being tossed sideways over thighs, GIs' hair flipping left and right, arms in the air. I was spellbound.

From the corner of my eye, I caught sight of Gwennie Morgan. She was in the far corner of the dance floor, jiving with her partner. He was significantly shorter than her and appeared to be bobbing furiously just below her bosom. She was red in the face and looked mildly startled, as if nothing in her life to date could have prepared her for this sudden thrill.

I scanned the room for Alwyn, the small, tight knot in my stomach grumbling. He was standing by the refreshment stand, beer in hand and staring at Gwennie.

Emrys was a few feet in front of him. To my surprise, it looked like he'd found a girl to dance with, but he didn't know the moves so instead of leading, he had his head over one shoulder, trying to watch the Americans so he could copy.

'There,' said Piotr, handing me a bottle of pop. 'For you.' I locked lips round the straw bobbing upwards and sucked. Lemonade. 'Where's Bethan?' he asked, his voice raised so I could hear him over the din.

'Coat check,' I shouted. I thumbed over my shoulder.

Piotr glanced down to my other hand. Gwennie Morgan's handbag was trailing from it. He nodded and took a glug from his beer. 'First I've had in ages,' he said, lifting the bottle upwards. 'As you would say, proper treat!'

I smiled and cast an eye back in Alwyn's direction. He was still staring at Gwennie dancing, and taking large, hungry gulps from his beer. He was making me nervous.

'What a queue!' declared Bethan, pushing her way back to us. 'I don't think I've ever seen so many people at a dance. It's such a squash I'm amazed anyone can move. Oooh,' she added, as Piotr handed her the bitter lemon, 'that for me? Lovely.'

They chinked glasses and drank. Piotr leaned in and whispered something into her ear. She took another small sip from her glass and shot me a quick glance. She whispered something back.

'Stay here where I can find you,' she shouted towards me. 'I'm just going outside for a bit. Need some air.' She mimed fanning herself and smiled, then, taking Piotr's arm, they headed back towards the door.

I watched them go, feeling a little disconcerted. I didn't know if I wanted to be left on my own. I looked around and noticed a group of GIs looking at me and laughing. One of them whistled and pointed down towards Gwennie Morgan's handbag.

I felt a flush of embarrassment. I wanted to do something with it, anything, so I didn't have to carry it a minute longer. I went up onto my tiptoes to see if Gwennie was still in the far corner but, unable to see her, I looked for Alwyn instead – he was still at the bar, having another beer, by the looks of it. Alf was with him, leaning against the pillar of the refreshment stand and talking animatedly, gesturing with an arm. Alwyn wasn't looking at him. I followed his line of vision and saw Gwennie Morgan in a tight clinch with the short American. They were dancing in a packed clutch of people, her meticulous topknot coming loose in the heat.

I pushed my way towards him.

'Oi, oi! Little man!' said Alf, seeing me emerge. 'Now, then. What's a fella like you doing with a bag like that?'

'It's Gwennie Morgan's,' I said, screwing my nose up. 'I feel proper stupid slinging it round. Fellas over there whistled at me.'

'Are you sure that wasn't because of your fabulous hairdo?' said Alf, taking a sip of his beer and throwing me a smirk.

'He's got his bloody hand on her arse,' said Alwyn, his jaw tightening.

I could feel him bristling, ready to blow. I knew my brother. There was a tension about him that felt dangerous, made me edgy. I looked back over my shoulder towards Gwennie. The little American was running his hands over her. I needed Piotr.

'Steady, now, Alwyn,' said Alf, his face turning serious. 'All these boys here, all of 'em, will be gone soon enough. Play the long game, man.'

'When have you ever known me to be patient?' said Alwyn, downing his beer.

'Never,' said Alf. 'But seriously, man ...'

Alwyn drained the last of his beer and slammed the bottle down on the counter behind him. Dragging the back of his hand across his mouth, he snatched Gwennie's handbag from me. 'Let's see how he likes this down his throat,' he grumbled and pushed himself roughly into the crowd. Alf made a lunge for the back of his shirt but Alwyn was too quick.

'Find Emrys,' said Alf, putting his own bottle down. 'And Piotr. Quick as you can. There might be some trouble.'

A nagging panic coursed through me and I turned, heart thumping, to weave my way back towards the last place I'd seen Emrys. Behind me, over the pulsing music, I heard a scream and the sound of something breaking. Male voices rose up and, above me, the band came to a slow, wilting stop. Whistles filled the air.

'Emrys,' I called out, 'Emrys!'

It was no good. People around me were pressing forwards to see what the commotion was. I was being squeezed in a direction I didn't want to go. I tried to fight the tide but I was pushed back towards the refreshment stand. I held back, allowing the press of people to go past me. Sounds of a full-blown fight were rattling off the rafters. I looked up, towards the stairs. 'Piotr!' I called out.

He was standing with Bethan at his side, both of them staring down. Bethan raised a hand to her mouth as another almighty crash sounded below them. Piotr, holding on to the railing, made his way downwards as best he could. Bethan scanned the room. She was looking for me.

I raised an arm and waved. 'Bethan!' I yelled. She saw me.

'Emrys?' she cried out. 'Where is he?'

There was another clatter, a loud, wooden crack, a scream.

I shook my head and made an exaggerated shrugging movement. She ran her eyes quickly over the room, skimming over the faces below her. Suddenly, she pointed. 'There, Ant!' I could see her yell. I followed her finger. She was pointing off to my left. I pushed my way forwards.

'Emrys!' I shouted, seeing him. 'It's Alwyn! He's having a fight!'

There was another almighty crash. 'Excuse me,' said Emrys, to the red-haired girl he was with. 'My brother's making a fuss. Where is he?' he added, turning to me.

'Down over b'there,' I said, my voice high and anxious. 'Alf chased after him. But you know what he's like.'

Emrys pushed past me and began to thread his way through the crush of people. Following him, I held on to the back of his trousers so as not to get lost in the squash and suddenly, having been pummelled left and right, I found myself popping out into an open circle.

'Christ, man,' yelled Emrys. 'Leave it!'

I let go of his trousers and looked up. Alwyn, his lip bleeding, was being pulled off the small American by three other Americans and Alf. Around us there were jeers, whistles.

205

'Come on, man,' Alf was yelling. 'Leave him be!'

Gwennie was retrieving her handbag from the neck of the man she'd been dancing with. The small fella was slumped and unconscious. He seemed to be wearing a chair. Alwyn, struggling to have another go at him, broke free and rushed forward, fist raised, but another American, big and muscular, stepped forward and with one punch had Alwyn down.

'That's enough, now!' he yelled, standing over Alwyn, fists poised and ready.

Alwyn shook his head and rolled over onto his side. Pushing himself up onto his knees, he pounced up, grabbed a glass from an adjacent table and smashed it on the back of a chair. Thrusting the broken glass, Alwyn moved forwards. The big American dodged sideways but was trapped against Gwennie and her collapsed dance partner. There was nowhere for him to go.

'No, Alwyn!' I cried, but the darkness was in Alwyn's eyes. He raised the glass, ready to grind it down. I felt a cold terror surge through my chest and then, suddenly, Piotr appeared from nowhere and struck the glass from Alwyn's hand with his walking stick.

'Never do something you'll regret, my friend,' he said, as Emrys and Alf jumped forward to grab him. 'Emrys, help get him out.'

'I bloody hate you, Alwyn Jones,' shouted Gwennie Morgan, who was now crying. 'Always ruining everything! That's all you ever do!' She bent down to push the hair out from the small American's eyes.

Above us, the bandleader clicked his fingers. 'Excitement's over, folks!' he shouted. 'Let's dance.' A small cheer went up, music rang out and everyone about us resumed dancing as if the short, violent interlude had never happened.

'Help me get him into van,' said Piotr, as they bundled Alwyn out from the building.

'Let me finish him!' yelled Alwyn, still struggling.

'For Christ's sake, man!' shouted Emrys. 'Pack it in, will you? What the hell were you thinking? Glassing someone? You could have been bloody killed. One of you versus two hundred of them? Are you bloody mad?'

'Where are the girls?' said Piotr, looking over his shoulder. 'Andrew? Robert?'

'It's all right,' said Alf, who had Bethan and Gwennie in tow. 'I've got the girls. The boys are coming up behind.'

'Gwennie,' said Piotr, as they bundled Alwyn into the back of the van. 'If you can bear it, sit in the back with him and try and calm him down.'

'I'll calm him down with the back of my hand!' cried Gwennie, dabbing at her eyes with a handkerchief. 'Evening ruined! Making a show of me in front of all those people! All I did was have a dance with the man! And he'll probably be dead in a fortnight,' said Gwennie. 'That's what he told me!'

I cast a quick look up towards Alf, who caught my eye and shrugged.

'Off to France, he said,' Gwennie continued. 'Crossing the Channel, fighting the Germans, expecting massive casualties on the first day, he said. Told me I'd probably be the last girl he ever kissed. And he was a virgin.'

'Gwennie!' yelled Bethan.

'Well,' cried Gwennie. 'It's wrong to send those boys off without letting them be men. I'd sleep with all of them if I could.'

'I'll kill 'em all!' screamed Alwyn, kicking at the side of the van.

'Right. That'll do,' said Bethan, her voice hard and stern. 'Get in the back of the van. You've made a right show of us, Alwyn. I can only apologise for my brother,' she added, looking towards Andrew and Robert. 'When girls are involved, he loses his mind entirely.'

'Don't worry,' said Andrew, jumping in and sitting next to Alwyn. 'We're from Texas. If we ain't brawling over women, we ain't Texan.'

I followed Bethan and climbed up into the front passenger seat with her. Alf started the engine and before anyone could come out from the town hall after Alwyn, he drove off and out towards the mountain pass back to Treherbert. There were no streetlights and the night sky was as pitch as molasses.

'The last time it was this dark,' said Bethan, staring out, 'Piotr crashed into the mountain.'

I looked over my shoulder towards Piotr in the back. He said nothing.

CHAPTER TWELVE

I didn't want to go back to school. I had no interest in it, none of us did. There was too much going on: Americans training up our mountain, wagons, the excitement of something building, something big. We wanted to sit on a rock and watch it all pass before us. Instead, we had nit inspection.

'There shall be no discussion about this,' barked Miss Evans, hands firmly on hips. 'You will all line up against that wall and nobody is to move until Nurse Blevin says so.'

Nurse Blevin, the dreaded nit nurse, was a mean-faced woman who came from the other side of the valley. She experienced no joy whatsoever from being in the presence of children and, armed with nothing more deadly than a toothcomb, instilled terror into our very depths. She was fleshy, squeezed into a dark-blue serge uniform, with a small, starched white paper hat pinned into her tightly wound hair. She bore the expression of a large, bored dog and rumour had it she had once found a child so infested with head lice, she'd put him in a sack and thrown him in the river. I don't know if I believed that. But looking at her, I wouldn't have been surprised.

Her method was startling and efficient: grab a child about the neck with the crook of her elbow, shove head into armpit, drag metal comb across scalp. It was as far removed from the notion of gentle nursing as you could get.

'It's like when they shear sheep, innit,' Fez said, edging along the side wall.

If you got the all clear, you were released and shoved away. If you were infested, you were pressed firmly up against the wall and handed a white card to be taken to your parents for your shame to be declared. Your head would be shaved then smeared with a mysterious ointment that left your scalp covered in purple spots. From that point on, you were the butt of all future jokes. In short, it was the very worst thing that could happen to you. The very worst.

'Have you been up behind the dip yet?' said Ade, who was lined up next to me. 'Massive great tent up b'there. It's where the Yanks have their tea, like. All the food comes in on a wagon. They haven't even got rationing!'

'Get away,' I said, casting a look down the line. Bozo had his head clamped into Nurse Blevin's armpit. He was pulling a strained, agonised face. 'I had some chocolate off one a few days back. It was proper horrible. Piotr said it's cos it's made not to melt.'

Ade nodded. 'I got some gum off one. We all did. Where've you been, man? Haven't seen you up the street or the mountain, like.' He stopped and looked at me, properly. 'What's the matter with your hair?'

I ran a finger through the front of my fringe. It was matted with three-day-old pomade and had taken on a strange, solid quality that I found mildly alarming.

'Emrys gave me a pompy,' I said. 'We went up the dance in Porthcawl on Saturday night. Alwyn had a fight. Lamped an American cos he had his hands on Gwennie Morgan.'

'Every lad in the valley's had his hands on Gwennie Morgan,' said Ade, running the back of his hand across his nose. 'Least, that's what my Mam says.'

'There was a proper band and everything. They were doing this crazy dancing. And I saw a black man.'

'I saw some proper black men 'n' all. They drive the trucks. I asked them. They're in the Eighty-ninth Quartermaster Battalion Mobile Transportation Corps. That's a long name, innit?'

I nodded.

'They're in charge of delivering supplies. I asked them that 'n' all. Then I told 'em all our fathers have black faces so we're not put off by 'em, like. Mam says it's best to put people at their ease. So I did.'

'Adrian Jenkins!' said Miss Evans, who was sitting, perched on the edge of her desk with her arms folded. 'Are you a wireless?'

Ade frowned. 'No, miss.'

'Then there is no need for a constant stream of chatter, is there?'

'No, miss,' replied Ade, screwing his mouth sideways.

'That reminds me,' I whispered. 'Me and Piotr went up the den. We found a radio. Piotr fixed it.'

'I know. We saw it up there,' said Ade, out the side of his mouth. 'Couldn't figure it out, though.'

'I can show you,' I whispered. 'We can go up later.'

'It's not there now,' muttered Ade, behind his hand. He was pretending to pick something out of his teeth.

'What do you mean it's not there?' I said, frowning. 'We left it on the bench. What you do with it?'

'Nothing,' said Ade. 'Went up yesterday and it's not there. I thought you'd taken it, like.'

I shook my head.

We looked at each other, puzzled. 'Well, who's …?' began Ade.

'Adrian!' barked Miss Evans. 'Move away from Anthony, please. Or you can stay late and do lines!'

'*He* was talking to *me*, miss!' protested Ade as he squeezed himself between Gwyn and Fez. 'I was only being polite and answering!'

'Not another word from either of you! Would you like a visit to the headmaster's office?'

No, we would not. I put my hands behind my back and leant against the classroom wall. Someone up the line was crying. I glanced up. Thomas Evans. He'd been given a white card.

'Now he'll catch it,' muttered Fez. 'He'll have to sit in the seat of shame and have himself scalped.'

'He's already in the seat of shame,' whispered Ade, nodding towards his wheelchair.

I suppressed a giggle.

Ade was tapping his foot against the back wall, his expression set and concentrated. He shot a quick glance towards Miss Evans. She was dealing with Thomas, filling out his white card. He leant forward and caught my eye.

'Eh, Ant,' he said, 'you reckon it's been nicked, like?'

'Who by?' I mouthed.

Ade shrugged then quietly thumbed towards Gwyn Williams. 'Maybe?' he mouthed.

I shrugged back. It had happened before. Gwyn Williams had been caught a couple of times snaffling stuff out our den. My heart sank a bit. Challenging him would mean scrapping him. My nose had only just stopped hurting. I didn't fancy another scuffle.

Ade had reached the head of the queue and was grabbed by Nurse Blevin, his thin, stick-like legs dangling down as she hoisted him into her armpit. Ade had wispy, fine hair and he gave out a small, pained yelp as she yanked the metal comb across his head.

'You're fine,' she growled, dropping him to the floor. 'Next!'

Gwyn Williams was before me. I really hoped he wasn't the culprit. I'd had no more trouble with him since I nicked the banana, so that was all squaresies. We hadn't seen him around much over the school holiday: Fez had heard his dad wasn't too clever, healthwise. When your life was underground, the lungs could only take so much dust and damp. When folk were dying, people retreated indoors. You didn't see them from one day to the next. You had to sit by the dying, stay with them, till the last breath. I didn't know if Gwyn Williams' father was long for the world or not, but all the same, I decided I wouldn't fight him just in case he wasn't. It didn't do to be squabbling when there was death in the air.

Gwyn got the all clear. My turn. I felt the tight clamp of the nit nurse's arm. She may have been as rough as an old pony, but she smelt of carbolic soap, all scrubbed clean, and her chest, my head squashed into it, was as soft as a pillow. 'What in the name of God's green earth have you got in your hair?' she said, trying to get her comb through my fringe.

'My brother put Brylcreem in it, miss,' I said.

'Brylcreem?' she said, in mild astonishment. 'Whatever for? It's like wet wool stuck in gorse. I can't get my comb through it, it's that matted.'

She stabbed at my parting with the teeth of her comb, the metal needles sharp and biting. It hurt so I bit my lip and clamped my eyes shut. Her breath was warm on the back of my neck. It was like being far too close to a cow, quietly huffing and tutting, her irritation coursing down through the comb. She gave a long, heavy sigh and then, her grip on me loosening, grumbled, 'I've done my best. No nits. Away with you. And next time, no Brylcreem.'

I slid away from her. Ade, who was standing, arms folded, legs spread slightly apart, shot me a wink. We were all right.

As first days back go, it hadn't been too bad. After the nit nurse, Miss Evans had handed out paper and we got to do some drawing. We had to do something that had happened over the holiday, so my picture was of Piotr and me up the mountain: Piotr was pointing up into the sky towards the red kite as it circled, while I stood next to him. I wasn't that good at drawing hands but it wasn't too bad if I had people pointing. I put his other hand inside his pocket.

Ade had drawn a picture of the plane crash. Most of the other boys had too. Bozo had drawn a rather gruesome tableau of the lined-up dead men. Fez had chosen to draw a packet of American gum.

'How's your Polish house guest?' asked Miss Evans. She'd asked me to stay back and help her pack away the crayons during break. 'Is he better? I heard he was hurt.'

'He's all right,' I replied, dropping some pencils into a pot. 'He had a twisted ankle. But I got him a stick so he's getting about fine now.'

'We should ask him to come and give a talk,' she said, pinning some of the better pictures up onto the wall. 'Tell us about his wartime experiences. If they're not too gruesome, that is. I expect he's well travelled.'

'He's been everywhere, I expect,' I said. 'Even Africa.'

'Africa? Goodness. Can you tell me where Africa is on the map, Anthony? Pass me up that picture. It's too far to reach.'

I picked the top picture on the pile and handed it up. Next to her, on the wall, there was a faded world map that hung on a red rope.

'Africa's there, miss,' I said, pointing to the continent.

'Long way away, isn't it?' said Miss Evans, pressing a pin into the corner of the picture. 'And where's his home? Can you point that out?'

'It's there,' I said, pointing upwards. 'Or at least, it was there. Before Hitler moved in and made it German.'

'It must be a great comfort that he has found such a friend in you,' she said, turning to look at me. I felt myself blushing. She placed her hand against the wall and stepped down from the chair. 'Have you thought any more about that chat we had, Anthony, the one we had with your mother?'

I shook my head.

'I thought as much. There's been too much excitement to be thinking about schooling. It's been lovely to see all you boys looking up to the soldiers, all the new people coming into the village. It's like the world has come to pay us a visit, isn't it?'

I nodded.

'When you're older, do you think you'd like to go and see the world instead of waiting for it to come to you?'

I nodded again.

'And do you think you'll get to see the world if you're set for a life underground?' She paused and fixed me with her eyes.

'Don't know, miss,' I mumbled.

'Look at this picture you've drawn, Anthony,' she said, holding up my drawing. 'Pointing up and away towards a free bird. Wouldn't you like to be like that kite? Going where she pleases? You won't get to do that if you stay as you are. Isn't it better for life to be an unknown adventure?'

I stared up at her. I felt conflicted in a way I had never been before. I had always known who I was: Davey's boy, set for a life underground. I might even have had my Father's tommy box, if Alwyn didn't want it. Or Emrys. But that was before. And now …

My eyes fell away from hers. 'I don't know,' I said, again.

There was a silence. Miss Evans turned away from me and placed my drawing back onto the pile. 'Where did I put those maths books?' she muttered, hands on hips. 'Ah. There they are.' She walked away from me, striding, confident. 'Thanks for your help. You can go join your friends now. Quite a decent football match on the go, by the sounds of it.'

I turned towards the door.

'You've got a week to make your mind up,' she added, not looking at me. 'Then I'll have to tell the Grammar.'

I turned to say something, but she was bent over, rummaging in a cupboard. I looked back again towards the map, then ran towards the corridor.

'Grammar boy?' said Ade, eyes wide. 'Get away, man? That means going to school for ever. Not for me. I'll be out of here next year. Job on, bob in pocket. A man should be in work, that's what my mam says.'

'You going underground straight away?' I said, drawing a line diagonally across a circle in my workbook. 'You'll be too young, man. Unless you want to work the ponies.'

'Nah,' said Ade, chewing the end of his pencil. 'Shopkeeping for me. I'm already delivering for Mr Hughes, ain't I? Work my way up. I'm on the bike now. One day, I'll be in the van. 'Ere.' He stopped and gave me a nudge. He stared past me out the window, his face suddenly etched with worry. 'Look out. All the mams are by the gates ...'

I glanced out over the playground. A gaggle of women were gathering, scarves on, heads tightly clustered.

'Miss,' said Ade, calling towards the front, 'look.'

Miss Evans, who had been writing problems up onto the blackboard, stopped what she was doing and glanced out towards the school gate. The chalk in her hand, hovering in mid air, fell to the floor unnoticed.

We all knew what this meant.

'Pack away your things, boys,' she said, quietly, taking off her glasses. 'Get home.'

The news was coming in dribs and drabs: some said a tunnel had collapsed at the pit, others that a fire was raging. Three dead, someone had heard, many more injured. The situation was sketchy; the only thing we did know was that stretchers were on their way.

All the women were out, standing on the flagstone steps of their houses, waiting. The mood was quiet, sombre. There was no larking about on occasions such as these; we all knew how hard the pain would bite.

'Not shoulder high,' said Bopa, who was standing on the pavement, waiting with my mother. 'Please, not shoulder high.'

We all stared towards the tinder track. Shoulder high was a phrase that landed like ice. When men were wounded, they were stretchered home at waist height. If they'd been killed, it was shoulder high. It was a sight I had only seen a few times, but it made your stomach plunge as you willed the stretcher away from your own front door. Bopa had lost her husband to the mountain ten years ago. He'd been digging a low seam, killed by a charge that had gone off by accident. 'Blown to bits,' Father had said. She didn't even have a proper body to bury. It left her bereft, more so, as she'd never been able to have children. Mam reckoned that was the reason she loved us so much. We were her family now.

I stood close to my mother, pressed tight into her, her arm wrapped about my shoulder, thoughts of Father, Alwyn and Emrys rattling through me. It had happened before that a woman had lost all her men to one seam. It was a story told on cold, dark nights when the mood was maudlin. It was the life of the pitman, the mountain's revenge: hew the black, but never forget it's man against an ancient land. 'We're stealing from her, remember,' Father would say. 'We're taking what is hers.'

I looked behind me into the hallway of our house. 'Where's Piotr?' I asked, my eyes flicking up to Mam.

She shook her head. 'Gone to see Captain Willis. He's been gone all day. Never mind that now, Ant.'

A cry went up. 'Here they come!' My mother's hand tightened on my shoulder.

Ahead of us, beyond the stream, men were coming down towards the village, walking wounded at the head, then beyond them, the first of the stretchers. Bopa's hand fell into my mother's, her grip tight.

'Emrys!' I called out. 'There's Emrys, Mam!' I pointed towards him. He was crossing the tinder track, filthy, as he always was, but he looked broken, as if the life had been sucked out of him.

'Oh, thank God,' said Mam, clutching her chest. 'Can you see Alwyn? Father?'

I shook my head.

'Shoulder high!' The cry went up.

Beyond my brother, I had the first sight of a stretcher aloft. I looked again at Emrys, his head bowed, and a surge of panic coursed through me. Where was Alwyn? Where was Father?

Down the street, women clung to each other as the stretcher approached, eyes wide with terror. Please don't stop here. Please don't stop. I swear I could hear my mother's heart beating.

Four men were bearing the stretcher. I strained to see who they were, but their heads were bowed, caps low over their foreheads.

'Is that Alwyn, Mam,' I mumbled. 'On the corner?'

She gripped my hand so tight, I could feel the blood squeezing out of it.

Women were crossing themselves, a few crumpling with relief as the stretcher passed. They were the lucky ones. I was willing the stretcher to stop. Don't be us. Please. Don't be us. Emrys was getting closer but he still hadn't looked up. Where was Father?

The stretcher-bearers came to a stop and an unearthly wail reverberated up the street.

'Oh, no,' said Mam quietly, 'it's John Reece.'

The stretcher had stopped. 'Poor Peggy,' said Bopa, her voice low. 'I'll go to her. You stay here. See your men home.' She squeezed my mother's upper arm and left us to join the surge of women drawn towards their stricken neighbour. I felt a stab of guilt. I turned and buried my face into my mother's side. I couldn't bear to look.

'Emrys,' I heard her cry. She pulled away from me and flung her arms about him. 'Where's Alwyn? Father?'

'It's bad, Mam,' his voice barely audible. 'Father's bad.'

I stared up at him, my chest imploding. 'How bad?' she said. 'Where is he?'

'The Americans sent ambulances for the worst injured. They've got a field hospital in Pontypridd ...' He stopped, his voice catching in his throat. 'His chest was crushed, Mam. They don't know if he'll live.'

Mam's hand involuntarily went up to her mouth. 'Oh, no.' The words slipped through her fingers like water.

'What about Alwyn?' I said, shooting another look down towards the tinder track. 'Where is he?'

'Broken wrist. He did it pulling Father out. He'll be fine. He's gone to get it set.'

'I have to go there,' said Mam, her eyes wild and determined. 'Ant, fetch me my bag and coat. Get me there, Emrys. I have to be with them.'

I'd never seen so many tents. Eileen Place Park, a flat field beyond the village, was rammed with green canvas. To our left, lines of soldiers were doing P.T.; beyond them, men were practising trench digging, and everywhere, groups of soldiers huddled around blackboards. Behind everything, a Nissen hut loomed large, and from it wafted smells I'd completely forgotten about. I lifted my nose into the air. 'Chicken,' I mumbled.

I was holding Mam's hand. It was something I hadn't done in years, but she had reached for it as we'd walked here with Emrys and I hadn't been inclined to let go. Emrys had a glazed look in his eye. We'd all been at the crash site, that night up the mountain, but when it's your own, your neighbours, your family, it bites in the soft spots. He was hurting.

'An explosion ripped through the tunnels,' Emrys said, as we walked into the encampment. 'A rescue team was sent down but the fire underground, it was so fierce they were forced back up. I volunteered to go down but the cage got stuck in the shaft, it was that damaged. Alf climbed out, slid down a guide rope. It was him who found Alwyn, dragging Father up a tunnel with one arm. They carried him together. By the time I got down there, they were trying to keep Father's spirits up, keeping him talking. But he was bad, Mam.' His voice trailed off and he stared off towards the top of the mountain. 'There were men still down there. They said they had to flood the shaft. Only way of putting the fires out. The pit'll be closed for months.'

Mam blinked. 'There's men still down there?' she said. 'But they can't. They'll be drowned.'

Emrys stood, staring at the coal on his hands as if it were blood. 'They've already done it.'

The three of us stood in silence. We didn't yet know how many had been lost, but in a small village, where everyone knew everybody, boy to man, every pitman down was a bitter blow.

'Where's Alf?' asked Mam, suddenly. 'Did he get out?'

Emrys nodded. 'He went with Father and Alwyn in the truck. I would have gone. But Alf said it were best if I told you what had happened.'

An American officer was crossing the field towards us. We didn't need to tell him why we were there, he was already pointing towards an open-backed wagon. 'You for Pontypridd?' he yelled. 'Jump into that. Leaving when we're full.'

It was a grim journey. Someone joked it was bonus training for the medical corps, but nobody had laughed. Mam didn't speak once, her knuckles white around the handle of her handbag. Her eyes were fixed, staring up towards the mountain. I stared too. Somewhere, in its depths, men were drowning.

'How long you reckon the pit's going to be shut?' said a woman sitting to my right. Her voice was low and anxious. 'Things are hard enough as it is with rationing. But with no wages ...' A quiet chorus of mumbles filled the wagon.

'Months,' said Emrys. 'At least.'

'How are we all going to manage?' continued the woman. 'No men working?'

'Let's just get everyone safe first,' said Mam, quietly. 'Then we'll worry about the money.'

The field hospital in Pontypridd had been set up behind the local schoolhouse, and as we pulled up, a line of children's faces, resting on forearms, peered over the back wall of the yard. A man wearing a white armband with a red cross on it was waiting for us. Beyond him there was a soldier in a bloodstained apron. He was leaning against a metal pole, the tail end of a cigarette burning between his lips. He saw us coming and with one last long drag, he tossed his ciggie to the ground.

He held his hand out.

'Captain Bundy. I'm one of the medics. Who have you come for?' Mam let her hand drift into his. She looked shell-shocked, lost.

'David Jones,' explained Emrys, taking over. 'I'm his son. This is his wife. That's my little brother.' He gestured down towards me. 'My elder brother should be here too. Broke his wrist.'

'Emrys!' I heard a voice calling. I looked behind Mam to see Alwyn, his hand in the air. Alf stood up in front of him and walked towards us.

Mam cast a glance towards the medic. 'It's fine to go,' he said. 'We've made him comfortable. He'll be pleased to see you.'

Mam gave a short, small smile and for a fleeting moment, the life came back into her eyes. 'He's over here,' said Alf, taking my mother gently at the elbow. 'You too, little man,' he added, gesturing for me to follow.

'If I could have a word ...' The medic steered Emrys to one side. I looked over my shoulder. He looked worried.

'He's broken three ribs,' said Alf, as he led us into the tent. 'He's been in a lot of pain. But they've given him something for that. He's had a blunt injury to the chest. So there might be a problem with his lungs. They won't know for twenty-four hours.'

Mam gripped Alf's arm a little tighter. 'How bad will it be if there is a problem?'

Alf ignored the question. 'He'll be ever so pleased to see you.'

We walked through a small maze of camp beds: most men were being treated for cuts and scrapes, and we could see cleaned swathes of bright white flesh shining out from the black. We knew all of them, and Mam nodded and smiled to everyone who caught her eye.

Fez's dad was having some stitches. 'Don't worry, Em,' he said, as we passed. 'He's a fighter.'

Alwyn was sitting on the edge of his camp bed next to Father. He had one arm in a sling. 'Don't touch it,' he said to me, nodding down to the fresh cast. 'It's not set yet. Hello, Mam.'

Mam leant down, her handbag dropping onto the floor beside him. She held his face in her hands for a moment and then turned to Father. 'Oh, Davey.' The words escaped out of her.

He was lying, eyes half-closed, his nose and mouth obscured by a heavy, dark mask. Thick elastic straps were digging into his cheeks, and below the mask hung a rubber balloon. I watched it swell then suck itself tight.

'He's on oxygen, Mam,' Alwyn told her, as she ran her fingers across Father's forearm. 'In case his lungs pack in. Best case – he's going to be bloody sore. Worst case – he could get pneumonia or go into respiratory distress.'

'What happens then?' asked Mam, casting an anxious glance at Alwyn.

'We do the best we can,' he replied.

I didn't know quite how I felt, standing there at the end of the bed. It was like it wasn't really happening, like I was up the flicks watching it on a big screen. Where was the orange peel? The fag ends flying through the air? I looked down at Father and a weight settled in my chest, the certainty of the grave. I had never seen him weak or vulnerable but now, as those frailties came knocking at our door, I knew my bones weren't ready for it.

Alf had pulled up a chair so Mam could sit by Father's side. He stood back and put a hand on my shoulder. 'All right, little man?' he whispered. 'He's made of strong stuff, your Father. He'll not go down without a scrap.'

I didn't want to cry but I felt a swell burning behind my eyes. I turned away and rubbed at hot tears with the back of my hand.

'Someone should go tell Bethan,' said Alf, behind me.
'Would you like me to do that for you, Alwyn? I'm sure I can cadge a lift off someone.'

Alwyn nodded. 'Thanks, Alf,' he said, quietly, 'I'd appreciate it.'

Alf reached for his cap and pulled it on. 'I'll be off, then,' he said. 'When he wakes up, tell him he owes me a shilling.'

A brief moment of laughter broke the tension, and with a short tip of his cap, Alf left us, a family that knew nothing except a life underground and the cold, hard shadow of the mountain.

'I'm so very sorry,' said Piotr, taking my mother's hand. 'I heard when I came from seeing Captain Willis. I went to find Bethan and one of the adjutants told me what had happened. If there's anything I can do …'

'Thank you,' said Mam, patting his hand absent-mindedly. 'Bethan, if anyone wants tea, can you get a brew on? I should go see Mrs Reece. Pay my respects.'

I'd never seen her look so tired. She was the hearth of our family, forever burning. Yet now, her strength diminished, she had something tiny about her, fragile. I watched her go and instinctively shot a glance towards Father's empty chair. The fire had gone out and Bethan, still in her uniform, was taking a shovel to the clinkers.

'Lend a hand, Ant,' she said. 'Fetch me in a bucket. Does everyone want tea?'

'I'll warm the pot,' said Piotr, walking towards the kitchen.

Alwyn settled himself on to the sofa, wincing as he sat. He took his cap off and threw it in my direction. 'Hang that up for us,' he mumbled. He leant his head backwards and let out a heavy sigh. 'Any more news, Emrys?'

'Tallyman says three men still down. Haven't heard who yet. Apart from John Reece. Four dead. One to bury.'

Emrys sank heavily into Mam's chair, his head falling into his hands.

'Christ,' said Alwyn, shaking his head. 'What a mess.'

'Come on, Ant,' said Bethan, again. 'I need that bucket.'

Down the hallway, a knock sounded, a familiar rat-a-tat-tat. 'Em?' called out Bopa.

'She's down with Mrs Reece,' called out Bethan, shovelling clinkers into newspaper.

'How's your father?' said Bopa, appearing in the doorway. 'I saw Beryl House, told me he was bad.'

'We don't know yet,' said Alwyn. 'He's been given morphine. It's knocked him out a bit. He hasn't spoken yet.'

Bopa folded her arms and shook her head. 'And they've flooded the mine. Whoever did that may as well have gone down and murdered them. Sacrificing men to save seams. I don't care how much coal burns, one lump isn't worth a man's life. Oh, *diawl*, look at your arm, Alwyn. Painful, is it?'

'Not too bad,' he replied. 'I'll live.'

Bopa gave a small, worried tut and then, looking round the room, frowned. 'Look at me, gabbling on when I could be making myself useful. Tea. That's what's needed. Leave it to me.'

'Ant,' said Bethan, turning to look at me. 'Bucket. Now. And bring some bricks in.'

The coal was stacked in the cellar out the back. Once a month the horse and cart would drop a ton of coal outside every miner's front door, and my mother would pull up all the rugs and mats. Being the youngest, I had to carry the coal through the house, out the back door, down the steps and into the cellar: large lumps used to build a wall, with the smaller bits thrown in front.

I hated going down there when the coal was running low: it was a mucky job, and you had to get right inside, the metallic smell deep into your nostrils. There was no door on the cellar and rats would nest there in the warm. If you caught a rat when it wasn't expecting you, you'd catch a bite, so as I ducked down and in, I took the hand shovel and gave the doorframe a few thumps.

Most of the small bits were gone so I had to take the pick and smash up one of the large slabs. It was always hard work but Father said it was good practice for when I went underground. It felt odd hewing coal in the circumstances, almost like a betrayal. Coal had put Father in hospital. I hated it.

I filled the bucket to its brim and picked up a few bricks to toss on top. On cold nights, they'd be laid around the hearth to heat through and then taken to bed wrapped in old socks. Posh folk had rubber bottles to keep them warm. We didn't.

'Anyway,' Bopa was saying, as I came back in, 'there's going to be a gathering up the chapel tonight at seven. Show respects, like. They've still got the coffins of them Germans up there. And your friends.' She nodded toward Piotr. 'Jones the Bible was saying he thinks the Germans'll be buried up at St

Athan. He doesn't want them in our cemetery. Don't blame him. Dunno what'll happen to the POWs. Do you?'

Piotr shook his head.

'Anyway,' continued Bopa, 'what with everything, we shall have to sit and stare at them. It's a grim old business, innit?'

The chapel was packed. It was tradition, whenever there was a death at the pit, for the village to gather as an act of solidarity. We'd managed to get the tail end of a pew, but with no more seats to be had, people were lined along the walls on either side, spilling out beyond the doors. There were a few Americans, the ones billeted locally, and their presence, though not expected, was nonetheless welcome. I glanced around me. Captain Willis had just arrived and was talking to Dr Mitchell. 'Nice of him to come,' whispered Mam.

Behind the lectern, the coffins of the dead airmen and Polish POWs were lined up. It was unusual to see coffins in the chapel: the Welsh liked to keep their dead at home. Two of the coffins, I noticed, were made from plywood, cheap stuff. Must be the Germans, I thought. Wouldn't want to waste good wood on them. Someone had made some little pennants, half red, half white, and hung them on the other three. I wasn't sure, but I guessed it was something Polish.

The chapel had one slightly battered organ, and playing it fell to an elderly woman, Mrs Onions, permanently hunched, always smelt of lavender and only knew three songs: 'Abide with Me', 'How Great Thou Art' and the Welsh national anthem. I don't think I'd ever heard her play anything else, even at Christmas. She was a notoriously slow player and every

Sunday, Emrys would joke she needed winding up, but that evening, as she played, there was no hilarity. The mood was sombre, sad and broken.

Jones the Bible was in serious mood: jowly, intense, burning with fire and brimstone. His jet-black suit ironed to precision, every button creaking at the seams. As the chapel filled, Mrs Onions played 'Abide With Me' as slowly as she possibly could. It added to the air of gloom. I looked about me. I'd never seen people looking more miserable.

Jones the Bible had entered through the rear door of the chapel and nodded to Mrs Onions to wind things up. Taking his cue, she delivered one last, elongated chord and then concertinaed herself into her usual hunched ball, hands on lap, ready to go again when required.

'We are gathered here,' the minister began, in that booming voice of his, 'under the saddest of circumstances. Only last week, we dealt with a tragedy above us' – he gestured towards the coffins behind him – 'and now, a tragedy below. One man, John Reece, taken trying to save others, and three other men unaccounted for, assumed dead,' he continued. 'Gareth Owen, Geraint Boyle and William Gayle, lives taken at the coalface. Our way of life, the price of coal, paid for in blood. Day-to-day comforts cruelly ripped away. The mountain makes fresh widows. Graves may take them, but never our memories. Long scars left behind. Deep in our hearts, we will remember them.'

He bowed his head and everyone around me instinctively followed suit.

'Where is the other coffin?' a voice asked from the back of the hall. Everyone turned round. It was Captain Willis, his face urgent. 'I'm sorry to have to do this, but this is important. There are five coffins. There should be six. Piotr.' He looked over towards us. 'You told me there were seven of you.'

Piotr shot a glance upwards, his forehead compressing into a frown. He shot a look in my direction, then back towards the coffins. His face contorted, as if trying to work out something impossible. Piotr glanced at me again. I could feel the tension.

A ripple of disapproval filled the hall.

'Sir, we are at prayer,' said Jones the Bible, his face reddening. 'Please. Sit down. This is neither the time nor the place. There were five bodies. And there are five coffins.'

'But Piotr told me there were seven of them in the plane.' Captain Willis' voice became more insistent. 'Captain Skarbowitz, please.'

'The Captain is right. There were seven of us,' he said, his voice slow and measured. 'I survived. There should be six bodies and six coffins.'

'We saw five bodies!' yelled Ade, standing up over to my left. 'We saw 'em. Three in Polish uniforms. Two in German!'

Piotr turned pale. 'There were three Germans. Three.'

'Oh, my God,' muttered my mother, clutching her face. 'There's a German up our mountain.'

CHAPTER THIRTEEN

It was chaos. All around me people were on their feet, shouting, gesturing, an air of panic and confusion adding to the dark and deathly shadow already hanging over us. My chest was pounding, and under the quick and leaping beat, a thin trail of excitement began to burn. The war was here, our own appointment with fear. Another stab of guilt: I liked it.

'Home Guard!' yelled Captain Pugh, standing up on a pew. 'Get home and get your uniforms on. If there's a German up our mountain, we're going to find him!'

'I'll run and get the rifle!' shouted Emrys, fired up.

'You've only got five bullets,' cried Ade. 'What if he's got a proper gun, like the Americans?'

'Stay where you are, Emrys,' said Alwyn, pulling him back. 'We need to think this through. This is going to take more than broomsticks.'

'Let us do it!' said Robert, gesturing towards himself and a few other Americans. 'We're trained for combat. We're properly armed. It's the least we can do after all your kindnesses.'

There were murmurs of agreement.

'Yes!' shouted Jones the Bible. 'The Americans know what they're doing. We've lost enough men. Let's not lose another to foolhardy notions of bravery!'

'But they don't know the mountain!' shouted Emrys, his face reddening. 'Not like we do. They won't know where to look, where someone might hide. We know that mountain like our own skin.'

'It's been over a week,' said Hughes the Grocer, stepping forward. 'Who's to say the fella is even still up there? If a German fell out of that plane and survived, he's either injured and most probably dead anyway, or he's long gone. And besides, he's not going to wander down into the village and ask for a cup of sugar. It's too late. Let's not risk a single man. We'll find him dead come winter. Mark my words!'

'But what if he's not dead?' yelled Bopa. 'What if he does come down into the village? What then? Do we want to wait and let our enemy pick us off? Or do we go up there and flush him out?'

'This is our village!' cried Emrys. 'Our home. It's up to us to defend it. Since when have Welsh men depended on strangers to keep their women and children safe?'

Murmurs of discontent rumbled through the chapel. He was right.

'Treherbert is full of strangers, but this falls to us. This is our responsibility.'

Yells of agreement rang around the chapel. Men were rallying, patriotic, proud, as if, suddenly, there was a focus for their collective frustration.

'Please!' said Dr Mitchell, holding both arms in the air. 'There's really no need for anyone from the village to …'

'With the greatest respect, Doctor,' shouted Emrys, 'there's every need. Now, who's with me?'

A cheer went up.

'I can fetch some pitchforks!' shouted Old Morris. 'There's some up the salvage!'

Hughes the Grocer ran a hand down his face. 'Listen to yourself, man! Have you all lost your minds? Let's all run up the mountain in the dark with pitchforks chasing the monster? We're not in bloody *Frankenstein*!'

Gwennie Morgan, who was sitting on the front row, stood up. She was breathing erratically and fanning herself with a hymn sheet. 'All I know is, there's a German up that mountain who is going to come down, at night, and murder us. Murder us in our sleep …' Her eyes rolled up and she crumpled downwards.

'Oh, *diawl*,' said Bopa, pushing her way towards her. 'She's fainted. Get some water from the font. Pass it up! Margaret! There's a cup b'there.'

I looked around me. Everywhere was uncontrolled and shapeless noise. People were arguing, their faces contorted. Over by the far wall, I saw Miss Evans, arms crossed, standing beneath a large wooden cross. Unfolding her arms, she took the collection plate and banged it against the wall.

Everybody stopped.

'One man!' she shouted. 'One man against us. Look around you! We're two hundred strong, even more with the Americans. One man cannot divide this village. One man is no greater part than we are together. He is on his own, he doesn't know where he is, he doesn't know how to get around and he certainly doesn't know how to get home. If anyone is going to be frightened, it's him. We shall not let him bother us.'

'There is a bloody German up our moutain!' cried Captain Pugh, throwing his arms into the air. 'He's not a bloody rambler that's got lost. A bloody German. And a German, I might add, who may well be here deliberately? A plane crash days before the Americans arrive? Don't tell me that's a coincidence?'

There were murmurs of agreement.

'Why did the plane crash?' shouted back Miss Evans, gesturing towards Piotr. 'Because the Polish took control of the plane. They were trying to escape. Do you really think if the Germans were planning something they'd come to Treherbert? Nothing ever happens here!'

'There is stuff happening here now,' shouted Ade, gesturing towards the Americans. 'The valleys are full of stuff happening.'

'And it still doesn't mean we shouldn't bloody kill him!' shouted Emrys. 'Germans are why we were digging that mountain so fast and hard. Germans is why the pit owners were cutting corners. Germans is why there's four of our neighbours dead.'

'He's right! We should find him and kill him!' shouted Old Morris.

Jones the Bible raised his hands. 'Let's not be hasty!' he cried out. "Thou shalt not kill!" The word of God is clear.'

'Sod God!' yelled Emrys, his face flushed with rage. 'My father is lying in a bloody tent fighting for his life. If there's a

German up our mountain, I'm going to find him and skin him like a rabbit. Now, who's with me?'

A cheer went up. I looked towards Mam and for the first time in my life, I saw hate in my mother's eyes.

'Kill him, Emrys,' she said, her teeth gritted. 'Get up that mountain and kill him.'

There was no stopping them. They were fired up, fury coursing through them. Long, brooding resentments finally allowed to spill free. If they could find this German, justice would be done. The ignominy of being left behind, forced down the pit, the cold, flaccid handshake of the coward – all these things would be wiped clean, forgotten, if they could spill blood on our mountain, a sacrifice for us all.

Emrys jumped up onto a pew. 'We'll need lanterns!' he yelled. 'Those who are coming, bring your Davy lamps! Ant, get the rifle from the outtie! Robert! Go tell your officers!'

'What do I tell them?' he shouted up.

'That we're going to find a German!'

Another cheer went up; the rabble was rousing. There was an air of collective hostility. It felt dangerous and exciting. 'Can I go, Mam?' I said. 'I want to.'

She shook her head. 'No, Ant,' she answered. 'This isn't for boys. Let the lads get it done.'

'We'll head up Pen Pych,' yelled Emrys, his chest thrust forward. 'Towards the crash site. Then fan down. Chances are he was hurt, like Piotr. If he's wounded, he'll be hiding. Let's flush him out.'

Piotr stepped forward. 'I can come with you,' he said, looking upwards. 'I can speak German. It might be useful.'

'We're not planning on speaking to him,' said Emrys, darkly, jumping down. 'Besides, your ankle's still bad. You'll slow us down. Sorry, Piotr. You stay with Bethan and Mam.' He patted him firmly on the upper arm then turned back towards the gathering pack. 'Let's get at it!'

I had never known a tenser night. We sat in the parlour, Bethan pacing. Mam darker than I had ever known her, her eyes fixed on the flickering flames in the hearth. I watched her for a while, losing herself in the constant comfort of the burning coal, her head tilted into an upturned palm. It was rare that she ever sat idle. There was always something to be done – mending, unravelling, darning, knitting – but now she was perfectly still, frozen in thought. Piotr sat in Father's chair, quiet, contemplative. There was little to be said.

There were so many places to hide up our mountain. The bracken was thick at this time of year. He could lie under it, this enemy of ours. Lie still and have a man pass right by him. Only the red kite would spot him under that. She'd find him, flush him out, tear his flesh. I thought about what Emrys would do if they found him. I thought of the skinned rabbits that had sat on our sink. I thought of the burnt flesh from the crash. I thought of a dead German being brought down the mountain like the carcass of a sheep.

I couldn't settle so I went to find Piotr, who by now was standing on the back step. He was smoking, one hand in pocket, and staring up into the night sky. I sat down and let my chin fall into my hands. 'Almost full moon,' he said, sensing my presence. 'When I was captured, I would stare up at moon and wonder if anyone I cared for was looking at it too. If you ever leave this valley,' he continued, sitting down on the step next to me, 'you can look at moon wherever you go and remember how it casts light across your mountain, or think of your mother, sitting here, as we are, gazing up. It can be comfort, knowing that however far apart you are, you can always look at same thing.'

I looked up. The moon was bright, its top half bleeding into the shadows. 'Do you think your mother is looking up at the moon right now? Like we are?'

Piotr shrugged. 'I don't even know if my mother is still alive. I've had no reply to that letter. Still. It may take time to reach her.' He took another, deep drag on his cigarette, the paper crackling as the tobacco burned down. 'Tell me,' he added, after a short silence, 'can you navigate by stars? Do you know how to do it?'

I shook my head. Piotr turned to me, his face filled with surprise. 'How can this be?' he asked. 'Mountain boy like you?'

'I don't know,' I said. 'I know some of the constellations. Like that one, the one that looks like a saucepan. That's The Plough.'

'Then you do know! Follow line down through constellation to lowest star. Wherever that is pointing is true north. Once you know that, you can never be lost again. What other stars do you know, Anthony?'

'Orion,' I said, pointing towards three bright stars in a row.

'Do you know story of Orion?'

'No,' I replied. 'Apart from he needs a belt.'

Piotr laughed. 'He was a great hunter, Anthony. A giant hunter who could walk the seas and carry men on his shoulders. But he had insatiable appetite for killing. He declared he would kill every creature on earth and for this, the goddess Gaia sent scorpion to kill him. And when he was dead, Zeus sent him to the stars to be remembered for all time. It's why you will never see the constellations of Orion and Scorpio in same sky. Enemies for all eternity.'

'Like us and the Germans,' I said.

Piotr took a last drag on his cigarette and threw the stub out into the garden.

'And what about his belt?' I asked. 'Did Zeus give him that?'

'No,' answered Piotr, shooting me a wink, 'his mother did. To keep his trousers up. Come, let's go back in. Take the ladies' minds off things. Perhaps we can play cards? Do you have pack?' He stood and dusted off the seat of his trousers.

'I think Mam's got some somewhere. We played Beggar My Neighbour one Christmas.'

'Beggar my neighbour? I don't know this game. You can teach me.'

I didn't know how long it was that we waited. We played cards for an hour or so, but I had settled next to Bethan on the sofa and must have drifted off into a sudden and deep sleep. Perhaps it was one hour, maybe three, the steady, thick tick of the clock on the mantelpiece marking the time, but I was jolted awake by the slam of a door. I opened an eye, momentarily confused as to where I was, to see Alwyn standing above me.

'Did you find him?' said Bethan, her hands gripped into a tight knot.

Alwyn shook his head. 'Got too dark. Cloud came over so we lost the moon. Emrys thought he saw something, let a shot go. But it was a sheep.'

'He's killed a sheep?' said Mam.

'No,' replied Alwyn, putting his Davy lamp down by the hearth. 'He missed.'

'Where is he?' asked Piotr, standing up to offer Alwyn Father's chair.

'Right behind me. Alf's with him. He's got an idea for going out again once it's light. Spreading out, like. That way we can cover more ground.' He melted into the armchair, his head flopping backwards. He gave a wince.

'You all right?' asked Piotr.

'Arm hurts a bit,' said Alwyn, gesturing towards his cast. 'It's not too bad, mind. Just tired. Christ, it's been a long day.'

He rubbed at his forehead with the tips of his fingers. I pushed myself up and swung my legs down onto the floor.

'What a night,' said Emrys, appearing in the doorway. He was holding the rifle and I could just smell the burnt residue of cordite. 'Thought I had him. It was a bloody sheep. I wouldn't mind but I've only got five bullets. I've only got four now. If you don't mind, Mam, I'll keep the rifle in the house for now. I don't want to leave it in the outtie. Just in case, like.'

He rested the rifle against the dresser and, reaching into his pocket, took out the four remaining bullets and tipped them into a cup on the dresser.

'Alf thinks we should head out in groups tomorrow. Captain Pugh's going to speak to the Americans. Teaming up, like. We know the terrain. They've got the firepower. The bracken's impossible. They've got flamethrowers. If needs be, we can burn him out.'

'Do you think there's school tomorrow, Mam?' I asked, drawing the back of my hand across my eyes.

She shook her head. 'No. Not now. Nobody'll want anyone far from sight. You get off up to bed, Ant,' she said, pushing herself up from her chair. 'We all should.'

Piotr picked up the fireguard and placed it in front of the hearth. 'Tomorrow I'll see Arthur Pryce. I might be able to give description. Might help catch the right fellow?'

'We'll catch him, no matter what,' added Alwyn, unbuttoning his jacket. 'German in Treherbert? He's got no chance.'

'Oh, if he's up that mountain,' scowled Emrys, turning to the doorway, 'he's a dead man. Of that be in no doubt.'

We all stood, a dead and heavy quiet sinking into the room. There was nothing more to be said. The manhunt was on.

Everyone was on high alert. Members of the Home Guard had gone door-to-door: all strangers were to be reported, however innocent. Suspicion was the order of the day. Better to be distrustful than for an enemy to slip through our fingers.

It was alien to us, this sense of unease. We were used to the oddities and sadness thrown up by our mountain, but to teach ourselves not to trust was a new and painful thing. We lived in a community with no locks, no forbidden spots. We lived by a set of rules, our own moral code, and the shame of transgression was enough to keep us on the straight and narrow. Bad things happen when you do something wrong. It was hardwired into us.

Mam was right, there was to be no more school until the German had been found. Finally, we were part of the war: there was a man on the run and we were going to find him.

'I reckon he'll be hanging round our den,' said Ade, splitting a long grass blade down its length. 'Think about it. There's tuck up there. And the radio's gone missing. None of us have got it, have we?'

We all shook our heads.

'We should tell someone 'bout that,' said Fez, kicking at a clinker by his foot. 'If he's got that radio, and you got it working, Ant, then he can send messages, like. Secret spy messages.'

'What do you reckon he's spying on?' said Ade, making a knot at the base of the twain blade. 'Gotta be the Americans, innit?'

Bozo nodded. 'Everyone's reckoning he's still up the mountain. But if he's spying, he's down here, innit? He could be in an outhouse. Or in the sheep dip sheds. They're not used till September. Nobody goes near 'em when they're empty. He'd have shelter, be near town, be able to creep about at night, like.'

'Yeah,' said Ade, his eyes widening. 'We should go check 'em out. Imagine if we find him first!'

'But he might have a gun. He might kill us!' said Bozo, his voice high and anxious.

'We've got a gun, remember,' said Ade, patting his shorts.

'And no bullets,' said Fez. 'They disappeared, 'n' all.'

I thought about saying something, telling them that Piotr had taken them, but decided against it. He had done it for our safety and to snitch on him felt like a betrayal.

''Ere, Ant,' said Ade, flicking me with the end of his finger. 'Your Emrys has got bullets, innit?'

'He's only got four. Used one last night. He put 'em in a cup on Mam's dresser. But that's all he's got. He'll never let us have any.'

Ade carried on weaving the long grass blades together. 'Got to get us some bullets. For safety, like. If we find him, we can't take him down with a Chinese burn, can we?'

'We should make a list,' said Fez, reaching into his pocket for a scrap of paper and a pencil. 'To catch a German, we have to think like a German. If we were lost here and wanted to stay hidden, where would we go?'

'I'd get on a bus to Cardiff,' said Ade. 'Nobody cares in a city. You can walk about right in front of people. They don't notice you.'

'Right under their noses,' said Fez. 'You couldn't do that in Treherbert, mind. Everyone knows everyone. Strangers stick out like a sore thumb. We need to think about all the buildings he could be in.'

'He might not be indoors,' I said. 'The weather's been good. It's not even rained. He could still be up the mountain. We know he is. He took the radio.'

'We should check out the den, see if anything else is gone. Maybe lay a trap. Leave some food. See if he takes it, like. That way we'll know. Plan?' said Ade, sticking his fist out.

'Plan,' we all replied, and down all our fists went, bumping in agreement.

*

Someone had been there. Of that there was no doubt. The den had a ransacked feel to it, as if a dog had gone on the rampage. Boxes were overturned, the bench was pushed onto its side, and our precious mountain treasure was scattered across the floor. 'Maps are gone,' I said, after a quick cursory check. 'Not our atlas, though. Just the maps we took out the plane.'

'That's curious,' said Bozo, kneeling down to pick up a plank of wood. 'The radio's back. Look.'

He heaved it onto an upside-down box and as he opened it, we gathered round. 'Looks like someone's had a right old hack at it,' he said, fingering some deep grooves in its side.

'Does it still work?' asked Ade. 'Give it a go.'

'You turn it on there,' I said, pointing towards a switch on the bottom right of the unit. 'Piotr showed me.'

'Stick it on, then,' said Ade, holding on to his knees with his hands. 'Eh, what if it's tuned in to the last person he was talking to? We might turn it on and hear Hitler!'

'Come on, Ant,' said Fez, nudging me. 'He's right. Might give us a clue, like.'

I picked up the headphones and slipped them over my head. 'Turn that,' I said, nodding towards a dial on the bottom left of the panel.

Bozo twisted it and a sudden crackle made me jump. 'Down a bit,' I said. 'It's too loud.'

Bozo turned the dial and the crackle evened out into a low hum. It was like finding yourself standing in a large, empty barn. There was no noticeable sound, but the silence had its own music.

'Can you hear anyone?' said Ade, leaning in.

'Nah.'

'Have you tried tapping that?' said Fez, gesturing towards a small metal armature. 'P'raps you need to tell 'em you're here, like.'

I let my finger rest on the small round button that sat at the end of the arm. I tapped it down. A sound. I tapped it again. Another one.

'I can hear something,' I said. 'But I think it's me tapping.'

'Of course it's you tapping, you idiot,' said Fez. 'That's for Morse code, innit? Tap it again.'

I made a few more random taps and waited. Still nothing. I shook my head. 'Nope,' I said. 'There's no one there ... Wait ... Hang on ... there's something.'

Sudden, organised, shape-shifting beeps came through: long, short, swift, slow, breaks, then again. Someone was trying to communicate with me.

'Can you hear that?' I said, my mouth agape.

Ade ripped the headphones from my ears and listened. 'Christ, man,' he said, his voice thrilling with excitement. 'You're talking to Hitler. To actual bloody Hitler.'

He dropped the headphone to his mouth and shouted into it. 'Up yours, Hitler! Up yours!'

'Don't be daft, man,' said Fez, taking the headphones to listen. 'He can't hear you. Tap back again, Ant.'

I tapped three times on the armature. Another series of beeps returned. Then nothing.

We all looked at each other, pondering our next move. And then they came again, a steady stream of dots and dashes, but as they continued, it was like an infection seeping, or standing too close to a fire. The noise felt dangerous, toxic.

'Turn it off,' I said, reaching for the switch. 'We don't know what we're doing. We might be giving them clues. I don't like it.'

I turned the radio off and sat back on my haunches, gripping my knees. The others looked at me. Ade was frowning. 'Let's not tell anyone about this,' he said, eyeing each of us in turn. 'If he's brought this back here, it's for a reason. Look at the place. He's coming here. He's looking for something. What stuff from the plane have we got stashed at home? P'raps we've got something he needs? And if we play clever, like, we can catch this fella in the act. We'll be heroes.'

'We can't not tell, man,' said Fez. 'This might be dead important, like. A radio that Germans speak through!'

'We can tell 'em after we've caught him. This is bloodsies, Fez. Proper bloodsies.' He reached into his pocket and pulled out his small penknife. 'Hands out,' he said, flicking the blade open.

We all held out one hand. Bloodsies was a promise that could never be broken. A do-or-die pledge. If you broke bloodsies, you were the very worst sort, a traitor, someone who would never be trusted again. It was death itself.

Ade quickly scratched each of our thumbs and, as the blood came, we placed our hands together, clasped tight so the blood came fast. I watched the thick velvet stream running down towards my wrist. 'Never tell,' said Ade.

'Never tell,' we replied.

Arthur Pryce was at sixes and sevens. In his ten years as the police officer in charge of Treherbert, he had never been this busy or confused. His pocket book, which I think I'd previously seen him remove only once, was now full, and the problem was, he didn't have another one.

'They come from Cardiff, see,' he said, as he tried to find a page he hadn't had to write on. 'So I'm waiting on a delivery.'

'Do you think you can remember what I say without writing it down?' asked Piotr, eyebrows raised in an attempt to be helpful.

A strange, baffled look wafted over Arthur Pryce's face. 'No,' he said, as if the very thought was utterly incomprehensible.

Arthur Pryce wasn't married. He didn't want to be, neither. Instead, he lived at home with his mother, Mrs Pryce, who, in the absence of a long-dead husband and a daughter who'd run off with a man in murky circumstances, was only too happy to devote her every waking hour to her son in uniform. 'A policeman,' she would say, 'commands respect. He's a figure of authority.' And then she would wipe something off Arthur's face with a wet hanky, because, after all, he was still her son.

'You haven't got anything I could use for official purposes, have you?' said Arthur, casting a hopeful glance at my mother. 'I have to write it down, see. To be proper.'

My mother gave a small, irritated sigh and stared off towards the kitchen. 'Well, you can't have Davey's Basildon Bond. That's for emergencies.'

'But it is an emergency,' complained Arthur. 'I've got no notebook.'

'It's Basildon Bond, Arthur,' said my mother, forcibly. 'That's for special emergencies. This isn't a special emergency. It's an unfortunate oversight. The two are very different.

I've got an old envelope somewhere. You'll have to make do with that.'

Arthur went to protest but there was little point. Men of Treherbert knew better than to ever pick a fight with a mam, so instead he sat, fingering the end of his pencil, looking forlorn and beaten.

'There you go,' said Mam, coming back from the kitchen and handing him a used envelope. 'You can write on the back of that.'

'Not very big, is it?' said Arthur, giving it a cursory examination.

'Then write in small letters,' said Mam, folding her arms.

'Any chance of a cuppa?' said Arthur. 'I haven't stopped all morning.'

'No,' said Mam, unrelenting. 'There isn't. Now hurry up and get this writing done, then I can be off to Pontypridd. Some of us have sick husbands to be visiting.'

Arthur blinked. Of all the men I knew in Treherbert, he was probably the least qualified to become a policeman, but Father often said Arthur's weakness was his greatest strength: everyone felt so sorry for him, nobody ever wanted to break the law.

'Right, then,' said Arthur, taking his pencil and licking the end of it. He had flattened out the crumpled envelope as best he could and rested it on the top of his thigh. 'Can you, Captain Skarbowitz, describe what the escaped German looks like?'

'I'm going to have to guess,' said Piotr, clearing his throat. 'Because I'm not quite sure which one it was. Ant tells me two of Germans he saw dead had severe burns to faces, so I don't think seeing bodies would help me much. Actually' – he stopped and cast a look in my direction – 'can you remember ranks of dead Germans?'

I was sitting by the wireless, staring up at the dresser. I'd been thinking about the cup of bullets and how I might take one, maybe two. Problem was, there was no way I could do that without getting a clouting from Emrys. It was too risky.

I crunched my face into a look of concentration. I'd only looked at the bodies fleetingly, but images flashed back to me: fallen photos, a hand raised in fear, blood congealed around nostrils. I clamped my eyes tight shut and tried to rewind my memories. Standing there, staring down, what did I see? The boots, the grey trousers, moving up, the tunic, half-open. Look to the sleeves, Ant. What was there?

'Stripes, I think. Three on one. Two on the other.'

Piotr nodded. 'Did you see flight jacket? Heavier thing. Made of leather?'

I shook my head.

'Then it may be navigator who escaped. He was wearing one. The others joked about it. Told him he always felt cold. They weren't intending to fly us far, you see. They didn't need full flight gear. And they weren't expecting to be flying into enemy territory.'

'Navigator?' repeated Arthur, trying to write that down. 'He'll know his way round maps, then. Which makes him dangerous.'

I opened my mouth to tell them about the maps that had gone missing from our den, but a sharp sting from the cut on my thumb held me back. I looked down. The wound had opened, a small trickle of blood weeping towards my knuckle. I lifted my thumb to my mouth and licked it. Never tell.

'He was average height, little on thin side,' said Piotr, brushing some lint from the knee of his trousers. 'Had hungry look about him. I think his nose may have been broken. It had a bend in it, here.' He tapped the bridge of his nose with a forefinger. 'Dark hair. Brown rather than black. Starting to thin. He had it greased down with something I remember being quite fragrant. It's funny how pleasant smells stand out when you're used to nothing but dirt.'

I remembered the sweet, deep smell of the cap I had found. How peculiar, I thought, to have the hat of a man we were hunting. If we had a bloodhound, I would press his snout into it. But we didn't have a bloodhound. We just had Arthur Pryce.

'Small, tight eyes, squinted as if he needed glasses. Drawn tight. Slightly hooded, haunted look about them. And I remember colour. They were black, lifeless. The sort of eyes you would never want to stare into to find love.'

He stopped and glanced towards Arthur.

'You probably don't need to write that bit down. I'm worried you're going to run out of envelope.'

'Yes,' said Arthur, stopping mid-sentence. 'I think I'll just write "small black eyes" and leave it at that.'

Piotr nodded. 'He had an unremarkable mouth, lower lip fuller than the upper. And he was clean-shaven. Having said that, few weeks up mountain may mean he's grown a beard. Actually, something I remember quite clearly now. He had a finger missing. On his right hand. The middle finger ended at first joint.'

Arthur looked up, his face brightening. 'That's an excellent detail,' he said, beaming. 'I'll definitely write that down.'

'I don't know if he had any other distinguishing features. To be honest, he was quite ordinary looking. A normal fellow. If it wasn't for the finger, I might not recognise him if I passed him in street.'

Arthur gave a solemn nod, sat back in his chair and sucked the end of his pencil. 'We'll recognise him if he's still in his uniform, mind. Although I expect he'll be quick to get out of that.'

'If I was him,' Piotr said, 'I'd lay low during daylight then go down into town at night. He'll need clothes and food. Whether he stays round here will depend on what he intends. If I wanted to get home, I'd surrender. His war is over. If he's here to gather intelligence, then he needs to stick to shadows.'

'He'll be killed before he can surrender,' I said, running my hand down into my wellington to deal with an itch. 'At least he will if Emrys and the lads get to him first.'

'Yes,' said Piotr, his voice falling. 'I expect he will.'

Mam reappeared in the doorway with her hair tied up tight and her coat on. She reached for her handbag and hooked it into the crook of her elbow. 'There's some cawl in the pot for your lunch, Anthony,' she said. 'Piotr too. But don't have all of it. The lads will want some when they're down from the mountain. I'm going to catch the bus to Pontypridd and see Father. I don't want you up that mountain, Ant, do you hear? I've told Bopa to keep an eye on you. Until that German's found, you're to stay in Scott Street. Promise me, Ant?'

I didn't say anything. I knew full well it was a promise I couldn't keep.

Ade had gathered us in the dark corner of a culvert beyond the baker's. The smell of bread baking – crisp, yeasty, warm, familiar – played the backdrop to something dangerous and unknown. Each of us had brought our own personal booty from the plane crash.

'It can't be the cap,' said Fez, nudging his head towards it, 'there's nothing important about a cap. If you were a spy, why would you care about a cap? You wouldn't. What else you got, Ant?'

'Couple of photos. Postcard. Magazine. This,' I said, holding out a thin tubular piece of metal. It had a tiny hook at the end of it.

'What is it?' said Ade, taking it from me to have a better look.

'Dunno,' I said. 'P'raps it's like a screwdriver, or something? Mechanical?'

'Let's have a look,' said Bozo, crowding closer. Ade handed the silver tube to him and he held it up towards the sun. 'Why's it got a hook?' he mumbled. 'What do you need hooks for?'

'Catching fish?' said Fez, staring upwards. 'Picking things up? Attaching something?'

'Try hooking it on something,' said Ade, looking around the culvert. 'There. Hook it on that line.'

Behind us there was a length of thin rope the baker used for hanging up muslin to dry. Fez reached up and gently placed the tip of the hook behind it. He let go and stepped back and we all stood staring at the small metal object gently swaying in front of us. Ade shrugged. 'Well,' he said, none the wiser, 'it hangs down. Why would you want a bit of metal that hangs down?'

I reached up to retrieve it, twisting the silver tube to the left as I did. The hook caught on the rope and I heard a small, distinct click.

'Did you hear that?' I said, going up on my tiptoes to pull it down. I looked at the hook. It had changed position. 'It's moved round,' I said, touching it lightly with my fingertip. 'What does that mean?'

'Pull it,' said Fez, standing at my shoulder and peering down. 'P'raps it's got something inside it?'

'Secret code, like?' said Ade. 'Go on, Ant.'

Pinching the hook between two fingers, I pulled upwards. There was another quiet click and something appeared from the base of the tube.

'Well,' said Bozo, 'will you look at that?'

I turned the tube upside down to reveal a small, corrugated metal rectangle, fully extended. I pushed the hook back down. It disappeared. I pulled it. It came back out again. 'What is it?' I said, looking to the others.

Fez took it and laid it in the palm of his hand. 'Has to be a tool for something. Special, like.'

'Dunno,' I said, tilting my head. 'It sort of looks like a key. But not one I've ever seen before.'

'Key for what?' said Ade.

I shrugged and stared down at the strange metal object in Fez's hand, and as I did, I was consumed with a feeling of cold and certain dread. No good would come of this. Of that I was absolutely sure.

'Must be something up in the den. Meet after tea. We'll head up there,' said Ade. He held his fist out. 'Bloodsies.'

'Bloodsies,' we replied. The pact sealed.

The news from Pontypridd was not good. Father was still on oxygen, heavily sedated. His breathing had got worse and the fear that pneumonia would set in was fast becoming a reality. All we could hope for was that he would somehow pull through. 'He's a fighter, Mam,' said Emrys, arms folded. 'He's given his whole life to that mountain.'

'That's what I'm worried about,' said Mam, sinking into her chair.

Alwyn was running a wet flannel across the back of his neck at the kitchen sink. They'd been up the mountain all day, sweeping through bracken, checking bogs, but all they'd found was the parachute Piotr had used when he'd leapt from the plane. 'We tore the silk up,' he called out to us from the kitchen. 'I got a bit for Bethan.' He gestured over his shoulder to a neat white heap of material on the parlour dresser. I picked it up, letting it melt through the gaps in my fingers.

'Enough for skirt, at least,' said Piotr, coming up behind me. 'So delicate,' he added, fingering its edge. 'And yet somehow it keeps a man in the air. Where did you find it?'

'About a mile from the crash site,' said Alwyn, reaching for a tea cloth. 'Wind would have taken it further but it was wrapped round some gorse. Mam says you saw Arthur Pryce today? You reckon this German would hand himself in if he wasn't up to no good?'

Piotr gave a small shrug. 'If I landed here by accident,' he said, with a small shake of his head, 'I'd surrender. If I didn't, I wouldn't. He's up to no good. Or he's already dead. That's my guess.'

I let my hand drift to my pocket. The metal tube was sticking into my leg. I wanted to tell my brothers, Mam, Piotr. But it was bloodsies. And that was that. Bad things happen. I wouldn't make that mistake twice. I tightened my fingers around it. The burden was mine.

'Bumped into Alf coming off the mountain,' said Emrys, tapping the end of a newly drawn cigarette against the mantelpiece. 'He's been up the pit. Three months closed, they reckon. Best estimate. Looks like Bethan's the bread winner now. Though I've got my Home Guard wages, mind.'

'Tuppence ha'penny?' said Alwyn, tossing the used tea cloth back towards the sink.

'Better than nothing, innit?' said Emrys, striking a match. 'And nothing is what we'll be bringing in. Till the pit reopens.'

'Hello, hello!' said a voice from the doorway. It was Arthur Pryce and he was smiling.

'A policeman, twice in one day,' said Mam, heaving herself out of her chair. 'If you've come back for that cup of tea, Arthur, then you're going to be sorely disappointed.'

'No tea, ta,' said Arthur. 'It's St Athan. They want you up there, Captain Skarbowitz. I gave them the description I wrote down, but I couldn't quite read my handwriting. So I just said "small black eyes and half a finger". Anyway, they've asked if you can pop up there. You can borrow the van, if you like? I don't need it.'

'They've taken their time getting interested, innit?' said Emrys. 'You'd think with what's kicking off they'd need the practice killing a German.'

'Rumour has it they're going to scramble a few Mosquitoes,' said Arthur, tucking his helmet under his arm. 'See if they can spot him from the air.'

'They'll not spot half a finger from the air, Arthur,' said Mam, rolling her eyes.

'No,' replied Arthur, with a nervous swallow. 'Still. I said I'd ask. Do you know how to get there, Captain Skarbowitz? I can't come with you. My mother's boiled a gammon.'

'I think I'll be fine. I remember way. Unless you want to come with me, Ant?' Piotr glanced over towards me.

A small charge of panic coursed through me. I couldn't go. I had to be up the mountain. I shook my head. To my relief, Piotr didn't protest.

'You can bring Bethan back,' said Mam, lifting her housecoat from the rack of hooks in the hall. 'She'll be glad for the lift.'

Piotr smiled. 'Then that's sorted. I shall take van.'

'Arthur!' sounded another voice from the hallway. We all turned to see Hughes the Grocer. He was panting heavily and had clearly been running. 'Arthur!' he called out again. 'It's Old Morris. He's had some clothes taken from the back of his salvage shop. Reckons it has to be the German.'

'How does he know?' said Alwyn, coming into the parlour, his face urgent.

'Because there's a bit of uniform stuffed behind a crate. Come on,' urged Hughes. 'I'll show you.'

Everyone surged towards the street. That was my cue. I slipped out after them, but instead of following them down Scott Street, I turned up, heading towards the dark of the mountain.

In one pocket I had the strange metal key. In the other I had four bullets, taken from the cup on the dresser.

We all needed to feel safe.

CHAPTER FOURTEEN

'Put the bullets in there,' said Fez, as Ade cocked open the pistol.

'Do they even fit?' said Bozo, frowning.

'Hang on,' said Ade, with a pout, his small fingers fumbling. 'It's fiddly.'

I was feeling anxious. 'Don't shoot unless you have to,' I said. If Emrys found out I'd taken those bullets, I was for it. 'When you're done, you have to give 'em back.'

'Stop frettin', man,' said Ade. 'If I have to shoot, it means we've got the German, and if we've got the German, we'll be bloody heroes. Nobody'll have our guts for a few bullets then, will they?'

Fez and Bozo murmured in agreement.

Ade tried to shut the pistol, but it was no good. The bullets didn't fit. 'Christ, man,' he grumbled. 'Wrong size, innit? We can't go without a gun. Ant, run back to yours and get Emrys' rifle.'

I looked at him, startled. 'I can't do that. Don't be daft.'

'It's fine,' said Ade, tucking the pistol back into the top of his trousers. 'He'll not notice, no how,' said Ade. 'We'll be up and back with the German before he even blinks an eye. Get on with it, man.'

I stood, frozen. This felt deeper in than I wanted to be. Borrowing bullets was one thing, taking the rifle was another.

'I can't,' I said, my voice quiet and pleading.

'If you don't, I will,' said Ade, his eyes insistent. 'Come on, Ant. It's no fuss.'

'Yeah.' Fez nodded. 'It's no fuss, man.'

Emrys had left the rifle leaning up against the dresser. The house was quiet apart from the steady, dull beat of the clock on the parlour mantelpiece. Something in the kitchen was quietly bubbling. 'Mam?' I called out.

Nothing.

I stood in the doorway into the parlour and stared at the rifle. It was only wood and metal, nothing, really, and yet it was everything. Father wouldn't want me doing this, of that I had no doubt, but this danger was something I felt incapable of turning from. I thought of Piotr. He'd take it and wouldn't think twice: a proper man who would risk all to protect his own. Somewhere, deep inside me, there was a knot of something brave. Get on with it, Anthony. Take the rifle.

I walked silently towards the dresser and placed my hand around its barrel.

There was a sudden noise from the back kitchen. I looked across to the doorway, frozen.

'Is that you, Ant?' I heard my mother call, and I was gone, running out of the house and towards the tinder track, the rifle heavy in my hands.

Dusk was rolling towards us from the hills. The air had turned cold and over a far mountain, bruised clouds were gathering. 'Rain's coming,' said Bozo, wind blowing through his hair.

'Good,' said Ade, throwing the loaded rifle over his shoulder. 'If he's out, he'll need to find shelter. Bracken won't save him from the wet.'

'Hughes the Grocer reckons he's been at the back of the salvage shop,' I said, pointing back down towards the tinder path. It wasn't too late to stop all this. An uneasy ache was settling between my ribs. 'That means he's in the village. P'raps we should look round there first, like?'

'Nah,' said Ade, picking up a small flat stone by his foot. 'If that thing is a key, we gotta see what it fits, innit? If he needs it, it's important, like. He'll not stop.'

A crow landed on a low branch overhanging the brook ahead of us. Ade put his weight onto his back foot and flung the stone at it. He missed, but only just, and the crow, with a loud caw, flapped off up the mountain. 'Right, then,' he said, rubbing his nose with the back of his hand. 'Let's get at it.'

A thin mist of rain, light but penetrating, had started to fall, making the jumper I was wearing heavy and damp. Bozo's spectacles kept misting over and every now and then he'd stop to wipe his one unplastered lens clean. There was little chatter. We wanted to keep quiet so we could be alert to every overturned stone, every crunch of bracken. I looked up for the red kite but she was nowhere to be seen. Dark clouds were rolling harder. She knew to stay out of it.

It took us longer to get to the den than usual. Ade insisted on checking every nook and cranny along the way. 'Tracks,' he told us, tapping the ground with a stick. 'We need to keep a look out for tracks.'

None of us knew how to identify a lost German's tracks but occasionally, one of us would point at a broken twig, a flattened patch of bracken, and we'd gather round it making suitable noises. But we didn't know what we were doing and even though I knew every step of this mountain, I had never felt more lost. In the distance, there was a grumble of thunder. The ache in my chest intensified.

The den was as we had left it. If the German had been there before, he certainly hadn't been there again today. Ade flipped open the old biscuit tin at the back. 'Sarnie's still there,' he said, his voice filled with disappointment. 'Mind you, he probably knows we're on to him. Taking the food would be too obvious, like. He's probably watching us right now.'

We all turned and scanned the darkening horizon. Shadows shifted at this time of night and stones became strangers. I wondered if he was out there, standing, looking at us, wondering what to do, thinking about what was in my pocket, thinking how he could take it. The small metal tube in my pocket felt like a lead weight. I didn't want the responsibility. If he came, I'd give it up gladly.

'Pass me that key thing, Ant,' said Ade, holding his hand out. 'Let's have a look at it again.'

I reached into my pocket and pulled it out, its brightness dulled in the drizzle. Ade lifted it from my upturned palm, regarding it in the same way Father sometimes looked into the back of his opened fob watch: his face full of wonder and curiosity. I stared at him and realised that Ade had a face I could never imagine old. Not like Bozo. Mam said Bozo had the face of a fifty-year-old man, ancient before his time, but Ade had something springlike running through him: the boundless energy, the sense that nothing was impossible.

'It has to be a key,' he said, pulling on the coiled hook. 'And a secret one at that. If it wasn't secret, like, then it wouldn't have a secret way of turning into one. And if it is secret, then that means that whatever it's meant to open is secret. That's what I think.'

'Yeah,' said Fez, tilting his head, 'but what's it meant to open? That's the point, innit?'

'Has to be something from the plane,' said Ade, turning back towards the pile of plundered items we'd ransacked a week earlier. 'Something with a hole in it.'

'What shape hole?' said Bozo, wiping his glasses again. 'It won't look like a normal keyhole, will it? That's not a normal key.'

'Dunno,' said Ade, squinting again at the small, corrugated rectangle. 'Sort of that shape, innit? Squiggly, like.'

'He had a good go at the radio,' said Bozo, pointing towards it. 'P'raps it's that?'

Ade flipped open the lid of the radio and stared down. 'Can't see anything that looks like a keyhole, funny or otherwise.' He peered closely at the deep gouges in its side. 'Nah,' he added. 'Nothing.'

Behind us, we heard the usual hum of the Mosquito squadrons heading off to who knew where. I turned and stood on the ridge, just making them out through gaps in the thickening clouds. The others, distracted, didn't seem bothered, so I saluted them by myself. It was unlucky not to.

Behind us, there was another deep rumble of thunder. The sky was blackening, the peak of the mountain disappearing into the dark cloak of the storm. The gentle drizzle that had accompanied us was gathering strength, and a thick blanket of rain began to fall. Instinctively, I returned to the shelter of the den. 'Golden sunshine', that's what Mam called Welsh rain. But there was nothing golden about this. It was grey, it was wet and it was ferocious.

'Just our luck,' said Bozo, staring out. 'Coming down in sheets. We're gonna get soaked.'

'If we're soaked, he's soaked,' said Ade. 'There's no such thing as bad weather. Just the wrong clothes.'

Fez turned and looked at him, frowning. 'But we're all in the wrong clothes. 'Part from Ant,' he added, pointing towards my wellingtons.

'I'm not bothered by a bit of wet,' said Ade, peering out into the slashing rain.

'I'm cold,' said Bozo, hugging himself. 'We'll never find him in this.'

'Stop mithering! Look. You two stay here. Keep a look out. Me 'n' Ant'll go over b'there. That way.' Ade pointed off towards a far peak. 'We can climb that ridge. Get a good look down the valley.'

'But it's almost dark, man,' said Fez. 'You'll be lucky to see the hand in front of your face in five minutes.'

'You're like a pair of old women,' said Ade, shaking his head. 'Come on, Ant, you with me?'

I wanted to say no, but the inexplicable tug of fate was calling me. I'd once watched Emrys thrust his hand into a pot he'd been told had a snake in it. He knew he'd be bitten. And he still did it. I pushed myself up from the bench.

'All right,' I said, quietly. 'I'll come.'

Ade took the lead. He was more nimble than I, lighter on his feet, and he scrambled up the hillside with the confidence of a goat. I was less agile, my wellingtons slipping on lichen-covered rocks, and as he climbed, ahead of me, I fell behind, staring down so I could tread a more secure path.

The rain was relentless, thick and bitterly cold. I could taste the last remnants of the pomade on my lips, washed away at last. Of that, at least, I could be thankful. Ade had stopped and was standing on a ridge above me. He had bobbed down into a crouching position, one hand resting on the butt of the rifle that hung down from his back. It was like the war films we had seen at the flicks where soldiers are moving forwards, the constant stop, start, stop, start of combat. We had spent hours on this mountain, playing war, and now here we were, doing it for real.

I was panting. It didn't matter how many times I climbed the mountain, my wellingtons took their toll. 'When's your mam gonna get you proper shoes, like?' said Ade, as I joined him. He nudged his head down towards my boots. 'Man can't get about in them. You're as slow as my nan. Imagine how fast you'll be when you get the right togs.'

I stood still to catch my breath, my eyelashes wet with rain.

'Ant!' shouted Ade. 'Hello? You're away with the fairies, man. Forget the rain. Keep your eyes peeled. We're coming up to the crash site.'

We were below a craggy outcrop and I pressed myself into a crevice for a little shelter. The wind had picked up and the storm was becoming ragged, unpredictable, dangerous. Everywhere, wild shadows flung themselves across the hillside. Everything was movement, chaos, wind whipping the rain sideways. Low clouds were dipping down, a rolling dense mist that wiped out the landscape. I wiped the wet from my eyes. 'I can't see anything, Ade,' I said. 'Fog's come down too thick.'

He joined me in the crevice and leant back against the rock, his face peering upwards into the storm. 'Wind's up, mind,' he said. 'It'll blow over. Look, there's gaps.' He pointed over to a patch of gorse still visible in the distance. 'It's coming and going. I could walk this mountain with my eyes shut. Fog won't stop me.'

I cast a glance sideways at him, seeing his face as bold and untroubled as it ever was. He was fearless, not a scrap of doubt etched into his face. Where had it come from, this certainty, this confidence? I thought of Piotr, alone in a French field, fighting his way towards fallen comrades, no thought of his own safety. This is how heroes are made, I thought. Bravery is simply not being afraid.

But I couldn't feel anything but afraid. I had taken my brother's gun, I was up the mountain when I had been told not to, and I was wet, cold and uncomfortable. I couldn't feel the thrill of the chase like Ade; I didn't want to find the German. I wanted to go home, see Mam and quietly return what I had taken.

The key jabbed into my thigh. The corner of my shorts had snagged on the rock behind me, and now yanked them tight to my skin as I moved. The short, sharp pain sucked me from the dark corridors of my thoughts. I was here and I was with my friend. It would have to be enough.

'What was that?' whispered Ade, pressing back into the rock face. 'Up there. Above us. Did you hear it?'

I shook my head. The wind was howling, bouncing off the boulders, whistling through the gorse. Then, suddenly, there was a small rockfall, leaving shards of flint scattered at our feet. Ade turned sharply and stared at me, wide-eyed. 'Up there,' he mouthed. 'He's up there.'

I could feel my heart pumping, blood throbbing between my ears. I was glued to the wall of the crevice. 'What shall we do?' I whispered, the words coming hard and fast.

Ade put a hand on the edge of the rock and, in one, quick, decisive move, peered round it and looked up. He darted back inside, a cat who's seen his mouse. 'I can see a leg,' he mumbled. 'But it's dark, didn't see his face.'

He silently removed the rifle from his shoulder and brought it round to his chest. Panic coursed through me. 'What you doin'?' I mouthed, frantic. 'Don't be mad, man, it might not even be him!'

'He doesn't know I'm here,' whispered Ade, slipping his finger over the trigger. 'I'll creep up on him. Only shoot once I look him in the face. You stay here. You'll never make it up this crag in them boots. Hold tight. I'll be back in a bit.'

'No!' I cried. 'Ade, wait …'

But he was gone.

I stared wildly at the edge of rock, longing for his face to slip back round it. I went to call out his name but my strength had gone, fear draining me of the ability to make even the slightest sound. I strained to hear, the beating of the rain drowning out everything. All I could catch hold of was the howling of the wind ricocheting off the rocks around me. I had to stand and wait, feeling every drop of blood pumping through me. Faster, faster. Where was he? Pumping. WHERE WAS HE?

A cry.

A shower of broken flints.

A shot.

The rifle skidded on the shale onto the ground in front of me.

Pumping. Pumping.

I gripped the rock behind me.

A thud. I stared. I stared. I stared.

And everything stopped.

I don't know how long I looked at him. All I was aware of was my chest heaving and one black, dead eye staring up at me. That face I knew so well. Frozen for ever.

Somehow I had to get him home.

Shoulder high.

CHAPTER FIFTEEN

I don't know how long I stood, pressed against the wet rock. I remember my breathing being quick and shallow, as if I was drowning. I don't think I blinked for the longest time. I remember watching his fringe dancing in the wind, like fresh grass, and wondering how something that was dead could be so alive. I remember being afraid that the German was still above me and would appear at any moment. Perhaps he'd kill me, too? Perhaps he'd take me, like a rabbit, and twist my neck, quick and sharp? I wished he would.

It was almost dark by the time I moved. The storm was still whirling, the miserable backdrop against which the end of our game would be played out. I took a step forwards, terrified, and glanced upwards into the driving rain. I thought I might see him, this German on our mountain, standing above me, waiting, but there was nothing but accusing skies.

I walked over to Ade's body, limp and sunken into the sodden ground. He was splayed, limbs scattered, so that he almost looked like a swastika. His face was over to one side, his eyes wide open, startled.

'Ade,' I said, hope still beating. 'Ade, get up!'

Dead bodies were grey and old. They had sunken cheeks, their hair was thin, they had a sweet, sickly smell to them, a sort of gentle rotting. Dead bodies weren't supposed to be young, full of mischief, brimful with larks. The order of things was broken. Broken.

I stood over him, staring down, my heart racing. I didn't know what was expected. The rain was seeping down the back of my collar, my eyes stinging from the liquid pomade. I turned and looked back over my shoulder towards the ridge above us. There was a stone that looked like a small tree trunk. Was that the leg that Ade had seen?

I bent down and picked up Ade's hand. It was limp, the fingertips blue. 'Come on, Ade,' I said, the words squeezing out of me. I felt desperate, longing for that staring eye to suddenly wink, for him to jump up, tell me he'd been pulling my leg.

But he didn't do any of these things, and I let go of his hand, watching it fall with a dull thud. And I stood, staring.

And I didn't know what to do.

I would have to remember everything. Every last detail. I would be quizzed on every moment. This was a scene I would have to revisit again and again. The way he had fallen, the shape of him, the small trickle of blood that quietly worked its way down from his nostril. Why we were up there …

I shut my eyes tight and felt into my pocket for the strange metal key that had sent us spiralling towards disaster. I hated it. Perhaps it wasn't a key at all? Perhaps it was just a random lump of metal that had fallen from the air with all the other day-to-day flotsam that rattles round an aircraft?

But I couldn't bear the thought. That it had all been for nothing.

I gripped the key tightly. I would have to tell. Have to tell about the radio, the key, the rifle, Ade's dead body. Father's words rang in my ears: 'It's always best to do what is right, rather than what is popular.'

I bent down and tried to lift Ade, but, lacking the strength, I let his body roll back into the wet grass. The pistol, stuffed so triumphantly into Ade's shorts, fell onto the ground beside him. I stared down at it and found myself wondering if I'd be standing here now if I had given it to Piotr when he'd asked. I picked it up, the wet metal heavy in my hand. I looked back up towards the ridge – still nothing – and quietly tucked it into my waistband.

I had never known sadness like it. The weight of it, thick and heavy in my ribs, like a boulder that would never be shifted. I had never been a crier, but now tears came freely, hot and pathetic, the slightest thing sending me back to that lonely, dark place where it was me, alone, standing in that crevice and staring. I would never be free of it, this scar across my heart.

I would find out later that Ade hadn't died of a gunshot wound. He'd broken his neck falling. Tripped or pushed? I couldn't say. Had I seen the German with my own eyes? No. I hadn't. But somehow, it didn't matter. It was my fault. I'd given him the rifle, the bullets. I'd gone with him, the coward who stood, back against the wall, watching his friend die.

I ran back to the den, rifle in hand, as fast as I was able. This burden was no longer my own, and my priority now was to get Ade home. A blind numbness had set in and I ran, oblivious to everything. All I knew was that I had to tell someone, and as I jumped down off the lip of the ridge above our den and crouched in the wet earth, rain coursing down my face, and looked up to see Fez and Bozo, I knew that the real horror hadn't even begun.

I will always wonder if they somehow knew, had felt it in the air. I remember hearing the words coming out of my mouth, but it was as if someone else was saying them.

'Ade's dead.'

They stood, staring at me, rigid. No doubt wondering, like me, whether this was just a grand lark or whether, if true, just how much trouble we were going to be in. I was fighting the urge to run and run and run and never look back; but knowing that, somehow, we had to take Ade home, kept me standing there, waiting for someone to say something.

'What you talkin' about?' said Fez, quietly, his head tilting slightly.

'Something went wrong,' I mumbled. 'He's up there. I can't carry him.'

'You're mucking with us, man,' said Bozo, his voice anxious. 'Pack it in.'

I shook my head, my eyes red from crying. 'I'm not,' I whispered. 'Please, help me.'

I led them to his body and the three of us stood, wind still howling, mourners at a grave not yet dug. It was so odd seeing the life knocked out of him. I would never again hear him calling my name. Never hear his clatter up our hallway. Never hear his rousing cry.

Bozo started crying. I remember that. He was scraping his hand across his face, the back of his forearm lifted to hide his eyes. Fez was shivering: he'd come up the mountain without a jumper. I was soaked through, but I don't recall feeling cold. I was deadened. That was something different.

We took him down the mountain, as carefully as we could. Fez and I carried him at his shoulders, Bozo holding his legs. A shoe had fallen off. We stopped to put it back on. We didn't talk much, apart from the odd 'Careful!' from Fez. It was like carrying a box of eggs. We didn't want to break him.

When we reached the tinder path, the dread came again. Until this moment, it had somehow not been real, but now, as we stepped into Scott Street, we had to tell grown ups. My stomach felt sour, my throat tight. Someone was walking towards us, and I knew that what happened next would happen fast, like a cloud covering the moon.

Things spiralled away. I remember the terrible, wounded cry let out by his mother. I remember her cradling his limp body. I remember women coming and surrounding her. I remember being stared at. I remember stumbling backwards and standing on my own, outside looking in. I remember an arm coming about me, being guided back home, my mother's hand clutching her face, Bethan crying. I remember standing, with Piotr, and handing him the pistol, and then crawling under my bed and seeing the picture of the shoes, glued to the wall.

And then the tears came. And I would never be free of it, this scar across my heart.

*

'Tell him everything you told me, Ant,' said Mam, her face grave and ashen. Piotr was standing behind me, his hand on my shoulder. Arthur Pryce was sitting on a corner stool, his helmet in his hands. He was staring down at his boots, the cowlick of his fringe dangling. Alwyn, Emrys and Bethan were standing to my right, gathered around the hearth. Bethan was still crying, her eyes red and swollen. Emrys hadn't looked at me since he heard, his arms folded tight. Alwyn had his one good arm resting on the edge of the mantelpiece. He looked exhausted. One thing after another. That's what this was. One thing after another. There was a tray of tea things on the occasional table, and in front of me sat Captain Willis, the nice man from St Athan. He had that attaché case on his lap again, and his pen was poised.

They had let me sleep. When we were first found, I had been in too much shock to be of use. Worn out, I had slept, and for a moment after waking up, I had forgotten it had all happened. I was curled in a ball, as I always was, and as I opened my eyes, there were the smart shoes stuck on the bedroom wall. And then the image of Ade's tatty plimsoll, falling into bracken, flashed up, hard and sharp.

And I remembered.

Who knew I had so many tears in me? The slightest kindness and there I was, off again, my cheeks hot and red, the swell of grief ebbing and flowing, as sure as the tides. My mother had held me tight. It wasn't the time for admonitions. I would punish myself later without anyone else's help. They just wanted to know what had happened and how.

I had finished telling the story, the linear version of how events had unfolded. Captain Willis had been kind and patient, taking care to ask his questions gently and without reproach. But it was time for me to tell everything, and I had to steel myself.

'So you're not sure Adrian saw anyone at all?' said Captain Willis, his pen hovering above official yellow-coloured paper.

I shook my head. 'He said he saw a leg, but there was nobody there when I looked. I heard a cry, then the rifle, then him.' My voice trailed off.

'But there might have been someone there?' he persisted. 'Because of the stones falling?'

I gave a small shrug. 'Dunno. Maybe. But it could have been a sheep.'

Captain Willis gave a small, encouraging smile and let his pen fall to the paper. We all watched him, every time he wrote something down. The words etched the matter into stone.

'And you had gone up the mountain thinking you might find this German on your own?'

This was it.

'Sort of,' I said, quietly 'But that wasn't all of it.'

I felt my mother's eyes upon me.

'There was a radio,' I began. 'It had come from the plane. And it was broken. And then Piotr had fixed it for us. To play with, like.'

'This is true,' said Piotr, coming to my defence. I felt his hand lift from my shoulder. 'A basic thing. I fixed crystal for him. I didn't think anything of it.'

Captain Willis paused and let his gaze settle on Piotr, hand floating in mid-air. 'You fixed the radio? So it could be used?'

Piotr nodded. 'This was before we knew there was someone up the mountain, of course.'

'Yes.' Captain Willis nodded. 'Of course.'

'Except we couldn't use it because it went missing,' I said, sitting on my hands. 'And whoever took it wasn't one of us.'

'Where do you think the radio went?' asked Captain Willis, watching every shift of my face.

'I don't know. But then it was back again. And our den was all done over. Like whoever took it was looking for something.'

'Looking for what?' pressed Captain Willis.

I reached into my pocket and pulled out the hooked metal tube. 'I think for this,' I said, holding it up. 'I think it's a key.'

Captain Willis laid his pen against the top seam of his notepad and took it from me. He frowned.

'You yank the hook at the end,' I explained, pointing.

Squeezing the tube at its middle, Captain Willis crooked his little finger into the hook and pulled. There was the familiar click and out came the corrugated rectangle.

'Well, I never,' he said. 'Curious. Seen this before, Captain Skarbowitz? See any of them use it on the plane?' He held it out for Piotr to take.

Piotr shook his head. 'No,' he said, tilting his head sideways. 'How do you open it, Ant? Show me.'

I took it from him, pulled the hook and twisted.

'I agree with Anthony. I think it's key,' he added, taking it back from me. 'But as to what it opens, your guess is as good as mine.'

'So you took this up the mountain to try and work out what it might open?' continued Captain Willis, his gaze falling back on to me.

I nodded. 'We wanted to work out what it fitted. But we couldn't. We knew someone had been up the den. Ade reckoned it was the German, and that he'd be hanging about. That's why he asked me to get the rifle.'

I shot a glance towards Emrys, but he turned his eyes away.

'For protection?' asked Captain Willis, his head down, writing. 'Or to kill the German?'

'Both, I think,' I said. 'But Ade wanted to kill the German. He wanted to be a hero, save the village, like.'

'And do you think he would have killed him, if you had found him?'

It was the first time I'd thought about it. Ade flashed into my mind, his ever-smiling face, dirt smeared on a cheek, sunlight kissing the tips of his hair, standing, gesturing for me to follow.

I shook my head. 'No,' I said, quietly, 'I don't think he would.'

Captain Willis gave another small nod and looked up towards Piotr. 'Would you mind?' he asked, gesturing towards the metal key. 'I'll have our fellows take a look at that.'

'Sorry,' said Piotr, handing it back. 'Trying to work out what might be for.'

'When the radio came back,' I said, 'it was pretty bashed up. We thought it might have been that. But we couldn't find a hole, like.'

'Hmm,' said Captain Willis, tucking the device into his inside pocket. 'Perhaps we should have that radio back, too? Apart from anything, can't run the risk of this chap using it to send messages back to Deutschland.'

'I can fetch it,' said Piotr. 'If it's back in den?'

I nodded.

'Thanks awfully,' said Willis. 'Safe rather than sorry, and all that. Well, Anthony, thank you for being so honest.' He took the lid of his pen and screwed it back on. The questioning, it would seem, was over.

'He's a murderer now,' said Mam, as Willis tucked the yellow notepad into his attaché case. 'You make sure they know they're looking for a murderer.'

'Well,' said Willis, his brow furrowing slightly, 'it's still not clear exactly what did happen to Adrian. He may have fallen of his own accord.'

'You tell them he's a murderer,' said Mam again, her voice quiet yet firm.

Captain Willis let his face soften, his mouth turning a gentle smile about the room. He stood, placing his cap squarely on his head, and took the attaché case by its handle.

'It's never pleasant,' he began, 'having to deal with such matters. Thank you for the tea, Mrs Jones. Take care of yourself, Anthony. You mustn't blame yourself. It was Adrian's scheme to head up into the mountain. You must remember that.'

'But I didn't stop him,' I said, standing.

'Sometimes,' Captain Willis said, his voice steady and true, 'it's not our place to stop others. You did what was asked of you. Soldiers have to do it all the time, and sometimes, brave men don't come home. Honour your friend by living your life well. That's all you can do.'

He held his hand out and I lifted mine into it. His shake was firm and sincere, and as I looked up into his eyes, I felt the boy in me fade, a shadow I once was slipping away from the light. His eyes turned to Piotr. 'I'd be grateful if you could retrieve that radio. I can come back tomorrow for it. Would that be convenient?'

Piotr nodded and held his own hand out. 'I shall make sure it's here.'

'Good. Then, until tomorrow. Anthony, Mrs Jones, Sergeant.'

Arthur Pryce rose and gave a small, polite nod, and we all stood in silence waiting for Captain Willis's footfalls to slip into the distance. 'I'll write up the report, my end,' Arthur said, fingering the rim of his helmet as the quiet descended. 'Word is, Captain Pugh is putting up a reward for the fella. Two hundred pounds, I've heard.'

'Two hundred quid?' repeated Alwyn. 'If I'd known there was that much money in sewing, I'd have packed up underground long ago.'

'Don't make jokes, Alwyn,' said Bethan, wiping her eyes again. 'It's not the time.'

'It wasn't a joke,' protested Alwyn. 'I mean it. Two hundred quid! Christ. I always thought old Pughsy was doing all right, like, but that's proper minted.'

'It's very good of him to do it,' said Mam, picking up the tea things from the small wooden table next to Father's chair. 'Everyone wants this man caught. Money concentrates the mind.'

I looked over towards Emrys. 'I'm sorry I took the rifle,' I said, trying to catch his eye. 'I thought it was the right thing to do.'

'Well, it wasn't,' he replied, his voice low and brooding.

'If it puts your mind at ease,' said Piotr, 'why don't you lock rifle in Bethan's wardrobe? It has small key. That way, it's out of temptation's way, whoever is thinking of borrowing it.'

Emrys nodded. 'Not a bad idea,' he said. 'You all right with that, Bethan?'

She gave a small shrug and blew her nose. 'You boys make your own minds up,' she said. 'I'm going to help Mam.' She wandered off into the kitchen.

Arthur Pryce was hovering, awkwardly, not quite sure whether his cue to leave had been and gone. 'It's all right, Arthur,' said Alwyn, reaching down to throw a lump of coal onto the fire. 'You can get off, if you like.'

'I'll get off, then,' he said, 'I need to check on Mrs Jenkins, anyhow. Dr Mitchell's been with her, but ...' His voice trailed off, not wanting to discuss the state of Adrian's mother in my presence. 'Yes. I'll get off.'

Nobody said anything for the longest time. The official bits were done. Now, somehow, we had to carry on.

As if we didn't have enough to deal with, news from the field hospital in Pontypridd was not good. Pneumonia, the dark unseen enemy of everyone who worked underground, had settled itself into Father's chest. It wasn't our way to have our own die anywhere other than home, and now, with the risk running high, Mam wanted Father back.

'I can ask Hughes the Grocer to lend us his delivery van, Mam,' said Alwyn. 'We can fetch Father back in that?'

'Don't be daft,' said Bethan. 'Honestly, Alwyn, you need your head screwing on. The Americans can send him home in an ambulance. Or would you rather Father came home in a bag of turnips?'

'Yeah, all right,' replied Alwyn, tense and testy. 'No need to be sarcastic. I was thinking out loud, that's all.'

'That'll do, you two,' said Mam, her face worn and sunken. She was reaching into her handbag for her purse. 'When do you get paid, Bethan?'

'Two weeks on Friday,' she replied, 'but we had kit to pay for. So it'll be about half than usual.'

Mam nodded and silently pressed her purse shut again. It struck me that Mam, having been told that Father might die, was still as practical as she ever was. I had never seen my mother cry, not once. Even when people we knew had died, she seemed to bear the burden, her natural stoicism battening everything down. I had no idea whether she was an emotional woman. I had no idea who she was at all. I knew she was our mother, my father's wife, but as to who Emily Jones was, deep down in that tiny corner that was just for her, I had not a clue. I had come home from school early once with a sudden and unexpected toothache, and had found her and Bopa waltzing together in the parlour, wireless on, faces set and serious. My mother had jumped when she'd seen me, and they'd sprung apart, as if it wasn't the done thing for women of a certain age to enjoy themselves. I'd shown her my tooth and she'd quietly led me off to the kitchen, unrolled a length of twine, wrapped it round the wobbling tooth and told me to go and stand in the parlour. Next thing I knew, there was a slam of the back door, a sharp pain in my jaw, and my toothache was gone. There was never any mention of dancing again.

Alf had volunteered to fetch Father home. He'd walked over, when he heard about Ade, and had taken me down to the bottom of our back garden. We had stood, staring up at the mountain, and he told me about his younger brother and how he'd shoved him down a spoil tip when he was little, for a lark. It had ended badly. He hadn't meant to hurt him, but he'd broken his back.

'It's what a boy intends that matters,' he said. 'What's in his head, his heart. A boy can't go through life with caution forever on his mind. It's not what pumps through the blood. A boy is built for the muck, scrapes, close calls, flying on any passing wind. If I'd been a lad, with this German up there' – he nodded upwards towards the towering hills – 'I'd have not rested at home. I'd have been scouring the green bits, the brown bits, the yellow bits, the purple bits and the black bits till I found him. You didn't go out that night thinking you wanted your friend to be killed, did you?'

I shook my head.

'No. You did not. And neither did he. Look at what happened underground. Four men dead. They didn't wake up that morning thinking they'd not bother because sometimes accidents happen. An accident doesn't announce itself. It just whips the rug from under your feet. And in that blink of an eye, you're gone.'

'What if it wasn't an accident, though, Alf?' I said, scuffing at a patch of rough grass at my feet. 'What if it was the German?'

'Then his withered soul will know no peace.'

He fell silent, his face turned upwards towards the morning sun. 'A grand day,' he said, closing his eyes. 'Look at us,' he added, giving me a nudge. 'Alive. On a day such as this. That's rare luck, little man. Rare luck.'

I tried to muster a smile, but everything still felt raw. I knew Alf was being kind, trying to lift my spirits, but I wasn't quite ready to receive it. I hadn't left the house since bringing Ade down the mountain. It suited me. I didn't want to face anyone, to have to explain again.

'Alf!' It was Piotr, standing in the arch of the back kitchen doorway. 'I've got delivery van from grocer! I can give you lift to Pontypridd, if you like?'

'Good man!' cried Alf back, raising his hand into the air. He turned towards me. 'That's me, then. Off to fetch your father. Remember what I said, little man. You'll be all right, you know. Trust me on this.'

He ruffled my hair roughly and sprang off towards the house. 'Coming!' he shouted.

I watched him go, slapping Piotr on the upper arm, smiling broadly, and I realised that Alf was precisely the sort of man Ade would have grown up to be.

The washing of linen usually happened once a month. It was too big a job for Mam to tackle weekly, but I always looked forward to it because the smell that wafted through the house was glorious. The fresh, sharp smell of soap and starch would cut through the prevailing wind of coal dust, a blast of cool air blowing away the cobwebs. Sheets were pressed into the tin tub with a long wooden pair of tongs, covered with boiling water and left to soak before Mam took her scrubbing board and thrashed the living daylights out of them. It was hard, backbreaking work, and she would stop every now and again, the sweat glistening on her forehead, and stretch backwards, hands on hips, to release the tension in her lower back. When she'd lathered the sheets, she'd take them out and rinse them under the cold tap in the garden; then, when all the soap was gone, she'd turn the sheet into a tight roll and twist it to extract the water before hanging it in front of the back kitchen fire to dry.

The house was suddenly a clatter of activity. Preparations for Father's return were in full swing. Bopa had come over to help Mam with the sheets, and Emrys had brought home another camp bed so that Mam could sleep on it rather than sharing the bed with Father. That way, she reasoned, if she needed to be up and down in the night, she wouldn't be disturbing him. Everything now was geared to settling in for the long, dark wait. Either Father would pull out of it, or he wouldn't.

He'd lost a lot of weight, his once rugged, solid frame diminished, his skin sallow and sickly. His face was etched with pain – anguished, even – and as Alf and Emrys carried him in, I felt tears prick again behind my eyes. I turned away, my bottom lip tense and trembling. Bopa, seeing me go, placed a hand on my shoulder. 'Don't cry in front of him, Anthony,' she said, quietly. 'It's time to be strong.'

He was on a stretcher but they would have to walk him up the stairs. It was either that or leave him on a camp bed in the parlour, and Mam wasn't having that. It was a terrible thing to see your own father being inched up a staircase. It was only eighteen steps but it may as well have been eight hundred.

Every step he had to stop, shoulders hunched, to catch his breath, the effort of raising a leg taking its toll. 'Lean on me,' said Alf, taking his weight. 'And tell us when you're ready.' And so it went. A nod from Father, a step, the sound of shallow rapid breathing, everyone would stop, wait, and start again. Mam was standing at the top of the stairs, her arms folded tight. She and Bopa had readied the room. Clean sheets on, bowls of water, hot and cold, flannels. The room smelled fresh, springlike, ready to be filled with the dank fug of sickness.

'Pass me that pillow, Ant,' said Mam, as the boys lifted Father into bed. He sank down, his head listing to one side, his eyes dull and lifeless. Mam lifted his head gently and rested it back against the extra pillow. 'Sit him up a little,' she asked Alf and Emrys, 'to help his breathing.'

He was clammy to the touch and seemed disorientated, and, as he sat up, he cast a look around the room as if he wasn't quite sure where he was. Mam held a cold wet flannel against his forehead. 'He's got a fever,' she said quietly, turning to Bethan. 'Ant, go get Dr Mitchell.'

I didn't need asking twice.

Half an hour later, Dr Mitchell slipped the stethoscope from round his neck and dropped it into his bag, his examination complete. 'I can give him some penicillin,' he said, reaching for his prescription pad. 'But that's all. If it's going to work, we'll see an improvement in three days.'

'And if it doesn't?' asked Bethan, her hand resting on the post at the end of the bed.

The question went unanswered. 'So,' said Dr Mitchell, standing up and handing Mam the prescription. 'Penicillin twice a day. If his fever is running, keep him cool. Open the window. If you can get hold of ice, use it. His heartbeat's running fast, that's to be expected with pneumonia, but if you notice his breathing becoming very quick and shallow, call me back.'

'Thank you, Doctor,' said Mam, fingering the corners of the prescription.

'Are you sure you want to keep him here?' Dr Mitchell added. 'I can arrange for a bed at the hospital, if it's too much?'

'Nothing is too much,' said Mam, shaking her head. 'We'll manage.'

Dr Mitchell fixed her with a small, silent gaze, picked up his hat and, with a polite nod, left.

Mam turned and handed me the prescription. 'Off you go, Ant,' she said, letting her other hand rest on Father's forearm. 'Let's get this started. You'll have to tell the pharmacist to put it on tick. We can pay him when we get Bethan's wages.'

'What shall we do?' said Emrys, hands tucked into his armpits.

'We shall wait,' said Bethan, sitting down on the end of the bed, her hand curling into Father's. 'We're here, Father,' she said, soft and gentle. Alwyn took up a spot in the corner of the room, sitting, elbows on knees. Emrys knocked open the window with the flat of his palm.

'I'll be off, then,' said Alf, unfolding the cap squeezed between his hands. 'Leave you to it.'

'Thank you, Alf,' said Mam. 'You've been a brick.'

Alf smiled and looked towards Bethan, hoping, from the looks of him, for a small gesture of kindness, but my sister didn't notice him. Alf's small, easy smile faded, and with a last nod to us all, he slipped away.

CHAPTER SIXTEEN

Piotr had got himself a part-time job doing deliveries for Hughes the Grocer. I was glad that it was Piotr who had taken over Ade's old job, but it was also a sad reminder. Still, with the drop in wages lessening the swell in Mam's pocket, Piotr had felt the urgent need to help out. We had looked after him, and now he would help look after us, he said.

'Why don't you go with him, Ant?' said Mam, bringing some sodden towels down to be washed. 'Do you good to get out for a bit.'

'You should,' said Bopa, her arms folded. 'You're looking peaky, Anthony. Boys are made for fresh air. Go get some. Besides, Piotr won't know his way around, will he?' She shot a look in his direction. 'Where's your first stop?'

Piotr looked at the crumpled piece of paper Hughes had handed him. 'Mrs Onions, Blaencwm.'

'Four potatoes, six carrots and a large white cabbage, am I right?' said Bopa, closing her eyes to concentrate.

Piotr let out an astonished laugh. 'Yes! How did you know that?'

'I've got the gift,' said Bopa, with a shrug. 'Try me with another.'

'All right,' said Piotr, casting a glance back down at his order list. 'Mrs Cadwallader.'

'She lives in the back room of her son's house. He doesn't like people coming to the front door, so you'll need to pass her order through the back window. Sprouts and green beans.'

'Yes! Mr Cecil …'

'Oh, him,' said Bopa, her voice deep and fruity. 'Bachelor. Likes to paint cats. Leeks. Cauliflower. Parsley. Peas when they're in season.' She stopped and fixed Piotr with an expectant grin. 'Well? Am I right?'

'Yes! Again! You're amazing, Mrs Jackson!'

'Now, the trick,' said Bopa, pulling my shirt collar out from under my jumper, 'is to not eat *all* the peas before you deliver them. Isn't that right, Anthony?'

I nodded.

'This is good advice,' said Piotr, 'and if I get too greedy, Anthony can stop me.'

The atmosphere at home was oppressive and downcast, and in the van with Piotr, I felt happily distracted. Since the war started, a lot of people had turned their gardens into vegetable patches, so deliveries were mostly for old folk who couldn't dig for themselves. Mam had had her own veg for a while, having dug over our own garden a few years back. She had a slim green book, *Cloches Versus Hitler*, that she treated like a bible. It was supposed to help her crop large varieties of vegetables through every month of the year, but, as Bopa pointed out, 'Mr Churchilll didn't reckon for Welsh slugs.'

What with every manner of crawling creature helping itself, we were more often than not left with vegetables that were half-chewed and mangled. Mam didn't care, mind. Once it was chopped, it didn't matter how ugly it was, she said.

'Want to come up mountain with me and get that radio?' asked Piotr, as we parked up outside the grocer's. 'I was thinking of going later. I've got to take some crates to Porthcawl first. Shouldn't take long. In fact, I'm giving Bethan a lift. She needs to hand over some papers. Want to come? There'll be lots of Americans to look at.'

I opened the door and jumped down, taking care to pick up the stolen pea pods we'd been enjoying. 'Dunno about the den. Feels weird. But I'll come to Porthcawl with you and Bethan.'

Piotr smiled. 'Great! Help me get some more crates in back, then we go pick up your sister.'

It was an uncommonly glorious day. A day with heat to it, dry and blazing. We loaded up the van then wound down the windows and I stuck my head out, enjoying the wind buffeting my cheeks and hair.

'You're like a dog, Ant,' said Bethan, laughing. 'You'll want a bone next, I swear.'

It was a relief to be out. Home had become so solemn and serious: everything was communicated in hushed tones, the wireless left silent, and Mam would sit for hours with Father, only leaving his side to make an endless stream of thin soups that she would attempt to dribble into his mouth. It was an unedifying spectacle, a vision of the end of a life. None of us expected him to pull through. We'd resigned ourselves to it. Miners with pneumonia didn't present good odds.

We hadn't seen much of Andrew and Robert, the two Americans billeted with Bopa; in fact, we hadn't seen much of the Americans at all. News had it they were off into the mountains, training and making final preparations. 'They must be going into France, mustn't they?' I said, as we passed a small convoy of large green trucks.

'Well, they're a long way from Japan,' said Bethan, pouting into her compact and applying bright-red lipstick. 'So I guess they're not going there.'

'What do you think, Piotr?' I asked, forming my left hand into a claw to catch the wind. 'It has to be France.'

'Of course,' he said, casting a quick glance into the wing mirror. 'The Germans are stretched. The Russians are putting up pretty good fight. It's right time to do it.'

I smiled. The thought that we were finally going to show Hitler what for had been a long time coming. 'Fez says his dad has got a loo roll with Hitler's face on every sheet.'

'Stop it!' cried Bethan, stopping what she was doing to glare at me. 'You've made that up.'

'I haven't,' I protested. 'Fez said his dad wipes his arse on Hitler every time he has a shit.'

Piotr bellowed with laughter. Bethan gave a small tut and turned back to fixing her lipstick.

'This, I would like to see!' said Piotr. 'Just the paper, of course. Not shitting.'

'Piotr!' yelled Bethan, thumping him on the forearm.

We grinned at each other. I stared back out the window, watching my fingers fill with the wind. The heather was out in full force in this part of the valley, the hillsides painted purple, with a strong, almost smoky aroma. You could make honey – rich, bitter and aromatic – out of it, if you persevered. One year out of five, you'd get good enough weather. I looked up into the deep-blue sky. The bees would be busy.

'Do you know, yet?' I said, turning back to Piotr. 'Whether you'll go too?'

'I don't. But I hope so,' he answered, his jaw tensing a little. 'But who knows what's in store for me? They still haven't managed to transport me to Scotland.'

'Well, I for one am glad they haven't managed to get rid of you,' said Bethan, clipping her compact shut.

'And I am,' I added.

Another large green wagon rumbled past us. 'Wonder when they'll leave?' I said, resting my chin on the lip of the window. 'For real, I mean.'

'When weather and moon is right,' said Piotr. 'But who knows when weather is right in Wales?'

'If you don't like the weather in Wales,' said Bethan, 'wait ten minutes. There'll be some more along shortly.'

He smiled. 'True enough. Now, then, I have two surprises. One, I have borrowed your Father's Brownie camera. I hope you don't mind, but I'd like memento of day. And two, I received wages from Polish army. Backdated, too. So not only have I got money to give your mother but I think, though I'm not promising, that I might be able to treat you both to ice cream. What do you think about that?'

'Ice cream?' I yelled, my eyes boggling.

'Yes. Ice cream.'

It was quite something that somebody, anybody, was able to lift our spirits, given the sadness that lay heavy over our roof, but in that moment, Bethan and I looked at each other and knew that we loved him.

Porthcawl was rammed. Mosquitoes and transport planes buzzed overhead, large battleships lay off the harbour, and everywhere you looked, soldiers were running up the beach, filling sandbags or building spurs. Bethan had dropped off some papers – more movement orders, she said – and, job done, the three of us decided to walk up the Esplanade. Gulls cried out, registering their protest from every vantage point: they were used to being the noisy ones round here, and here they were, being outdone.

'You could take us to the Seabank,' said Bethan, linking her arm through Piotr's. 'It's that big white hotel there on the corner. The one with the red roof.' She pointed off into the distance. 'It does teas and things.'

'Does it do ice cream?' I said, fiddling with Father's camera.

'Probably,' replied Bethan, tossing her hair. 'Be careful with that, Ant. It's not a toy.'

Piotr had let me carry Father's camera and said I could take three pictures. I wanted to choose wisely, so I stood and stared down into the viewfinder. I was hoping to see the destroyers sitting in the bay, but all I could see was a dark smudge.

'I can't see anything,' I said, my mouth curling upwards at one corner.

'You've got your finger over hole,' said Piotr, taking it from me. 'Here. Let me show you how to hold it.'

The camera was a Brownie 620, a black-leatherette-covered metal box with rather smart geometric designs in nickel chrome and black enamel on its front. Father had taken part in a fishing competition and won it for catching the largest trout. Mam hadn't been that impressed, because she didn't see the point in it. Apart from weddings, there was little reason to have a camera. It was an entirely unnecessary luxury. Mam would rather he'd been allowed to keep the trout. 'You can't eat a camera,' she said when he brought it home. Nobody had disagreed with her.

'There are two viewfinders, here and here,' said Piotr, showing me. 'And a shutter release lock, here. See?'

I nodded.

'Do you know what shutter release lock is?'

'No.'

'It doesn't matter. You look there, press that, and hey presto, you've taken a photo. Here. You try. Take picture of me with Bethan.'

He handed me the camera and grabbed Bethan, who squawked with delight. 'I haven't fixed my hair!' she protested as he pulled her into him.

'Let the wind take it!' Piotr laughed. 'Now keep still.'

I stared down and found them. They were leaning against the white-painted railings of the promenade, behind them the backdrop of a glistening sea. Bethan curled into him like a cat finding a warm lap. If the beach hadn't been full of vehicles and men and the rag and bones of war, it might have made for a nice picture. I took it anyway, smiles frozen for evermore, a moment captured. I looked up.

'Taken it,' I said, beaming. 'That's my first ever photograph.'

'Well, then,' said Piotr, 'take next two, and then it's my turn.'

I turned back towards the expanse of beach to my left, the sea breeze pummelling my hair, the brine sharp in my nostrils. I wanted to get a picture of all the battleships out at sea, but the viewfinder was restrictive.

'Hey!' a voice called up at me from the beach. I unsquinted my eye and looked down. 'No pictures!' It was an American sergeant, his face scowling.

'It's okay,' said Piotr, stepping forward and waving down. 'He means no harm. It was my fault. He didn't know it wasn't allowed.'

The American made a low grumble, hands squarely on hips. 'Fine. But take better care! This is a secret operation!'

Behind me, Bethan gave a small snort. 'Secret operation,' she whispered, 'Stretching for as far as the eye can see. Come on. Let's go to the Seabank.'

The Seabank Hotel was the swankiest place I had ever been. There was wallpaper and silver cutlery and curtains with satin bows. 'Look,' I whispered, pointing down, as we were shown into the dining area. 'What's that?'

'Carpet,' said Piotr.

I stared down and frowned. 'How come it doesn't get dirty?'

'It probably does,' said Bethan, following me.

'Makes the floor all bouncy, doesn't it? It's weird.'

'Bay view table?' asked the waitress, looking over her shoulder towards Piotr as she led the way. She was petite, wore a short black dress with a white apron, and had pale blonde hair tied up into tight curls.

'Yes, please,' said Piotr.

Reaching a table by the window, the waitress stopped and gestured with her arm at the bay view. 'I'll bring the menus presently,' she told us.

'See that,' said Bethan, pointing to some land in the distance as we sat down. 'That's Somerset and Devon.'

I stared out of the window in the direction Bethan was pointing. I didn't really know what Somerset and Devon was, but I tried to look enthusiastic all the same.

The restaurant was empty. Turned out the hotel was being used as a billeting base for the Americans, and with them all out training, we had the place to ourselves.

'They're all off to France,' said our waitress, returning with the menus and handing them to us. 'Going in days, they reckon. I'll be glad of it. They've been a handful, to say the least.' She stood attentively and reached into her pocket for a small notepad and pencil. 'Anyways, what can I get you?'

'Do you have ice cream?' asked Piotr.

'Yes we do. Vanilla. Two scoops or three?'

Bethan and I shot each other astonished looks.

'I think three scoops all round,' said Piotr, grinning.

'I forget,' said Bethan, as the waitress wandered off towards the kitchen. 'Hotels and restaurants aren't on rationing. You can get whatever you want, if you've got the money.' She shook her head with wonder. 'Three scoops! I can barely believe it.'

I sat, elbows on the table, chin resting in my upturned palms, and stared out of the window. A large transport plane was flying overhead, making the windows buzz, its large lumbering frame prowling slowly off over the channel. 'They're on the move, aren't they?' I said, straining to see the last of its tail wing. 'It's like when the starlings gather at dusk. You know they're off.'

'I've got an idea,' said Bethan, chipping in. 'Why don't we pretend, for half an hour, at least, that there's no war. We're just here, in this hotel, and we're going to eat ice cream. And it's going to feel normal, like it used to. And we're not going to think about what's going to happen. And we're not going to think about anything gloomy or dark. We're just going to think about ice cream. And what a glorious day it is. Deal?' Her eyes were bright and sparkling.

'Deal,' said Piotr, placing his hand over hers. They both looked towards me.

'Deal,' I said.

The ice cream came in a cut-glass bowl set on top of a miniature doily in a saucer with flowers round its rim. Three scoops of creamy vanilla ice cream – the proper stuff, not the thin, watery business we'd had for the past five years, but proper, thick, stick-to-the-top-of-your-mouth ice cream that you had to suck off the spoon. The three of us sat in total silence, occasionally shooting each other ecstatic looks.

'I want to lick my bowl,' I said, as I swallowed the last spoonful. 'Can I, Bethan?'

She shot a look over her shoulder. The waitress was behind us, folding napkins at another table. 'Go on, then,' she whispered, 'but do it quick, while she's got her back to us.'

I picked up my bowl and shoved my face into it, licking my tongue into every crevice of the cut glass.

'Told you he was like a dog, didn't I?' said Bethan, nudging Piotr.

'I'm bit jealous,' said Piotr, picking up his own bowl. 'Keep a look out. I'm going in.'

Bethan gave out a small gasp of shock as Piotr began ravenously licking out his own bowl. She shot a panicked look back in the direction of the waitress.

'Go on, Bethan,' I said, running the back of my hand across my lips. 'You've got loads left in there. We might never have ice cream again. Not if Hitler wins.'

'No,' she whispered back, her eyes frantic at the thought of the impropriety. 'I couldn't possibly!'

'Go on,' said Piotr, with a wink. 'We've done it. Now it's your turn.'

She glanced between us, her mouth curling into a smile. 'Oh, all right,' she said, eyes filled with mischief. She picked the bowl up and tentatively licked the inside rim.

'You all done, I see,' said the waitress, suddenly appearing at Bethan's shoulder, a tray under her arm.

'Sorry,' replied Bethan, trying to compose herself. 'I was just ... well ... goodness, this is delicious, isn't it?'

'Will there be anything else?'

'Just bill please,' said Piotr, trying to stifle a laugh.

The waitress stacked our empty bowls and saucers onto her tray and sauntered back to the kitchen.

'You've got ice cream on end of your nose,' said Piotr, dabbing at it with his napkin.

Bethan's forehead fell into her hand. 'I've never been so embarrassed,' she whined. 'Of all the things to be caught doing.'

But I couldn't be of any help. My ribs hurt from laughing.

*

'How's Father?' said Bethan, throwing her handbag down onto the settee.

'No change,' said Alwyn, who was sitting in the parlour, trying to polish a shoe with his one good hand. 'But then, he's not worse. Mam's up there. Try and get her to take a rest, Bethan. She's looking ragged.'

Bethan nodded and turned to go upstairs. 'Thanks for a lovely morning, Piotr,' she said, softly, her hand brushing against his. 'We had such a time. Proper treat.'

Piotr nodded and watched her trot up the stairs.

'Pretty girl, my sister, ain't she?' said Alwyn, glancing up towards Piotr. He made a thick, hawking noise in the back of his throat and spat onto the toe of the shoe wedged between his knees. Piotr blinked and looked back towards him, an unspoken understanding between them.

'Well,' said Piotr, a small, awkward smile resting fleetingly on his lips. 'I should get up the mountain. Fetch that radio.'

'No need,' said Alwyn, taking his blackened brush to the toecap. 'Emrys went up there with that fella from St Athan.'

'Captain Willis?' said Piotr. 'He was here?'

Alwyn nodded. 'Seemed daft to make him wait. So Emrys took him up. Looks like you've got the rest of the day off.'

'Where's Emrys now?' I said, picking an old comic out from a heap of newspapers.

'Up the Labour Club. There's going to be a village meeting about this German. People are twitchy. Want to know what's being done.'

'What time?' asked Piotr, reaching into his waistcoat pocket to check his watch, and I remembered searching the mountain for it – his father's watch – and was happy that we'd found it.

'Three-ish. But Home Guard's in charge. So more ish than three.'

'Thanks. I'll get van back to Mr Hughes. See you up there.'

I flicked open my comic, my eyes drawn towards a favourite escapade of Desperate Dan. He was stopping Hitler's warships with a giant magnet and shooting his planes down with a peashooter. I sat reading, the only noise the occasional spit and scrub from Alwyn.

'You see anything funny going on with Bethan and our friend,' said Alwyn, his voice low and careful, 'you tell me.'

I didn't look up.

'Are you listening, Ant?'

I felt a prickle of something awkward creeping up the back of my neck. I squirmed on my seat, refusing to look up. I knew my brother. When he decided he didn't like something, there was no turning back. He would have it out of me.

'Dunno what you're talking about,' I mumbled, eyes firmly down.

'You know full well what I'm talking about, boy. And with Father incapable, it's down to me to keep an eye on things. Do you understand?'

My brain was a jumble of noise as I panicked, determined to stop myself saying the wrong thing. There was something between Piotr and my sister; I knew it, but to tell Alwyn would feel like a betrayal. Allegiances were shifting. Never tell.

'Ant!' he growled. 'Do you understand?'

Above us, there was the sound of footfalls on the stairs. 'Enjoy your ice cream?' said Mam, running her hand over the top of my head.

I looked up at her and nodded. She looked drawn, dark rings under her eyes. She mustered a smile. 'Good. Good.'

'You going up the Labour Club in a bit, Mam?' asked Alwyn, tucking his polishing brush into a small bucket. 'Bethan can stay here.'

She shook her head. 'No, I want to stay with Father. You can tell me what's said. What's to be done, anyway? We should set fire to the bracken and burn him out.' Her voice sounded tight, angry.

Alwyn mumbled in agreement. A flash of that night in the rain came to me, Ade's face looking up towards the rockfall, his excited eyes, telling me he'd seen a leg, slinging the rifle forward. I blinked and Mam's voice drifted in.

'Ant? Did you hear me? There's rabbit stew in the pot. If you're going out, have a bowl before you do. And be up and see Father. You've not been in to him all day.'

The walk to my parents' bedroom was one I had done a thousand times, but now every step was filled with dread, my legs heavy and reluctant. It wasn't that I didn't want to see Father; I was just anxious that I would see him in a state I wouldn't want to remember. The imprint of him in my mind was of a strong man, tall and broad, waistcoat on, sleeves rolled back to the elbows, active: an oak of a man. Yet with every visit to his bedside, that memory was being eroded.

Bethan was wringing out a flannel in a bowl, the sound of the water falling through her fingers gently filling the room. I went to the side of the bed, one hand on the metal bedstead at the end, the other hovering awkwardly over the patchwork quilt. The quilt was the only thing Mam had ever inherited; it was her solitary richness, left to her by her mother, who had stitched it by hand during one harsh winter when the snow, so the legend went, was as high as the bedroom windows. It was lovely to lie on, eyes shut, letting your fingers journey across the different textures: rough calico, smooth cotton and that one patch of something velvety.

Father's eyes were half-closed, his breathing laborious. His jaw lay slack, his mouth slightly drooping to one side. His hair was pressed flat against his forehead, and he gave off a faint odour that lay somewhere between stale sweat and rotting fruit. I stared at him. He was forty years of age. His hair was still jet black, not one fleck of grey yet to trouble him. I wanted to see him old, white hair cut close at the nape, a cap covering a bald patch, trousers held up with braces that were starting to look a little big, hair creeping out from his ears, shoes that were always polished properly to put the youngsters to shame, twinkling, watery blue eyes folded into smiling creases, a half-drunk pint and a game of dominoes, then showing another boy, perhaps my son, how to thread a worm and catch a fish. It wasn't the death I feared; it was the absence.

'Pass me that glass, Ant,' said Bethan, placing the cool flannel on Father's forehead. 'He needs some more penicillin.'

I reached for the small tumbler half-filled with water that sat on the bedside table. Bethan was pouring a livid pink liquid into a spoon.

'Father,' she said, bending in to him, 'open your lips a little. It's for the medicine.'

He gave out a small moan, not of pain, more of mild irritation that we were trying to keep him alive. I came round the bed and stood at Bethan's shoulder, watching the viscous syrup slipping onto Father's tongue. He grimaced at the taste: bitter, filthy stuff. 'Here,' said Bethan, taking the water from my hand. 'Sip this.'

He tried to lean forward, but he didn't have the strength. 'Help me sit up,' he whispered, his eyes clamped shut in discomfort.

Bethan put down the glass and took him under one armpit. 'Give us a hand, Ant,' she said, shooting me a quick glance. I edged forwards and took the weight of Father's forearm in my hands. It was lifeless, dense, and as Bethan heaved upwards, I pushed it up and back, as I would a stubborn log that wouldn't settle on a fire. Father leaned into Bethan's side and she sat on the edge of the bed, arm about him, holding him up. She gestured towards the glass of water with her eyes and I took it once more, holding it up to Father's lips.

'Here's your water, Father,' I said, tilting it carefully so he could drink.

His eyes squeezed tight shut then opened lazily, reluctantly. 'Thank you,' he managed and then fell back into Bethan like cloth dropping to the floor.

I had to turn away. It was the first time he had ever said that to me.

The meeting was at three. Captain Pugh was in charge and was busy shuffling papers, Arthur Pryce was putting out some chairs in a line on a raised dais, and Captain Willis was towards the back, head hunched in conversation with another man in uniform. He looked like an American. I strained to see. Between them was our radio.

We knew it was serious. There were women in the Labour Club, a first apart from that time Mrs Harris had marched in demanding her husband stop drinking his wages up the wall and get home.

'Bloody filthy,' said Bopa, sweeping a forefinger across the nearest surface. 'Look at that!' She presented a pitch-black fingertip. 'It's like a pigsty. Is that why you've got us all up here? So we'll take pity on you and start cleaning?'

'There's a mop up the back!' shouted Hughes the Grocer, gesturing with his thumb. 'Make yourself useful, Bopa!'

A smattering of laughter filled the room.

Bopa folded her arms and arched her back. 'I'll make myself useful, Mr Hughes. With my boot up your backside!'

A mock roar of shock went up and, against the hoots, Hughes put his arms in the air to show he'd already given up. There was no point trying to outdo the women of Treherbert; they were indomitable. Mam said that was where Mr Churchill was going wrong. He should send a bus filled with Rhondda women to Berlin. They'd sort Hitler out in five minutes flat.

A series of sharp raps echoed about the room as Captain Pugh banged a tankard on the table in front of him. 'Right, then!' he shouted, as the soft chatter fell away. 'Let's get this started. Have all the ladies present got a seat? Malcolm, get up, lad. You don't need to be sitting. Unless you're expecting.'

'Expecting what, Mr Pugh?' answered a puzzled-looking Malcolm, who was then cuffed on the back of his head with the nearest cloth cap.

I looked around the room. There was the usual huddle of Scott Street kids down the front, some sitting cross-legged, others leaning against the corners of tables. I could see Fez, but not Bozo. Thomas Evans, still in his wheelchair. We caught each other's eye and exchanged a short, almost embarrassed smile. Alf was over by the window, Emrys next to him. Alf looked relaxed, one arm draped high across a ledge; Emrys seemed less so, arms tightly folded. Alwyn was over to my left, deep in the circle of some pitmen, no doubt giving them an update on Father's condition, and Piotr was standing with Mr Hughes, hands tucked behind his back.

'Now, you don't need me,' began Captain Pugh, shuffling the papers in front of him, 'to tell you the seriousness of the recent incident that occurred up the mountain. Nor do I feel the need to explain the sorrow we all feel at the passing of young Adrian.'

Murmurs of approval rumbled around me.

'Mrs Jenkins,' Captain Pugh continued, looking down at a chair to his right, 'please accept our deepest sympathies. We shall spare nothing in finding who did this. Of that, be in no doubt.'

I pressed myself up onto the toes of my boots. I could just see the back of Mrs Jenkins' head. She was slightly hunched, flanked by other women, and as a resounding 'Aye' filled the air, she nodded her head in appreciation. I sank back down and looked around me. I didn't want to be seen staring.

'If I may, Captain Pugh,' said Captain Willis, standing up, 'I feel obliged to say, as unpopular as this may be, that it is the RAF's view that this German is no longer here. If that is the case, then it shouldn't be greeted with regret.'

'What you talking about, man?' called out someone leaning against the bar. 'Course he's not gone. There's what happened with the boy, and the clothes found at the back of Old Morris's salvage shop.'

'That's true!' shouted Hughes. 'Stuffed behind some boxes. Probably left there after he murdered the boy!'

'Although,' chipped in Arthur Pryce, clearing his throat, 'the clothes found at Old Morris's turned out to be old Polikoff tunics. I don't think Germans wear those.'

'The point is,' persisted Captain Willis, 'it's not conclusive that anyone did kill Adrian Jenkins, let alone a rogue German. I know this isn't what you want to hear, but please, I must urge restraint.'

He was right. It wasn't what people wanted to hear. Discontent boiled through the room.

Captain Pugh raised his hand for quiet. 'That'll do!' he yelled. 'That'll do! That's one man's view! As for me, I think the German *is* still up our mountain. Truth is, we don't know. One of us is right and one of us is wrong, but, by God, I don't want to take the chance. Let's play safe. If there's an enemy up there, then let's find him.'

A rousing cheer filled the room.

'Why can't the Americans find him?' shouted Bopa, gesturing towards the third man in uniform. 'Why aren't they out there looking?'

Captain Pugh glanced towards the American officer.

'Ma'am,' he began, rising to his feet, 'we simply cannot spare the resources to look for one man. Our boys are gearing up for something big. And I agree with Captain Willis. There isn't enough evidence that anyone is up there. If I was him, I'd be a hundred miles away by now, and in the absence of anyone actually seeing the fella, we can't spare men to chase a shadow. I'm sorry.'

Cries of 'Shame on you!' and 'Disgraceful!' rattled uncomfortably about the room.

The American sat back down again and exchanged a small, awkward glance with Captain Willis.

'Look,' said Captain Pugh. 'We're not convinced. But that doesn't matter. We don't need the RAF. And we don't need the Americans. If we want to keep on looking, then that's our business. I've put up a reward of two hundred pounds. We know the mountain; we know the gullies. We know the outhouses that might provide shelter. All we need do is remain vigilant. If you see a stranger, stop him, bring him in to Arthur. Only someone up to no good is going to kick up a fuss. Pitmen have got time on their hands right now, with the mine out of action. Organise yourselves. Walk the mountains. Check the streets. Question everyone who comes into the village. If this German is still here, then he'll show his hand. And as for the children, no going up the mountain until further notice.'

A peal of young disappointed groans sang forth.

'No,' said Captain Pugh, shaking his head. 'I shall not be swayed on this. From now on, there'll be a member of the Home Guard on duty by the tinder track. He'll be stopping anyone under sixteen from heading up. Until we're absolutely sure this chap is gone, it's too dangerous.'

The mood was different from before. That evening in the chapel, when we'd first realised a German was missing, had been heady, exciting, even, but now there was no relish, no young men calling for wild heroics. We were as much in the dark as we ever were. Perhaps this German was long gone? Perhaps we were all fretting over nothing? It was as though you could feel the village retreating behind a wall. It was us, not them. Not the RAF, not the Americans. It was *us*, born and bred, our mountain, our home, and a thorn was troubling at our feet.

The meeting wrapped itself up pretty quickly: the Home Guard would set up further searches of the mountain, men from the pit would take up vantage points on ridges, keeping a look out for movement or anything suspicious, like fires burning at night or things going missing from the village. Everyone else was to keep an eye out for anybody they'd never seen before. The village was on lockdown. Doors were to be kept shut.

'It'll be like looking for a needle in a haystack,' said Alf, as we walked home. 'That's the problem. If the fella's up there, he can see men coming, hide, then creep out, stay in the exact same spot. Unless we've got men up there all day, every day, and stretched across the whole mountain, we've got no chance.'

Alwyn gave a heavy sigh. 'I dunno,' he said. 'Maybe the RAF fella's got it right? Maybe he is gone?'

'Better be safe than sorry, though, Alwyn,' said Emrys, scuffing his hobnailed boots on the flagstones. 'That's what Pughsy said. He doesn't want to chance it. And I'm with him. And we'll do it ourselves. We don't need help from outsiders.'

'Way I like it,' said Alwyn. 'Been too many outsiders hanging round as it is.'

I cast a look towards Piotr, who was walking with me behind them, but if he was offended, he didn't show it.

*

'I need you to help me make cheese,' said Mam, handing me a bottle of sour milk.

'But that takes ages, Mam,' I protested, taking a sniff into the bottleneck.

I recoiled. Milk made me gag at the best of times, but when it had turned, it was a singular evil.

'Please, Ant,' she said. 'I'm up to my eyes. It's all hands to the pump.'

I poured the milk into a large, porcelain bowl and went and sat on the back step, bowl wedged between the heels of my wellingtons. Pulling the neck of my jumper up over my nose, I began to whisk. You had to do it until the milk started to curdle. It took for ever.

Behind me, Mam was getting out a roasting dish. I cast a glance over my shoulder. It'd been a while since that had come out.

'Are you roasting a rabbit, Mam?' I asked, changing hands as the ache in my upper arm began to burn.

'Pork,' she replied, opening the larder door and pulling out an enormous joint. 'And before you get excited, it's not for us. It's for the Women's Guild Annual Dinner. I'm doing the cooking for a bit of extra cash.'

My heart sank. This would be torture. Mam had done the odd bit of cooking for the Guild before. It meant something huge and delicious gently roasting in the oven, and an afternoon of hell for the rest of us. The house would be filled with smells that made your mouth water and your stomach rumble. There wasn't much that could break a pitman, but the sight of caramelised meat sitting in a pool of its own gravy could reduce Alwyn to tears.

I watched as Mam took a knife and scored triangles into the skin; salt next, plenty of it, and then she laid the joint on top of some roughly chopped onions and carrots. Sage leaves were squeezed into the cracks of the scored skin and butter pressed around the meat to keep it moist and flavoursome. What I would give to sit down in front of a plate of that pork, I thought, knife and fork in hand, napkin tucked into the neck of my shirt, fat running down my chin. I stared back down into my bowl. Still no curdling.

'You're killing me, Mam,' moaned Alwyn, an hour later. The house was a heaven of meaty vapours. 'It's making me want to wander about with my tongue hanging out,' he moaned, 'licking up the air.'

I was still stirring. One tiny lump had looked like forming half an hour ago, but it turned out to be a bit of bread that had fallen in. My arms were hurting like hell, so I put the bowl down for a bit so I could watch Mam.

She'd lifted the pork out of the oven and was spooning juices up its sides, a thick, golden, sizzling liquor. 'You mustn't get the skin wet, mind,' she said, as I leant in for a deep sniff. 'We want that to crackle up nicely, don't we?'

I nodded. Quite why, I didn't know. I wasn't going to get the benefit of dry-as-a-bone crackling. I hated these women of the Guild who were going to be chomping down on it. Chances were they'd leave it anyway, what with it being fatty. The thought made me furious.

'Oh, giz a bit, Mam,' begged Alwyn. 'I've got a bad arm, like.' He pulled a face and gestured towards his cast with the end of his nose. 'It'll cheer me up, wannit?'

'If he gets some,' I said, muscling in, 'then I should have some 'n' all, Mam. I've not grown properly yet. I need it.'

Alwyn shoved me in the shoulder. 'Get away,' he snarled. 'If there's scraps, they need to go to people who need proper building up, not lost causes.'

'That'll do, you two,' said Mam, taking her oven gloves and sliding the pork back into the oven. 'If you're lucky, I'll let you have some bread and dripping. But you'll have to wait. Have you curdled that milk, Ant?'

I shook my head. She turned and frowned at me. 'How long have you been whisking it?'

'Hour. Thereabouts.'

'Have you put the vinegar in?'

'No.'

'And the rennet? Did you add that?'

I shook my head.

'Where have you been stirring it?'

'Back step.'

'Ant!' she exclaimed. 'It won't turn unless you've got some heat under it.'

She lifted up the bowl and transferred the milk into a pot. 'There,' she said, lifting it onto the stove. 'Get the vinegar and rennet in, and then you can stir it. It's my fault. I should have paid more notice to what you doing. I thought you were sitting outside staring at the clouds.'

'Brain made of cloth,' said Alwyn, giving the back of my head a clout.

With everything in and some heat underneath, the curds formed quickly, and I spent the rest of my time fingering them out from the whey. I liked how they felt in my fingers, the chalky beads rolling across my palm. Mam salted the curds, so they'd be preserved, then moulded them into round balls, wrapping them in little muslin bags and hanging them outside the back door, their milky drips popping off the steps. 'Wartime Cheddar,' that's what Bopa called it.

'Right, then,' Mam said, wiping her hands on a tea cloth. 'I think you've earned a treat.'

She reached for her oven gloves and opened the stove door, the sound of sizzling meat bouncing around the kitchen. A large smoky cloud billowed out, and my mouth filled with saliva. The joint looked amazing: beautifully browned end bits and crowned with a mighty golden crackling. She took a small knife and tapped it. Rock solid.

'Pass me the bread knife, Ant,' Mam said, as she took two large forks and lifted the pork onto an oval display plate.

Tucking a loaf into her armpit, she took the knife and carved off a thick slice. 'There you go,' she said, handing me the bread. 'You can dip that in the gravy, Alwyn! If you want dripping, you can have some!'

It was like nectar: thick, greasy, heady nectar. I loved how the bread looked just after a dip: deep brown at its tip then lightly golden towards the edge.

'Who needs fancy meals?' said Alwyn, sucking on a crust. 'All you need to die happy is a chunk of bread and some liquid fat.'

'Don't tell anyone,' said Mam, in a conspiratorial whisper. She was holding out three small squares of crackling. 'One each.'

I took mine and popped it into my mouth: syrupy, salty, crispy skin. Alwyn and I smiled at each other. 'It's like a meat sweet,' I said, rolling it round my tongue.

'God,' he said, 'that was magnificent.'

'Right,' said Mam, crunching down, 'let's get this up the Guild.'

The Women's Guild met once a month at the Social Club at the top of the village, near Tynewydd, and we dropped the pork off in a large function room at the back. I wasn't paying attention to anything much, and Mam had fallen into casual conversation with Enid Simpkins, who lived in the next road over: nothing of particular interest, just a general round-up of people's state of health.

'Gallstones,' said Enid. 'I couldn't believe it. Who's got a diet to give them gallstones, these days? I'm telling you, Emily, they're on the fiddle. Mind you, they're clamping down on unauthorised food ...'

I turned and looked down towards the end of the street. Three men were coming. To be more specific, Hughes the Grocer and Old Morris had hold of a third man who, by the looks of him, appeared a bit roughed up.

'Mam,' I said, tugging at her sleeve to get her attention. 'Look.'

The pair of them followed my pointing finger.

'What's all this, then?' said Enid, her eyes narrowing.

People were coming out from their houses, some women holding carving knives aloft. The man looked terrified, his nose was bloodied, his lip thick and split. Hughes and Morris had a tight grip on him and were bundling him up the street, yanking him upwards when he stumbled.

From a side street to our left, Arthur Pryce appeared. He was running and had his truncheon out. 'Where is he?' I heard him shout.

'We've got him, Arthur!' yelled Hughes, pulling up the man again. 'We've bloody got him!'

I looked again at the man between them. He was almost unconscious. One of them, probably Mr Hughes, had clearly given him a proper wallop.

'Oh, my God,' said Enid, grabbing Mam by the shoulder. 'They've caught the bloody German.'

CHAPTER SEVENTEEN

'Come on, Mam,' I cried, picking up pace and running towards them.

'Oh, God,' she said, behind me. 'They'll tear him limb from limb.'

Catcalls filled the air and the man, pummelled by passersby, ducked as a small, rotund woman shoved forwards and slapped him hard about the face. He reeled backwards, his brown trilby flying sideways and rolling into the gutter.

Mr Hughes and Old Morris were holding people off as best they could, but punches were coming in thick and fast.

'Stop it!' yelled Old Morris. 'Arthur! Hurry up!'

Arthur, who was running as best he could, reached for the whistle in his top pocket. He tried to blow but was so out of breath that instead of a fulsome blast, there came a thin, half-hearted squeak. As we got closer, Mam held me back, gripping me by the upper arm.

'Hold back, Anthony,' she said, her voice tight and grave. 'There's a dangerous mood. This could get nasty.'

I stood staring at the man. He was clean-shaven, apart from a small, functional moustache. His hair, though ruffled, was well kept, thick on top, greased to one side, short and trim above the ears. He was wearing a light-grey three-piece suit, shirt with a starched collar, and a perfectly knotted blue polka dot bow tie. I frowned. Where had a German hiding up a mountain got all that from?

I glanced down at his hands. He was carrying a small case but, as he was buffeted about, that was knocked to the floor too. The lock cracked and the case fell open, revealing a host of papers that began fluttering up into the breeze and twirling away down the street behind him.

'Get back, please!' shouted Arthur, trying to push his way through the tight, angry circle of people.

'Let him through!' yelled Old Morris, holding up his arm to prevent another blow coming in.

'Now, then,' said Arthur, panting. 'What have we here?'

'We've caught the German, Arthur,' said Mr Hughes, his face set and serious. 'I had to punch him. He's a bit on the wobble.'

'How do you know he's German?' asked Arthur, bending down a little to take a better look at the fellow's face.

'He talks funny and he's in weird clothes,' said Old Morris, pointing a bony finger towards the man's face.

Arthur frowned and straightened up. 'Where did you find him?'

'Walking down the road from Blaenrhondda,' said Mr Hughes.

'The road from the train station?' asked Arthur.

Mr Hughes and Old Morris exchanged a small, suddenly worried glance.

'Yes,' said Old Morris. 'But no matter. He's the German, all right.'

The man, who was still bleeding from his bottom lip, looked up towards Arthur. 'Can I have a handkerchief, please?' he said, thickly.

'He can speak English,' said Enid Simpkins, nudging my mother. 'Bloody tricky bastard!'

He cast an exasperated glance in her direction. 'I can assure you I am not. Please. A handkerchief?'

Arthur reached into his pocket and handed the fellow a square of blue cotton. 'It's all right, gents. Let him stand up.'

Mr Hughes and Old Morris released their grip, and the man, dabbing his lip with the handkerchief, straightened up. 'I'd like you to arrest these men,' he said, gesturing towards the pair of them. 'I have been assaulted. And that woman there as well,' he added, pointing towards the woman who'd slapped him.

'Arrested?' cried Old Morris. 'For saving the village and fighting the enemy? Why, the very brass!'

'Nobody's getting arrested for punching a bloody German!' shouted Mr Hughes, taking a grip of the man's upper arm a second time. 'You're from Germany!'

The man shrugged him off and pushed Mr Hughes away from him with a forcible shove to the chest. 'I am not from Germany. I am from Rye. I'm from the Ministry of Agriculture.'

'He's lying!' shouted someone towards the back of the crowd.

'Grab that case, someone!' shouted Arthur, pointing towards the papers billowing down the street.

Mam gave me a shove. 'Go on, Ant,' she said. 'Lend Arthur a hand. Chase them papers for him.'

I ran past the tightening circle. Some people were already backing off, embarrassed that a terrible error may have occurred. Others were edging in, reluctant to admit the mistake. The case was resting against the kerb, a file tumbling out. Gathering it up, I shoved the file under my arm and chased the remaining loose papers making a bid to escape.

'Here you are, Arthur,' I said, squeezing back into the centre of the group. I turned and had a closer look at the stranger. His nose appeared broken and he looked furious. If he was a German, I thought, he was very brilliant at looking like he wasn't one.

'Pass me that,' he said, gesturing for the case.

'Don't give it to him, Arthur!' shouted a woman behind Old Morris. 'Those are German top secrets!'

Arthur picked one of the loose papers and had a squint at it. 'It doesn't look top secret. Or German. This is a letter about cabbages.'

'I'll take that,' said the man, stepping in and grabbing back his case. 'I shall make an official complaint about this. Mark my words. This won't be the last you hear of it.'

'Who you going to complain to?' shouted Enid Simpkins. 'Hitler?'

Another woman made a shushing noise.

'Here,' said the man, reaching into his inside breast pocket. Everyone flinched as if he might be about to pull out a gun. When a wallet emerged, there were audible sighs of relief. 'My card from the Ministry. That's me.' He shoved it towards Arthur.

'James Montgomery. Enforcement Officer. Ministry of Agriculture,' read Arthur, slowly.

'Does it look faked?' asked Old Morris, stepping forward. 'Excuse me,' he said to the man, 'I want to get a better look.'

'I bet you do,' said the man, his jaw tensing.

'No,' said Arthur, turning it over. 'It looks pretty real. Well. Sorry about that, Mr Montgomery. We've got a German on the loose, see. People are a bit tense.'

'Tense? They're out of their minds,' Mr Montgomery yelled, glaring at Mr Hughes.

'What you here for, anyway?' said Arthur, handing back the card.

'I am here to stop the unauthorised selling of eggs,' the man declared. 'But now I've been treated so abysmally, I shall be taking a very dim view of anyone selling any produce without the appropriate licences.'

There was another audible gasp.

'That man there,' said the woman who had slapped him, 'that's Mr Hughes. He's the grocer.'

Mr Hughes stared at the woman in disbelief. 'Don't tell him that!'

'Oh, really?' said Mr Montgomery, wheeling about to stare at Mr Hughes. 'Well, perhaps I'll start there. Take me to your shop. I want to see all your books.'

'Bit late, innit?' said Mr Hughes, his face crumpling. 'It's almost five o'clock. Look, I didn't know you were from the Ministry. I thought you were from the Third Reich. I wouldn't have hit you, otherwise.'

'To your shop, please,' said Mr Montgomery, his voice hard and insistent. 'And I shall deal with the rest of you later.'

We stood, dumbfounded, and watched as he marched Mr Hughes off in the direction of the grocer's. There was a brief moment of silence.

'I'm glad I hit him,' said Old Morris. 'He's an arsehole.'

And finally, everyone had something they could agree on.

With the mountain out of bounds, we had to make a different sort of fun. Bozo had emerged from his self-imposed exile and he, Fez and I met by the sheep dip pens, the first time we'd been together since that night up the mountain. We were more subdued than usual, but that was to be expected. It felt odd for the three of us to be without Ade. He had been the driving force, the engine that drove us forward. Now, with him gone, we felt rudderless and unglued. There was a sense of awkwardness, too, as if none of us knew quite how to address what had happened.

'All right?' I said to Bozo as he wandered over. He gave a small shrug and pushed himself up onto the wall I was sitting on.

'S'pose,' he said. 'You all right?'

'S'pose,' I answered, picking at some lichen.

Silence descended and we stared off towards the Americans' Nissen hut in the field beyond. At our feet, Fez was making a cairn of stones, finding flat-sided pebbles and layering them on top of each other. We sat and watched him, none of us saying anything. For a while, we hung about, waiting for the Americans to come and be fed, but it was taking too long. Besides, they might not be back before nightfall, if at all. We needed to do something else.

'Three days till school again, Mam says,' said Fez, standing up and dusting off his hands. 'They reckon they'll have caught the German by then. Be weird without Ade, wannit?'

I hadn't thought of that: the empty seat that would be beside me, the window, with my name carved into the sill. I was suddenly consumed with regret that Ade hadn't carved his own name there. I wanted solid reminders that he'd existed. I didn't want to forget.

'Oi!' came a cry from below us. We all turned. It was Thomas Evans, sitting in his wheelchair. 'Shove us up! I can't do it over grass!'

I jumped from the wall and ran down towards him.

'Christ,' he said, as I hunched over and began to push, 'I'm bored witless. I need a caper. Come on, lads. Let's go up the spoil tip.'

'Are you mad?' said Fez, frowning. 'You can't get up the spoil tip with your leg in plaster. Besides, that's how you got like that in the first place.'

'I can't break it if it's already broke, can I?' protested Thomas. 'Come on! I can sit on my arse and shuffle myself up.'

'Don't be daft, man,' I said, 'you're bust up enough as it is. Leave it be.'

'At least take me up the mountain a bit?' whined Thomas. 'Please, lads? I haven't seen anything other than bricks in weeks.'

We all stared down at him. We'd never tried to get a wheelchair up the mountain before.

'I've got sherbets ...' he said, tapping a lump in his pocket.

'What flavour?' asked Fez, narrowing his eyes.

Thomas met his gaze. 'Lemon.'

'Right, then,' said Bozo, jumping down from the wall. 'Let's get at it.'

It took all three of us to get him onto the path that trailed up behind the spoil tip, Bozo and Fez taking either handle, with me pushing between them. It was hot and heavy work, and by the time we'd got him onto the first ridge, we were drenched with sweat.

'Christ, man,' said Fez, throwing himself down onto his back. 'What you been eatin'? Bricks?'

'Giz a sherbet, then,' said Bozo, sitting on the grass, one hand held up.

'Ain't got none,' said Thomas, with a shrug. 'I was lying.'

Bozo shot him a scandalised look. 'What? You better be muckin'.'

'I'm not muckin'. Got nothing. Look. Handkerchief. That's it. You can eat that, if you like?'

'You're a bloody shit, Thomas Evans,' said Bozo, scrunching his face into a knot.

'You'd never have pushed me up if I hadn't fibbed, innit?' he protested. 'You try havin' a broken leg. It's bloody borin'.'

I shook my head but I couldn't be cross with him. I leant back against a tussock and looked out over the village, the Nissen huts, the tents, the streets rammed with military vehicles. The last time we'd been up here, we'd been on the slag heap with Ade. It felt so long ago, another lifetime. I had sat here then and thought how our village would never be any different, and here we were, three weeks later, our world turned upside down.

'What shall we do now, then?' said Bozo. 'I'm not pushing this bastard up any higher. He can roll down on his own, for all I care.'

'Climb that?' said Fez, spitting at a grass stain on his knee. He pointed off up the hill. There was an old metal crane, a dilapidated thing that was of no use to anyone other than for scrambling, crawling and hanging off.

'Yeah, all right,' I said. 'Last one up is Hitler's arse!'

'Hang on!' yelled Thomas, as we scampered off. 'What about me?'

'Eat your invisible sherbets!' shouted Bozo.

We clambered up towards the crane, dodging rabbit holes, avoiding tussocks. You could swing yourself onto it from a metal ladder that jutted out at a weird angle. It was buckled by the weather and boys hell-bent on breaking things, but from the ladder, you could snake yourself upwards through a maze of poles and struts that left your hands and the insides of your knees red with rust.

I pulled myself up onto my favourite spot, a crossbar you could sit on and be lord of all you surveyed. I glanced down the hill and waved towards Thomas. He stuck two fingers up at me. Below me, on the crane, Bozo was bringing up the rear behind Fez. 'You're Hitler's arse, Bozo,' I said, picking at a tooth.

'Christ!' he yelled. 'I'm always Hitler's arse. We need someone fatter and slower in this gang. I've got no chance.'

'Should have brought Thomas, then, innit?' I replied.

Fez was swinging from a pole below me, his knees lifted up so that he had the appearance of a large, slow pendulum.

'See if you can get right up the top, Ant,' he said, gazing up between his arms. 'The very top, mind.'

I looked above me. A lot of the poles were rusted through, no good for swinging on; but like on the spoil tip, there was always a path of greater resistance. I stood up on the crossbar and grabbed another above my head. Using that, I pulled myself up, groin resting parallel to the bar, and slung my left foot up to the side. Hooking my heel over the top, I pushed up and grabbed the next bar above.

I stopped and looked down; Fez and Bozo were sitting on crossbars, watching, their lower legs swinging back and forth. I could feel rust on my hands, that course, bitty sensation that would leave my hands smelling metallic for days. I cast a look around for my next move. There was a pole jutting to my right, below it a large hook. I reached out for it but my fingers couldn't quite get a grip, so getting myself into a crouched position, I pushed myself off the bar and leapt, but the pole was slimy to the touch and my fingers, as they grabbed it, slid downwards.

'Look out, Ant!' the boys called out below.

I wasn't going to be able to hang on. I cast a quick look downwards to see what I could grab a hold of, but it was too late. My fingers fell away from the pole and I dropped.

There was a short, sharp yank, a ripping noise, and then I fell again, bouncing off a pole to the right and landing on the ground between the crane's four feet. I was face down, the wind knocked out of me, but nothing was hurt other than my pride. Above me, Bozo and Fez were in hysterics.

'Never mind Hitler's arse,' cried Bozo, 'we can see yours!'

I reached down to the back of my shorts and felt soft, damp flesh. I cast a look over my shoulder. A large hole had been ripped out, and my backside was exposed. 'Oh, no, man,' I muttered, pushing myself upwards. 'How am I going to get home like this?'

Fez was doubled over. I was trying to re-attach the flap, but with no success. 'P'raps we can get a snap?' he howled. 'Put it in the chapel newsletter?'

Bozo roared with laughter. I stood, my face crumpled into a picture of despair and embarrassment. 'Ah, leave off,' I complained. 'How am I gonna get home, like? I can't walk down Scott Street with my arse hangin' out!'

Fez and Bozo had jumped down and were collapsed on the floor in front of me, both weak with laughter. I frowned and looked back down the hill.

'Thomas Evans,' I muttered, an idea coming to me. 'Get up, you two. Come on.'

'Fuck off,' shouted Thomas, as I pulled him up out of the wheelchair. 'I can't walk home. Are you bloody mad?'

'You're not walking home,' I said. 'Fez and Bozo are going to carry you. I need your chair. We'll call it quitsies for you trickin' us.'

'I've got a broken leg!'

'Leave off, man!' yelled Fez, grabbing him under his armpit. 'You wanted an adventure. Ant can't be walking up Scott Street with his arse for all to see. Let him sit in your wheelchair!'

As Bozo and Fez heaved him up and got either side of him, I sat myself down. 'Right, then,' I said, with a nod. 'Brakes off.'

'No, wait,' said Thomas, slinging his arms about the boys' shoulders. 'There's a knack to ...'

'Oh, shit,' I yelled, and off I sped, rattling towards certain oblivion.

My next problem was getting upstairs without Mam finding out what I'd done. I didn't have another pair of shorts, so unless I wanted to wander about in nothing, I was going to have to find a needle and thread, get upstairs, and somehow stitch my shorts back together.

I tiptoed up the hallway and peeked quickly into the parlour. Mam's sewing box was next to her chair. I ran lightly over and rifled through it until I found a reel of dark cotton. I slipped it into the palm of my hand and unhooked a needle threaded into the felt underside of the lid.

Gently and quietly, I backed out of the room. Mam must be in with Father. I'd have to slip up the stairs without making a sound.

Taking hold of the side rail, I eased myself onto the first stair. The second had a telltale creak so I stretched my leg upwards to the third. I took the fourth, then the fifth and sixth, and then stopped. I reached up and peeked through the banisters. I scanned left. There were feet, four of them: facing each other and very close. I moved up another step and took another look. My eyes bulged. Bethan was kissing Piotr. Right outside our parents' room.

'Bethan!' came a call from the kitchen. Mam was downstairs after all. 'Can you give me a hand with these shirts?'

I glanced down, then up again. Bethan pulled away from Piotr. He had his arms about her waist.

'Coming, Mam!' she called back.

Quickly, I hopped back down the stairs, leapt over the creaky step, and ran towards the front door. Taking the handle, I opened it and then closed it loudly.

'I'm back!' I yelled, turning back into the hallway. Bethan was halfway down the stairs.

'You're as mucky as the devil,' she said, casting a look at me. 'Tin bath for you, later.'

I gave her a lopsided grin, hands held tightly behind my back. I waited, letting her go through to the parlour, and then ran up the stairs. Piotr was standing, one arm resting against the doorframe of Father's room. He turned. 'Been getting up to mischief?' he asked. 'Your father's sleeping. Try not to wake him.'

I nodded and began to sidestep into my bedroom. Piotr frowned. 'Is something wrong?'

I shook my head. 'No … I … well, see ya.' I leapt into my room and closed the door.

I was breathing heavily, a small trail of sweat working its way from my forehead towards my ear. I slammed the cotton and the needle down onto a blanket folded at the end of Alwyn's bed and slipped out of my shorts. They looked terrible. I held them up to the window; the hole was so big, I could see the entire mountain through it.

The door opened and I clutched the shorts downwards.

'Anthony,' said Piotr, 'you all right? What's happened?'

'Nothing,' I said, swiftly.

'Anthony?' said Piotr, coming in. 'What's wrong?'

I sighed and stared down at my hands. 'It's my shorts,' I explained, gesturing towards them. 'I've ripped the seat out of them. I need to fix them before Mam sees.'

'Here,' said Piotr, holding his hand out. 'Give them to me. I can sew quite well, actually. Let me see if I can do it.'

He reached towards a pile of Alwyn's dirty shirts that lay strewn over the back of a chair. 'Put that on,' he said, throwing one to me. 'It'll cover you up. Don't worry. I'll turn round. Tell me when you're ready.'

'Mr Hughes thought he'd caught the German this morning,' I said, as I pulled Alwyn's shirt over the top of my own. 'But it wasn't. It was a man come to make everyone stop selling illegal eggs and vegetables.'

'I know,' said Piotr, his back still to me. 'I was at back of the shop when Mr Hughes came in with him. He tried to give him sack of potatoes to apologise.'

'Did he take it? You can turn round now.'

Piotr took the torn shorts from my extended hand. 'No. The man told Mr Hughes that was bribery and he'd take great pleasure in reporting him for it. Goodness. That really is quite a rip. Did you say you had cotton?'

I pointed towards the needle and reel.

'Will he really report Mr Hughes?' I sat down on Alwyn's bed next to Piotr. 'He had a heck of a lamping. I wouldn't blame him for being so cross.'

Piotr had broken off a length of cotton and was tying a knot at one end. He licked the other and then, with one eye closed, he threaded the needle.

'All right,' he said, his face concentrated, 'let's see if we make amends.'

He pulled the ripped section taut and began to sew. 'Sometimes men have to make show of things so as not to lose face. He was pretty furious. But he'll get home, his wife will feed him, he'll realise odd things happen in war, and he'll wake up tomorrow with more important things to do. Men do what they have to. So, no, I think Mr Hughes will be fine.'

'I hope so. Mr Hughes was only doing what he thought was best.' I watched as Piotr criss-crossed the thread. His fingers were swift, dextrous. 'How come you can sew so well?'

'Just picked it up. When you're in army, you have to be able to fix things, not just jammed guns or broken-down engines, uniform too.'

'Emrys has a got a uniform,' I said, 'but he can't sew.'

'He doesn't need to sew. He lives with his mother. Here,' he said, handing me the needle and the shorts. 'I'll teach you. Take needle in your right hand between your thumb and forefinger. And with other hand, take a good firm hold of your shorts. Follow line of rip, and thread needle through so that you bring hole together. That's all there is to it. Do that all way round until you no longer have a hole.'

'Thread's got tangled,' I said, my head bent over in concentration. 'Won't pull through.'

'Be gentle with it,' said Piotr, 'sewing takes patience. It's why women are so good at it. Slow and steady. With every stitch, hole gets smaller.'

'Thank you, Piotr,' I said, looping the needle. 'My brothers never show me how to do things.'

'Well, they don't know how to sew, so ...'

'Not just sewing,' I added. 'You've taught me lots of things.'

He looked down at me. 'I'm glad you feel this way. It's important to me that we are friends. And we are friends, aren't we, Anthony?'

I looked up and nodded. Piotr smiled back at me and patted me on the back. 'Good. This won't take long. Not now you've got the knack. When you're done, how would you like to come to cinema this afternoon for early matinee? I'm taking Bethan.'

I stared up at him and narrowed my eyes. 'Are you and my sister sweethearts, like?' I asked.

'Let's say she's my friend, too,' he replied. 'Just a prettier one than you. Come with us. We always have such fun, we three. And who knows how much longer we can have fun? Say yes. Please, Anthony?'

'Yes!'

My shorts had come up pretty well, all things considered. They were a slightly odd fit but I'd get used to them, and until Mam had any money for anything other than feeding us, they would have to do. There was a new film on at the Gaiety, *Gaslight*, with a lady called Ingrid Bergman. I didn't think much of the poster. It said it was a melodrama, which I didn't understand, but other than that there wasn't much to go on.

'Gaslighting,' explained Piotr, as we stood queuing for the tickets, 'it's form of psychological abuse.'

'He won't know what psychological is,' said Bethan, who was rooting around in her handbag. 'Where's my purse? Could have sworn ...'

'It's all right,' said Piotr. 'My treat.'

'I do know what psychological means,' I chipped in. 'It's stuff to do with your mind. It's what a psychiatrist tries to cure. If you've gone off your rocker.'

Piotr's eyebrows raised in admiration. 'See!' He beamed. 'I know a clever fellow when I see one. You're entirely right, Anthony.'

'What sort of abuse, anyhow?' said Bethan, clipping her handbag shut and tapping at the bottom of her upturned curls with her fingers.

'It's when victim is gradually manipulated into doubting what is real.'

'Like what?' I asked, frowning. 'How can you make someone not believe something that's real, like?'

'We'll have to watch the film and find out. Hello, Gwennie. Three sixpence seats, please.'

'Oh, hello,' said Gwennie, pursing her lips. 'Hello, Bethan. How's your father keeping?'

'Not too bad, thank you,' said Bethan. 'He's not getting any worse. That's the main thing.'

Gwennie nodded and handed over the three small cardboard tickets. 'I'm devastated, thanks for asking.'

I exchanged a small, puzzled look with Bethan.

'My beau is leaving,' Gwennie said, taking a small dotty hanky from the inside of her sleeve and dabbing at the end of her nose. 'No doubt to be killed by the wretched Germans. I am abandoned, Bethan. Abandoned.'

'Leaving?' I said, stretching up to rest my elbows on the sill of the booth. 'When?'

'Days!' declared Gwennie. 'Maybe tomorrow. Who knows? I shall be a widow!'

'But you're not married, Gwennie,' said Bethan.

'Doesn't matter. I shall be a metaphorical widow, which, in many ways, is worse.'

'He might be all right, you know,' said Piotr, kindly. 'Not everyone who goes into combat is killed. I wasn't.'

'He's got no chance,' persisted Bethan, shaking her head. 'He can't cross a room without hitting a shin. I don't know why I fell for him. But I did! And now he's leaving! Oh, by the way, Bethan, I'm telling you this in the strictest confidence, you understand. Don't mention this to Alwyn, will you?'

Bethan gave a small snort. 'Don't worry, Gwennie, I won't. Always best to keep your options open.'

Gwennie gave a small, tight smile and then, looking over Piotr's shoulder, shouted, 'Next!'

'Here,' said Piotr, handing me my ticket as we walked towards the doors. 'That's for you. You can choose where we sit.'

'Piotr!' a voice called from behind us. We swung round. It was Alf. He looked agitated, his chest heaving. 'Mrs Jones said I'd find you here. You have to come with me, now.'

'Get off, Alf Davies,' said Bethan, stepping forward. 'He's taking me and Ant to the pictures. He's bought our tickets and everything.'

'No,' said Alf, his voice tight and urgent. 'You don't understand. We've found the German.'

Bethan rolled her eyes. 'Yes, I heard about this morning,' she began. 'That poor man. Who've you captured now? A postman from Cardiff?'

'Bethan,' said Alf, his voice low and quiet, 'I've been sent to fetch him. A man's crawled off the mountain. Captain Pugh found him. He's pretty bashed up. Broken leg, bullet wound, the lot. He's in uniform. He's unconscious.'

'Unconscious?' said Piotr, stepping forward. 'So he hasn't spoken?'

Alf shook his head. 'Nothing but groans and mumbles. I reckon he's been up that mountain the whole time, nothing to eat. He must have broken the leg coming out the plane. He's as weak as a kitten. You're the only one who's seen him, Piotr. You have to come. They've got him in the Labour Club. Captain Willis is there, waiting for him to wake up. They've sent for Dr Mitchell. Once they've got some morphine into him, they might be able to get some sense out of him.'

I don't think I'd ever run faster. Alf led the way, Piotr at his heels. Behind me, Bethan, chased by Gwennie, was making after us. Was it really true? Was this the man we'd all been looking for? Word had travelled fast and the front doors of the Labour Club were crammed with people trying to get in. Captain Pugh was holding them back, rifle braced across his chest.

'I've found him!' Alf called out, as we ran up to the steps.

'Let them through,' shouted Captain Pugh. 'Come on, step to one side. Official business. Malcolm, you take over here, keep everyone back. Have the rifle.'

He unhooked the gun from his shoulder and handed it over to a rather startled-looking Malcolm. 'If anyone tries to get in,' he whispered, 'do I shoot them, then?'

'No, Malcolm,' whispered Captain Pugh. 'You can't. It's got no bullets. Just make a show and look like you're in charge. Captain Skarbowitz,' he added, turning back to us. 'Follow me.'

It was a peculiar scene. An area had been cleared in the saloon bar, with a large table placed in its centre. A man was lying on it, one leg bent and unnatural looking, the other splayed to one side. An arm was hanging off the edge of the table, limp and lifeless, while the other was draped across his face. There was a patch of something dark and brown across his tunic, long-dried blood, by the look of it. Sunlight was beaming in from a high window, illuminating the room in soft tones. The mood felt solemn, almost devotional, and as I saw him, I didn't feel what I expected. There was no anger, no need for revenge. I was simply filled with sadness.

Captain Willis was standing, hands held tightly behind his back. Hearing us enter, he turned, his face grave. 'Well, looks like I was wrong. I don't think there's any doubt we have our man,' he said towards Piotr. 'He's in a pretty bad way. By the looks of that leg, gangrene has already set in. Curiously, he's got a bullet wound in his chest. How he's survived this long, I'll never know. All the same, take a look at him, would you? Formal identification and all that.'

Piotr nodded and approached the table. Lifting the man's arm that lay across his face, he took a good look at him, then placed the arm lower, across his chest. He turned back to Captain Willis. 'It's him,' he said, quietly.

I crept forward, wanting to see the man's face. It would make things easier if he looked mean – tight, tiny eyes, jutting cheekbones, a scar that proclaimed great evil – but he had none of these things. He looked terrible, his skin yellowish and sweating. His lips were cracked from dehydration, his cheeks sunken, but his jawline was square and true. His nose was neither bent nor hooked, instead it had a refined quality, thin and tapering, and his eyes, half-open, were framed with noticeably long lashes. He may have been in a reduced state, but he was clearly a handsome man. He gave out a small moan and his face rolled away to his opposite shoulder.

'Has he said anything yet?' said Captain Pugh.

Captain Willis shook his head. 'He's in shock. We'll get Dr Mitchell to give him some morphine, then we might get some sense out of him.'

'Piotr,' said Bethan, resting a hand on his forearm. 'Go fetch Mam.'

Piotr nodded and slipped quietly out the back.

We all stood, our eyes fixed on the man's mouth. We had our German. Now all he had to do was talk.

CHAPTER EIGHTEEN

Emrys was being held back.

'Let me at him!' he shouted, his face red and looking fit to burst.

'Calm down, man!' yelled Captain Pugh, gripping him by the shoulders. 'Look at the state of him! One punch and you'll kill him.'

'What's the matter with you? Protecting a German? Think of who you are, man!'

'Please,' said Captain Willis, stepping in, 'he may have vital information that might help our boys about to leave. Hurting him further won't help them. And look at him, he's going nowhere.'

'Be the better man, Emrys,' shouted Captain Pugh, struggling to hold him back.

'Emrys!' said Bethan, placing a hand on his shoulder. 'Father wouldn't want this. Let your rage go.'

Emrys' eyes were wide, his face filled with anger. He stared at Bethan, his frustration burning deep, and with a roar, he tore himself away, kicking a chair across the room as he did. We knew to let him be.

Malcolm wasn't doing that good a job of keeping people out, and neighbours were creeping in, talking in hushed tones, filling the spaces in the saloon bar and waiting for the man to come round. Bopa crept in behind me.

'*Diawl*,' she said, taking first sight of him. 'Terrible state. Wassup with him? Hurt, is he?'

'Broken leg, parched half to death. Bullet wound, too, apparently,' whispered Bethan.

'Bullet wound?' said Bopa, shaking her head. 'He must have a will of steel to still be alive.'

'At least we can put one theory to bed,' said Captain Willis, his voice soft and low. 'There's no way this man killed a child. He can barely move, let alone stand. He couldn't have pushed Adrian Jenkins off that ridge, and certainly no way could he have run away. I know you blamed yourself, Anthony,' he added, casting a look down towards me, 'but if you can, take comfort that Adrian's death was truly an accident.'

Bethan put her arm about me and gave me a small squeeze.

'I never thought,' whispered Bopa, who had pushed further forward to get a better look, 'that I'd feel sorry for a German. But, *diawl*, that's something terrible. Christ, when Dr Mitchell gets here, I wouldn't be surprised if he takes him out the back and hits him round the head with a spade like a wounded badger. Put him out of his misery, like. What's he called?'

'He hasn't spoken yet,' murmured Bethan.

'I'd sit with him, hold his hand, for comfort,' said Bopa, folding her arms. 'But it doesn't seem right, somehow, what with him being the enemy, 'n' all.'

The room was now packed with familiar faces: Mr Hughes, Old Morris, Jones the Bible, my teacher Miss Evans, Fez, Bozo, Arthur Pryce. It had been true: there had been an enemy among us, but now there was a comfort in us being together, a village reunited. I looked back towards the table, the man's chest lifting and dropping, the forefinger of his left hand twitching, the occasional low, wounded moan.

Mam had arrived with Piotr, and he led her through the crowd so that she could stand with us. She caught sight of the man lying on the table and gasped, her hand rising to her mouth. 'Is he dead?' she whispered.

'Not far off,' said Bopa, leaning in. 'He's breathing very shallow.'

It was odd, this reverential hush. Only this morning, the same people had been trying to murder a man from Rye whose only crime was to turn up in Treherbert wearing a spotted dickie bow. Yet here they now were, heads dappled in muted sunlight, gathered about a dying man, caps in hand, as if they were witnessing a profound mystery. It was terror. That's what it was: terror of anyone or anything different; terror of change. The war had come, the pit was closed, our habits tossed and broken, and this man was the embodiment of all that: the bogeyman captured.

'Let me through, please,' said a voice behind us. I looked over my shoulder. It was Dr Mitchell, his face a little red, his breath hot with something alcoholic. He pressed past me and stood still, staring at the empty vessel in front of him. 'Oh, my,' he mumbled, placing his bag onto an empty chair.

'His leg is badly broken,' said Captain Willis, stepping forward. 'He's dehydrated, cold and clammy to the touch.

He's disorientated and feverish. He's been mumbling but nothing coherent. What I need is for you to bring him round so I can speak to him. Dr Mitchell, I must impress upon you the urgency of this matter. If this man was sent here to gather intelligence, we need to find out why he was here, what he knows, and what he has communicated back to Berlin.'

'Yes, yes,' Dr Mitchell muttered, reaching for a handkerchief in his jacket pocket. He wiped his forehead, his hands trembling. 'Has anyone given him water?'

'No,' replied Captain Willis.

'I need to get some fluids into him if he's going to …'

'Doctor,' interrupted Captain Willis, 'I need him awake. Fluids will have to wait. Give him pain relief and a stimulant.'

'But that might kill him,' retorted Dr Mitchell, his voice tight and anxious.

'Please, Dr Mitchell,' insisted Captain Willis, 'this man could die at any moment. I have to speak with him. Needs must.'

Dr Mitchell adjusted his spectacles. He was a village doctor who dealt with coughs, colds, the odd outbreak of mumps. Like all of us, he was not prepared for the stench of war, the ruthlessness of it. Needs must. We all knew what it meant. Wake up the German long enough for him to talk and then let him die.

I looked up towards Piotr. His face was concentrated, his gaze fixed, one hand deep in his jacket pocket. He looked down at me, his gaze intense and serious. 'Don't worry, Anthony,' he whispered, and placed his free hand on my shoulder.

Dr Mitchell reached towards his bag and pulled out his stethoscope. 'Actually,' he said, with an embarrassed twinge, 'listening to his chest is entirely redundant. I'll just ... ummm ...' He folded the stethoscope back into the bag and, instead, pulled out a hypodermic needle and syringe, along with a small vial filled with a clear liquid. 'I can give him morphine,' he said, quietly. 'For the pain. And then' – he cleared his throat – 'I can use smelling salts to bring him round.'

Captain Willis nodded.

I watched as Dr Mitchell upturned the vial and inserted the needle into it. Tapping it with his forefinger, he pulled down the syringe until it was full, and then, discarding the empty vial, he let a little of the morphine shoot out from the needle's tip. Rolling up the man's sleeve, he searched for a vein and then plunged the needle into his arm. The German gave out a small moan and shuddered, his eyes rolling up into his head.

'How long till that takes effect?' asked Captain Willis, looking at his watch.

'About a minute,' answered Dr Mitchell. 'There's no point administering the salts until he's not feeling that leg. You'll get no sense out of him.'

Captain Willis leant forwards and put his hand on the German's shoulder. 'Can you hear me?' he asked, his voice a little louder. 'My name is Captain Willis. I am an officer with the RAF. You are in my custody. Do you understand?'

'He may not even speak English,' Dr Mitchell muttered, dropping the syringe back into his bag.

All eyes were on the German, his left hand twitching, his head rolling on his shoulders.

'Do you understand me?' said Captain Willis, again, staring down at him.

The German's lips moved and a barely imperceptible 'Yes' squeezed itself out.

A cloud of low mumbles rolled through the room. Captain Willis held his hand up. 'Please, everyone,' he began, 'I must ask for silence. It's imperative that I hear everything this man has to say.'

Everyone fell silent.

'Can you understand everything I am saying to you?' said Captain Willis.

I took a step sideways so I could see the man's lips. Piotr was next to me, his eyes fixed on the same point. The German's mouth opened and closed; a sound like a short breath panted out. Captain Willis gave a curt nod and straightened up.

'Good,' he said, turning to Dr Mitchell. 'When you think the morphine has taken effect, let him have the salts.'

The atmosphere couldn't have been more tense. People behind me were straining to see and hear, all eyes blazing towards the German lying on the wooden table.

Dr Mitchell glanced at his watch. 'I can try with the salts now,' he said, his hand reaching once again into his bag. 'You may want to sit him up.'

Captain Willis nodded and put an arm under the man's shoulder. 'Can you help?' he said, turning towards Alf. 'Take the other side.'

Alf stepped forward and, together, they heaved the man upwards. He gave another groan, his head flopping downwards onto his chest.

Dr Mitchell moved closer and unscrewed the top of the small, dark-blue bottle in his hand. 'Turn your heads away, gentlemen,' he said to Alf and Captain Willis, 'so you don't get the fumes.' Then, taking the bottle, he wafted it quickly under the man's nose, back and forth, back and forth.

A greater groan went up, a protest at being roused from his torpor, and as he flinched away from the sharp, acrid smell, Alf and Captain Willis took his weight to support him. His head fell back to an upright position, resting against Alf's upper arm, and slowly, painfully, his eyes began to open.

'Can you hear me?' said Captain Willis, his face leaning in towards the German's.

The man blinked and gave the tiniest of nods.

'Do you know where you are?'

The German's eyes flitted around the room. He reminded me of a landed trout, the way their eyes seem to blaze with confusion on finding themselves out of water. He shook his head and a weak 'No' fell from his lips. 'Water,' he said, gripping Captain Willis's forearm. 'Please, water.'

'Can someone pass me some?' called out Captain Willis.

Mutters rippled through the crowd and a glass of water was passed forward from the bar. Emrys took hold of it and handed it to Captain Willis. He lifted the glass to the man's cracked lips and gently tipped it, trickling the water into his mouth. The German closed his eyes, as if the sensation of something cold and wet was a relief greater than any he had ever known. He nodded and Captain Willis set the glass to one side.

'What were you doing?' Captain Willis spoke slowly and clearly. 'Why did you come here?'

'German,' the man whispered.

'Yes, but why were you sent here?'

'German … in … radio.'

'What's in the radio?' said Captain Willis.

'Mission. German,' he mumbled, his eyes closing again.

'Doctor, more salts, please,' said Captain Willis. 'Arthur! Is that radio still at the cop shop?'

'It is!' called Arthur from the side of the room.

'Run and fetch it, fast as you can.'

'I'll go, Arthur,' said Emrys, pushing towards the door. 'I can run faster than you. Where is it?'

'Behind the counter,' shouted Arthur. 'Next to the biscuits.'

Captain Willis reached into his inside pocket and pulled out the metal key. 'Have you seen this before? Do you know what it does?'

'Opens …'

Dr Mitchell wafted the bottle of salts under his nose.

'Ahhh.' He let out another groan of complaint.

'What does it open?'

'German … in … radio … in … radio … He shot us.'

'Sorry?' said Captain Willis, frowning. 'Who shot you?'

'German … shot us … before crashed.'

'Shot who? The POWs on the plane? But you're not a POW. Are you saying another German shot you then crashed the plane deliberately?'

The man shook his head. 'German …' he mumbled again.

'I know you're German,' said Captain Willis, almost comfortingly.

'No …' the man whispered, grabbing Captin Willis' arm. 'Polish …'

Captain Willis shot a puzzled look towards the doctor.

'Your name,' Captain Willis asked, looking back towards the man in his arms. 'What is your name?'

The man swallowed, opened his eyes, and looked up towards Captain Willis. 'Skarbowitz ... Piotr.'

I frowned.

Captain Willis glanced over to where I was standing with Piotr. The doctor looked over his shoulder. 'He must recognise him. It'll be the morphine. He's confused.'

'No,' Captain Willis said again, '*your* name.'

'Piotr Skarbowitz. Polish. I am Polish.'

Alf looked towards Piotr. 'Why's he saying your name?'

'He's delirious,' said Piotr, his hand digging deeper into his pocket.

Captain Willis lifted the man's head and pointed it towards Piotr. 'Can you see that man?' he said, pointing towards him. 'Who is that man?'

The man's eyes flitted erratically then settled on Piotr. He swallowed and, gripping Captain Willis, whispered, 'German ... Hartmann ... German.'

I heard the shot, the screams, I saw the man's chest judder backwards, I saw Alf and Captain Willis splattered with blood, and then I felt the hand gripping me about the back of my neck.

'Nobody move,' said Hartmann. 'Or I kill the boy.'

CHAPTER NINETEEN

Everyone was screaming. It happened fast. I was dragged, swiftly, towards the far end of the room, away from the villagers, a gun pressed to my temple. My head was pushed down into my chest. It hurt.

'What are you doing?' I called out. The hand tightened its grip. I let out a pained yelp.

'Be quiet now, Anthony,' said my captor. 'There's a good boy.'

'Who are you?' I yelled. 'I don't understand!'

'Let him go!' I could hear Bethan screaming. 'Piotr! Please!'

'Piotr is dead,' said the voice above me. 'Everyone, please, remain calm and I promise that no harm will come to you.'

'Calm?' I heard Alwyn shouting. 'Are you bloody mad? What the hell are you doing? You've got a gun to a child's head! Christ, man! You've been living under my father's roof. We took you in. Who the fuck are you?'

'I am a captain in the Waffen-SS. Gerhard Hartmann. You have been very kind. Don't take this personally, but I have a job to do. Now, please, I would like everybody to get well back. Oh, and Arthur, there is no point in running to your police station to call for help. I have cut the line. If you want to do something useful, get these people out of here. If I do not get what I need, I will kill the boy. Have no doubt on that matter.'

I blinked. He was going to kill me? What? My breathing was rapid and I felt a wave of nausea billow through me. I tried to look up but he was gripping me hard, forcing my eyes downwards.

'Bethan!' I called out. 'Help me!'

'What the fuck is this?' It was Emrys. He must have returned with the radio.

'He's bloody German SS, Emrys,' I heard Alwyn shouting. 'He's called Hartmann. Gerhard Hartmann. The fella on the table's the real Piotr. He shot him,' he said, pointing at Gerhard. 'He's got Ant. Says he's going to kill him.'

'What the fuck?'

'Please, whatever your name is,' said Bethan, her eyes watering. 'Let him go. If we've meant anything to you, let him go.'

'Put down the radio, Emrys,' replied Gerhard, his voice cold and clear. 'And step away. Get back, please, or I will kill your brother.'

'Like hell you will!' yelled Emrys, surging forward. I could just see his feet, running forwards. Gerhard dragged me sideways and the radio smashed against the wall behind us.

'No!' I heard Bethan scream. 'Emrys!'

I could just see him. He was about ten feet away. Panic surged through me. The grip on my neck tightened and the barrel of the gun, pressed roughly into my temple, lifted. I heard a shot. I flinched, my mouth gasping for breath. Emrys stopped in his tracks; his hand dropped to his abdomen. He stood, startled, his eyes rapidly blinking. 'What you do that for?' he said, opening out his hand to reveal a patch of blood spreading across his shirt. He looked at me, looked back towards Bethan, and then his eyes rolled upwards and he fell to the floor.

'No!' I cried out. 'No!'

A wail rang out behind him. Gerhard twisted me again and I couldn't see what was happening. I felt pained, guttural sobs choking out from the back of my throat. How was this happening? Blind terror filled the room; I could feel it, taste it. I wanted to be sick. I raised a hand to my mouth and retched.

'What sort of monster are you?' Bopa's voice rang above the din. 'Let that boy go! What man takes a child? A child who trusted him?'

I could hear Bethan crying. She was mumbling Emrys' name. I strained to hear a response. Had he killed him?

'He has only fainted,' said the voice above me. There wasn't a trace of anxiety. 'I have shot him in his side above his hip. Apply pressure to the wound. Quickly, Dr Mitchell. You can save him if you're prompt.'

'Bethan ...' I heard a small, pained cry. It was Emrys.

'Quickly!' Bethan called out. I could just see him. Emrys was on the floor, his eyes wide, his breathing shallow. Bethan hitched up her skirt and ripped at her petticoat. 'Everyone,' she yelled. 'Pass me anything you can to stop the bleeding!' She knelt, pressing the clean white cotton into his wound. She looked back over her shoulder, her eyes filled with fury. 'How could you?' she said, her voice trembling. 'You're a bastard. A bastard!'

Stop the bleeding … I still had sphagnum moss in my pocket … 'Please!' I called out, reaching into my pocket. 'Please … give him this.' I waved the small amount I had in the air, my face still turned sharply down towards the floor.

'Drop it, Anthony,' said Gerhard, his voice cold and firm.

'Please!' I pleaded. 'He's my brother!' The butt of the gun came down sharply on my wrist and, as I let out a cry of pain, the moss fell. I cradled my stricken hand, wincing from the blow.

I heard a boot scrape across the floor. 'There,' said Gerhard, 'pack that into the wound. Now, Captain Willis, I'm afraid I need your help.'

'Never,' he replied, his voice steely and determined. 'Let that boy go. What you're doing is monstrous. These people cared for you.'

'There is no time for sentimentalities,' Gerhard retorted, sharply. 'I'm afraid I'm rather up against it. The clock is ticking. I have no wish to kill anyone here but if I have to, I will. I have plenty of bullets. Now, Captain Willis, please. You will need the key that has puzzled you for so long.'

'Don't do it!' yelled Alwyn. 'Let him kill us all!'

'I will if I need to,' interjected Gerhard. 'Captain Willis, the key. Take it to the radio. It's a little bashed up but this is of no matter. Open it. Towards the back on the front panel, there is a small red socket. It looks as if you might push a cable into it. Unscrew it. Underneath it you will see an opening. Push the key into it and turn to the left. Do it now.'

He twisted me round again and allowed my head to lift a little. Captain Willis was standing directly in front of me, arms out as if ready to catch a falling object. Beside him, the dead Piotr Skarbowitz stared upwards, his mouth carved into an expression of anguish. On the floor, Bethan, Alwyn and the doctor were working on Emrys. Where was Mam? I wanted to see Mam.

Alf, his eyes darting, stepped out from behind Captain Willis. 'Piotr, Hartmann, whatever your name is,' he began, 'you can get away from here. There's a jeep right outside. We don't want any trouble with you. But, please, man, I'm begging you, leave the boy out of it.'

'No,' said Gerhard, his grip tightening on my neck once more. 'I'm afraid that won't be possible. I have much to do in the next hour and I'm going to need him. Now, Captain Willis, as I asked, please. I have many more bullets in this gun. Don't make me use them.'

Terrible, moaning cries filled the bar. Women, who had brought this man cakes, shaken his hand, welcomed him into their homes, stood clutching their faces in dismay. I caught sight of Bopa, the most indomitable woman I had ever met, standing stock still, frozen in horror. Where was Mam? I wanted Mam.

Captain Willis looked around the room.

'You are vastly outnumbered,' he said, his voice low and purposeful. 'Think very carefully before you make your next move.'

'I have thought carefully, Captain Willis,' Gerhard replied, his voice haughty. 'I have thought of little else for over a year.

If you would like me to kill people in this room, then I will. But they are not professionals like you and I. Let's leave them out of it, shall we? Now, please, I won't ask you again. Open the radio. If you don't, I will shoot another person, and this time, I won't be so precise.'

More cries of panic echoed through the room.

'Everyone remain calm,' shouted Captain Willis. 'I don't think he's bluffing. A trapped rat will do whatever it takes to escape.' He held the key out in his open palm. 'There,' he said, turning to Gerhard. 'Take it.'

'I'm afraid I can't take it,' said Gerhard, his voice almost light. 'To do so would mean releasing either the boy or the gun. I am prepared to do neither. You will do as I have asked. Unscrew the red socket and insert the key. Do it now.'

Captain Willis's eyes narrowed as he surveyed the scene. If he was thinking how to get us all out of this, then he had to think fast. 'All right,' he said. 'The red socket, you say?'

'Stop stalling,' said Gerhard, gesturing with the gun towards the radio. 'You know what I asked.'

Gerhard pulled me backwards and my leg hit the side of a table with a dull thud. The radio was lying on the floor of the raised dais to our left, the lid smashed off it. Captain Willis had to walk past us to get to it. I caught his eye. 'You'll be fine, Anthony,' he said, passing me. 'Just do as he says.'

Stepping up on to the dais, Captain Willis stared down into the lid of the radio and tried to unscrew what appeared to be a cable socket. 'It's stiff,' he said, frowning. 'I'm not sure if I can …'

'Keep trying,' said Gerhard.

Captain Willis tried again, his face straining as he gripped the socket. 'It's moving,' said Captain Willis, with some relief. He unscrewed it and lifted it out. 'There a hole underneath it.'

'Insert the key into it, please,' said Gerhard.

Captain Willis took the metal tube and lowered the flattened corrugated end into the hole. With a twist to the left, there was a click and a section in the side of the radio slid out. 'It's some sort of metal tray,' said Captain Willis, looking up.

'Pull it out,' said Gerhard.

His jaw tensing, Captain Willis lifted the small, rectangular drawer out from inside the radio and opened it. 'Papers,' he said, his teeth gritted as he picked them out from the tray. 'False papers, passport, flight order! Damn you, man! What the hell are you planning?'

'No need to trouble yourself with what my orders are,' said Gerhard. 'I wouldn't want to worry you.'

'This is a flight order for a Mosquito bomber!' yelled Captain Willis, staring into his hands. 'God help us. Of course. No German bomber could get anywhere near a sensitive target. They'd be blown out of the sky. But a Mosquito? One of ours? It can fly over anything it wants! That's why he crashed the plane, having filled it with POWs. So he had a brilliant cover story.'

'What's he going to bomb?' called out Bopa. 'Why would he need to crash a plane here and pretend to be a POW? Why didn't he do it in London? Or Cardiff?'

'Because this is where the Allied Chiefs of Staff are secretly meeting,' said Captain Willis, his face etched with fury. 'God damn you, man! He means to bomb Allied Command!'

'Take the papers out and place them at the end of the table,' said Gerhard, unmoved. 'Then move away and take off your uniform.'

'What?' protested Captain Willis. 'I'm not removing my clothes!'

'I'm afraid you have to. It was the one thing I hadn't yet managed to acquire. But no matter. I'll simply take yours. Take them off, Captain Willis, and place them on the floor in front of the boy.'

I watched as Captain Willis reluctantly began to remove his trousers. Alf had moved into my eye-line and was staring at me intensely. My mind was racing, a jumble of pained confusion, fear and betrayal. I understood nothing. Was he taking me in a plane with him? Was I ever going to see my family again? I took a great, gulping gasp of air. I was forgetting to breathe.

'Please,' said Alf, his voice low and pleading, 'take me instead. I won't do anything to try and stop you. Take me instead of Anthony. He's just a boy. He looked up to you. Don't do this to him, please.'

'Always trying to be the hero, Alf,' replied Gerhard, 'for which you have my respect. But the boy comes with me. Shirt and jacket as well, please, Captain Willis. There's a good fellow.'

Captain Willis was now standing in his vest, pants and socks, his uniform in a heap at my feet. It was a humiliating spectacle not lost on the villagers behind him.

'May God forgive you,' shouted out Jones the Bible. 'One day, you shall be judged by a higher power than me. Shame on you. Shame on you.'

The villagers, realising that this drama was reaching its conclusion, began to hurl insults. It was all they could do.

'I hope you rot in hell, you bastard!' yelled Old Morris.

'Coward!' cried out Hughes. 'Stinking coward!'

'Pick up the papers, Anthony,' said Gerhard, ignoring the taunts that were coming thick and fast.

I reached over to the table where Captain Willis had left the small pile of documents and picked them up.

'Put them in the inside pocket of the jacket on the floor,' he added, his grip on my neck still tight and unforgiving.

I cast a glance up towards Captain Willis, who was wrapping himself in a blanket that had been passed to him by Miss Evans. Everyone else in the room was paralysed, sheep caught unawares by the wolf. With Gerhard's grip on my neck a little less unforgiving, I was able to scan the room again for a sight of my mother. I could see a huddle of women, bent over, a pair of shoes slightly splayed. She had collapsed.

'Inside the jacket, please, Anthony,' said Gerhard, his voice insistent. 'Then pick up the clothes.'

'We've got to stop him!' yelled Bopa. 'We can't let him take Anthony. Arthur! Do something!'

There was the beginning of an angry surge, and Gerhard shot again, this time into the air.

'No!' shouted Alf, holding his arms up. 'Don't do anything. Please! Everyone, stay calm. For Christ's sake.'

'Listen to your friend,' warned Gerhard, as I bundled Captain Willis's uniform into my arms. 'Now, if you please, all of you, back out in front of us. Slowly. Do it now. Leave Emrys on the floor, Bethan. You can come back for him later.'

The hand on the back of my neck was starting to sweat, the barrel of the pistol tight against my forehead once more. I wondered if his other hand was sweating, whether the wrong twitch of a finger would send a bullet into my brain.

The uniform felt heavy in my arms, a lead weight of treachery. Fleeting moments came back to me: the moment I had first seen him; laughing with him as we sat reading *The Dandy*; showing me how to shave: the ice cream, the photos, sewing up my shorts, the moon ... How could I ever look at the moon again?

How was it possible that somebody who just ten minutes ago was my dearest friend was now my deadliest enemy? And yet, somehow, I believed if I could look into his eyes, we would see each other. We would see each other properly, and he would remember who I was. He wasn't going to kill me. He couldn't.

'A little faster, Anthony,' he said to me, pushing me forwards as the villagers backed out from the room.

Everyone had done as he asked, and the villagers were now standing in the street, tense and wretched. Behind them sat Captain Willis's jeep. Gerhard bundled me towards it.

'Step away from the jeep,' Gerhard shouted, 'right back.'

'You're a bastard!' shouted Old Morris, as Captain Willis encouraged them all backwards. 'A yellow-bellied custard-spined shit! I hope your cock drops off!'

Similar taunts filled the air. Captain Willis was trying to hold people back, but the yelling was sharpening mettle. It was as if people were coming to their senses. In the saloon, they'd been dazed, bludgeoned into submission by a sharp, swift shock, but now, with the fresh mountain air coursing through their lungs, they were waking up. One of their own was in danger, and it was time to fight back.

'Open the door,' Gerhard shouted. 'Get in!'

I reached for the handle and pressed down. The door swung open and Gerhard shoved me hard into the jeep, leaping up behind me. Still holding me at the neck, he momentarily lowered his gun in order to turn the key in the ignition. It was my only chance. I shoved him sideways as hard as I could, and the gun clattered down into the footwell.

'He's dropped it!' I yelled. The villagers surged forwards.

'Get out, Anthony!' yelled Alf, running towards me.

I reached for the door handle but a fist came crashing across from my right. My face smacked into a metal strut to my left, snapping my head backwards. I cried out.

I lifted a hand to my forehead; blood was trickling down into my eye. I could hear yelling, the sound of a gearstick grinding, Alf shouting my name followed by a gunshot, more screams, and then the jeep lurched away at speed. I winced and looked down into my hand. It was covered in blood. I turned and looked back towards the people I loved, but, run as hard as they might, there was nothing I could do to stop them fading into the distance. I looked towards Gerhard. I only had one thing to say.

'I hate you.'

CHAPTER TWENTY

I didn't want to cry in front of him but the tears came hot and fast, my hands clenched into fists buried against the back of my eyelids. The deception was so callous, so calculated, I was engulfed by it. I felt crushed, devastated that I could have been so stupid. I let out a long, guttural wail, my face upturned towards the sky. I hated him. It terrified me how much I hated him. He was a soul made from tar, a malevolent cancer. How could I ever have believed him, this foul and wicked man?

He was driving fast, his face set like stone. I wanted to hurt him. I wanted to kill him. Enraged, I raised my fists and with a livid yowl, I turned on him, pummelling at him as best I could. He held me off, pushing me back against the jeep door. 'Anthony!' he shouted. 'Stop this! Stop!'

'I hate you!' I yelled, my fists flying at him. 'I hate you! I hate you!'

He slammed his foot on the brake and we both jerked forwards then snapped backwards, slamming into our seats. I felt both his hands on me, pinning me down. He pressed on top of me, a large forearm coming down across my chest as he reached behind the seat to pull out a length of rope.

'No!' I shouted, as he grabbed my wrist. I spat at him.

Roughly, he yanked at my other wrist and, pulling them both together, wrapped the rope tightly about them. I tried to scramble upwards, pushing with my feet against the bottom of the windscreen. There was a sharp burn in my wrists and I let out a pained yelp. My arms were jerked downwards and I felt his hand snatch at my ankle. I was still kicking, frantic to escape. With my free leg, I shoved my boot into his face. His head snapped to the left and, sensing I was keeping him off me, I pushed again, harder. He let out an angry bellow and a fist came down into my jaw.

Everything went black.

Something hurt. Everything hurt. I could taste blood, and my tongue found its way to a loose tooth. I was tied down, my ankles roped to my wrists, and I was lying in the deep shallow of the jeep. We were still moving. I rolled onto my back and looked up. Blue skies, a few faraway clouds; it was a lovely day. We must be up the mountain pass, I thought. I could smell the heather.

I felt dazed. The punch had been quite something. I'd been hit before, of course, but by people my own size. Being lamped by a grown man was quite a different matter. I tried to raise my hand to my mouth, but the rope stopped me. I let my head drop back onto the floor of the jeep, a dull ache sweeping through my body. I could feel dampness around my groin. I looked down. I'd wet myself. I was going to die.

The jeep was slowing and I felt it swing to the left. There was a jolt, a series of jerks and then the sound changed. We were on grass. He'd left the road. I heard the crunch of the handbrake and the coarse juddering of the engine falling silent. I rolled against the backboard so I could better see him. Was this it? Was this the moment he was going to kill me?

I could see the back of his head. He looked down to his right, opened the door and got out. He shot me a glance, a cursory, almost irritated look, as if I was a terrible inconvenience. I blinked and winced. The right side of my face felt swollen, my upper lip puffy. I tried to wriggle free of the rope, but it was no good.

'Get on with it, then!' I yelled at him. 'If you're going to kill me, do it!'

'I'm not going to kill you, Anthony,' he replied, not looking at me. 'I'm sorry I had to hurt you.' He reached down into the footwell on the passenger's side and pulled out Captain Willis's uniform. 'I don't expect you to understand what is going on. I don't expect you to be anything other than angry. I am doing what I must.'

'How could you do it?' I cried, the tears coming again. 'How could you do that to me? To Bethan? To my brother? Mam? Father? You're a bloody German. A bloody German!'

'Yes,' he said, pulling off his tank top and shirt. 'I am a German. I love my country, Anthony, just as you love yours. We are enemies, and yet, we are not. Not really. And I want you to try and remember that, when this is done. I must do things for my country that I have been asked to do. You believe in duty and honour. My duty means that I must betray people I have grown fond of. I do this for my country. That is my honour. Can you understand that?' He slipped off his trousers and tossed them to one side.

'No,' I yelled, 'I can't understand it. All I know is you've been a viper, a sneak. You've lied to us. You're the worst person I've ever met.'

He bent down and pulled on the uniform trousers. They were a little loose at the waist. He zipped up the fly and, before fastening the button, pulled on the light-blue shirt. Tucking the bottom of the shirt into the trousers, he looked at me again. 'One day, when you are older,' he began, his voice a little softer, 'I hope you can forgive me. War makes monsters of the most mild-mannered of men. Please, Anthony, I mean you no harm.'

'No harm?' I laughed. 'You've shot me brother, you've kissed me sister and you've punched me tooth out.'

'Sorry about that,' said Gerhard, pulling on Captain Willis's jacket. 'Think of it as a battle scar. You'll be able to tell endless tales about it.'

A fury raged through me. He was being calm, normal, as if this was of little importance to him, as if he didn't care. I wanted him to feel the pain inside of me; I wanted him to burn with it. I tried to kick against the side of the jeep, but every movement was agony.

'Don't fight it, Anthony,' said Gerhard, pulling out the papers I'd placed in the inside pocket of the jacket. 'Resistance will tighten the knot. You'll hurt yourself more.'

He stood up straight and cast a quick glance through the wad of documents. He pulled out one that was a faded yellow, threw it down onto the passenger seat then tucked the rest back into the inside of his jacket. He looked back towards me. 'I have to do something to you now, Anthony,' he said. 'Try and stay calm.' He reached down and picked up the shirt he'd been wearing. Taking a firm hold of it, he grabbed one sleeve and ripped it from the shoulder.

A stab of panic surged through me. I felt clammy, nauseous, but he was right: every time I struggled, the pain intensified. My eyes were wide and staring, fear blazing out. He reached into his pocket. He was getting the gun. This was it. I closed my eyes.

I was pulled upwards, his hands deep in my armpits. He pushed me into a sitting position, my back resting against the side of the jeep. I couldn't look at him. I wouldn't look at him. I buried my chin into my chest, my eyes clamped shut.

'Open your mouth, Anthony,' I heard him say.

I shook my head.

'Please,' he said again, 'it will be easier if I don't have to force you.'

I shook my head again.

His hand gripped me under my jaw, tight like a vice, his other hand pushing back against the tip of my nose with the flat of his palm. Oh! The pain! Instinctively, I arched backwards, my head turning upwards, and as it did, I felt his fingers creeping over my bottom lip and onto my teeth. I opened my mouth a fraction and bit down hard.

'Aaaargh!' he yelled. 'Anthony! The more you fight, the more I have to hurt you!'

He pinched my nose hard and yanked my head backwards. I let out a cry of pain and as my mouth opened, I felt something being shoved into it. I choked.

'Breathe through your nose, Anthony,' said Gerhard. 'Don't panic. You will be able to breathe, even if you can't make a sound.'

The material in my mouth hardened into a wet ball and before I could spit it out, he had taken the torn sleeve and tied it tight over my mouth. He stood back and shook out the hand I had bitten. His eyes narrowed. 'Bethan said you were like a dog. You can stay sitting up or I can lie you down. Which would you prefer?'

I tried to yell at him but all that came out was meaningless muffles. I kicked out in anger, forgetting that every strain pulled the ropes tighter. I buckled with pain.

'Anthony,' he said, his voice tinged with frustration. 'If you lie still, it won't hurt. Do you want to sit up? Or lie down?'

My eyes were red and swollen from crying. The despair that coursed through me felt like poisoned blood. It was grief, an ache of sorrow that consumed me. I let my head fall back onto the wall of the jeep behind me and sobbed.

'Stay sitting up, then,' said Gerhard, reaching for the rolled-up tarpaulin that was tied above me. 'I haven't got much time left. I'm putting this over you now. You'll be perfectly safe where I'm taking you. You won't see me again, Anthony. I wish you well.'

I watched as he unrolled the green canvas and looped small rope ties through its holes. Bit by bit, the sheet tightened down. He didn't look at me until the very last. I was staring up at him, lost, bewildered. He met my gaze and in that moment, we saw each other.

And then he pulled the rope tight.

It wasn't entirely dark. Small beads of sunlight were shining down through the holes in the tarpaulin. The engine rumbled back into action and my body was flung roughly as the jeep reversed over uneven ground. There was a bump, then a crunch of gears and we were moving forward. I blinked, allowing my eyes to adjust to the dimmer light. I looked around me. I couldn't wriggle myself free, that was clear, but perhaps there was something else? Something I could use?

I could guess where we were going: RAF St Athan. He was going to steal a Mosquito bomber. That was clear. Was Captain Willis right? Was he going to bomb Allied Command?

I let my head rest against the backboard. It was hard to swallow with the ball of cloth in my mouth, and the muscles around it were starting to ache. I thought about Emrys, wondered if he was all right. I thought about Alf, running as fast as he could as the jeep sped away from him. I thought about Bethan and Mam. They'd be worried sick.

Maybe they'd fetch the Americans, try and rescue me? But the only Americans not up the mountain were peeling spuds. They couldn't catch him with a vegetable knife. I thought about Hughes the Grocer's delivery van. They could use that, if Gerhard hadn't thought to sabotage it. He'd thought to cut the phone line from the cop shop, so the chances of the van being driveable were slim. He must have done everything he needed when he was sent to fetch Mam, including fetching the pistol I had given him. I had given it to him! He was one step ahead of everyone. He always had been.

My body slid over to the right. We were turning. We must be at the base. The jeep slowed to a halt. I heard a voice.

'Hello,' I heard Gerhard shout, 'flight order. Been sent over by Strategic Command. What about this weather? Fine day for flying. You can almost imagine there isn't a war on!'

'Ha!' I heard a voice replying. It was coming closer. 'That'll be the day. Strategic Command, eh? Here, you got wind of when it's all kicking off, then?'

I realised why he'd sat me up. I couldn't kick the side of the jeep. I needed to make my presence known. I had to stop him.

'All hush hush, I'm afraid,' he said, in a cut-glass English accent. 'But it won't be much longer, I can tell you that.'

'It's worse than waiting for a baby,' said the voice. 'Making the lads proper edgy, like.'

I had one chance. If I slid myself downwards, I could slam my feet against the side of the jeep, and if I did that loud enough, then maybe the sentry at St Athan would hear it. The thought of a German in a British bomber allowed to fly unchallenged to his target was unthinkable. I tried to stretch my leg but my wellington couldn't reach. It was no good.

'Anyway,' said the sentry, 'you'll be wanting the airfield. Follow the road round; you can leave your jeep near the squadron huts. Anyone there will direct you to Operations.'

'Thank you, Sergeant,' said Gerhard.

I had to make a noise, any sort of noise. I tensed my stomach muscles and flipped myself upwards from my buttocks, raising myself no more than an inch from the jeep floor. I let myself drop and a small metallic bang shuddered through the jeep. I stared upwards, straining for a response from the sentry, but the noise had been masked by a crunch of gears and the gravelly roar of the engine. We were on the move again. It hadn't worked.

And then I realised how stupid I was.

I was wearing wellingtons. He had tied my wrists to the ankles of my boots. If I bent towards my ankles rather than trying to pull back, then I was able to provide a little slack, enough slack to allow my foot to try and slip out. If I could get onto my knees, I might have a chance. I rolled onto my side, pressing the top of my head into the wall of the jeep behind me, but the exertion was taking its toll, a dull ache beginning to throb through the centre of my neck, a warm, clammy film of sweat creeping its way around my body. In order to maintain the slack long enough for me to wriggle my foot out of the tethered wellington, I would have to lower my shoulders and push my hands towards my shins. The effort was excruciating.

It wasn't working.

Don't give up, man. I said it to myself again and again. Sweat from my forehead was dripping down my nose. I bit down on the cloth in my mouth, the stale saliva bitter on my tongue. I pressed my eyes closed. Sucking air greedily through my nostrils, I pushed my bound wrists down towards my ankles. The muscles in my shoulders and upper back screamed in protest, and, taking my weight on one knee, I tried to raise the other so that I could lift my leg out from the wellington. My body, contorted and throbbing with pain, was begging me to stop. I had one chance, I kept telling myself.

Managing to lift my left knee high towards my chin, I could feel the wellington wanting to slip in the other direction. I could feel the grip on my ankle loosening. The further I pushed my wrists towards my feet, the easier it became. The tension across my back was unbearable. One more push and, suddenly, my foot slid up from the base of the boot, my toes wriggling past the knotted ankle. I brought my knee up until it touched my chin. My left foot was out.

I felt ecstatic; adrenalin surged through me. Shifting my weight onto my left leg, I repeated the process. With one leg free, my right foot was out from the wellington in a matter of moments. I turned onto my backside and ripped at the torn shirt sleeve tied about my mouth. The jeep was slowing. The knot was unyielding and I couldn't get my fingers into it. I tried pushing the sleeve upwards. Too tight. The jeep came to a stop and I heard the door open and close.

Hurry, Anthony!

My fingers scratched at my face, pressing into my cheeks so I could drag the sleeve downwards. I tugged at it violently, an edge came over my ear, and in that split second, I yanked the bind downwards. I clawed at the mass in my mouth, spluttering and retching as it came out. I gasped, sucking in deep gulps of air, and then, with my chest heaving, I threw back my head.

'HELP!' I screamed. 'HELP!'

My hands were still tied together, the wellingtons dangling. I had no idea where Gerhard had parked the jeep. For all I knew I was in the middle of a field. I turned myself around and started scrabbling at the small rope ties that held down the tarpaulin. I had to get out, find someone.

'HELP!' I yelled.

My lungs were still adjusting and my chest convulsed, bending me over with a sharp, agonising pain. I waited for the spasm to pass and then lifted myself up again. Gerhard hadn't taken his time with the knots and I found that once I had managed to pull them through the hole, I could undo them quickly. Four ties undone and I pushed the tarpaulin up with the flat of my hand.

'HELP!' I cried again.

I forced myself upwards, fighting the cramp in my lower legs. The jeep was parked against the wall of a building with no windows; ahead of us lay grass, and beyond that a hangar. I swung around, desperate to see someone, but there was nobody. I let out a small, pained moan, lifted my right leg up onto the lip of the jeep and swung myself out, stumbling over the dangling wellingtons as I landed. Scooping the wellingtons into my arms, I ran, barefoot, towards the hangar.

There had to be someone, anyone! I glanced to my left as I crossed a thin gravel path. Wincing as the stones bit into the soles of my feet, I could see a green hut about 200 metres away. I stopped and looked back towards the hangar. The sound of a thick, heavy throbbing was coming from it and, to my horror, the nose of a Mosquito bomber began to emerge. I ran towards it, Gerhard clearly visible in the cockpit. I tried to run with it, the wind from the propellers slicing through my hair.

'STOP HIM!' I yelled into the wind, my voice evaporating in the din.

I looked back into the hangar. Empty. Gerhard was taxiing down to the runway. I'd have to make a dash for the green hut. I kicked down, my legs carrying me as fast as they were able. I glanced back over my shoulder. He was almost at the end of the runway. Where was everyone?

I reached the hut, my chest bursting. Grabbing the knob, I flung the door open. A group of men, sitting, relaxing, reading papers, smoking pipes, all stopped and looked up.

'Please,' I panted. 'Help me. The plane. The plane on the runway. There's a German in it.'

'What?' said a man in full flight gear, getting to his feet. 'What the hell has happened to you?'

I'd forgotten what I must look like. The right side of my face swollen, eyes crimson with tears, drenched with sweat, a shirt sleeve hanging around my neck and my wrists, bound with rope from which hung a pair of dangling wellingtons.

'Please,' I said, near collapse. 'He's been sent to bomb something. You have to stop him.'

The man cast a puzzled look over to the others. 'How did you get in here? Call down to the sentry hut, Hutchins, see what's what.'

He looked back down towards me. 'Who tied you up like that?'

'He did!' I yelled. 'Please! You have to believe me! He's taking a Mosquito!'

Another man behind him ran to the window and shoved it open. In the distance, there was the sound of propellers.

'Christ, sir, there's someone on the runway!'

'Sentry hut says fella presented flight papers. RAF, he says,' shouted a man in the far corner, hugging a telephone to his ear. 'Looks legit.'

'He's not RAF! He's a bloody German!' I yelled.

'Morse code just come in, sir,' said another man, running in behind me. 'Captain Willis in Treherbert. German on loose. Taken boy hostage. Sent to steal a Mosquito. Kill on sight.'

'Jesus,' said the officer in front of me.

As one, the men leapt to their feet and pushed past me. Gerhard was on the runway, the Mosquito picking up speed. I turned and ran out after them, watching as they sprinted towards gun posts at the edge of the field. A wind blew across my face, billowing down from the mountain, the hint of heather still dancing at its edges. Leaping over sandbags, the men swung machine-gun barrels skywards. My eyes darted back to the runway. The front wheels were lifting, the deep, heady pounding of the propellers pulsing through the air. He was up and climbing.

A fast, steady beat of bullets thumped through the air. It was so loud, I wanted to cover my ears, but I couldn't. I don't think I blinked, my eyes fixed rigidly on the Mosquito bomber climbing, climbing. He was going; he was getting away. I looked back towards the guns, pounding back and forth, and a stab of panic surged through me. And I remembered looking up into his eyes. We saw each other. He was my friend.

'Don't hurt him,' I heard myself muttering. 'DON'T HURT HIM!'

I snapped my head back towards the climbing Mosquito. He had tied me up, he had punched me, he had betrayed us all, and yet … A sharp, explosive boom ripped across the sky, a bright blast of light, and the Mosquito faltered. The engine spluttered and, like a Christmas cracker, it snapped into two, spiralling towards the ground.

Someone yelled 'GET DOWN!' and I turned, crouching to the ground, covering my head with my hands, sprawling in an instinctive act of self-preservation. Behind me, there was a loud blast, followed by a shower of small thuds around me, and as the noise settled, I opened my eyes and looked over my shoulder at the inferno burning.

I felt no joy.

CHAPTER TWENTY-ONE

Father died on a Sunday afternoon in June. It had been a beautiful day, warm, a pleasant breeze, the sort of day I could have spent wandering the mountain before coming home with burnt cheeks and a red nose. He had been unable to eat anything for the best part of a week, and we had watched him diminish a little more with every passing day. His fading was slow but relentless, and there was nothing we could do about it. It had been a long wait, since the accident down the pit. Death had lingered at our door, refusing to either come or go. We had closed in, staying near to Father at all times, Mam rarely, if ever, leaving his side. Neighbours brought round stews, the odd loaf of bread, and we scraped by, day by day, just waiting.

Father's last words, far from being weighty or historic, were, 'Lemonade? Lovely.' He had whispered it on seeing Bethan carrying up a pitcher. She'd placed it down on my mother's dressing table and poured out glasses for me, Alwyn and Emrys. Father hadn't wanted any, but he smiled as Emrys gulped down a glass. It was a small, tiny moment that made us feel, if only for an instant, normal.

It was hot in Father's room that day, sticky and oppressive, and Bethan, Alwyn, Emrys and I had gone out to stand on the front step for some air, the events of the past two weeks still dominating our conversation. We'd stood there for a good while, watching the comings and goings of the street: women huddled in twos and threes, arms folded, moaning about rations or the weather or how their husbands, with no pit to go down, were driving them mad; kids playing, acting out the newsreels from France; unoccupied pitmen coming off the mountain, rabbits slung over their shoulders, a trout or two if they'd been lucky. Life, all around us, going on, and the four of us, draped around our front door, glasses of lemonade in hand.

Alwyn still had his arm in plaster. It was driving him mad with the itching, so he carried a broken-off length of beanpole that he could shove in to relieve the maddening prickles. Emrys' gunshot wound had turned out to be superficial. Bethan's quick-mindedness in stopping the bleeding had certainly saved him, a fact she intended to never let him forget, but the bullet had, in fact, gone straight through him, missing everything significant. It had been found a few days later, embedded into the side of a chair, whereupon it was tossed into a pint glass and put into the Labour Club's trophy cabinet, an object that would be revered for years to come.

Bethan was inconsolable after Gerhard's betrayal and had struggled. She felt ashamed and foolish, but Emrys took it upon himself to lift her from her doldrums, explaining that Gerhard had pulled the wool over all our eyes, and that nobody had seen it coming. All the same, she took it hard. We all did.

I'd been right about Gerhard sabotaging Hughes the Grocer's van. He'd yanked out the ignition motor wires so it couldn't be started. Captain Willis had run to it in his vest and pants, only to discover it was useless. Old Morris had offered up a pair of dilapidated bicycles instead, but was shouted down by just about everybody, whereupon Captain Willis had had the bright idea to spark up Gerhard's own radio and wire a message to RAF St Athan.

It was all we talked about in those days and weeks after it happened: how none of us had guessed, how completely hoodwinked we'd all been. We relived the scene in the Labour Club over and over, wondering what his target might have been. Alf reckoned Captain Willis was right, that he'd been sent to bomb the D-Day commanders, Mr Churchill and the American lot. He might have been right, but we'd never know for certain.

I became a local celebrity for a while, my picture on the front page of some papers, arms folded, expression a little strained, standing proudly in my wellingtons. Captain Willis had arranged for me to get a medal for bravery. I didn't know if I deserved it. I hadn't felt brave at the time – I'd felt anything but, in fact – but Mam said bravery is an instinct some people have and others don't. If you do anything, she said, it's still better than doing nothing.

Eventually, as with all things, life returned to a normality of sorts, even if we weren't where we always had been.

'Gwennie Morgan's had a letter from her GI beau,' said Bethan on that hot Sunday afternoon in June, taking a sip of lemonade from her glass. 'So he's still alive.'

Emrys raised an eyebrow. 'Oh, that's good to know, innit? *Diawl*, they took a pounding, by the sounds of it. Does she know where he is?'

Bethan shook her head. 'Nah, he's not allowed to say, is he?'

'Quiet round here without 'em, innit?' Emrys scuffed the toe of his shoe against the base of the flagstone step. 'Never thought I'd say it, but I miss 'em. They might have been loud, but they was all right, wannit? Bet you miss the gum, Anthony?'

I shrugged. The Americans had left two days after Gerhard had been killed. We'd watched the *Pathé News* newsreels. The Allied troops had landed on beaches in Normandy. Turns out the Germans were expecting them to land at Calais so, catching them unawares, our lot were able to get stuck into France. I wondered if the Germans' mistake was down to Gerhard telling Captain Willis to do just that. Part of me hoped it was, and that he'd been secretly on our side all along, but deep down, I knew he wasn't. I hated myself for it, but I missed him.

It was something we all felt but didn't dare speak of. We missed him, his sense of adventure, the spark in his eyes, his kindness, his generosity. I had to force myself to remember that even if he had taught me how to shave, he'd still put a bullet in my brother, and my brother's my brother, however annoying he is. Blood comes first.

'Christ, it's itching bad today,' moaned Alwyn, grinding his broken beanpole into the gap between his arm and his cast. 'It's murderous. There's a bit b'there I can't bloody reach. It's driving me mad, it is.'

'Must be bad,' said Emrys, sticking his hands in his pockets. 'You didn't even flinch when Bethan mentioned Gwennie Morgan.'

'She's not the only girl in the valley,' said Alwyn, trying to reach in further with his makeshift scratcher. 'Besides, now my brother's been shot by a German, I can have whatever girl I fancy. I'm practically famous, innit?'

'Not as famous as our Anthony,' said Bethan, ruffling my hair.

'Yeah, well,' said Alwyn, 'he's too young for girlfriends. So bad luck on him.'

I drained my lemonade, the sharp citrus twang buzzing off my tongue. There was a game of doggy and catty playing out further up the street, the cries of the young lads echoing off the terraced walls. I wondered if Gwyn Williams was among them, still picking on kids smaller than himself; or if his own father's poor health had changed him for the better. I was sitting on the flagstone, elbow on one knee, wondering when I would be back at it with them, when the life I knew would return. I wondered if it ever would, whether it was even possible.

'Hey!' said Emrys, giving me a thump. 'Look at that! By God. I've never seen that before.'

I followed his finger, pointing up towards the rooftop opposite. It was the red kite, sitting on the high ridge. I'd never seen it this close, and I cupped my hands over my eyes so the sun bouncing off the bricks wouldn't blind me. Emrys was right; I'd never seen a bird of prey off the mountain or so low into the village.

'Perhaps she's had babies,' I said. 'Needs all the food she can get.' She looked magnificent, her white head atop dark-flecked russet wings, the yellow beak hooked between pale eyes lined with black.

'She's beautiful,' said Bethan, staring upwards.

Alwyn whistled, and the kite, for a fleeting moment, looked down towards us. I fought the urge to wave, as if somehow we might see each other and she might know me, but the noise had unsettled her, and, unfurling her wings, she beat them upwards into the air, two great white flashes burning on their undersides.

'What a bird,' said Emrys. 'They can have lambs, you know. Swoop down and take 'em.'

'Pity she can't swoop down and take you,' said Bethan. 'Here, pass me your glass. Let's go back up.'

Father's breathing had changed: long gaps when it was almost as if he was holding his breath followed by thick, rasping exhales, his lower jaw slack, bottom lip drooped and wet with drool. It made him look ugly, these final hours, something I would come to resent. Perhaps the greatest hardship in watching someone die is having those last days burned into your memory. The man in the bed wasn't my father. He was the shadow of him, a person I didn't want to remember.

We had gathered round, Mam sitting on a stool at his side, holding his hand, the rest of us sprawled about the room, tightening in as the gaps in the breathing became ever wider. I pulled myself up onto the bed and sat next to him, my eyes never leaving his face.

'Look,' said Mam, her voice low and hushed, 'look at his fingers.'

She held up his hand. The tips of Father's fingers were turning blue. She rubbed them gently between her own as if her warmth could somehow stop the inevitable. I looked back towards Father's face: the frown that had carved itself into his forehead began to relax; the breathing, that had been so heavy and pained, lightened. Nobody spoke but everyone leant in to lay hands on him.

'We're here, Davey,' said Mam. 'We're all here.'

Two short, shallow breaths, then a long gap. I glanced down towards Father's arm, a long trail of blue snaking its way up towards his elbow. I looked back at his face, the pain ebbing, one last sip of air, as if tasting a long favourite drink, and he was gone.

The tears came freely. Mam's head was buried into his side, her shoulders heaving. Bethan was sprawled over his lower legs, her face etched with the weight of sadness. Alwyn, standing at the end of the bed, crumpled downwards, his hand holding on to Father's ankle, as if somehow, wherever Father was going, he could follow. Emrys, cheeks wet with sorrow, draped an arm about Mam, and I slid myself down onto the bedspread and nestled into Father's body, laying my arm across him so I could catch those last whispers of warmth. I had never held him while he was alive. It would be my only regret.

He was buried a week later. The undertaker had come the night Father had died and taken him, his body leaking all the way to the front door. It was a final indignity, an unnecessary cruelty, and to spare Mam the upset, I had taken a rag and cleaned the mess myself. He had been brought back to us two days later, tidied into a suit, his face strangely pink as if he'd been for a bracing walk in a stiff breeze. We'd all stared at him and wondered if he was actually dead.

The coffin was laid out in the parlour, top off, and we had taken it in turns to sit with him as the steady stream of neighbours came in to pay their respects. Many brought cakes, or small cuts of meat. Some of the men, my Father's workmates, brought a few shillings. Mam would get no money from the colliery owners, but, as a pit widow, she would receive a lifetime supply of coal. She may have been hungry but at least she'd be warm.

The atmosphere in the house was muted and reverential. Mam seemed in a daze as if, after a period of round-the-clock caring, she didn't quite know what to do with herself. I'd catch her looking at me, puzzled, as if she couldn't place who I was or why I was in the house, and then she'd remember and hurry to the larder to find some scraps to feed me with. It was a strange time, a different sort of waiting. Father was there, but he wasn't. It felt like we were holding on to him before we had to give him back.

On the day of the funeral, people from the pit and the street had gathered, pressed into our parlour and kitchen, spilling out onto the pavement outside. Alwyn and Emrys stood either side of Mam, and I cleaved into Bethan, straining to catch a last glimpse of Father before the lid was put back on and I would never see him again. Jones the Bible had stood in front of the hearth and given a suitably sombre eulogy. A few women dotted about the room wept quietly; men stood, caps in hand, heads bowed. I thought about Gerhard. I didn't know what had become of his body or if he'd even been buried: the life of a man, unmarked and forgotten, the sum total of his parts never to be celebrated.

As we sang 'Abide with Me', the lid to Father's coffin was gently slotted back into place. As the wood slid over him, I felt a dark melancholy descend. There was no return. He now belonged to the mountain, and it was our burden to return him.

Coffins went in and out from a house through the parlour windows. It was a valley tradition brought on through necessity. Pit houses were all so small and narrow that it was impossible to turn a coffin from the hallway into the parlour, so in and out the window they had to come. If anything, it added to the drama of the occasion, made it more solemn, somehow, and I stood, silently, watching as my brothers joined the undertakers to take Father out, feet first.

The coffin was taken to Treorchy Cemetery, set into a high hillside of the mountain. I climbed the steep incline, my hand tight inside Bethan's, and stood, looking down into the hole that would take my Father from us forever. It was odd to think of his body down there, out of sight, never to be seen again. Death was such a hard thing for the living. There was no hope to it.

I remember sounds: a few men singing, the midday pit siren howling in the distance because nobody had bothered to turn it off, the quiet clicking of coins being turned in the pocket of a mourner. But above all, I remember my mother's face, carved with woe, anguish burning through her. She'd been strong for all of us for long enough, and as Father was lowered down, she crumpled delicately downwards, as if her bones were made from paper.

It was the single saddest thing I would ever see.

CHAPTER TWENTY-TWO

I took the exam two weeks later. Miss Evans had got a special dispensation from the Grammar school and they'd allowed me to sit their entrance paper on my own, one Wednesday in early July. It had rained that afternoon, and the classroom was filled with the metallic smell of a recent downpour. My classmates had all left, scurrying home as the rain slashed down, and I had sat, head resting in my upturned palm, watching temporary waterfalls cascading down from loose guttering. As the rain snaked down the window, my eye was drawn to the windowsill, my name carved into it. It didn't feel right and so I took my compass and etched another name next to it.

ADE

Blowing the sawdust out from the carving, I ran my thumb across the newly fixed legend:

ANT and ADE

It was better.

'Are you ready, Anthony?' Miss Evans asked me, opening a large envelope that contained my examination paper. She cast a look up towards the clock on the wall. It was four o'clock. 'You'll have an hour and ten minutes to complete the Arithmetic paper. Then I'll give you the English Reproduction paper. You'll have fifteen minutes to read it and then you'll have to write the passage in your own words. You get fifty minutes for that. Do you understand? Have you got enough ink? Blotting paper?'

I nodded. I'd placed an inkpot at the top of my desk. Beside it sat a battered fountain pen that had been my father's but was given to me by Mam when it was clear there wasn't going to be much in terms of fancy bequests. I didn't care. I only wanted something to remember him by. The pen would do just fine. Alwyn had been given Father's tommy box and Emrys had been given a tie clip he'd been fond of. Bethan, who didn't have much left to choose from, took Father's *David Copperfield*.

'I'm going to place your paper in front of you,' explained Miss Evans, walking towards me. 'Then when I say, turn it over and begin. Good luck, Anthony. Take your time with your answers. Think before you write. You'll do just fine.'

She placed the paper in front of me. It was thick, stapled at the seam, and I caught a faint smell of something carbolic and antiseptic. She glanced up again at the wall clock. 'All right, Anthony. Turn over.'

I reached down towards the paper and flipped it over. Across the top, in large capital letters, it read: 'RHONDDA EDUCATION COMMITTEE. COMPETITIVE EXAMINATION FOR ENTRANCE

TO SECONDARY AND CENTRAL SCHOOLS, 1944.' I felt a surge of something nauseous. I hadn't thought of it as a competition, but there it was in black and white. I stared down. Question one.

An aeroplane left its base at 9.00 a.m. and flew to an aerodrome 1500 miles away at a steady speed. It came down, took one and a half hours to refuel, and then returned at the same speed to its base, where it arrived at 11.00 p.m. Find its speed in miles per hour.

I blinked and reached for my pen. I'd fill it up first. Thinking time. *If a plane left its base at 9.00 a.m. and arrived at 11.00 p.m. 1500 miles* ... I reached for the notebook I'd been given to write down my answers. My pen gave a little, hungry slurp. I dabbed the nib on the blotting paper and, with a determined hunch of my shoulders, began.

The time slipped through my fingers like melted butter. Before I knew it, Miss Evans had taken away the Arithmetic paper and handed me the English Reproduction. At the top of the first page was the title: 'The Grizzly Bear'.

I am a Rocky Mountain silvertip grizzly. I can stand up with my back to a tree and, biting over my shoulder, make my mark fully nine feet above ground. I am not afraid of anything that hunts in the woods, barring human beings with guns. I would drive men from my mountains if it were not for their rifles. They take advantage of us poor bears. Being afraid to come into close quarters, they stand off a fair way and shoot at us.

I closed my eyes and fixed the words in my mind. *I am not afraid of anything that hunts the woods, barring humans with guns.* I stopped and stared out the window. The dark cloud had lifted, the rain stopped. I cast a look out across the mountain.

'I've read it,' I said, turning to Miss Evans. 'I'm ready to write now.'

She came a week later, knocking at our door, and Mam had let her in and they both sat, drinking tea in the parlour, until I returned from an errand to the baker's. I walked in, loaf tucked into my armpit, and Mam had stood up, her face soft and welcoming.

'Miss Evans is here,' she said, needlessly. 'She's got some news for you, Anthony.'

Miss Evans placed her cup back into its saucer and rose from the chair. 'I've heard back from the Grammar, Anthony. Would you like to know how you got on?'

'S'pose,' I said. A small explosion of butterflies released itself into my stomach. 'Yes, please.'

'You've got a Special Place, Anthony,' said Miss Evans, beaming. 'That means all your fees are paid. Only the cleverest boys are offered them. I'm very proud of you. Well done.'

She stepped forward, her hand extended. I took it and shook, the butterflies fluttering gently skywards.

'What about the uniform, though?' I asked, casting an anxious look towards my mother. 'The shoes? We can't afford them.'

'It's a Special Place, Anthony. Everything is paid for. It's all going to be taken care of. Your mother will be sent vouchers and she'll be able to get everything you're going to need with those. Uniform, stationery, books, equipment, everything.'

'And shoes?' I asked again.

Miss Evans nodded. 'And shoes, yes.'

'Smashin',' I said. I didn't know what else to say. My mother was dabbing at her eyes with a handkerchief.

'You'll never have to go down the pit, Ant,' she said, smiling through her tears. 'An educated man, in our family. Your father would have been very proud.'

Yes. He would. A wave of sadness coursed through me, and I glanced up towards the mantelpiece. We had one photograph of Father, the only one taken of him on his beloved Brownie camera. He was standing, jacket slung over one shoulder, sleeves rolled up, hand on hip and laughing, his hair blowing in the wind, and behind him, our mountain.

'He knows,' said Mam, catching my glance. 'He knows.'

A lady from the Education Board came to visit Mam. She was a thin, shrewish woman, tight lips and curls, in a meticulously pressed two-piece. She smelled of Parma Violets and had an air of anxiety about her, as if she needed to eat more meat. She had lots of forms for Mam to fill in. I don't know what they all were, but it rattled down to making sure we were as poor as we said we were. Once she was suitably satisfied of our impoverished state, she made me stand up and unfurled a cotton tape measure from her handbag. I stood, back against a doorframe, and she measured my height, my chest, my waist, my cap size, my inside leg and my feet. She didn't say much. Instead, she made a few scribbles in a small red notebook and then left without wanting tea. Mam didn't like her. I'm not sure I did, either.

The rest of the summer passed without incident. Fez, Bozo and I would head up to the den, sit on the ridge and watch the Mosquito squadrons like we always did. Occasionally, there would be bomb raids on Swansea or Cardiff, and we'd sit watching the sky illuminate in the distance, but they were increasingly infrequent. Hitler was on the back foot. Allied forces were pressing further into France. The war was as good as over, Fez reckoned.

The pit remained closed. It would be another two months before it re-opened. There was disquiet in the village as the pit owners refused to give anyone wages until they were all back at work. It made a lot of people sour and resentful, and many lifelong pitmen decided never to return. Alwyn was still having trouble with his wrist. It had mended badly and if he went back, he'd never be allowed underground again. He hoped he might get a job as a tallyman, but like Emrys, he was looking around for other work. The big news was that he'd met a girl called Frances at a dance, and I suppose you'd call them sweethearts. Mam liked her; she seemed to calm him down. It was what he needed, she said: a sensible girl with thick ankles.

Emrys had managed to get work with a local decorator's. The boss's son had been killed somewhere in France, and he'd been keeping his job open for him till he came back, but now he wasn't, well, it was different. Emrys had a trial period, learning the ropes, seeing if he was any good with a paintbrush, but the fella liked him and they made the arrangement more permanent. He used to bring home the long strips of wallpaper-edge cuttings for the kids in Scott Street to use as race tape and, for a while, he almost became popular.

Bethan was promoted at RAF St Athan and became secretary to one of the majors. There was some talk of moving her to London, but she didn't want it. Like our teacher Miss Evans, she loved our mountain too much; and, more importantly, she wanted to be near Mam.

With the pit closed and no pitmen in the house, Mam took a while to adjust. The daily routine she had set her clock by was gone, but it was a hard habit to break. Occasionally, I would hear her, still getting up at five in the morning to light the fires and get everything ready, only to realise she'd forgotten she didn't need to do it; but she kept herself busy, did some more cooking for the Women's Guild, and started playing cards with Bopa, a pastime, declared Alwyn, that would end in nothing but ruination.

I was all right. It had been such a strange, upsetting summer. I missed Father, I missed Ade, but every time I went up the mountain, I felt them with me. They would always be part of our mountain, as would I. It was us, and we were it. I felt excited about my future, going to the Grammar school. Fez told me I better not turn into a pooho, but Bozo said loads of the Grammar boys were on Special Places. He reckoned there'd be lots of boys like me.

It was the last week of August and I'd slept in, one of those thick, drowsy mornings when you can't get yourself out of bed. Bethan was back in her own room but I was still underneath Alwyn and Emrys, and I'd woken thinking I hadn't looked in my shoebox for a while. I reached over and dragged it towards me, sliding the lid off as I did. *The Dandy* was still there and I picked it out to have another look at it. As I lifted it, something fell out and onto my chest. It was a photograph, the one I'd taken of Gerhard and Bethan at Porthcawl. I frowned. I hadn't put it there. I stared at it, remembering how much I had loved him that day, and how I'd thought I could never be happier. I looked at his face, that large, toothy grin beaming out at me. I stared at it, and, struggling not to cry, I threw it down. But as I did, it flipped over. There was something written on the back. I picked it up again. It read:

For my friend

'Ant!' A yell came from downstairs. Mam. 'Come down, please,' she continued. 'There's something here for you.'

I stared again at the photo. He must have left it here for me to find. His words came back to me: 'I am your enemy, but not really.' And, finally, I understood. It was this war that had raged over us, not him. To think I had longed for it to come. We all had. And then it did. Be careful what you wish for.

'Anthony!' my mother called again.

I tucked the photo back into my shoebox and crawled out from under the bed. I pulled on my shorts, dragged a dirty shirt down over my shoulders and slipped my feet into the ever-dank wellingtons. I never did manage to get rid of that rubber ring round my shins. Maybe, one day.

I trudged downstairs and walked into the parlour. Alwyn, Emrys, Bethan, Bopa and Mam were there, all standing.

'Wassup, like?' I said, rubbing at my still-sleepy eyes with a fist.

'Look over b'there, Ant,' said Mam. She pointed towards the far end of the parlour, and I turned.

Hanging from an unused picture hook was a brand-new school uniform. Navy blue shorts and jumper, white shirt, blazer with a cream trim, complete with school crest, a striped tie, socks with the same cream trim and a cap dangling from the top.

I looked back towards Mam, my mouth gaping open.

'Careful, Ant,' said Bopa, 'shut your mouth or people'll think you're a fish.'

'Well, get it on,' said Alwyn, gesturing back towards it. 'If we're going to have a genius in the family, I want to see what he looks like.'

'There's shoes too,' said Mam, her smile spreading. 'On the floor underneath. Go on, try them on.'

I had never seen anything more beautiful. Black leather lace-ups, polished to within an inch of their life. I picked them up, the wonderful, deep smell of brand-new leather filling my nostrils. I let my hand run over them, caressing every contour.

'Are they really mine?' I said.

Mam nodded.

I kicked off my wellingtons and reached for the socks. They were soft and warm, and I pulled them up, snapping the tops just under my knee. I quickly pulled on the rest of the uniform, and then, taking one of the shoes, I loosened the laces and slipped my foot down into it. It felt strange. Years of rattling about in loose, rubber wellingtons, and now my feet were held, supported. I couldn't fathom it. I stood and stared down at my new shoes. I never wanted to look at anything else.

Behind me, a voice came from the doorway. 'Well, well! Look at this! Little man! You're a dandy and no mistake!' It was Alf, come to pick up Bethan.

'Doesn't he look amazing?' she said, leaning up to give Alf a kiss.

'You'd never think he smells of mould,' said Emrys, smiling.

'Not any more, he won't.' said Alwyn. 'Not in those togs. You look right proper, Ant. Right proper.'

I looked up towards my family and smiled. 'Can I go out, Mam?' I asked. 'I won't get it dirty.'

'Mind you don't,' she said. 'Go on, then. You can go and show your pals.'

I stepped out onto Scott Street and stared down again at my shoes. There was only one thing I wanted to do. I looked up towards our mountain, thoughts of Ade and Father beaming through me, and I ran.

ACKNOWLEDGEMENTS

First and foremost I need to thank my father, Anthony Williams, on whom much of this book is based. A lot of young Anthony's story is based on my father's own experiences of growing up in Treherbert during the war years. I am also indebted to my Aunts Jean and Gwennie and my uncles John and Gary who helped with Welsh spellings, reminded me of the Nit Nurse, told me what it was like to go underground and taught me the rules of Catty and Doggy.

A lot of research was required and *A Moment in History* by Bryan Morse, the story of the American Army in the Rhondda in 1944, proved to be invaluable in helping me get my facts right.

The cigarette card that Anthony reads from is a Wills Cigarette Card called Rubber Clothing.

The song the boys sing as the Mosquitoes fly off on their mission is 'Wish Me Luck As You Wave Me Goodbye', a song written by Harry Parr-Davies and made popular by Gracie Fields.

The copy for the Regal Shoes ad stuck on Anthony's wall was taken from a vintage magazine ad.

Appointment with Fear was a real show and the extract that appears in this book is taken from an episode broadcast on May 18 1944. It was called 'The Clock Strikes Eight' and was written by John Dickson Carr. I have spliced and edited much of it but you can still listen to the entire episode on the internet. It's suitably melodramatic.

Bopa reads extracts from the instructional pamphlet 'Instructions for American Servicemen in Britain'. This is from the 1942 edition and was issued to all American personnel by the War Department.

Cloches versus Hitler is also a real book that was very popular at the time. It was written by Charles Wyse-Gardner.

Anthony's exam paper is the real one that would have been sat that summer in 1944. It was issued by the Rhondda Education Committee.

I also need to thank many followers on Twitter who, apart from keeping me going as I was writing the manuscript, helped me out with various small queries, but special mention must go to Lynne Clark who helped me out with some RAF St Athan intel.

Enormous thanks must also be showered without reservation upon my wonderful team at Ebury – my amazing editor Jake Lingwood, his assistant Emily Yau and my brilliant copy editor Samantha Bulos. All of you keep me on the straight and narrow and make me better than I am. Thank you.

I am blessed to have a wonderful agent in Sheila Crowley at Curtis Brown who looks after me so beautifully and takes me for the best lunches. Don't ever leave me.

And last but not least, to my darling Georgie, who puts up with everything.